The Art of
Seduction

The Art of Seduction

KATHERINE O'NEAL

BRAVA

KENSINGTON PUBLISHING CORP.
http://www.kensingtonbooks.com

For Machi

Prologue

What am I going to do?
The question burned in Mason Caldwell's mind as she walked the drenched and dreary streets. She was soaked through, her light brown hair freed from its pins by the force of the gale, her overcoat clinging clammily to her body. But she'd long since ceased to care, or even to feel the discomfort. The rain as it lashed her seemed the outward manifestation of the tears she wouldn't allow herself to shed, as if the sky itself mourned for her on this night when all her hopes and dreams had come to nothing.

The elaborately embossed envelope from the Exposition Committee had arrived that afternoon. Her hands trembling with excitement, she'd torn it open and unfolded its single page. But it was only her own letter of application with the word REJECTED stamped across it in brutal crimson letters—all eighteen submissions. Not even the courtesy of the form letter of rejection she knew other artists had received.

Remembering it now, the humiliation singed her cheeks.

Utter failure.

Not even the slightest glimmer of a silver lining to grab on to.

Again, the question gripped her. *What am I going to do? What* can *I do?*

It had been pouring for over twenty-four hours, the worst storm she could remember in her five years in Paris, battering the roof of her one-room flat and the cobblestone street below like an army of horses' hooves barreling by, hour after hour, with no end in sight, as she'd wracked her brain for a solution. Something.

Anything.

And now she walked the streets alone. It was past three in the morning. Here and there the last of the night's drunken revelers passed her by, arms thrown around each other, reeling giddily, oblivious to the downpour. A few prostitutes huddled in doorways, yawning or casting disgusted glances at the deluge, which was bad for business. Mason looked at them with new eyes as she passed. What circumstances had driven them to sell themselves on the streets to any passerby? Had they, too, come to Paris thinking they could conquer the world?

She walked on. The gas lamps sizzled and sparked in the rain, casting an eerie, shifting light show on the pavement before her. Or was it she who was weaving? She couldn't tell. In her agitation, she'd eaten nothing since noon. And then tonight, in an effort to cheer her, her friend Lisette had taken her to the Café Tambourine and had coaxed her into drinking absinthe to dull the pain. The highly intoxicating, acrid liqueur had done nothing to deaden the sense of emptiness and loss and had only made her feel drugged and heavy limbed. It no doubt accounted for the sensation that she was weaving like a leaf in the torrent.

She was so wrapped up in her dilemma that she lost track of her surroundings until she found herself approaching the Pont de l'Alma, a bridge that spanned the Seine. It shouldn't have surprised her, for she came here often. It afforded the most spectacular vantage point to watch the progress of the dazzling new construction project going up on the Left Bank.

La Tour Eiffel they were calling it. She peered through the darkness and thought she could barely pick out its distinctive silhouette. It was nearly completed now, except for its crown, a graceful colossus of iron and steel—a tower of industrial lace—that was causing controversy among the conservative French elements who thought it ugly and couldn't wait to tear it down.

But it had seemed to Mason a symbol of hope because it had been commissioned for *L'Exposition Universelle Internationale* in two months' time, the same World's Fair in which Mason had naively hoped her paintings would be exhibited. All the world would be coming to Paris for what promised to be the grandest showcase of industry and art in the history of France. It was her last chance. After all her rejection, she'd dared to believe that its art selection committee would finally be the one to recognize her talent.

What a colossal fool.

She closed her eyes and stood, hands on the stone rail of the bridge, face tipped back, allowing the shower to cool her fevered skin. She'd been so certain that she was on the right path. But she was only a cliché, after all, a pathetic joke: one more American who'd come to France determined to make it as a painter. Convinced, like all the others, that success and recognition would come if only she believed with all her heart and soul.

She'd started out with such hopes. Five years ago, grieving the death of her mother and desperate to leave behind the pain and despair, she'd taken her modest inheritance and had come to Paris—city of exiles, expatriates, and refugees. A city where you could start over and no one asked about your past. A city that appreciated artists and offered them freedom and support. Here, she'd had her first look at the controversial giants of Impressionism: Monet, Renoir, Degas. Looking at their work, she felt that she'd been struck by lightning. As a girl, her mother had taught her to paint and had taken her to art shows. But the works her mother loved had seemed dry, remote, antiquated. This new style was alive and modern, full of color and light. It spoke to her as nothing ever had before, and she knew she must answer its call.

For five years she'd followed a blissful crusade, playing with novel contrasts of color, experimenting with bold compositions and themes, and developing her own signature style. She'd flattered herself into believing this unique vision was so fresh, so daring, and so innovative that she might be taking Impressionism itself in a revolutionary new direction. Over the last year, she'd summed up this exciting personal breakthrough in eighteen canvases that she'd worked on day and night to finish in time to be considered for a place in the art pavilion of the Great Exposition.

But when she took a sampling to the Boulevard art galleries, hoping to gain their support, the dealers were unanimously appalled. Most of them hadn't even been kind about it.

"But, Mademoiselle, these paintings are revolting!"

"I would lose my reputation were I to give my support to such atrocities."

"Tell me, please, who would want such a thing hanging in their salon?"

The hardest to hear had been Monsieur Falconier, because he'd taken the time to bluntly explain his objections. "The style is simply impossible. Impressionism is difficult enough for the buying public to accept, and this goes beyond Impressionism to . . . I do not know what. The central figure in each of the paintings is appealing, I admit, rendered with a certain Renoiresque charm. But you've surrounded her with chaos and violence, a world that seems deliberately distorted to show its ugliness. You will receive no support for works such as these. They will be laughed at—no, jeered at. Please to take them out of my sight at once!"

Even with this harsh rejection, she'd clung to her hopes for the Exposition. It was well known that the judges were looking to represent not just the Salon painters and the Impressionists who were beginning to struggle their way into the main-stream, but the true avant-garde as well. So she'd submitted her work, rallying herself to believe in her vision, praying with every moment that passed that her canvases would be understood . . . appreciated . . . telling herself that all of it would have been worth it if only one person in all the world would look at her work and say, "Yes, I see."

But it hadn't happened.

And now she was left with nowhere to turn. She'd run out of options.

She felt more than humiliated. She felt angry and betrayed. The men who judged her did so through the veil of their own prejudices. As always, they were unwilling to accept a new vision, a new style. Especially the vision of a woman.

How could she have been so blind? To even *think* they would look upon her work with anything but contempt. It was her father all over again. *Your painting is a waste of time. It will only bring you heartache.*

She still felt the sting of his words. All these years later, the wound had never healed.

As she did so often in times of dejection, she thought again of her mother. The sad, gentle woman who'd painted as a way of escaping an intolerable existence. "Be careful what you wish for," she'd warned Mason, "because you may well be given it. But it won't be given in the way you think it will. You must be willing to pay the price."

She would have taken success any way she could get it, would have paid any price. But her mother had been wrong. Wishing . . . hard work . . . perseverance . . . nothing had made any difference.

Had her father been right all along?

She was shivering in her saturated coat. Leaning on the rail, she looked down into the inky waters of the Seine. She could hear it rushing far below her, the current stronger than she'd ever seen it. She closed her eyes, feeling faint, feeling strangely as if she were melding with the river, becoming one with it. She knew the feeling must be caused by the effects of the absinthe, but somehow it seemed more than that. "I need help," she whispered to the river gushing below. "I can't do any more myself. I need . . . help."

She didn't know how long she stood there repeating the phrase over and over in her head. But after a while she became aware that the rain had slackened. It seemed to her that something had changed. She lifted her eyes and suddenly was struck by the beauty all around her. She turned, glancing east toward the lights of the city, misty in the rain, glistening indistinctly in the distance as the majestic Seine cut its way through the heart of the city like a ribbon of quicksilver.

And then, like a mirage, a figure emerged from the mist and rain, coming toward her across the bridge. The figure of a woman encased in a colorless cloak, holding the hood about her head against the wind as the cape flapped behind. Mason watched her approach, wondering if the absinthe was playing tricks with her mind. Was she seeing things?

But the phantom spoke in French, calling, "Are you in trouble?"

Mason looked around, wondering where the woman had come from. "No, Madame, I'm fine," she answered, also in French. "But thank you for your concern."

"I know better."

Mason turned away, assuming the woman would walk on. But she didn't. Her voice rose again above the sound of the elements. "You feel that all is hopeless. That you have been beaten down so far there is nowhere to turn. That no one understands your pain. That the Seine, with her sweet embrace, is your only friend. Your only solace. Your only solution."

Stunned, Mason glanced down at the raging river, then back again at the woman. *She thinks I'm going to jump!*

"No, Madame, you misunderstand."

But the woman continued as if Mason hadn't spoken. "The temptation is great, is it not?" she called into the wind.

"To leave the world you know behind. To become one of the faceless who give their last breath to Mother Seine."

The words shamed her. It had never occurred to her to take the easy way out. But still, she'd been indulging in a riot of self-pity and that had never been her way.

"No," she declared, straightening her stance. "You're perceptive to see that I have problems, but they haven't beaten me. Not yet, anyway."

"Then I envy you," the woman said, lowering her hands so the wind blew back her hood. For the first time, Mason saw her face. She carried all the sadness of the world in her eyes. Eyes like Mason's mother. "I wish that I, too, had your resolve. But, unfortunately, my strength is at its end."

With that, the woman smiled tenderly at Mason, then, with startling swiftness, mounted the balustrade and hurled herself headlong into the river.

It was such a shock that it took a moment for Mason to realize what had happened. When she did, she leaned over and saw the cloaked figure being carried away like a matchstick in a storm drain.

Mason's mind darted about in a panic. *I've got to do something, but . . . what?*

She stared down into the rushing water, which suddenly seemed so far below her, fighting the numbness of her mind, trying desperately to think. *I'm a good swimmer. I can save her.*

She had to try. Wrenching off her shoes and coat, she straddled the rail, took a deep breath, and let herself drop feetfirst from the bridge.

The moment she hit the water, she knew she was in trouble. The icy current, far more violent than she'd supposed, began to pull her downward so she could barely keep her head above the surface. She sputtered and coughed the water from her lungs. Lack of food and the effects of the absinthe had left her with no reservoir of strength. As she tried to ignore her own peril and swim toward the rapidly careening woman, the tide shifted suddenly and forced her in another direction.

Mason swam for all she was worth. *I have to keep trying. I can't let her die like this.*

Soon her struggle to reach the woman became symbolic of her own resurrected will to survive. The two became one: Her refusal to bow to crushing defeat fueled her determination to beat the river and pull the woman from its grasp.

But it was all she could do to stay afloat. The Seine was stronger than even her fierce will. With mounting panic, she reached for one of the severed tree limbs rushing by, but it sank under her weight.

She was already dangerously exhausted. The woman was now completely out of sight. She tried to force her arms and legs to move, but they were dead weight.

Suddenly, the truth loomed before her. She was going to drown.

Panic choked her. She shook off the lethargy, scratched and clawed to summon some latent strength, to battle like a fury her inevitable end. But it was no use. The current dragged her down, her clothing weighing her like a stone.

As she realized the futility of her struggles, alarm gave way to a resignation that dazed her more than absinthe ever could.

I'm twenty-five years old and I'm going to die.

But then another realization swept through her, more powerful than the last.

She'd never even been in love. She'd never found the one man who could cherish her for who she really was, who could believe in her for no reason except that he loved her with all his heart and soul.

And that, she knew now—when it was too late—was the true tragedy.

She couldn't let it happen. She had to fight for another chance. Her lungs were about to burst. *Help me,* she prayed once again. With a surge of desperation, she shot upward, breaking the surface and taking a deep, rasping gulp of air.

But as she did, something heavy crashed into her, cracking her head. She reached for it, flailing, hoping to use it to keep afloat. But her arms lost all sensation and the world spun madly as she felt consciousness begin to slip away.

Her last bitter thought as blackness stole upon her was of the cruel irony of fate.

I ask for help and this is what I get!

Chapter 1

I must be in heaven.

Mason stepped from the carriage and into a perfect world. The rain was gone and it was a glorious Parisian day, the sky a brilliant blue, the air shimmering and dappled with fleecy clouds. The merest trifle of a perfumed breeze rippled through the bare branches of the trees that lined the fashionable Rue Lafitte.

And there before her, a line of people awaiting admittance to the Galerie Falconier stretched all the way down to the Boulevard Haussmann. A placard beside the entrance displayed, in French, words that seemed to have been snatched from a dream:

Exhibition of Paintings
By the Celebrated
American Impressionist
Mason Caldwell

As she took in the scene, she caught her reflection in the gallery window and almost didn't recognize herself. She was corseted and bustled into a concoction of the palest pink, topped off with a playfully insouciant hat sporting ostrich feathers. Swathes of lace cascaded down in a veil to delicately obscure her face. Her newly dyed black hair made her look faintly exotic, masking her usual fresh-scrubbed country appearance. She liked the change. It made her feel so mischievous that she had to resist the impulse to spin about in glee.

Lisette stepped out behind her. "Are you ready for this, *chérie*?"

Mason looked at her friend. She was an effortlessly beautiful woman of twenty-two, raised on the streets of Montmartre—and wise to all its ways, despite the childlike innocence she exuded—with a tumble of sunshine blond hair, a pouty smile, and a lithe yet curvaceous body that was a prime attraction of the Cirque Fernando, where she was the featured trapeze artist.

"Ready?" Mason took an excited breath. "I've been ready for this all my life."

The dreamlike atmosphere continued as they entered the gallery. Auguste Falconier, the same man who'd said such scathing things to her before, now actually rushed forth to usher her in with welcoming arms. "Ah, Mademoiselle Caldwell, at last! The invited guests are all here and, as you have seen for yourself, the public outside clamors for admittance. Those inside are so eager to buy the paintings that the moment the preview is over, they will be trampling over one another to give us their money!"

He gestured past the foyer into the salon beyond. What she saw inside was just as she'd always imagined it: a crowd of wealthy patrons circulating with champagne in hand to admire her canvases, which were tastefully displayed throughout the high-ceilinged rooms of the former Second Empire row mansion.

"Allow me, Mademoiselle—may I call you Amy?"

Lisette nudged Mason and she started at the sound of the still-unfamiliar name. Rousing herself, she answered, "Yes, of course. By all means, call me Amy."

"Then, Mademoiselle Amy, allow me to show you our most heart-wrenching tribute to the artist, your late sister."

He led them to a glass display case. Inside was a collection of well-used personal effects: paint box, palette colored with rich smears of dried oil paint, tin can filled with brushes, stained smock, broad-brimmed straw hat, and in the center, a coat and a pair of shabby brown shoes.

"The shoes were those left by your sister on the bridge before she ju—" He corrected himself hastily, "Before she entered immortality. A last-minute idea on my part. I find them indescribably touching. Somehow they speak of her dedication, her poverty, and in the end, her desperation and tragedy."

Mason regarded the grimy shoes—the leather faded and worn, the toes scuffed from numerous painting expeditions in the Oise River Valley—and had to put her hand over her mouth to keep from smiling. It was too funny. She had other, nicer shoes, but none she'd have chosen to ruin on a midnight walk in the rain.

I'd love to see the look on this phony's face if he knew I wasn't the sister Amy just off the ship from America, but the dear departed herself.

Falconier allowed a moment of reverential silence before speaking. "I cannot tell you what an honor it is to represent an artist of such innovative genius as Mason Caldwell."

Lisette, rolling her eyes at the hypocrisy, put a hand on a shapely hip and spoke for the first time. "Genius? Was it her genius you referred to when you called her style impossible? When you told her to get them out of your sight?"

The proprietor drew himself up in outrage. "*Mais, pas du tout!* I said no such a thing! If someone of my staff dared to utter such defamation, I will discharge him from my employ immediately!" He turned to Mason with both hands on his heart. "I can say, Mademoiselle Amy, in all humility, that I recognized the monumental gift of your sister from the first."

Lisette, who feared nothing and no one, shook her head. "Ooh-la-la!"

"But come, everyone is eager to pay you their respects."

Falconier marched off, full of his own self-importance. Lisette put a hand on Mason's arm, waiting until he was out of range, then whispered to her, "Remember. You've never been to France before. You do not speak a word of French."

When they caught up to Falconier, he said, "I realize, Mademoiselle Amy, that you are still raw from your tragedy, but we have some gentlemen of the press here who are panting to talk with you about our beloved Mason. And it is always wise to strike while the iron is hot, *n'est-pas?* So if you don't mind, please to follow me."

He didn't pause long enough to see whether she minded or not, but proceeded into the main salon where a group of gentlemen stood waiting with pencils and pads in hand and eyes hungry to embellish a story that was fast becoming the rage of Paris.

Mason had always dreamed of being the center of attention, all eyes on her, pencils poised to jot down every word she uttered. But it had been such a rush to pull herself together for this charade that she hadn't had time to fully formulate her story.

Don't slip. Don't let them suspect who you really are.

As she joined Falconier, she dabbed her eyes with her veil, as if brushing away a tear, and said with a feigned air of sorrow, "Yes, it's been quite an ordeal. But if it will help the legacy of poor Mason, of course I'll tell them whatever I can."

As she spoke, Lisette translated for those in the group who didn't understand English.

Falconier cleared his throat. "Gentlemen of the press, may I present Mademoiselle Amy Caldwell, the sister of our late-departed and much-missed artist. And with her, the lovely Mademoiselle Lisette Ladoux of the Cirque Fernando and Folies-Bergères. She was, as you know, a close personal friend of the artist and her primary model."

A thin man with a goatee began the proceedings. "Mademoiselle Caldwell, I am Etienne Debray of *La Gauloise.* May I ask, why do you think it is that your sister's work was so unappreciated in her brief life?"

Mason considered the question, then spoke slowly, "I know little about art, but I think her paintings may have threatened the people who always want things to remain the same."

"Why do you think there is such interest in her now?"

"I'm sorry, I can't answer that. Perhaps it's just that her time has come."

As Lisette translated, Mason noticed a man standing by himself several yards behind the reporters, staring at her with a penetrating gaze. The first thing she noticed was his size. He stood a full head above the rest of the crowd, with prominent wide shoulders and large hands that offered a captivating contrast to the ease with which he wore his expensively tailored suit. He'd forsaken the beard Parisian men favored and was clean-shaven, emphasizing the sculpted line of his jaw. He was the most arresting man she'd ever seen. But it wasn't just his individual features—dark hair, wide forehead, thick brows atop piercing dark eyes, vertical creases on either side of his mouth—that made him so. As handsome as he was at first glance, it was the energy he projected that riveted her attention, one of action and excitement, and the promise of adventure. It hit her like a physical blow. Raw. Feral. Brazenly sexual.

For a moment, she lost track of what Lisette was saying. Why was the man looking at her this way? She'd never seen him before, but he was inspecting her with a cheeky sort of intimacy. She felt positively naked beneath his unflinching scrutiny and had to resist the urge to adjust her clothing. Was it possible that he recognized her? But no, she'd taken great pains to change her appearance—dyeing her hair, wearing carefully applied cosmetics, even chopping off the long eyelashes that were her most noticeable feature.

She dragged her gaze away and forced herself to concentrate.

Another reporter asked, "But, mademoiselle, there is no precedent for what is going on here today. Surely much of the interest is due to the harrowing circumstances of your sister's demise. Such a wretched death for one so young, so beautiful, so talented."

Someone piped up with, "But it has done wonders for her career."

There were some snickers from the spectators who'd gathered round.

Falconier held up his hands. "Please, gentlemen, have some respect!"

The questioner added, "I certainly meant no disrespect. I only meant to point out that there is a quality to her life and death that seems to move people in a way that I have never seen before. She never had a patron, never sold a painting, never had the slightest encouragement from what we can tell. And yet she worked on, giving everything to her art, including, finally, her life. That is the mark of a true martyr, a . . . Joan of Art."

As he coined the phrase, a silence descended on the crowd, as if suddenly realizing that they were a part of something larger than what had first been apparent.

Mason, taken aback by this, wasn't sure what to say. She glanced about at the dumbstruck crowd. As she did, her gaze met and held that of the man standing on the fringes. He gave a slow, single nod of his head that baffled her.

"*Jeanne d'Art*," repeated one of the reporters. "*C'est formidable!*"

The newsmen were now writing furiously. As they finished, another of them asked, "What are your plans for the paintings?"

Mason waited for Lisette to finish translating before she answered, "Monsieur Falconier will try to sell the eighteen here today—"

The intriguing man at the back shook his head, distracting her. She stumbled, then continued, "With the stipulation that, should the committee deem them acceptable, they be made available to be displayed at the World's Fair this summer. I understand they turned her down once, but Monsieur Falconier seems to think in light of the recent publicity . . ."

"Are there more paintings?"

Mason hadn't expected the question. But on impulse, she said, "Yes, many."

As she translated, Lisette tossed her a quizzical frown. This wasn't part of the plan.

Falconier looked pleasantly startled. "Really! But this is *magnifique*! And where are they?"

Thinking on her feet, Mason said, "My sister shipped them back to me in Massachusetts. I could have them sent over if anyone wanted to see them."

Falconier had brightened considerably at this news. He rubbed his smooth, white hands together, and his eyes sparked with the glint of avarice. "Want to see them? The world will *demand* to see them! And you may rest assured that the Falconier Gallery will be the enthusiastic broker for these masterpieces."

Lisette couldn't help but smile at his greed. "How kind of the monsieur," she quipped.

One of the reporters was nibbling thoughtfully on his pencil. "What do you surmise will happen to all this interest? Will it continue to grow?"

"I can answer that question."

Mason turned to see Lucien Morrel, the city's foremost art critic. She'd read his reviews and respected his opinion for years. He'd been instrumental in the careers of Renoir and Degas in the days when the art establishment had turned a blind eye to the revolution in painting that was going on all around them. Now he was about to pronounce judgment on her work. Unconsciously, she held her breath.

"In two weeks' time," the learned man proclaimed, "this Mason Caldwell will have been completely forgotten. Her current notoriety is entirely without substance or merit. Her technique is sloppy, the subject matter tends toward the macabre, and her colors bear no relation to the physical reality they're supposed to convey. In short, her work is not art. It is an *affront* to art. This morbid interest in her is due solely to the fact that she surely realized she had no talent and, having come to this astute recognition, ended her life by flinging herself from the Pont de l'Alma. A romantic notion that at present has the bourgeoisie swooning and lining up to see her paintings, but that is all. Parisians are notorious for loving a good suicide. No, no, my friends. What we are experiencing here is not the discovery of a new master; it is a carnival sideshow."

Lisette turned to Mason, her eyes brimming with consternation. Mason waved a hand, silently telling her not to bother to translate. Hearing it once was enough.

Mason turned away, feeling flushed and overheated, wanting nothing more than to bolt from the crushing rejection.

But at that moment, her gaze once again found the handsome stranger at the back. He was still watching her. Now he slowly shook his head, then rolled his eyes. His meaning was clear. He was telling her that the revered Monsieur Morrel was talking through his hat. The warmth of it flowed through her, coursing courage and a badly needed jolt of appreciation through her veins.

Caught off guard by the critic's denunciation, Falconier had turned white. But he was saved from having to react by a sudden shuffling in the crowd and a harsh male voice calling out, "Where is Falconier?"

All eyes turned to a man of medium height, slim but well built, with slicked-back black hair and a distinctly disreputable air. It was the infamous gangster Juno Dargelos. As he and two burly bodyguards moved their way, the elegant bystanders parted in a flurry of scandalized whispers.

Spotting the proprietor, Dargelos called out, "I will buy them, Falconier. All the pictures of Lisette."

Seeing him, Lisette raised her face to the ceiling and cried out, "Oh no! Not again!"

The intruder peered at her like a love-struck spaniel, and

said, "Did you think I would let anyone else possess the pictures of my darling turtledove?"

With a stamp of her foot, Lisette fired back, "How many times must I tell you, Juno? I am not your turtledove, and never will be!"

The presence of the gang chieftain provided a delicious new twist to the story. The reporters jumped on it, firing questions at him.

"Eh, Juno, what are you doing so far from Belleville?"

"You don't own the police in this part of town, after all."

"Haven't you heard that Inspector Duval has sworn he will not rest until the day he packs you off to Devil's Island?"

Dargelos extended both arms toward Lisette in a gesture worthy of a Puccini hero. "For the woman I adore, I would *swim* to Devil's Island and back."

As Lisette groaned, Mason took the opportunity to steal away. She looked around, trying to spot her silent advisor, but he'd moved on. Finally, she saw him in the farthest corner of the salon, his back to her.

As Falconier nervously protested that most of the paintings featured Mademoiselle Ladoux and he couldn't possibly sell all of them to the man—"I have regular customers here, Monsieur, whom I must honor!"—Mason made her way to join the fascinating stranger. As she neared, she realized he was staring at one particular painting. Like the others, it featured an idealized young woman surrounded by nightmarish imagery: a world of chaos in which line and form were exaggerated to create a sense of menace. But unlike the others, the figure at the center was herself. Her only experiment in self-portraiture.

It showed a figure—Mason herself—kneeling in the foreground with her Prussian blue dress falling in soft folds about her hips, her naked back to the viewer. Her long hair, light brown with touches of gold, tumbled down her back, leading the eye to a heart-shaped birthmark on her upper right flank. She was glancing over her shoulder as if she had just become aware of the viewer's presence, acknowledging it with the hint of an enigmatic smile. There was no source light or shadows, but the figure seemed to glow from within. On one side of the frame, a grove of leafless, misshapen trees stretched their branches to the sky as if in agony. On the other side, an overturned canon jutted into the air beside a path that snaked into a succession of distant hills, one of which was covered with tombstones. Falconier had labeled it *Portrait of the Artist.*

The man was gazing at it with rapt attention. She watched him for a moment, thinking he would continue on to the next painting. But he didn't. He just stood there, as if in a trance.

Finally, she walked over and joined him. This close, she could feel the heat of him, as if he radiated some vital energy all his own. It made her feel keenly aware of the new dress caressing her skin.

He must surely feel her presence, as she felt his, but he didn't show it. After a moment, she asked gently, "What do you think of it?"

Without looking away, he said, "I think it's a revelation."

It was a marvelous voice, deep and rich, decidedly upper-crust British, but with the faintest trace of a Scottish burr. He pronounced the word *revelation* with an inflection all his own, drawing out the vowels as if savoring them on his tongue. A sensual voice, one that sent shivers up her spine.

"You heard what the critic Morrel said," she reminded him tentatively.

"Morrel's an idiot."

She was slightly shocked to hear this contemptuous appraisal.

"They tell me he's the last word on what's acceptable in art."

He still hadn't looked away from the painting. Now he gave a careless shrug. "Morrel's had his day. But the world has passed him by. He wouldn't know an innovative work of art if it bit him on the—" He turned then and gave her a roguish grin that deepened the creases in his cheeks. "But not to worry. He'll come around."

He said it with a conspiratorial confidence that was absolutely thrilling. She looked at him more closely now. There was a glint in his dark eyes that seemed to invite her in. She couldn't decide if that twinkle was truly wicked or just the contrivance of a charming man. He seemed so self-assured with such a sexual magnetism that her breath quickened. His face was an odd mixture of contrasts, elegantly handsome yet strangely rugged, with a touch of danger about the mouth— a compelling combination. Looking at that mouth—so full, so blatantly carnal—she found herself unconsciously licking her lips.

"The artist was my sister," she said as much to anchor herself as anything.

"I know. You were pointed out to me."

He fixed his eyes on her with flattering assessment before returning them to the painting.

After an awkward silence, she ventured, "You said it was a revelation. What did you mean?"

"I mean it's one of the most extraordinary personal visions I've ever seen."

She strained not to show her excitement. "Why?" she asked as casually as she could.

"First of all, no artist has ever portrayed the anxiety of modern life quite so imaginatively or vividly. The backgrounds of each of these works conveys menace—images of the ugly, the grotesque, the terrible. And yet, the sheer passion of her technique, and the expressive flourish of her color, transforms them into something almost beautiful."

Mason's heart began to thump. He was getting exactly what she was after!

"Moreover, the threat of the backgrounds is further neutralized in each of the paintings by the central image of a young woman. These women exude a beauty, a purity, a moral strength, and an awareness of their own sensuality that transforms the misery and peril of the world around them. At first, the paintings seem pessimistic. But the longer one looks at them, the more obvious it becomes that they are intensely hopeful and life-affirming. Look at this one. Obviously painted in the catacombs, the woman is surrounded by stacks of human skulls. A more unsettling reminder of our mortality you'd never want to see. Yet she's by far the most powerful thing in the painting. A power that makes even our destiny of death seem beautiful."

Mason's heart was racing now.

He gestured again toward her self-portrait. "But for me, this is the most captivating of them all. She's painted herself in what appears to be a battlefield. A horror that has brought her to her knees and stripped her bare. And yet, she's rising from her knees, from the ashes, and giving us that exquisitely enigmatic hint of a smile. What is she telling us?"

Mason looked away from the painting and into his eyes. "You tell me."

"She's telling us that the beauty of art can transcend and purify the horror of the world. Hardly the message of a woman about to kill herself, I admit. But that's her tragedy. She succeeded in her mission, yet she didn't know it." He shook his head sorrowfully. "I wish I'd known her. I wished I'd been able to tell her just how magnificently she succeeded."

Mason couldn't believe what she was hearing. For the first time in her life, she felt completely understood, accepted, appreciated.

"Who *are* you?" she gasped.

"Me? I'm nobody."

"Are you a critic? Or an artist yourself?"

He chuckled, a deep rumble that seemed to emanate from his massive chest. "I'm not a critic or an artist or a collector. Just a chap who hangs about the art world. You might say

I'm just an appreciator of art. But I know the real thing when I see it."

"You must have a name."

He smiled, showing a flash of straight white teeth. "Garrett. Richard Garrett."

He extended a large hand that made hers seem miniscule in comparison. The touch of his firm, warm flesh sent a jolt through her senses.

"And your name is . . . ?" he prompted when she just stood holding his hand.

"Ma—" She caught herself just in time. She was so befuddled, so swept away, that she'd almost slipped and told him her real name. Shaking herself, she amended, "I'm Amy Caldwell from . . . Boston, Massachusetts."

"Well, Amy Caldwell from Boston, Massachusetts, I'd say you have a bit of a dilemma on your hands."

"Dilemma?"

"I assume you saw all those people lining up outside to buy your sister's paintings. Tomorrow they'll be able to sell them for five times what they paid for them today. And the day after that, those people will be able to sell them for *ten* times what *they* paid. There's a phenomenon afoot and you need time to sit back, assess the situation, and find the proper strategy for dealing with it. Were I you, I'd stop this sale right now before it gets started."

Mason looked across the room and saw that Falconier was about to open the doors to the public and begin the sale. The gangster Juno Dargelos had already taken three canvases featuring Lisette off the wall and was waving a fistful of francs at Falconier's back as Lisette continued to berate him for embarrassing her this way.

Uncertain what to do, Mason glanced back at Garrett and asked, "Stop it? But isn't that a bit like leaving the bride at the altar?"

"Better that than a life of regret brought about by the

wrong decision. Just go to Falconier and say, 'I've changed my mind. The sale is off.'"

She cast a glance at the gallery owner who was unlocking the door, then back at Garrett.

His gaze pierced her.

"You'd best hurry," he stressed, "before it's too late."

Chapter 2

Stop the sale? Before it even got started? On the advice of a complete stranger?

After all she'd gone through, shouldn't she just be grateful to be selling anything at all?

But then . . . this wasn't just any stranger. It was almost as if he'd been sent here by destiny to hold up a beacon to her future. Could there be more in store for her than selling a few paintings at bargain prices?

She had no way of knowing. Her life, since that tumultuous night on the Pont de l'Alma, had been a kaleidoscope of bizarre events that had taught her one thing: What had seemed like the worst catastrophe of her life might well have turned out to be the best thing that ever happened to her.

Two months ago, on the city's stormiest night in living memory, Mason was flailing in the Seine when suddenly something cracked her in the head. She'd lost consciousness, assuming those were her last moments on earth. But when she awoke sometime later in the night, she found that she'd somehow managed to hook her arm around whatever flotsam had struck her. Either she'd managed to pull herself up with her last ounce of strength, or she'd been saved by a fluke of that same fate she'd earlier cursed. She had just enough presence of mind to heave herself on top of it and out of the frigid water before she'd blacked out once again. After that, there was a sense of moving in and out of consciousness as the rapid current carried her cascading through the night.

When she awoke—God only knew how many hours later— it was in a warm bed under a fluffy down comforter. A woman's face appeared above her and a kind voice asked, "Are you awake?" Mason tried to respond but couldn't. She didn't have the strength to move her lips. A moment later, she sank back into the darkness.

She was vaguely aware of tossing feverishly and kicking off the covers to cool her burning skin. She had bleary memories of moving in and out of the light and of some sort of vile medicine being forced down her throat, bringing with it another heavy sleep.

Then one morning she awoke to a room full of sunshine to see the woman sitting in a chair, mending a stocking. Mason tried to push herself up, but was so weak she fell back into the pillows, exhausted and lightheaded. Finally, she asked, "What happened? Where am I?"

She heard a cry. "She's awake! She's all right!" Then the shuffle of footsteps as the family quickly gathered round her bed—the parents, two boys, a little girl, and a toothless grandmother. They all spoke at once, making a fuss, rejoicing in her recovery.

The woman who'd been sewing said, "Dr. DuBois says something hit your head in the water. He says it was a miracle you didn't drown."

"Where am I?"

"Rueil-la-Gadeliere."

Groggily, Mason placed the name in her mind. Renoir had painted there. But it couldn't be! It was fifty miles downriver!

"How long have I been here?"

"It has been nearly four weeks since the good Lord brought you to us."

"Four weeks!"

Again, she tried to sit, but her head swam sickly. The kind woman helped her back, adjusting her covers as she introduced her family. They were the Carriers, farmers who lived at the edge of the river. They'd chanced to spot her sprawled on top of the massive tree limb as it had floated by the morning after the storm. In their launch, they'd pursued and rescued her. They were a poor and simple people, and seemed to her blurry eyes as if they'd just stepped out of a painting by Millet. Pere Carrier assured her that they were happy to take care of her and wanted nothing in return.

"And the woman . . . the other woman . . ."

They exchanged puzzled glances, and the father said, "There was no other woman with you."

Mason felt a heavy sadness. She'd wanted so badly to help that poor nameless soul on the bridge. Madame Carrier saw the tears that slipped down her cheek and gently stroked her hair back off her face. "There, there. You've been very ill. You must rest and not worry. You will stay with us and let us care for you until you are yourself again."

Choked with tears, all Mason could do was nod her gratitude. Madame Carrier gave her some more medicine and before long, she'd once again drifted back to sleep.

Three days later, Mason awoke with more strength. She managed to get out of bed and stand for a few minutes. Every day she increased her time out of bed until finally she was able to take walks around the nearby village.

The Carriers were wonderful. They accepted her as a member of the family and gave no indication that they wanted her to leave. As her strength returned, she found herself enjoying being protected within the bosom of this family and being away from the life she'd left in Paris.

It was an idyllic retreat. Her gratitude at having been so miraculously spared blotted out any thoughts of the past or feelings of failure. The air had never smelled so sweet; the sky had never seemed so blue. She savored every moment of life, putting off thinking about where she would go from here. She had no commitments in Paris and she'd told Lisette she might go to Auvers, a village on the Oise River where she often retreated to paint, so there was no need to notify her. For now, it was enough just to be alive.

But then one day she decided to walk into the village. She'd been away from Paris for just over seven weeks by then and had lost a great deal of weight. She barely resembled herself, but she felt wholly refreshed, bursting with energy and robust with health.

Then she saw it: her name on a newspaper lying on an outside table at the local café. She snatched it up and hastily began to read.

The article told the story of how the late American painter Mason Caldwell—whose body had washed up on the shore of Neuilly, just outside of Paris, on the eighth of February— was becoming a posthumous celebrity. The Parisian papers had been in competition to glamorize what they were calling her suicide. According to them, she'd thrown herself from the bridge with the desperate romanticism of Madame Bovary. That was remarkable enough, but even more astonishing was the fact that dealers were actually competing to acquire the right to sell her paintings!

Stunned, she stumbled back to Chez Carrier and, without telling them what had happened, announced that she must return to Paris at once. Asking no questions, they gave her five francs, and she set out to correct the ghastly mistake.

On the riverboat back to the city, the scenario of what must have happened played through her mind. The woman on the bridge that night—the one she'd tried so hard to save— had drowned and her body, which was found more than a week later, had been mistaken for Mason's. She tried to remember her face, so briefly glimpsed when the wind had blown back the concealing hood. Who was she? She must have some family who Mason should contact and tell the sad news. Nearly two months later, they must be out of their minds with worry. Her message would be a blow, but at least they'd know what had really happened.

It was late by the time the now nearly complete Eiffel

Tower came into view. Passing the fairgrounds below it, she saw the silhouettes of dozens of new buildings for the upcoming Exposition that had sprung up in her absence. She looked around her at the once-familiar sights of her adopted city and felt lost and alone, like a stranger. This wasn't the Paris she'd left behind. This was a Paris where Mason Caldwell was no longer alive.

She had no idea how to go about accomplishing what suddenly seemed like an overwhelming task. All she knew was that she needed to go to someone—now, at once—who would be happy to see her. She needed to be welcomed back from the dead.

She needed Lisette.

Mason's childhood had been isolated and lonely, and she'd never had a close friend before Lisette. They'd met shortly after Mason had arrived in Paris. She'd outfitted herself with art supplies and had set out to *La Grande Jatte,* an island in the Seine where the bourgeoisie went to enjoy their leisure time. She'd set up her easel, plopped her straw hat on her head, and picked up her brush. Everything at the ready, she'd looked about, wondering what to paint. Women dressed in their Sunday best strolled unhurriedly along the paths or picnicked beneath the trees. Men, in top hats or derbies, lounged in the shade, watching the sailboats glide along the river. Children frolicked on the grass or waded along the banks, their squeals piercing the air. Typical Impressionistic motifs. She was looking for something different, but she didn't know quite what.

Then she saw Lisette. She was a child-woman with a tumbled tangle of luxurious gold hair that seemed to glow in the fulsome sunshine of summer. Half a dozen dogs of all sizes and breeds surrounded her, panting in anticipation as she raised a small ball she held in her hand. She was barefoot and was laughing as the two poodles leapt into the lake. Hiking up her skirts, she'd run playfully in after them, picking them up in both arms and smothering them with heartfelt kisses, completely mindless to the fact that they were soaking her pretty yellow dress. She was effortlessly elegant and earthy all at once, delighting in the movements of her own body, completely unconscious of the effect she was creating.

At this point, Mason hadn't found the artistic vision that would later so possess her. But one look at the carefree young woman made her realize that she'd found something special. A Greek goddess for the modern age, a new kind of woman full of light and color and sensual grace.

She found, when she introduced herself in halting French, that Lisette was a trapeze artist and acrobat. When Mason asked if she would model for her, the young woman wrinkled her nose in distaste, then reconsidered and said with a shrug, "*Et bien*. Why not?" Mason was so satisfied with the results of the sitting that, several weeks later and after many frustrating afternoons of painting plaster casts and bowls of oranges, she decided to seek out her reluctant model at the Folies-Bergères, where she'd said she was currently appearing. This time Lisette refused. But several days later, she appeared at Mason's Montmartre flat and said, rather haughtily, "I have nothing to do this afternoon, so you may paint me."

As Mason worked in a lightning flash of inspiration, she realized she'd found the subject she'd been looking for—one who somehow fit into the vision she was struggling to formulate. She still couldn't explain to herself exactly what place Lisette would occupy in this grand scheme, but she'd never felt more at one with the creative force than when painting her.

For her part, however, Lisette seemed cautious of the young American artist and kept her distance as the French were wont to do, occasionally agreeing to pose, but demanding a fee and offering nothing of herself but her physical presence. Then one day, Mason was shopping for vegetables in the market at Les Halles and was in the process of paying the vendor when she heard a familiar voice behind her. "What are you doing? Do you not know this man is charging you three times what he would charge a French customer for that pathetic head of lettuce?"

Before Mason had time to answer, Lisette had attacked the vendor in a hand-waving tirade of French, snatched some coins from Mason's hand, and exchanged them for the lettuce. "You need someone to take care of you," she'd pronounced contemptuously.

Over the following weeks, their acquaintance entered a new stage. Not quite a friendship, but something more than the indifference Lisette had previously extended. Several times she dropped by with no warning and took Mason out shopping for food and clothes, and once she led her by the arm to the building's concierge and told her in no uncertain terms that the American would no longer be paying such an inflated rent for her "miserable hovel." Another time she gave Mason a ticket to the Cirque Fernando where she was performing. Mason had marveled at the ease, agility, and breathtaking charisma with which she'd flown through the air on her trapeze. But Lisette still didn't give herself in real friendship. Mason assumed she never would. She kept most people at an emotional distance and reserved most of her affection for her dogs.

Several months later, however, Mason stopped by Lisette's apartment on the Boulevard de Clichy, intending to borrow a cloisonné vase she'd given Lisette and wanted to use for a still life she was painting. Lisette was out of town, on a long tour with the traveling circus that was taking her all over France and into Italy for most of the summer, and couldn't be reached. When she went to the concierge to ask admittance to Lisette's rooms, she discovered that the old woman, a friend of Lisette's, had passed away a week before. The building had been inherited by her son, a worthless brute whose unwanted advances Lisette had rebuffed time and again in no uncertain terms. In revenge, the new landlord was in the process of transporting her beloved ménage of dogs, which the late concierge had been caring for, to the Paris dog pound, where they would soon meet their demise.

"You can't do that!" Mason insisted.

"I certainly can. She didn't pay her rent in advance."

"I'll pay her rent," Mason told him.

"It's too late. I've rented her rooms to someone a little more appreciative, and those mongrels are on their way to the meat grinder."

Mason raced to the pound and managed to rescue the seven animals just in time.

A month later, at the end of her summer tour, Lisette appeared at Mason's door utterly distraught with tears streaming down her face. She'd been to her apartment where she'd been gleefully informed by the new landlord that her darling brood were long gone. After flying into the man in an attempt to scratch his eyes out, she'd gone to see Mason. "That beast sent my babies to their execution."

Mason was about to reassure her when, behind them, there was a bark of recognition. A light came to Lisette's eyes. She rushed past Mason into the room, dropped to her knees, and the seven dogs attacked her joyfully, jumping up on her, licking her face, as she screamed in delight. She kissed their faces, crying uncontrollably, and as she did, she noticed that they'd been freshly bathed and each had a bright red ribbon tied about its neck.

Slowly, Lisette disengaged herself and rose to look at Mason in bafflement. "You . . . You saved them!"

"Just in time. That bastard really had it in for you."

"But you don't even like dogs."

Mason smiled. "I didn't think so. I've never had one. But I've sure grown fond of these guys."

"But . . . you kept them for a whole month. Walked them, fed them, bathed them . . . all that time and trouble . . . What made you do it?"

"I couldn't very well let them die," Mason told her. "They're part of *you*."

Lisette looked at her for several moments. Then she stooped and picked up a small Pekinese puppy and offered him to Mason. *"Pour toi,"* she said, for the first time using the familiar form of French, the *"toi"* reserved for family and friends.

Deeply touched, Mason realized there was no more precious gift Lisette could bestow. But she shook her head. "I couldn't take Monsieur Fu. He's your baby. Just let me visit him from time to time."

Lisette hugged the puppy to her chest. She never said another word about what had happened. But from that moment on, she became that devoted best friend Mason had never had as a child. She knew, without having to question it, that come what may, Lisette Ladoux would always be there, loving her with the fierce devotion of a true sister.

So it was natural, in this extraordinary situation, that Mason would race to Lisette, knowing how she must have suffered on hearing the news of her "death."

She used the last of her borrowed money to take an omnibus to the Cirque Fernando at the base of the Montmartre butte. Lisette would just be finishing her performance about now and would soon be walking her dogs home. Wishing to avoid a scene in the circus auditorium, Mason waited outside for her. Momentarily, she saw her friend leave the building behind her pack of leashed canines. Knowing her route, Mason stood in place, waiting for her to pass. But it was the dogs that recognized her first, barking greetings and pulling Lisette toward her. Lisette was about to scold them when she saw the object of their excitement. Her doelike brown eyes registered first shock, then recognition, then teary relief, all in an instant. Trying to keep herself from exploding with happiness, she whispered, "I'm not dreaming, am I?"

"Not unless I'm dreaming, too," Mason smiled.

"But I saw you!" Lisette cried. "They made me look at what was left of your poor swollen body!"

"That wasn't me. That was a woman I jumped in trying to save."

Lisette grabbed her and began covering her face with kisses, giving her the welcome she'd so needed. "I should have known you could never do such a thing. But I thought it was you. It looked so much like you, the same coloring, the same height. . . . It broke my heart. How . . . Why . . . ?"

Mason pulled away. "I'll tell you all about it, I promise. But for now, tell me what's been going on here. I read in the paper that—"

"*Zut!*" Lisette remembered. "*Les journales!* That was my fault. I was so desolate at the thought of you dying like that, so miserable, so unappreciated. I only wanted to make it up to you somehow. So I went to the papers, where they know of me from the circus, and I told them your sad story. I wanted you to have a little bit of the fame you deserved."

"Fame." The word sounded so strange in connection to her that it was jarring.

"Yes," Lisette cried, "they love your paintings now! And can you believe it? I sold three of them!"

"You sold my paintings?"

"You can't believe how eager people were to buy them. I sold them for five hundred francs each!"

Mason had to pinch herself. Five hundred francs!

"The galleries are fighting to represent you. I gave the rest of them to Falconier because he offered the best terms. He bought back the three I sold and he was hoping to show them all the day after tomorrow."

"My own show?" Mason took a moment to savor the idea. "But all this attention . . . it's because they think I'm dead, right?"

Lisette shrugged. "I suppose. The story has swept the city. You know how we French love a romantic tragedy."

"But will they still be interested once they know I'm alive?"

"We'll soon see, no?"

But Mason's mind was charging ahead. "What if we *don't*

test it? What if I conveniently stay dead for a while? Until after the show. Maybe once people see the paintings, what they'll care about is the work and not the 'romantic tragedy.' And then I can return from the dead. I was recuperating in the country, I had no knowledge of what was going on in Paris . . . I might just as well have discovered the mistake after the show as now."

"But you didn't give me a chance to finish. Falconier can't show the paintings."

"What do you mean he can't show them? You said you gave them to him."

"The police now say he can't show them. You didn't leave a will, so no one can say for sure who owns them. Until it's settled in court, Falconier can't open the show. He's going out of his mind."

Mason took a minute to consider this. Then a mischievous smile began to tug at the corners of her mouth. "What if I had a sister? As my only living relative, she'd inherit the paintings. What if you suddenly received a letter from this sister, who you didn't know I had, saying she'd read about poor Mason's demise in the Boston papers and was about to embark for France to settle her affairs? What if you cabled her aboard her ship telling her about the show and she cabled back her permission to go ahead with it?"

"But you don't have a sister."

"I do now."

All at once Lisette saw the beauty of it and met her smile. "Wouldn't that be a terrible thing for us to do?"

"Terrible."

"We've got to do it, yes?"

"I don't think there's any power on earth that can stop us now, do you?"

Lisette clapped her hands. "This is going to be such fun!"

Early the next morning, Lisette went to Falconier and told him the story they'd concocted. Overjoyed, the gallery owner rescued the pile of invitations that hadn't yet been tossed into the fire and whipped his staff into a frenzy of preparations. "We open in two days," he proclaimed.

"You should have seen him," Lisette told Mason later in her frilly bedroom overrun with stuffed toys and live dogs. "He was so delighted that he insisted on putting the sister up in his suite at the Jockey Club on the Rue Scribe. That's one of the best addresses in town, you know. *And* because he was so desperate to show the paintings, I told him he had to cover the sister's expenses while she's here. Look at this! A letter of credit! All the money we need to dress you right. I already spoke to Madame Tensale, who will bring a selection of clothes this afternoon."

"That's perfect!" Mason cried excitedly. "We'll give the sister an entire wardrobe, the kind of things I never wore. Create a whole new image for her."

"Silks and feathers and all sorts of pretty things," Lisette agreed, "instead of those plain clothes you wear. We'll pretend we're playing dress-up."

That settled, they pondered how best to proceed with the transformation.

"I can cut bangs," Mason suggested, peering at herself in the vanity mirror. "That's a start, but it won't be enough. We could dye my hair. How do we do that?"

Lisette gave her a defensive pout. "Me? How would I know? My hair is completely natural." Mason answered her with a mock frown, which brought on a fit of laughter from Lisette. "*Ça va*," she conceded. "I know a place where we can get some chemicals. We will dye your hair dark, no? Like a gypsy."

"That's a start." Mason searched Lisette's vanity for a small pair of scissors. With them, she cut the eyelashes on one eye to half their length.

Lisette screeched. "Your lovely lashes! You've killed them!"

"They'll grow back," Mason assured her, repeating the process on the other eye. "I cut them once when I was young just to see if they would grow back. They did, even longer than before. This is the one way I can guarantee that people won't recognize me."

"It's true," Lisette teased. "It wouldn't occur to anyone that you would do such a stupid thing."

They threw themselves into the planning like Sarah Bernhardt preparing for the Comédie Français. The extensive amount of weight Mason had lost added to the disguise. They took the initials from Mason's first and middle name— Mason Emily—and twisted them a bit to form the name Amy. Once they'd purchased the new wardrobe, they packed it into steamer trunks and had them sent to the Jockey Club. Then, with Mason in full costume, they went to Gare St-Lazare, where they hired a finer coach and took it to the Opera Quarter as if Miss Amy Caldwell from Boston, Massachusetts, had just arrived on the train from Le Havre.

They giggled most of the way there. What they were doing was outrageous, but after all, it would only be a brief charade. Once the show was a success, Mason Caldwell would come back to life and her sister Amy would conveniently disappear forever.

Chapter 3

As the show was about to open to the public, Mason was faced with an important decision. Falconier had already unbolted the doors and people were beginning to stream in. Halting the sale at this point wouldn't just be a major inconvenience for everyone involved, it would be considered an affront, particularly inconsiderate in light of the false start-and-stop Falconier had already endured. And yet . . . What if this Garrett was right? She had no way of knowing. Stopping the sale, as he suggested, required a cheeky daring that certainly appealed to her, but it also called for a confidence in the popularity of her work that, up to now, was completely unwarranted.

What to do?

She scrutinized Garrett. "You really believe there will be that kind of demand for these paintings?"

Without hesitation, he answered, "I do."

She glanced back at the dealer, who was ushering in the waiting crowd. "Falconier will have an apoplexy."

Garrett arched a brow. She detected a challenge lurking in his amused smile. "Would you like me to do it for you?"

There was something hidden in the smoky depths of his eyes that captivated her, beckoned her, told her she could . . . What? Trust him?

In that moment she made her decision. "Thank you. I'll do it myself."

She swiveled on her feet, marched over to Falconier, and announced, "I'm stopping the sale."

He wheeled in alarm. "Stopping the sale!"

"Just until we can better assess the real value of the paintings. There's just more interest here than I know how to deal with."

"*Mais c'est impossible!* It cannot be done, Mademoiselle! As you see—"

"I know. But think about it. If we wait, and the interest continues to build, you might end up with three or four times the commission you'd get today."

A thoughtful look crossed the dealer's pasty face. "It would be unprecedented, to be sure, and yet . . . They *are* your paintings now, so . . ." He gave a Gallic shrug. "So I suppose I must do as you wish." He lowered his voice and shook his head in appreciation. "You Americans. So shrewd at business, *n'est pas?*"

He clicked his heels together and gave a crisp clap of his hands. "*Messieurs et mesdames,*" he called. "Gentlemen and ladies, you are welcome to view the paintings, but for the time being, they are no longer for sale."

The announcement was met by a roar of protest.

"Not for sale! I've been waiting in line for three hours!"

"But this is an outrage!"

"How can this be? The paintings are not for sale?"

In that instant, Dargelos the gangster stepped forward. "You can do what you wish with the rest of them, but I am purchasing these three pictures. Here is your money." His henchmen clustered around him to make the point.

Lisette stormed to Dargelos and grabbed hold of the paintings, pulling them away. "You stupid oaf! These are not for you!"

"But, sugarplum, who should own them but he who loves you with all his heart?"

Someone else called out in a maligned tone, "So you bow to ruffians but deny the decent citizens of Paris!"

Another called, "You close the door on the public so the speculators can move in and make money off the dead woman, eh?"

This seemed to strike a chord in the crowd and instigated a chain reaction of pushing and shoving as people rushed to the walls, took possession of the nearest painting, and began to form a queue behind the gangster with billfolds in hand.

Falconier gulped, screwed up his courage, and called over the noise, "Monsieur Dargelos, I respectfully remind you this is Rue Lafitte, not Belleville. If you do not put down those paintings at once, I will summon the police."

"Police?"

The word was picked up by others and echoed through the incredulous crowd.

"That goes for everyone here," Falconier declared.

Instead of quieting what was becoming a mob, it enraged those already inside and panicked those who were coming in the doors. Afraid they might be locked out, they began to push their way in. Within moments, there were so many people that there was no room to move or even breathe. More people, caught up in the agitation, were bolting over others in an effort to squeeze inside.

By now Falconier was shrieking for order. But the horde was not to be dissuaded. Mason looked about her at the ensuing bedlam. But instead of feeling fear or trepidation, her face was aglow with an amazed, delighted grin.

They're fighting over my paintings!

Outside, the sharp sound of a police whistle pierced the air. Obviously, some of Falconier's staff had run for help. This only added to the chaos.

This is getting better and better!

Mason turned in a semicircle, taking it all in, relishing

every rousing moment. She had to battle the impulse to laugh out loud. Never in her wildest dreams could she have imagined such a spectacle, and all on account of her paintings!

But then she noticed a different sort of upheaval before her. The crowd began to part in a channel that was rapidly moving her way from the direction of her self-portrait. And then she saw Richard Garrett towering above the throng, coming toward her with a determined gleam in his eyes.

What is he doing?

As he drew closer, she could see that he was firmly and resolutely taking the arm of each person who stood in his way and moving them aside to create a path for himself. His actions were decisive, even aggressive, but he kept up a litany of polite salutations, uttering each with a wry twinkle in his eyes. "Excuse me. Thank you very much. Lovely hat, Madam. We'll move you just there, shall we?"

Until at last he'd brushed away the bystanders that separated them, scooped Mason up into his arms, and swept her through the multitude toward the front door and safety. Large, magnetic eyes with a touch of irony in them crinkled in amusement as he spoke. "I don't always get this chummy on first acquaintance. You'll forgive me, I hope."

Before she could reply, the police swarmed inside, whistles blaring, pushing their way through. As they did, the wall of people surged like an angry sea, teeming in alarm, nearly knocking Garrett off his feet. He swerved her around, and as he did she was nearly pitched from his hold.

She felt herself tumbling. But then, like an athlete, he righted himself and his arms tightened about her, catching her fall. He heaved her up and into his embrace so powerfully that she had to throw her arms about his neck. And then, like a whirlwind, he swung her around, knocking others out of his way, and swooped her through the melee.

She kept hold of him dizzily, feeling the bump of bodies strewn in their path, feeling the rigid, corded muscles of his arms anchoring her to his chest. His shoulders were so wide they seemed like the rampart of some medieval fortress protecting her.

Before she knew it, he'd stormed out the door and up the sunlit street, away from the gallery, from the racket, from the crush of human bodies and greed.

As he set her down, she swayed on her feet. The whole experience had left her feeling breathless and exhilarated. She'd never experienced anything like this in her life. It was extraordinary enough to don a disguise and watch as people went berserk for her work, but on top of that, to be appreciated, *understood*, by such an incredible man who'd literally swept her off her feet . . . She couldn't believe it.

As they strolled toward the Boulevard Haussmann, Mason stared up at Richard Garrett with dazed fascination. But then it occurred to her that she was being ridiculously transparent. One look and he would read her dazzled feelings in her eyes. She lowered her newly trimmed lashes, trying to get her bearings and think of something to say that wouldn't sound as giddy and girlish as she felt inside.

Garret saved her the trouble. Grinning, he said, "We appear to have caused something of a commotion."

She smiled at the understatement of it—so charmingly British—and replied, "I hope I did the right thing."

His gaze flicked over her. "What can I do to persuade you?"

The gleam in his eyes was warm and vaguely suggestive. It curled her toes. She swallowed hard and said, "You understand, Mr. Garrett, that I don't know much about the business of art." A slightly disingenuous statement, but basically true.

"My name is Richard. And it just so happens I know quite a bit about this peculiar business. I'd be happy to be your guide. If you'd permit me, of course."

Again, his gaze swept over her, promising all sorts of delicious possibilities. Clearly an overture, but what sort: business, pleasure, or both?

"My guide," she repeated, liking the sound of it. "That's very kind of you. I'm sure there's a great deal you can teach me." Looking at the breadth of his shoulders, she felt a shiver race up her spine. "About art," she added, then almost kicked herself.

"Splendid. We'll start right here then, shall we?"

He stopped in front of a picture window displaying large canvases in gaudy frames. "This is the Onfray Gallery, the most successful in Paris. Tell me. What do you see here?"

She forced her attention away from him to try and focus on the paintings in the window. What would Amy Caldwell—who knew nothing about art—say about them? "Well, they're not very colorful, are they? All brown and grey. And they all seem to be pictures of . . . historical events . . . mythological scenes . . . pompous businessmen straining to look success-ful . . ."

"Precisely. This is what we call academic art. It's what gets displayed in the Salon every year—that's the government-sponsored art show. It's also what the critics rave over and well-heeled patrons buy. Let's walk on, shall we?"

They continued down half a block until they came to what Mason well knew was the Durand-Ruel Gallery. This window was filled with vibrant canvases by Monet, Degas, Pissarro. "But twenty years ago," he told her, "there was a revolution in painting."

"Impressionism."

"Yes, this gallery is one of the few that handle Impressionist paintings. What do you think of it?"

"After what we just saw, they're like a breath of fresh air."

He gave her a pleased smile. "With new, brighter pigments available in collapsible tubes and trains to take them out of town and into nature, artists were no longer bound to their studios. *En plien air,* they discovered they could capture the fleeting color and light of the scenes before them with a real-ism and beauty that had never been known before."

She'd never heard anyone who wasn't a painter speak on

the subject with such enthusiasm. "You like Impressionism, don't you?"

"I love everything about it. Its color, its beauty, its celebration of everyday life. It seduced me, and I believe it's destined to seduce the entire world. To become to our descendants what the art of the Italian Renaissance is to us today. But, I'm sorry to say, that's a minority opinion. And twenty years after it first startled the Parisian art world, it still hasn't broken into the mainstream."

"To my eye, Mason's work doesn't seem to have much in common with these Impressionists in the window."

"You're right. The new generation of avant-garde artists have absorbed Impressionism into their sensibility and are going beyond it. Experimenting with the psychological aspects of color. Exploring the symbolism inherent in nature. The critics call these new artists Neo-Impressionists. Their work is even less appreciated than the Impressionists. The only place you can see their paintings displayed is in the back rooms of a few Montmartre cafés."

"Is that what Mason was—a Neo-Impressionist?"

"Technically, yes. But that hardly sums up the impact she might well end up having."

"Impact?"

"She might be what the Age of Impressionism has always needed and never had."

"And what's that?"

"A larger-than-life figure. You see, one of the reasons Impressionism has never caught on is because it's never produced an artist who has captured the world's imagination with the force of a Michelangelo or a Leonardo. But something in Mason's life seems to appeal to people on this profound and personal level. Maybe your sister will be the artist Impressionism has been waiting for."

Mason was so staggered that she stopped short. "You can't be serious!"

"I'm deadly serious."

It was too much. His intoxicating words—his assurance—surged through her veins like an aphrodisiac. Suddenly all of it—what had happened at the gallery, his praise and approval, his vision of her potential—came crashing together to create in her a single overriding feeling, a desire she'd never come close to experiencing before.

I want this man . . .

I want him now!

She looked up and watched as the corner of his mouth slowly crooked into a smile. A devilish smile, as if he'd read her mind and knew exactly what she was thinking.

She felt herself redden and turned away. His effect on her was irresistible, this shamelessly handsome man, erudite, witty, with a voice that could melt chocolate and an animal magnetism that oozed from his pores despite the veneer of cultured sophistication. Her desire for him was so intense that she was having trouble catching her breath.

"But tell me," he said. "What are your plans?"

"Plans?" She couldn't seem to figure out what he was asking.

"For the future," he elaborated. "Falconier will pull back the paintings for a bit, quadruple the prices, and no doubt sell them in a matter of minutes. Which will leave you with a valise full of francs. What then?"

"I don't know. I suppose I'll go back to America."

And Mason will miraculously reappear.

"A pity, that. I was hoping you'd stay for a while."

His voice had taken on a husky timbre, hushed, intimate. Was she imagining it, or was he looking at her the way a hunter looked at his prey?

"Why would I want to do that?" She hadn't intended it to be a tease, but the breathiness with which she'd uttered it gave it a sassy quality.

"It occurs to me that we have a great deal in common. I should like to . . . deepen our acquaintance."

His tone was deceptively casual yet edged with determination—the polite vanguard of a will not to be denied.

"Deepen?"

Oh, God, did I really say that? It sounded like the invitation of some Pigalle tart.

"You don't object, I hope? Because the truth is, I find myself in the throes of a most peculiar urge."

"What sort of urge?" she gulped.

The dark eyes, hooded and penetrating, seemed to bore a hole in her. "The urge to do whatever it takes to keep you in Paris."

"Whatever . . . it takes?"

What am I doing?

She knew where this was leading, but she couldn't seem to stop herself.

He leaned toward her, close enough that she could almost feel his lips with hers, and repeated firmly, "*Whatever* it takes."

Chapter 4

Garrett raised his hand and momentarily a large gilded coach drawn by four white horses pulled up before them. The words LE GRAND-HÔTEL were lettered on the side. It had apparently been waiting for him outside the gallery and the driver was monitoring the progress of his and Mason's stroll.

Garrett took out his billfold, withdrew a hundred-franc note, and handed it to the crisply uniformed man who sat out front in the driver's box, the reins taut in his white gloved hands. "Drive," he commanded. "Don't stop till I tell you on pain of death. Understand?"

"*Certainment, Monsieur.*"

Garrett opened the door and held his hand out to Mason. She hesitated for the briefest of moments. If ever she was going to turn the tide, it would have to be now. She looked up into his eyes and saw there a kind of fierce glare. It wasn't so much that he was inviting her inside as commanding her to enter his domain. All the while his eyes bore into her; his mouth, with the full lips, looked pagan and wicked, and almost predatory. She could feel his energy engulf her, wholly masculine, unconscionably rife with a sexuality that made no apology and asked no quarter. There was something about his unflinching concentration that mesmerized her. It was almost as if she were in the throes of some uncontrollable power. But the truth was, if he was some kind of sorcerer who rendered women to putty in his hands, she didn't care. Because she wanted to step inside, to taste of the forbidden fruit he dangled before her.

Mason took the hand he offered. His touch melted her in a pool of yearning. He handed her up into the coach, a grandiose affair plush with emerald velvet–lined walls and thickly padded matching seats. The woodwork was painted white and gilded in the style of Louis Quinze, and the door handles appeared to be made of gold. He lowered the shades on all sides so they were sheltered from prying eyes.

The coach was luxurious and could easily hold a family of eight. But Mason wasn't thinking of her opulent surroundings. She was watching the way Garrett moved, as sleek as a panther, as self-assured as a battle-seasoned gladiator. He turned to her as the vehicle rattled off, swaying on his feet.

As he saw her lounging back in the cushions, he halted abruptly, his eyes roaming the length of her as if envisioning every line of her femininely concealed curves. The hard-edged gleam almost made her swoon.

If he didn't touch her soon, she'd burst into flames.

He crossed the length of the coach in two strides, took her shoulders in his hands, and hauled her to her feet. Her breath left her as she collided against the massive weight of him. And then his arms were around her, pinioning her to him, holding her tight as he dipped his head and took possession of her mouth. She swayed beneath the ambush of his kiss, no nonsense now, zeroing in on her with blistering passion. She was wedged so closely against him that she felt every sex-hardened ridge of him pressing into the excruciating throbbing between her thighs. She tilted into him as the carriage picked up speed and felt her head reel. His hands began to move on her, touching all the sensitive hollows and swells, scorching her breasts, moving down the length of her back to come up behind and press her buttocks in his palms. Desire flared hot and luscious, piercing her, igniting responses that left her feeling flushed and defenseless as his tongue sweetly ransacked her mouth.

Oh yes, the whole of her body seemed to sigh. *This is just what I need.*

Without warning, he dropped back onto the seat and took her with him with a possessive tug so that she fell into him, straddled on his knees, her own knees on either side. His mouth still searching hers, he slid her closer until she could feel the immense stiffness of him against the spread softness of her female core. Already combustible, her loins ignited and she whimpered into the prison of his mouth.

Too soon he took his lips away. He kept her pinned to him with one hand, and with the other unbuttoned her bodice with the sure hand of a man accustomed to breaching such obstacles. He jerked the fabric aside, baring her breast. Then he grabbed a handful of her hair in his massive fist, pulled her head back, and bent to capture her nipple with his mouth.

Awash in pleasure so intense it was almost painful, Mason threw her head back against the crush of his clenched hand and moaned, abandoning herself, feeling him rock her against him harder, faster, the friction building in succulent spirals, her breast pulsing in the moist ardor of his mouth. There was something forceful, demanding, thrilling in the way he held her trapped where he wanted her, moving her at his own will. The deep, coiling hunger welled inside, leaving her feeling famished, incinerating all conscious thought like the blast of a furnace running at full heat. This was ecstasy she hadn't counted on. She'd decided she'd wanted him, whatever the cost. But there was no question that he was the one in control. She'd become a feather in the force of his domination.

It was sweet agony. She couldn't take the torture of having him, sheathed and flint hard, teasing her so unremittingly as he spread his knees to open her to him wider still. Her breath was like a blowtorch in her lungs, her body bursting to life under his puppeteer's hands. She wanted to feel him inside her, surrounded by her. She'd never felt so explosive in all her life, a hair trigger perilously close to discharging with the slightest touch.

She reached up and clutched his head in her hands. "Don't make me wait. I can't."

His mouth twisted in what seemed a knowing smile, but it only served to accentuate its seductive cruelty. He knew the effect he was having on her. And he was enjoying it. He was relishing the sight of her, rumpled now as her hair, tangled in his fingers, spilled free of its pins beneath the perky bonnet; her eyes glazed with desperate passion; her breasts, damp and swollen now, bared to his unsparing gaze.

His eyes narrowing, he took the bonnet in hand and snatched it off, tossing it aside. Then he cupped his hands beneath her armpits, grazing her breasts as he did and sending shivers up her spine. Lifting her off him, he gave a mighty heave so she went sprawling across the coach to the opposite seat. She gasped, surprised, sinking into the cushions like a discarded rag doll.

He stood, filling the enclosed space, having to stoop to keep from banging his head. He came toward her slowly with a rapacious tread. Bending, he put his hands up under her skirt, finding her legs and grazing them upward, upward, so the cascading pink skirt rose in his track. She felt the power of his touch everywhere, on her calves, her knees, along her tingling inner thighs. Then he took hold of the waistband of her undergarments and, with one savage jerk, yanked them down. The air was cool on her exposed sex as he swiftly removed her undergarments and sent them flying to land on her forgotten hat.

Her legs moved to close automatically, but he shot up and stepped between them, arresting her progress. He stood over her and began with calculated motions to undo his trousers.

She watched, transfixed. He pushed aside the expensive material and took himself in hand. Her breath stopped completely. He was magnificent. Revealed this way from the confines of refined clothing and sophisticated bearing, he stood like some primitive beast of pleasure, hard, colossal, divinely shaped. It wasn't the cock of a gentleman. He looked rugged and all man.

"Spread your legs for me," he instructed, the words sounding exquisite in the richly rolling vowels that seemed to taste every syllable.

She did so unhurriedly, making him wait, feeling utterly exposed as his eyes took in every detail of her, sprawled before him like a Palais Royal whore. She caught the light of appreciation and wanted more. So she drew her legs up so the heels of her boots were on the seat at either side of her, and put her hand where his eyes were avidly feasting.

She was so wet that it startled her. Her fingers grew slippery as she played with the folds, opening them to his view. And now it was his eyes that grew glazed, making her feel depraved and beautiful all at the same time.

He was on her in a single pounce, thrusting her legs back so she was propelled wide open. He lowered himself to her, rubbing the bare clit with the velvety head of his erection, replacing her hands. She cried out in an agony of urgency, ready to explode, curling into him, coaxing him to come inside.

It's been so long. Too long.

But, no. It was never like this!

He kept his hands on her legs, holding them widespread. But he eased himself into her slowly, so slowly, one excruciating inch at a time, so she could feel each successive motion, the deliberate easing of himself into her snug warmth, tantalizing, teasing, and yet driving himself in with a resoluteness that said, *This is where I belong.* As if he wanted her to *know,* with his measured invasion of her, that this was where he was meant to be.

She'd never felt so possessed, so taken, so claimed in all her life. It seemed to her that all the world was suspended in ravishing anticipation.

Needing to hold on to something, she reached her arms back and grabbed on to the top of the seat cushion behind her with both hands, stretching herself before him, shifting her hips up to meet him, to try and take control. To hurry his penetration.

But he felt her designs. As if to show her who was really in command, he drew out until the supple head was teasing her slick opening. Then, with one single ram, he plunged inside.

She cried out and felt his hand clamp itself over her mouth. And then he was plundering her with vigorous thrusts, again and again and again, filling her so completely, so sublimely, that she felt she'd go insane. He leaned into her, his mouth at her ear, his breath hot and luscious, and said, "Go ahead and scream. You need to scream, don't you? When was the last time a man made you scream?"

She surrendered unequivocally and screamed into his hand. Outside the rumbling coach, Paris passed by. Ladies strolled the streets with parasols perched, and children frolicked with puppies in the parks. But in here, in this lavish, sheltered haven, she was screaming out loud because this man—this *unbelievable* man—was slamming into her like a battering ram and driving her wild.

She came on his cock, spasming on him, around him, consumed by him, engulfing him deeper and deeper, as deeply as it was possible to take him, feeling shivery and glorious, swimming with pleasure, with joy, with life-affirming bliss.

Then she was being moved. Her head was spinning so that she didn't know where he was taking her, and didn't care. Mason found herself lying back along the length of the seat, Richard's raging erection still inside. He moved like a shot and he was on her, never ceasing his delivery of each delicious thrust.

She clung to him now, sinking into a whirlpool that sucked her down, down, until he sent her spiraling once more. He caught her cries in his mouth this time, tasting them, the proof of her elation at his hands.

"What are you doing to me?" he rasped in her ear.

And she answered, like a woman possessed, "What are you doing to *me*?"

Some remnant of cognizance swam to the surface of her mind. *I'd like to paint him. I'd like to put on canvas the way he makes me feel.*

As if he'd divined her wish and understood, he took her face in his two large hands and gave her a deep, poignant kiss.

They spoke no more, except with moans and groans and sighs. But she opened her eyes and found him watching her wondrously as if he, too, were rocked to the foundation of his being. Their eyes met and a spark of something raw and real passed between them. She felt her spirit soar staring into the mystery and mastery of his eyes.

In that instant, all pretense vanished. She lay beneath him as her true self, feeling that they looked, not into each other's eyes, but into their very souls as they came together now, unflinchingly naked and revealed.

In the hushed and intimate aftermath as their breathing slowed, they held one another close, neither wanting to let the magic end. Mason's heart was beating as it never had before. She felt riveted by an emotion she couldn't comprehend.

But it had to end. It was inevitable that they'd slowly, painfully, become aware of their surroundings, of the swaying of the coach, of the heated sheen of their skin. Of the silence that was so dense that it seemed a new and previously unheard sound.

Richard moved away too soon, standing stiffly, assembling his clothing as he looked down at her with a stirring affection in his eyes. "Where are you stopping?"

He asked the question as if he could think of nothing profound enough to say. She had to think what he meant. She had to pull herself together, to recall the outside world. Once again, she had to remember the role she was playing.

"The Jockey Club, on Rue Scribe," she croaked, as if she hadn't spoken for a year.

He arched a brow. "The Jockey Club? Isn't that a private hotel?"

She eased up into a sitting position, righting her now badly wrinkled skirt. "Falconier keeps a suite there. He offered it to me while I'm in Paris."

"Then we're neighbors. My hotel is directly across the street."

Their eyes met and she breathed softly, "Yes, I know." Then added, "I saw the hotel's name on the door of the coach."

He rapped on the ceiling, lowered the window, and called to the driver to tell him where to go.

Then, with great solicitation, he busied himself in tidying her up, grinning sheepishly—endearingly—as he attempted to replace the pins in her hair, putting her bonnet gently on her head, watching as she awkwardly stepped into her undergarments as the coach shimmied from side to side.

When they finally stopped, he said, "We'll meet tomorrow, shall we? To . . . continue your education."

She smiled bashfully, delighted by the prospect.

He gave her a mock frown. "In art, I mean. I can show you Montmartre. We can walk through Mason's world."

"I'd just as soon take this enchanted coach."

He laughed, a deep, rich, rumbling sound that made her feel all tingly inside. "I have some business in the morning, but I'll have a coach pick you up and bring you to meet me. Shall we say one o'clock?"

She nodded. She couldn't seem to stop smiling.

He bent to kiss her forehead, then opened the door and handed her down in front of her hotel. "Until one, then."

She watched the coach lurch away, an antiquated fantasy from another age, like the carriage that had taken Cinderella to the ball. Hugging herself, she marveled at what had just transpired. It had all happened in a fever. She felt both shattered and exhilarated.

She'd come to Paris to live the life of a Bohemian, wanting to savor all that life had to offer so she could capture it in paint. But in many ways, that life had been a fraud. Because she'd never really felt the passion she'd been after. None of her earlier explorations had seemed real.

But *this* was real. She didn't know this man, didn't know anything about him. But the communion she'd felt with him was more meaningful, more fulfilling than any she'd ever known.

She was already dying to see him again. But a walk through Mason's world . . . It complicated things immensely.

Because she wasn't who he thought she was.

And she was already beginning to wish he knew the truth.

Chapter 5

Garrett bolted up in bed, his heart racing, his body bur-
nished with sweat. He was surrounded by darkness, so
silent that all he heard was the sound of his own ragged
breath. What was happening?

The nightmare.

Quickly, he turned on the lamp. Fumbling, he reached for
the book of color reproductions he kept at his bedside and
opened it. The page he'd turned to featured a Chardin still
life: a silver goblet, a bowl and spoon, three pieces of fruit on
a tabletop. He forced his mind to sink into the tranquil picture, and it calmed him.

They were the curse of his existence, these nightmares.
He'd had them every week or two since he was a boy, and
though they'd varied in detail, they were basically the same.
Trapped in apocalyptic darkness, desperate to escape, surrounded by unseen terrors, reaching out for him, pulling him
back. In the distance, a dim blue light—so radiant, so pure—
that he knew it was his salvation from this pit. But the harder
he tried to get to it, the faster it receded from him, until he
was struggling with all his might, the light vanished completely, and he was engulfed by the unspeakable. Then he
jolted awake.

When he did, he felt as terrified as he had in the dream.

Until he could turn on the light and find a piece of art to look at. To soothe him, to bring him back to reality.

He tossed back the sheet, threw his legs over the side, and rose naked from the bed. Stepping over to the dresser, he took the pitcher of water in hand, holding it high, letting it pour down like rain over his head. It cooled his throbbing head and washed away the last remnants of the dream, trickling down over every tight muscle of his body. With his hands, he plastered back his wet hair, then rubbed the water over the sinews of his chest, his fingers ruffling the thick damp hair. Then he went back to the bed and sprawled upon it, his naked body still taut from the stress of the dream, letting the world settle itself around him.

Gradually, it came back to him. Paris. The Grand Hotel. The gold suite. And, finally, the extraordinary day he'd just experienced. Just when he thought he'd seen it all and the rest of his life was going to be routine, a day like this one came along.

He'd been asked to come here to have a look at the Caldwell paintings and the phenomenon that was building around them. Frankly, he hadn't expected much, so it had all taken him by surprise.

He still wasn't sure what to make of it. But as he lay there, reliving the experience, he was even more sure that, buried in this phenomenon, was an enormous opportunity for him.

Then he thought of the woman and felt himself stir once again. She, too, had taken him by surprise. Christ Almighty! He'd just intended to lay on a little charm. But the situation had exploded into one of the most intense carnal experiences of his life. Something about her brought out the beast in him, stirring feelings he couldn't even define. For someone who liked to be in control of every situation, she was a perilous proposition. He'd have to be careful with this one.

Had his overture been an unwise move? In retrospect, probably so. Why had he made it, then? Obviously, because she said she was leaving and he had to prevent her from slipping out of his fingers. Still, she'd been more than he'd bargained for. Once again, he cautioned himself to be careful.

Well, here I am. What am I going to do now?

Some decisions had to be made.

For some time he remained there, propped against the pillows, letting things play out in his mind, beating down erotic thoughts that kept popping up about the delicious interlude in the coach, knowing there was no way he was going to walk away from this.

Suddenly, the spark of an idea hit him. An ambitious idea. An outrageous idea. So ambitious, so outrageous that he couldn't take it seriously, but . . . he couldn't let go. It would take patience, meticulous planning, all his skill and dedication. But maybe . . . just maybe . . .

Slipping into a robe, he felt such a surge of creative satisfaction that he knew he was hooked.

He walked the long path to the double doors and threw them wide, opening up the bedroom to the sitting room beyond. A sliver of light stealing through a crack in the curtains helped him see the shapes and shadows of the tasteful furnishings of the suite. He yanked back the drapes, letting in the golden glow of the lighted façade of l'Opéra across the street. His fourth-floor French doors put him in line with an exhilarating view of the gilded angels that graced the rooftop of Garnier's palace, as if they were soaring before his eyes.

He looked at them for a moment, these muses that seemed to have been placed there just for him on this auspicious night. Then, going to the bar and pouring himself a brandy, he pulled a chair to the window and sat facing it.

He stayed there for the rest of the night, sipping the brandy slowly as his eyes caressed the view and his mind began to unfold his exhilarating plan.

Mason awoke the next morning feeling strangely happy and at one with the world. It was such an unusual feeling that, for a moment, she couldn't figure out why. Then she remembered. The show . . . the riot over her paintings . . . and him . . .

Richard Garrett.

She stretched her limbs, smiling dreamily, feeling the sweet afterglow flood through her. Snuggling deeper into the feathery folds of the bed, she luxuriated in the majesty of her good fortune.

Her discretely luxurious surroundings served to reinforce the dreamlike sensation. Falconier's suite was a large, high-ceilinged space at the front of the block-long building consisting of two levels: a comfortable sitting room with a mezzanine bedchamber above overlooking it. Striped wallpaper of cranberry and plum created a backdrop for the maroon and hunter green furnishings. Pictures of celebrated race horses adorned the walls.

But for Mason, the most extraordinary aspect of it was the fact that her phenomenal streak of good fortune had placed her directly across the narrow Rue Scribe from the Grand Hotel and Richard Garrett.

As if it was meant to be.

She heard the key turn in the door downstairs and sat up in bed. Then she heard Lisette's voice, "Thank you, *mon cher*."

A young male voice answered, "But it is my pleasure, Mademoiselle Lisette. I have delighted in your artistry many times at the circus."

"Aren't you sweet," Lisette said. "Here's something for your trouble."

"Oh, no, Mademoiselle. I could never accept anything from you. Meeting you is honor enough."

"I'm up here," Mason called when she heard the door close.

"Still in bed?" After a moment, Lisette appeared coming up the spiral stairwell. She looked at Mason, lying in bed with her hands above her head, bathed in morning sunlight streaming through the windows, a satisfied smile on her face.

"I'm a woman of leisure," Mason sighed.

"Where did you go yesterday? I looked for you every-where. Then I had to go to work."

Mason stretched again, savoring the feel of her body against the cool sheets. "I was swept away by Apollo."

"What Apollo was that?"

"Didn't you see me with him? The tall Englishman? I don't know how you could miss him. He made every other man there look like Toulouse-Lautrec."

Lisette blew a dangling strand of hair out of her eyes. "I only saw Dargelos trying to make my life miserable, as usual. But tell me." She flopped down on the bed beside Mason. "What man is this?"

"Like I said. A god."

"But *who* is he?"

"His name is Richard Garrett."

"And who is Richard Garrett?"

"Who knows? Who cares? He has something to do with the art world. But, Lisette, he loves my paintings. He under-stands them."

Lisette turned over onto her stomach, peering closely at her friend. "I do not think that is what put the smile on your face, *chérie*."

"No! He ravaged me! It was wonderful."

"Ravaged you?" Lisette tucked her chin into her hands. "Tell me!"

Mason shifted up in the bed, too excited to lay prone any longer. "You remember what it was like when I first got to Paris? When I wanted to taste the Bohemian life . . . those conceited painters you set me up with? Well . . . it was nothing like that. Richard Garrett swept in like a knight on his charger and showed me what I've been missing. And here's the really strange part. That night in the river, when I thought I was going to drown . . . I thought about this man I'd never known. It was as if I was wishing for him to appear. And then, out of the blue . . . he does. It's as if fate heard all my wishes that night and decided to grant *all* of them to me in one fell swoop. Here, pinch me so I know I'm not dreaming."

Lisette was laughing. "He was that good, eh?"

"It's not just that. Well, he was, yes. He was *astonishing*. But it's more than that. He *believes* in me! You should hear the things he says, the way he talks about me. When I listen to him, when I see myself through his eyes, it's as if all the things I thought were wrong with me disappear. He makes me feel that everything that's happened to me happened for a reason, to make me what I am. That what I am may be worthy, after all; someone I could learn to love. No one has ever made me feel that way before. It's such an amazing feeling, Lisette, that I almost don't know what to do with it."

"I've never seen you like this. You're falling in love with this man."

"Am I?" Mason tried the thought out in her mind and felt it answered in the sudden flitting of her heart. "I suppose I am."

"*Chérie*, I am happy for you. But you do have a teensy little problem, no?"

"Problem?"

"He thinks you are your sister."

Mason grinned. "That is a problem, isn't it?"

"What are you going to do?"

"I'm going to tell him the truth."

"And . . . You don't think that will make a difference? You *have* tricked him, after all."

"He's so crazy about the paintings, he'll be ecstatic to find out I'm alive."

"If you say so. But you'd better be very careful about how you deliver this exciting news. You don't want to make him feel like a fool."

"That's a good point. We're going for a walk this afternoon. He's going to take me on a tour of Montmartre and show me 'Mason's world.' If I wait until afterward, he *will* feel foolish. So I have to tell him right away." She rolled the covers around her hands, thinking. "I know! You can help me."

Lisette sat up. "Oh, no."

"You know men. Here's what we'll do. We'll go to breakfast. We'll go to the Café de la Paix—"

"The Café de la Paix! That's the most expensive place in Paris!"

"I know. But we'll sign it to Falconier. It's the least he can do for us. I feel like celebrating. And while we're at it, you can help me figure out just the right way to tell him."

Mason and Lisette's celebratory mood was tempered when they reached the lobby. Lisette put her hand on Mason's arm to stop them short. A distinguished, grey-haired man had just come through the door and was looking around, as if to get his bearings.

"What is it?" Mason whispered.

"That man. He's Inspector Duval of the Sûreté. The most feared flic in all of Paris."

Mason paled. "Policeman?"

"Yes, someone you definitely do not want on your trail."

As she said this, the inspector noticed them. Smiling pleasantly, he walked toward them.

Lisette's hand tightened on Mason's arm. "What does he want with us?" she muttered.

As he came before them, still smiling, there seemed nothing threatening in his demeanor. He looked, in fact, like a kindly grandfather. He removed his hat and gave a slight bow.

"Mademoiselle Amy Caldwell, I believe. From America." He spoke in English, which was accented but fluent.

"Yes," Mason answered cautiously.

"I thought you must be, as you are in the company of your sister's friend. I am Honoré Duval of the Prefecture de Police. I am here to extend the condolences of the French nation on the loss of your sister. If I might be of assistance in any way during your stay here, I hope you will call upon me."

Mason could sense Lisette's tension beside her. She smiled sweetly and said, "Thank you so much, Inspector, but I don't think that will be necessary. My sister's friends have been extremely generous and have been helping me through this difficult period."

He watched her closely for a moment, as if studying her, and she could see, beneath the benign exterior, the eagle eye of a man whose profession caused him to suspect hidden meanings in small details. He remained silent for several awkward moments.

Lisette put some pressure on Mason's arm, prompting her to leave. But before she could move, the policeman said, "I wonder if I might ask a somewhat indelicate question."

The smile froze on Mason's face. "Of course. Ask anything you like."

His eyes swept down the chartreuse dress she wore. "Is it not the custom in your country to wear mourning on the loss of a family member?"

It was a detail she'd forgotten in the rush to pull off the masquerade in time. She needed to think fast.

"It's not quite as strict a custom as it is here on the Continent," she stalled. Then the answer came to her. "Besides, my sister hated black. She considered it the *absence* of color. If you look closely at her paintings, you'll see she doesn't use black. She would have hated for me to wear something she so despised."

He gave no response. The awkwardness continued.

Finally, he asked, "May I share a personal feeling with you?"

"Please do."

"Mademoiselle, in the past year, my office has investigated two hundred and fourteen suicides within the Paris city limits. Of those, all but four left some sort of suicide note, or at least a final word. It seems extremely odd to me that your sister, who devoted her life toward expressing herself, would depart this world without a word . . . or any provision for the paintings she obviously loved so much. It simply goes against all my instincts to believe this could happen."

The hair on the back of Mason's neck prickled. Forcing herself to assume an air of calm grief, she said, "All I can say, Inspector, is that nothing about my dear sister was conventional."

"True, true. Artists are a world unto themselves. I hope I have not unduly alarmed you with my little observation."

"Not at all, Inspector. I appreciate your interest."

He took her hand and kissed it gallantly. "Let me assure you, Mademoiselle, if the death of your sister is not what it appears to be, I will find out. And if that is the case, I will prosecute the person responsible to the full extent of the law. That, Mademoiselle, is my promise to you."

Chapter 6

Mason rumbled along in the coach on the Boulevard de Clichy. At any other time, she would have been enjoying its plush surroundings, reliving the ecstasy she'd experienced here the day before. But now that it was upon her, she was nervous about telling Garrett the truth. And the incident with the policeman had unsettled her.

Over breakfast, Lisette had said, "Duval knows something."

"He doesn't know anything," Mason had argued. "How could he?"

"He suspects something, or he wouldn't have come here."

"The suicide note. Why didn't I think of that? It would have been so easy to scribble something."

"Details are that man's specialty. They say he loves to sink his teeth into the little things you'd never even think of. And once he does, he never lets go. He's like a bulldog."

Mason had lost her appetite. "I get the picture, Lisette," she said testily.

But Lisette leaned across the table and hissed softly, "France has the toughest penalties for fraud in all of Europe. Juno knew of a man Duval nailed for cashing one of his mother's war-widow pension checks after she died. A first offense! And he ended up spending *ten years* in Santé Prison."

Now the coach was pulling up in front of a building on

Place de Clichy, close to the Hippodrome. Garrett stood in the doorway of the building shaking hands with a man. The sign on the window told her it was a realtor's office. When he saw the coach, he excused himself and hurried toward her.

She took a breath, remembering the speech she'd rehearsed, trying to quell her trepidation. When he opened the door and helped her out, she said, without preliminary, "I have something to tell you."

"That's a coincidence. I have something to tell *you*. How's this for an idea? The Mason Caldwell Pavilion."

He caught her completely off guard. "What?"

He was nearly vibrating with excitement. "The Mason Caldwell Pavilion—at the World's Fair."

"But the paintings were turned down by the Exposition."

"They'll change their minds. And even if they don't, we'll do it independently. A pavilion of our own with nothing but Mason's paintings in it."

"But . . . that's impossible."

"Far from it. Courbet did it at the 1855 Fair, and Manet again in 1867. Only our pavilion will be bigger and grander. I know plenty of people in the art world with money to spare who might very well be talked into contributing to such a noble venture. I've already put some feelers out this morning."

Incredulously, she asked, "Is that why you were at the realtor's?"

"No, I was there to buy the building where Mason had her studio in Montmartre."

"You *bought* the building? But . . . why?"

"Because it's hallowed ground. It should be preserved as a museum. A place where people can come and pay homage."

"You're joking!"

"Not in the least. This can happen if you and I take the necessary steps and work together now. I've been up all night thinking about this. It hit me out of nowhere, like a thunderbolt, and I've never been more excited about anything."

"But . . . a pavilion . . . buying the apartment building for a museum . . . isn't that a little . . . extreme?"

"I told you, your sister is special, unique."

"But there are many unique artists out there."

"You still don't understand, Amy. It's not just her art. It's her *life*. Walk with me while I explain."

He hooked her arm through his and began to walk down the wide boulevard to where it dead-ended at the Hippodrome and Rue Caulaincourt. "Richard, I need to tell you something—"

"Wait. Let me get this out while it's still fresh in my mind. Mason worked for years without selling a single painting. She suffered crushing poverty, near starvation, and nothing but rejection. And yet she believed in herself and her vision, and nothing stopped her. She didn't care about commercial success or what the critics said about her. She always found the energy and means to put oil on canvas day after day after day, no matter what, oblivious to the opinion of the world. She was a paragon of honesty, purity, and dedication. She really *was* a Joan of Art."

Mason squirmed beside him. It wasn't true. She'd never been that poor. She'd suffered bouts of laziness. God knew she was full of self-doubt. And she desperately wanted commercial and critical success.

"But the thing that gives a genuine epic quality to her life," he went on, "is her death. The suicide. It breaks our hearts that anyone so talented, so courageous, could come to that point. Yet, at the same time, it gives her story a mythic power and resonance that will echo down through the ages. It's almost as if the unconscious part of her genius realized that her mission was complete, her entire life was a work of art, and the suicide was necessary to complete it with a poignant, bittersweet flourish."

Mason's heart was sinking. He was saying that the suicide was *vital* to the legend, and the legend was vital both to the appeal of the paintings and to his fascination with them.

He guided her across Rue Caulaincourt. "What I'm trying to tell you, Amy, is that Mason is something new to art. The artist as outsider, heroic idealist, martyr. I believe this idea has the power to shake the world. *If* we make it happen— you and I. If we nurture the legend. If we present her work to the proper critics in the proper way. Above all, if we can gather her work and display it before the adjudicaters of public taste who will come to the Exposition from all over the globe this summer, then . . . it *can* happen. It *will* happen!"

Dear God, how can I ever tell him now?

She looked up and saw before her the gates of the Cimetière de Montmartre. What were they doing here? He led her along an uneven cobblestone path lined with gloomy mausoleums and sarcophagi. The monuments were stained black with soot, some of them cracking with age and neglect. As the walkway took them down a flight of stairs, the sun went behind a cloud and a chill wind whipped them. She felt oppressed by the macabre energy of the place and shivered with dread.

On the lower level, he finally stopped before a simple, square headstone, this one new and unstained. Mason stared in shock at its epitaph.

Ici Repose
Mason Caldwell
1864–1889

"It was all her acrobat friend could afford," Garrett said, "but I rather like it. The simplicity of it seems to fit Mason so much better than all these gaudy monstrosities."

Mason was staring at the headstone, stricken. She hadn't expected this. She hadn't thought about it, but of course they had to bury that poor woman from the bridge somewhere.

It was bloodcurdling, seeing her own name in a cemetery, set in stone. It seemed to give a permanence to what she'd considered only a brief charade.

As they stood there, he offered her his hand. "Will you join me in this quest, Amy? As my partner? Will you help me give Mason the immortality she deserves?"

Mason had left the cemetery in a kind of a trance. She hadn't taken Richard's hand and had made no commitment to him. Numb with shock, she'd babbled, "I don't know . . . seeing Mason this way . . . I have to go think." Then she'd turned and reeled away from him, nearly running up the stairs.

But in this traumatic moment, she'd made no effort to pull off her mask the way she'd steeled herself to do.

How could she? It would ruin everything. He wouldn't understand. He was so wrapped up in the glory of her tragic young death that he'd be appalled by what she'd done. The truth would rob him of something he considered exquisite and profound. He saw her death as noble, epic, mythic. It almost seemed to be the thing about her that he loved the most.

There was no question in her mind now that, if she told him the truth, he would walk away and never forgive her.

And she would lose everything she'd always wanted in the process.

But what was the alternative? Take his hand? Be his partner? Remain Amy Caldwell?

It was impossible . . . just impossible.

Hours passed. She walked the streets, wrestling with her dilemma. She knew where she wanted to go, but she was trying to resist its lure. But eventually, it became too much of an effort. She couldn't stay away.

She crossed the Seine and headed down the Left Bank until she reached the Champ de Mars and the fairgrounds. The work crews had just left the various construction sites for the day. The cordoned-off area, with its signs warning her not to enter, stretched out before her like some sort of half-finished fairyland. And here—among all this rising splendor, in the midst of the glass-domed Palaces of Machines and Fine Arts; the reconstructed Cambodian village and Egyptian Bazaar;

the exhibition halls; gardens and restaurants representing countries from all the corners of the earth to accommodate the culinary, scientific, and artistic appetites of the 32 million people expected to attend the fair—Richard Garrett wanted to construct a temple dedicated entirely to the art of Mason Caldwell.

Think what that would do for the family name. All those nasty people who'd looked down their pious noses at the Caldwells. How could she possibly say no? Didn't she owe it to her mother, if nothing else?

But how could she possibly say yes?

To do that, she'd have to be willing to stay dead, assume the identity of this nonexistent sister, paint in secret, pretending that whatever new work she finished had been a discovery from the past. Not just for two weeks, not just for a month, but *for the rest of her life!* To never tell the man she loved who she really was. To always have to lie to him, trick him into believing what he needed to believe.

And then there was the matter of the policeman, Duval. Who knew what he suspected? If she stopped now, if Amy disappeared and Mason resurfaced, she could likely get away with what she'd done. But if she continued the deception and got caught, as surely she would . . . What had Lisette said? The toughest fraud laws in Europe. Ten years for a minor offense. More shame. More humiliation. More scandal for the Caldwells of Massachusetts.

No, no, no.

It was out of the question. To even think about continuing this perilous game was madness. It would require nerves of steel. The cunning and confidence of a master criminal. The acting skills of a Sarah Bernhardt.

But if she didn't do it . . .

She would lose this miraculous opportunity, this answer to her prayer for help that night on the bridge. *And* she would kill any chance of keeping the only man she'd ever met who she knew could fill the empty space in her soul.

Mason . . . or Amy?

An impossible choice.

But . . . What if she *could* do it? Take the risk and seize it all. The thought gave her a tingling sensation of daring.

She walked past a Mediterranean-looking building and crossed to the middle of the plaza made by the four corners of the Tower's base to stand directly beneath it. She'd never been so close to it before. From a distance, there was no way to appreciate the massive scale of it. She looked up and felt it soaring above her, the tallest structure on Earth. The naysayers had all declared that it would never stand, that the forceful winds of the Île-de-France would send it toppling to the ground before it could be finished. But here it was, flying in the face of their ridicule, a symbol that anything that could be imagined could be accomplished.

Tomorrow, England's Prince of Wales would officially inaugurate the monument and would be granted the honor of being the first to ride the elevator to the top. Crowds would gather to celebrate the occasion. A grandstand had been built where speeches would be made and the royal party would enter the elevator.

But tonight, the Tower was hers alone.

Darkness was descending. Mason was looking all around her, marveling at the network of iron girders, at the grace and beauty of the crisscrossing ribs, when her gaze came to rest on the stairway that zigzagged its way from the north base of the Tower just behind the grandstand all the way up to the first level. Seized by an impulse, she walked to the base and found that the stairwell was unblocked. She stood there a moment, pondering it. *Do I dare?*

She stepped to the opening and looked up. It was growing darker and she couldn't see very well, but it didn't look especially intimidating. Why not go up and have a look?

She began to climb the metal stairway, her heels making a hollow, clanging sound. It was a steep incline, but scaling the Montmartre butte every day for five years had made her legs strong, and she effortlessly climbed higher . . . higher . . . back and forth as the staircase shifted direction at regular intervals.

Finally, she emerged on the first observation level. It was deserted. She was amazed that she'd made it this far. Was there no one to rush out and arrest her for trespassing?

She stepped to the rail and looked out on the view of the Champ de Mars below her and the dome of Les Invalides to her left. It was completely dark now and stars were beginning to sparkle in the sky. She felt positively wicked being here. Then the thought hit her.

Could I go even higher?

She looked around until she saw the entrance to the next level of stairs. This was a narrower spiral staircase that wound almost straight up. Feeling even more wicked, she began to ascend the staircase. Higher, higher, higher . . . She was breathing hard now, but it was strangely fulfilling. She lost all track of time, until finally she emerged on the second observation level. She went to the rail and beheld the same view, but from this height, it was even more spectacular. She'd never seen anything more stunning. The gaslights had come on, and Paris was spread out below her in its nocturnal magnificence.

It suddenly struck her just how much she loved this city. Twenty years before, it had been in ruins from the disastrous Franco-Prussian War and the civil strife that had followed it. But it had risen from the ashes to once again become the first city of the world. This fair was the showcase of that resurrection, and this spectacular tower was its symbol. Tears of pride came to her eyes as she thought of it. She was filled with a surge of appreciation, power, and possibility.

Why not go all the way? To hell with the Prince of Wales. Who better to be the first to scale the Tower than someone like me?

Once again, Mason began to climb. The stairs grew steeper, narrower. She lost herself in the rhythm of her footsteps clanging on the metal. Up . . . up . . . into the very sky. Panting now. Climbing, climbing, climbing. Her calves began to ache, but she didn't care. A cold wind began to hit her, but she found it bracing. The sensation was almost sexual. She couldn't stop herself now if she wanted to. Higher, higher, higher . . .

Until the stairs ended. She was at the summit: 919 feet high, 1,665 steps!

She leaned against the rail, trying to catch her breath, which was burning her lungs. It was pitch-black around her, but the lights of the city formed a carpet at her feet. Looking down on it gave her a swell of exhilaration.

Truly, anything was possible.

"Young woman!" A male voice behind her startled her. She whirled to find a bearded man holding a lamp. He'd just come out of the small enclosure at the pinnacle. "What on earth are you doing here?"

Caught up in her sense of accomplishment, she said, "I might ask the same of you."

"I'm Gustave Eiffel, and I built this tower you are trespassing upon. And who, may I ask, are you?"

Who was she?

Time to decide.

Holding out her hand to him, she said, "My name is Amy."

Chapter 7

A week later, at a center table in the opulent dining room of the Grand Hotel, Mason and Richard were entertaining a balding, heavyset man in his late forties wearing pince-nez glasses perched on a bulbous red nose. They'd just finished a five-course meal of the finest French cuisine, during which they'd been served by a small army of waiters. Now they sat back in sated contentment with coffee and brandy before them.

Their guest was Stuart Cuthbert, the Paris correspondent for the *London Times* and a long-time acquaintance of Richard's. The single topic of conversation through the sumptuous meal had been Mason Caldwell. Mason, since making her decision, had embraced her deception and was rather enjoying it—the refined surroundings, her new lace-trimmed evening gown, the hushed tribute Richard was paying the late, tragic painter whose reputation he'd dedicated himself to build. His sense of mission radiated off him like rays of the sun.

Though she and Richard had spoken several times over the past week, it had been only briefly, long enough to cement their partnership and solidify their plans. He'd been busy petitioning the stubborn Exhibition officials and other bureaucratic powers of the Parisian municipal government who weren't keen to allow a previously unknown American painter—and a woman at that—to have her own extravagant showcase in the shadow of the Eiffel Tower. As he moved around Paris like a man on fire, there had been no time or opportunity for anything personal. Now, she was savoring the luxury of watching him and being in his relaxed, assured presence.

For most of the meal, Richard had monopolized the conversation, giving the journalist what amounted to an extravagant sales pitch. But now, with the instinct of a skilled negotiator, he realized it was time to sit back and let the other man have his say.

Cuthbert took a sip of coffee and swallowed. "There is one point you've neglected to mention. The riot in the gallery."

Richard raised his brandy snifter and studied the amber lights as he swirled it with deceptive casualness. "Oh, that. I assumed you'd read about it in the local press. People seemed to lose their heads. It wasn't pretty, but it shows the fanatical devotion her paintings inspire. Even so, I'd hate for you to make that the focus of your article."

Cuthbert peered at him through his spectacles with the defensiveness of a professional being told his business. "What *should* be the focus of my article?" he asked stiffly.

"What I've been telling you. Her amazing work and her martyred life. Do you know what they're calling her? Joan of Art."

He jotted it down, but shook his head doubtfully. "I don't know, Richard. Every year some dabbler or other comes to the surface that everyone is excited about, and six months later, no one can remember their names. How can we know she's the genuine article?"

"You've known me for a while, old man. Have you ever heard me talk about *anyone* this way? I'm more sure of this than I've ever been about anything in my life. I would stake my reputation on her paintings alone. But what we have here is more than just a body of sublime work. In living the way she did, and in taking her life, Mason Caldwell has created a saga the likes of which we've never seen."

Cuthbert turned to Mason. "Why do you think your sister took her life?"

Richard answered for Mason. "I believe she took her art to its absolute limit. And when she reached that point, there was nowhere else to go. The suicide was a deliberate act of self-martyrdom, a statement to a cruel world that doesn't appreciate the sensitive and the vulnerable. The only possible conclusion of a life lived solely for artistic expression."

Cuthbert took a few notes, then looked up at Mason. "Miss Caldwell, what can you tell me about your family?"

In the last week, she'd prepared herself for this, but it was still an agonizing subject. Her family wound was an open sore, and she had no intention of venturing beyond a few half-truths. "There's not much to tell, really. My father was a casualty of America's civil war. My mother had a small inheritance that we lived on. After she passed away five years ago, Mason and I split that inheritance. She used her half to come to Paris."

"Were you and your sister close?"

"When we were young, but our interests were different, and when she moved to Paris, we lost contact. She did, however, write me about a year ago asking me if I would store some of her paintings."

"What do you speculate made your sister dedicate herself to art? What gave her that tremendous drive to express herself?"

It was a deeper question than she'd expected. She glanced at Richard to find that he was watching her as if he, too, was interested in hearing the answer.

"Our mother was an amateur painter, mostly landscapes. Her great desire was to bring a little beauty into the world. But that ambition was frustrated. No one understood. Our father never approved and thought she was wasting her time, and the people in the community thought she was odd, even un-Christian, and scorned her from their society. Finally, it broke her heart." Her voice cracked a little. She hadn't meant to reveal so much truth. She took a steadying breath and added quickly, "I suppose Mason was trying to vindicate our mother. . . ."

She paused, hoping the subject would be changed by another question. But Cuthbert said, "Then the figure in the paintings is her mother. And the backgrounds represent the narrow forces that cast her out."

"I suppose," Mason answered. The analysis was making her uncomfortable.

Cuthbert thought a minute, then shook his head. "It's compelling, I admit. But the question remains: Will the woman be more than just a flash in the pan?"

"Surely you can see it." Richard's voice was husky with emotion. "The story of Mason Caldwell touches a chord of human existence that is potent and elemental. In attempting to validate and exonerate her mother, she has personally assumed that rejection and humiliation in a way that's almost Christlike. And in the end, she suffered more than her mother ever had. It's a sacrifice we all can feel in our souls. Who of us hasn't known, at some time or other, such isolation and despair? Who hasn't felt what it's like to be alone in a hostile world with nowhere to turn, no one to talk to, no one to listen to our troubles? No one to love. Never hearing the sound of another voice. Never having someone beside us to say the simple words, 'I understand?' Everyone who stands before her paintings will feel her loneliness and her pain and see their own suffering in it. But what they will feel even more strongly is the transcendent power with which she transformed that loneliness and pain into the healing, uplifting glory of her art. No painter of our century has the potential to have *that* kind of impact on people."

A profound stillness settled on the table.

Shifting in his chair, the journalist cleared his throat and asked, "Then what exactly is your plan for presenting the paintings?"

Richard wrapped an arm around the back of his chair,

once again assuming a more composed demeanor. "Basically, what we hope to do is to take the eighteen paintings now at the Falconier Gallery and add to them another dozen or so that Amy has stored back in the States. There are also a number of paintings that Mason gave away or exchanged for food over the years. We'll try to acquire these as well. So, ultimately, we hope to have the entire Caldwell Collection in one place, exhibited in its own pavilion at the fair. Naturally, this will all take some time. The exhibition officials are making it difficult. But I'm confident we'll prevail. And knowing your way with words, I'm certain your article will go a long way toward changing their minds."

Cuthbert chuckled at the presumption. "But the fair opens in a month. How can you possibly get the paintings and build the pavilion in that short time?"

"We can't make the opening, obviously. But the fair will go on for months, and its spiritual opening won't come until the fourteenth of July. That's when the real excitement begins. They'll be celebrating the Republic's hundredth birthday with special exhibits, a reenactment of the storming of the Bastille, and a pyrotechnical display so spectacular that they're having to import boatloads of fireworks from all over the world. We hope to be up and running some time before that monumental moment. My target date is the twenty-first of June, the summer equinox."

"And then what? Where will the paintings go from there?"

"That's up to Amy. As Mason's only living relative, they belong to her. Naturally, I hope they will ultimately find their way not into the hands of speculators or private collectors, but to an institution that will honor them and share them with the world."

"What about the French government? You know, of course, that their law entitles them to match any outside offer for a French painting so the best works stay in the country."

"I know. But even though they were painted in France, the Caldwell paintings are by an American artist."

"That may be, but these French . . . they're odd bits about such things. They may have a different idea about that."

Mason had never heard about this. "You mean . . . even if someone buys one of the paintings, the French can match the offer and keep it here?"

"Only if the painting is French," Richard assured her. "There's no precedent for seizing a painting by an American artist, even a longtime resident."

The waiter presented the bill, which Richard signed and handed back as Cuthbert jotted a few lines in his notebook. Cuthbert closed the notebook and smiled. "I have to admit it, Richard, this is quite a story."

"I thought you might find it so. Naturally, I wanted you to have it first. When do you think it might run, old chap?"

"I can't say. We shall have to see what my London editors make of the story." He turned to Mason. "It's been a pleasure meeting you, Miss Caldwell. I must say, you make a gracious representative for your sister."

Richard, his eyes shining with pride, said, "Doesn't she, though?"

Mason stood in the lobby, watching as Richard walked Cuthbert out. She was trembling. She hadn't revealed much, but she'd spilled enough of her family secrets to feel vulnerable and exposed. Her mother. Why had she told them about her? Couldn't she have made up some story that didn't cut so close to the bone? The empty hollow inside her had opened up a crack, the same hollow she'd thought all this would fill. She hugged herself, trying to quell the shaking. She had to get hold of herself before Richard returned. If he saw her like this he'd ask questions she didn't want to—couldn't—answer.

But he was walking toward her, a grin softening the flinty contours of his mouth. Taking her shoulders in both hands, he said, "You were magnificent."

"Was I?"

"You gave him—and me—precisely what we needed."

Mason avoided his gaze, shutting out the pride beaming in his eyes. "You made Mason sound like some kind of saint."

"Well . . . Wasn't she?"

She tried to swallow the lump in her throat. "I don't think she wanted to be thought of that way."

"That's what makes saints. Their humility. In any case, the night was a success. We're a formidable team, you and I."

She looked up into his eyes, saw the spark of desire, and realized the process of manipulating the hardened journalist had excited him.

"You're shivering."

She hadn't realized she was still trembling. "I'm cold," she lied.

His hands tightened on her shoulders. "Come upstairs with me," he invited softly. "Let me warm you up."

She wanted suddenly to be held . . . to be reassured . . . to be loved. To have the hole inside her once again filled with the warmth of his appreciation.

She nodded and went with him to the grill elevator. As it ascended, he took her hand and traced the palm with his finger. She felt her body leap to life.

Suddenly, she couldn't wait. The memory of their passion in the coach flooded through her and her feeling of emptiness transmitted itself into a longing of the flesh. He saw the simmering hunger in her eyes and leaned toward her, bringing his mouth a mere inch from hers. He didn't kiss her, and the fact that he didn't made her want him to all the more. The nearness of him, the clean masculine scent aroused her, anticipation turning to liquid heat. He took her hand and placed it on his groin. She felt him, hard and coiled, in her palm. His desire washed over her, banishing the memories and unwanted despair.

"I can't wait to have you in my arms," he whispered.

His words were like music soothing her soul. She, too, was impatient now. The whir of the elevator grated on her nerves. Too slow . . . too slow . . .

At last it stopped. Holding hands, they rushed down the wide, empty hall. The colors flashed before her eyes, the red, black, gold, and green of the thick carpet, the emerald hues of the walls. The gleaming rich mahogany of the double doors to his rooms as he turned the key in the lock. The muted golds of the vast, dim sitting room, lighted only by a single lamp. This room alone was larger than her entire suite, sumptuous with Second Empire furnishings, sometime haven of princes and kings.

And then he was lifting her in muscular arms, sweeping her through, his urgency now a palpable presence. He swept her through another set of double doors and into his bedroom, kicking the door closed behind them. Swallowed by darkness, his private domain smelled ever so faintly of him.

He laid her on the bed, following in one swift move so he came on top of her, his erection grazing her between her thighs. He kissed her madly, his mouth grinding into hers, his tongue quickening her pulse as he roamed her with his hands, feeling her through her clothes.

She moaned helplessly, suddenly so hot, she felt nearly delirious with yearning. She clung to him, running her fingers through his crisp hair, pulling his head to her and whimpering now as the force and possession of his touch, and his demanding kiss, made her head spin. She felt drunk on the taste of him. His hands running over her curves as if he could never get enough of the feel of her, causing her blood to boil in her veins.

She reached between their twined bodies, touching the rampant erection, and he groaned in her mouth like some sort of unleashed beast. She loved the feel of him in her hand, so large, so stiff, pulsing with the energy of life.

She wanted him inside. She wanted it so badly she knew she couldn't wait another minute. She began to tear at the fastenings of his trousers, frantic now. Wanting him to hurry . . . hurry . . . to fill the ache inside with his virile strength.

He shoved her hand away. Somehow, still ardently kissing

her, he got himself unsheathed. And then he was hiking up her skirts, wading through the barriers of petticoats, brushing them aside. Yanking off her undergarments with a savage tug. His hands found bare flesh, igniting her lust. He pushed her knees open and plunged inside.

He filled her so suddenly, so fully, that she cried out. She was so juicy, she took him easily, as big as he was, feeling him slam home with a jolt that sent her heart galloping. He thrust into her powerfully, masterfully, swallowing her cries with his mouth, holding her so tightly she could barely breathe.

His relentless drive carried her away, escalating her excitement, until she felt she was levitating in his arms. She exploded on his cock, delicious spasms that spiraled one into another, cracking her open, washing over her with a rush of emotion that brought tears to her eyes. She clutched him desperately, loving him so deeply, so completely, that she felt herself a part of all living things. As if her soul had shattered and was spreading all around her like a shower of shooting stars.

She wished, with all her heart, that this moment would last until the end of time.

As if sensing it, or feeling it himself, he didn't stop. He increased his thrusts, pounding into her like a honed athlete, propelling her to orgasm again . . . and again . . . and again . . . until all her senses were filled with nothing but him.

Only then did he allow himself release. Waiting for her, for that sublime moment when her heart began again to race out of control and she felt herself losing it once more . . . only then did he join her, holding her wrapped in his enclosing arms, pinned to him, taking them both to a climax that was sweeter and more fulfilling than anything she'd ever known.

When it was over and she felt wondrously complete, limp with swimming joy, he stayed lodged inside her, holding her as his breathing slowed, clutching her to him like something precious beyond measure, swelling her heart as she, too, held him for dear life.

Minutes passed. She became aware of a clock somewhere in the room delicately ticking away the time. And then his heated breath at her ear. "Holy Christ!"

He moved then, dislodging himself, taking away his warmth and weight. He stood, turning his back to her, running his hand along his sweaty brow. A faint stream of moonlight illuminated him, his large frame so treasured to her love-softened gaze.

He stood like a statue, rigid and still. And then, so softly he might not have even known he spoke aloud, he rasped, "I can't do this."

She pushed herself up with effort, her body so depleted it didn't want to move.

"What can't you do?"

He turned to her. She could see his face faintly, so achingly handsome, but twisted by some inner torment she didn't understand.

"This." He gestured toward her. "It's too much—I hadn't counted on—" He stopped abruptly, as if he'd said too much. He was staring at her as if she were some sixteenth-century witch who'd stolen his senses.

Suddenly, she understood.

He was falling in love with her.

And he didn't want to.

She rose from the bed and went to put her hand on his arm. It felt like iron. "It's all right," she soothed.

In the moonlight, he pierced her with his gaze. "This can't happen again."

"Of course not," she said.

His eyes narrowed to slits. "We have a mission. We have to concentrate on that. We can't afford to become . . . distracted."

She'd never before been such a distraction to a man that it frightened him. She couldn't contain the smile that spread across her face.

"I mean it," he told her sternly.

"Of course you do."

"It won't happen again."

"Of course it won't."

He grabbed her shoulders and shook her. "It—won't—happen—again," he ground out.

"Never."

She tiptoed to kiss his cheek. As she did, she put her hand on his cock. It was flaccid, but at her touch it hardened instantly.

He jerked away from her, turning his back once more. "Please," he groaned, "go."

"Of course I'll go."

"And stop saying 'of course.'"

She gathered up her things, then went to stand before him. Kissing her fingers, she reached up and touched them to his mouth.

"Of course," she smiled.

Chapter 8

Uncertain of Cuthbert's commitment to the story, Richard left for London the next morning to lobby his editors. Mason welcomed the reprieve because she needed the time away from him to do some of the new paintings that would be "shipped from the States." She also wanted to give him time to miss her. But as it turned out, over the next few days she felt no inspiration to create the new works, and it was she who missed him—achingly.

Time and again, she found herself going to her window and looking out at the back façade of the Grand Hotel. She thought of his suite where she'd found such bliss, only to be pushed away, and she felt his absence keenly.

Finally, she was sick of it. She had to get away.

The timing was perfect. The Cirque Fernando had just ended its current season and wouldn't start up again for another few weeks, so Lisette would be free to come along. They would go to the country and paint.

She sent a message to Lisette, bundled up all the painting equipment she'd bought the morning Richard had left town, then went to the offices of E. Larue, Real Estate Agent on the Boulevard Montmartre, and told him she wanted to take a lease on the villa in Auvers-sur-Oise that her sister Mason had rented the summer before. Using Falconier's letter of credit, she paid three months' rent in advance. This would afford her a place to go in the months ahead to be alone and paint in secret.

The next morning, Lisette met her at the Gare St-Lazare with all seven of her dogs in tow. She was delighted to leave town. "It will give me a chance to get away from that pesky Juno. Ever since he saw your paintings of me, he hounds me like never before. Every day, flowers. If I see another bouquet of red roses, I will lose my mind. Boxes of candy. Poems."

Mason laughed. "Juno Dargelos, the king of the Apache gangsters, writes poetry?"

"Pooh! He can't write his name. He must have made some destitute poet do it for him."

Mason studied her friend. "He seems so devoted to you. You take lovers at the drop of a hat, but this man who's considered a romantic Robin Hood by half the shopgirls in Paris, you won't give the time of day."

"What he did, I can never forgive."

"It must have been something awful."

"More than awful. Disgusting. But enough. I refuse to discuss it!"

The train took them through the northern outskirts of the city, over the Seine at the town of Asnières, which the Impressionists had immortalized in their art. Once they'd navigated the confusion of cramming more than half a dozen dogs into a single compartment and had settled down, Lisette pulled some grapes from her hand luggage and gave half of them to Mason.

"I asked around about your man," she said.

"You asked about Richard?"

"But of course. I've never seen you so smitten with a man, and I worry about you. After all, you don't seem to know much about him."

"What did you find out?"

"Not much. He moves around Europe going to art shows and mixing with high society. Lives in hotels. Comes to Paris several times a year. He has money, but no one seems to

know where he gets it." She tossed a grape to one of the ter-
riers. "He's a mystery."

"What about women?"

"Oh, lots of women. But none for very long."

"What kind of women?"

"Mostly society types. An Italian contessa who never got
over him. Some English heiress. That sort of thing."

"No wife stashed away, I hope."

"*Mais non!* If I'd found that out, I would have shot him
for you." The dogs were up again, all begging for grapes,
which Lisette tossed to each, smiling her affection.

Mason mulled this over. "I suppose you think this is all a
little crazy, don't you?"

"Crazy? What's crazy about spending the rest of your life
pretending you're a sister you never had so you can be with a
man who wants to spend his life promoting your paintings,
which you have to paint on the side because he can't know
you're alive? What's crazy about that?"

The absurdity of it caused Mason to laugh.

But Lisette wasn't smiling now. "The only thing that really
bothers me about your little *comédie* is that flic Duval. He's
no one to trifle with."

"I'll just have to be careful and not do anything to rouse
his suspicions. I'll only paint in Auvers and leave all my
equipment there so I won't leave a trail for him."

Fifty minutes later, they arrived in Auvers-sur-Oise. It was
a charming village of old stone houses with thatched roofs
that stretched for several miles along the picturesque Oise
River, rising in a series of terraces from its banks to a plateau
of wheat fields that seemed to stretch to infinity. In the early
days of Impressionism, Cézanne, Pissarro, and Berthe
Morisot had painted extensively in its fields and rustic lanes
and along its willow-draped riverbanks. The cost of living
was much cheaper here than in Paris, and Mason had found
it both economical and inspirational to spend several of her
summers here.

The villa was located a mile or so upriver from the hamlet itself in a sylvan setting. They had a boatman row them from the landing just below the train station to the small private dock stationed between two large willows with dangling leaves that floated lazily in the water. Across a grassy expanse, the house with its black shutters stood by a huge oak tree with a swing attached. The rooms inside were tiny, in the French tradition, but numerous enough to house Mason, Lisette, the art supplies, and all the dogs. It was a peaceful retreat that looked as if it had sprung from a Louisa May Alcott story. But just as they arrived, the sky clouded up and it began to rain.

The rain kept up for the next three days and nights. Lisette was in a lethargic mood, and Mason had to struggle to make herself pick up a brush. She hadn't worked for months and she'd been looking forward to it, but the dreary weather dampened her spirits, and the lack of momentum made her feel nervous and rusty. She forced herself to finish three canvases in the style that had so captivated Richard, but she felt disconnected from the process and the work gave her none of the satisfaction and sense of escape that it had before.

To add to her uneasiness, she couldn't stop pining for Richard. Was he thinking about her as he went about his business in London? Or was he trying *not* to think about her? It didn't seem possible that he could shut her out of his mind completely, as much as he might want to. Not after the explosive lovemaking they'd shared. But then she remembered all those other women—the contessa who'd never gotten over him. Had she, too, been convinced he was in love with her? Had he said to her, in that tormented way, *I can't do this?* Thinking about it kept her awake nights, tossing in her bed, with the rain beating incessantly on the roof.

The warmth of a beam of sunlight streaming through the lace curtails awakened her on the fourth morning. Rising from bed, she could see that the gloom had passed and it was a delightful April day. Birds were chirping, the crocuses were suddenly in bloom, and the world, bathed in the golden light that had brought painters to France for the past 400 years, seemed newly born. Thrusting her top floor window open, she leaned out and took in a cleansing breath of the crystal air, feeling the familiar stirring inside that told her she was ready at last. She was itching to paint.

She ran into Lisette's room in her bare feet and pounced on her bed, startling the dogs who lay sprawled about her, shaking her awake. Lisette sat up, muttering, her blond hair tangled and cascading about her shoulders, and held a hand to her eyes to shield them from the flood of morning light. "What time is it?"

"Who cares what time it is? It's a new day. A new world. Out of bed, lazybones. I want to capture this beautiful morning before it goes away."

They hastily packed a picnic lunch and spent the day down by the river. Mason had no stomach to attempt another "typical" Caldwell picture. She just wanted to paint Lisette in the joy of nature, to capture the quality of light on her face as the willow fronds blew around her in the gentle breeze. All at once, the enjoyment of painting returned to her.

They had a marvelous time together, like two children frolicking barefoot in the fields beneath the invigorating sunshine. They laughed and talked of nothing and everything the way they'd done in the old days before Mason had disappeared. They ate their picnic lunch on a blanket spread out beneath the willows, nibbling brie and bread and sipping wine, tossing tidbits to the ever-present dogs who performed the tricks Lisette had taught them in her spare time.

While playing with them, Lisette had stuck out her fleshy lower lip and given her mane of blond hair a shake. It gave her the look of a petulant child, and yet, with her lithe, sexual body, the effect was extraordinary. Mason had captured elements of this look before in earlier canvases, but she'd never seen it so striking or fully realized, this innocent, pouty sexuality.

"Stop!" Mason cried. "Stay just as you are. Don't move a muscle."

She brought over the canvas she'd been working on and began to make revisions. After a while, as it was beginning to come together, she said, "Lisette . . ."

"Hmmm?"

"You know about men."

"Some," Lisette shrugged. "It's so cozy here, I could just go to sleep."

Mason sat back to survey her work. "After years of constant practice, I finally feel that I'm beginning to know something about art. The finished products don't always live up to the image I first had in my head, but they're coming closer."

"*Oui.*" Lisette sounded as if she was already falling asleep.

"Painting is familiar to me. But I know absolutely nothing about the art of seduction."

"What's to know? You just show the man your ankles and he won't leave you alone."

"There has to be more to it than that."

"I don't know. I never seduce men. They always chase after me."

Mason tried another tactic. "You know how I feel about Richard, right?"

"I know you've lost your head."

As she painted, she told Lisette about what had happened with him the other night. "He wants me, but he doesn't *want* to want me. How do I get around that? I need something foolproof. Something he can't resist."

"Ah! Like a magic potion?"

"Well, yes, in a way."

"I know just the thing. Perfume."

"Oh, come on."

"Bah! You think I'm joking? What do you think gives French women their legendary allure? Are we more beautiful than you?"

"*You* are more beautiful than anyone."

"Have you ever seen a likeness of Madame Pompadour? Or Madame du Barry? Homely as doorposts! But they smelled like goddesses. Scent is the greatest of all aphrodisiacs. Every French woman knows that."

"I hardly think you would ever need a perfume to drive a man wild."

"No? When I need to be devastating, the first thing I do is go to see Madame Toulon. She is more than a concocter of perfume, she is a sorceress. She creates for me a scent men can't resist."

"Could she do that for me?"

"But of course."

Mason wasn't convinced. "I find it hard to believe a strong-willed man like Richard Garrett, with his confidence and experience with women, could be swayed by a mere perfume—"

Abruptly, Lisette held up a hand. She straightened up and peered into the distance. "This man of yours. Is he very tall? Dark like Lucifer?"

"I guess you could say that. Why?"

"I think he's here."

Mason shot around to see a figure coming their way from the road by the house. They were some distance from him, but Lisette was right. Richard!

In a panic, she looked at the scene around her: the canvas, the paints, the easel, the smeared smock she was wearing. Trapped!

"What are we going to do?"

"You hide everything," Lisette told her, leaping to her feet. "I'll stall him."

With that, she pointed toward the oncoming figure and called out a command in French. At the sound of it, her pack of dogs, who'd been dozing contentedly in the shade, went barking across the field after him. They surrounded him, jumping up on him, nearly knocking him down, while Mason frantically grabbed the canvas, the easel, her paintbox and pallet, and tossed them all in a jumble under the blanket. She ripped her smock off, saw the pigment stains on her dress, and stepped out of that as well, stuffing them under the blanket with the rest of the incriminating evidence. She hurriedly arranged the picnic things on top, then turned to see what Richard was doing.

He'd crouched on his haunches and was holding out his hand for the dogs to sniff, trying to make friends with them. They were responding too quickly. In another moment he stood and his new friends led the way toward the two women.

Mason looked down at her hands and saw stains of geranium lake and chromium yellow. Glancing about, her gaze came to rest on the riverbank still muddy from the rains. He was coming closer by the second. "Quick," she told Lisette, "take off your dress and come with me."

Lisette obeyed and they hurried to the riverbank where Mason bent to bury her hands. Standing, both hands full of mud, she slung some at Lisette, who shrieked at her. "What are you doing?"

"Pretend we're having a mud fight," Mason urged, "so I can hide my hands."

"Ah, *oui*." Lisette followed suit, flinging it at Mason. Soon they were upon one another, rubbing mud on each other, laughing like two maniacs.

"I can't think when I've seen a prettier sight," a deep voice greeted.

They looked up at him, two women clad in petticoats and covered in mud. He was dressed in sporting clothes, casual yet immaculate and crisply tailored, looking every inch the gentleman off for an outing in the country. He'd removed his hat and a lock of dark hair fell rakishly over his forehead. As he noticed the way Mason's damp, mud-splotched shift clung to her curves, his eyes darkened and his lips parted. He looked absolutely delicious. Mason had to fight the urge to run to him and throw herself into his arms.

Instead, remembering the necessity to keep her distance,

she picked up a huge glob of the muck, straightened with a taunting grin, and said, "Come and join the party." With that, she hurled it at him.

He stepped aside deftly and it sailed past him. "Not just now, thanks all the same."

She wrinkled her nose at him. "Spoilsport."

"The country air does odd things to people."

"Ah, but you're breathing the same country air. Sure you won't change your mind?" She approached him, looking as if she might pounce on him at any second, head-to-toe mud and all. He backed away, which, of course, was exactly what she'd hoped he'd do. The farther he kept from her, the less likely he was to see the paint on her hands.

"How did you find me here, anyway?" she asked.

He shrugged. "A bit of detective work. It wasn't too difficult."

His words sent a chill through her. She glanced nervously at Lisette. "Mason used to come here to paint sometimes. She wrote me about it."

"Nice to see the two of you getting on so well. I should imagine Mason would be pleased."

"Oh, Lisette's a dear," she said quickly. "I asked her for directions to the place and she dropped everything to bring me here herself. We've been having a little vacation. Just us and the dogs."

Some of those dogs had run in after Lisette and knocked her down so she sat in the mud as they crawled all over her.

"Apologies for invading your privacy, but I need to talk to you," Richard said.

"Let's go back to the house. I want to wash up." She turned and began to walk, leading him away from the scene of the crime, thinking regretfully of the ruined painting beneath the blanket.

"What about your things?"

"Oh, Lisette will get them. What did you want to talk about?"

He'd been looking quizzically at the oddly shaped blanket, but her reminder distracted him and he caught up to her. "Have you made any progress on shipping the paintings from America?"

"I'm working on it, but it will take some time." The mud was beginning to dry on her hands, making her worry that the paint might show through. She thrust them behind her back and said, "I did, however, manage to find three paintings that she exchanged here for food."

Genuinely excited, he said, "Excellent! I can't wait to see them."

"You came all this way just to ask me that?"

"You're right. There *is* something else. Something important. Next week, a man is coming to town whom I'd very much like you to meet."

She couldn't concentrate, feeling vulnerable as she still did from coming so close to being caught in the act. "All right," she said distractedly.

"Shall I bring him here?"

"Oh, no. I mean it's such a long way. I'll go back to Paris." They'd reached the house and she stood back, gesturing for him to open the door. "Go on into the front parlor." She pointed the way. "I'll get cleaned up and bring the paintings down."

Upstairs, she hurriedly stashed all her painting equipment in one of the spare rooms. She washed off the mud and used turpentine to remove all traces of paint, then washed her hands again. That done, still in her petticoat, she checked herself out in the mirror. Her hair was falling about her shoulders in a disheveled way that made her look ready for bed. Her loins began to tingle.

With any luck, he'll have to stay the night!

She'd intended to change into a clean dress, but, remembering the way he'd looked at her in her shift, she decided against it. Instead, she slipped into her laciest new petticoat—the tight one that accentuated all her curves—leaving the top two buttons open as if she'd been in too much of a hurry to finish. Her cleavage peeped through just enough to afford him a glimpse of hidden treasures. Then she fluffed her hair and carried the three paintings she'd completed downstairs.

As she entered the parlor, he turned from looking out the window and froze. His gaze came to rest just where she wanted it—on the swell of her bosom. It seemed to her that his face paled a shade. His throat moved as he swallowed.

"Sorry to be so long," she said. "I tried to hurry."

He shifted his weight to his other foot. "Perhaps you hurried a bit too much. Haven't forgotten something, have you?"

She glanced down at the flimsy lace with its pink bow. "Oh, this? Does it bother you? I mean, you did just see me in my petticoat out there, so—But I could go change, if it makes you nervous. I just thought you'd like to see the paintings as soon as possible."

"I do. And I'm not the least bit nervous."

"Of course not."

She set the paintings up against the wall opposite him for his inspection, bending as she did to provide him a glimpse of her backside. When she turned to him, he was frowning and his lips were pursed tightly. He waved his hand in a sardonic gesture, indicating for her to move out of the way.

"Oh, sorry. I didn't mean to distract you."

"Like hell you didn't."

She moved aside, suppressing a smile. He stepped over to the paintings, put his hand to his jaw, and studied them carefully, looking at them for an unusually long time without comment. One of them, another version of Lisette in the catacombs, he picked up and held to the light. Then he set it down again, still saying nothing.

She came up behind him, looking over his shoulder, coming in close so her breasts flattened against his back. It was so delicious to be near him again. She felt a shudder go through him before he stepped away.

"Well?" she asked.

"They're good." His voice sounded tentative. "But not as good as her best work. These must have been painted early on. Before she was fully up to speed."

This annoyed her. *All those miserable hours painting the damn things.*

But she felt no attachment to them. He was right. They weren't her best.

She put her hands behind her back, clasping the palms together, and stepped into his sight line. Once again, his gaze drifted, as if on its own accord, to her cleavage, which was now all but thrusting out at him. "It's getting late. I suppose you'll be needing to stay the night. We have plenty of rooms. You won't even have to share yours with one of the dogs."

"No," he said too quickly, too violently. Then, collecting himself, he added in a carefully modulated tone, "As tempting as that may be—with or without the canine companionship—I have some pressing business in town. I'm going to rush and catch the last train back. I have a chap waiting with his wagon who'll return me to the station."

"The last train isn't due for an hour yet. Are you sure you wouldn't like some . . . refreshment first?"

His eyes flicked to her bosom and away again. "No. Thank you, no."

With that, he bolted out of the door and down the path toward the road as if the furies of Hades were after him.

She fell back against the doorjamb with a sigh.

I guess I'm going to have to get some perfume, after all.

And then, belatedly, she wondered, *How did he manage to track me down?*

Chapter 9

They left Auvers a day earlier than Mason had intended. She'd tried to throw herself into the work again, but it was no use. She simply didn't feel like painting. And she couldn't stop thinking of Richard, so obviously attracted to her, tempted by her, and running down the path from the villa to prevent himself from giving in to her. She felt encouraged by the difficulty he was obviously having, and she was determined now to move in for the kill. But first, she decided she'd take Lisette's advice and see what the sorceress Madame Toulon could do for her.

Lisette took her to see the *parfumeuse* that same afternoon. Her shop was located on Île-St-Louis, the smaller of the two islands in the Seine that made up the geographic center of Paris. It was a diminutive boutique at the end of a dead-end lane. Its front window was dominated by an incongruous poster for such an establishment: a garish advertisement for Buffalo Bill Cody's Wild West Show, which would play at the Champ de Mars throughout the run of the fair. Exposition fever reached even to this elegant enclave.

Inside, it was meticulously clean; the walls were lined floor to ceiling with shelves supporting untold hundreds of multi-colored glass vials. In the center, a huge overstuffed pink velvet ottoman sat beside a rococo table.

Madame Toulon herself was a miniscule woman in her

later years with bright green eyes that twinkled when she saw Lisette, her favorite customer. *"Mon chou!"* she exclaimed, kissing her on both cheeks. "My day is now complete."

"I have a most special challenge for you, *maman*. This is my friend Ma—" She corrected herself, "Amy Caldwell, from America. She is in need of your genius."

"But she is most fetching," Madame said, looking Mason over with her practiced eye.

"Still, there is a man who is determined to elude her."

"But no, no, *no,* that will never do." Madame began to roll up her sleeves. "Come, my child."

They sat together on the ottoman and the elder woman looked Mason over more closely.

Lisette, enjoying the moment, pulled up a chair and beamed at Mason.

"Tell me, little one, what scent are you now using?"

"Nothing."

"Nothing?" She turned to Lisette. *"Rien?"*

Lisette shook her head incredulously.

"But this is sacrilege! No wonder you are having trouble. Well, then, we start from the beginning." She took Mason's hand and gave her wrist a delicate sniff. "Tell me about this man who is so foolish he thinks he can escape your charms."

"Well, he's English—"

"Sacre bleu! This gets worse and worse! Oh, well. What does he like? What does he do?"

"Mostly he's a connoisseur of art."

"At least *that* is in his favor. What sort of art?"

"All kinds, I think. But he likes Impressionism most of all."

"Ah! Now I begin to like this man. We will find just the thing that will drive a connoisseur of art wild."

She clapped her hands. A young assistant appeared and followed behind her as Madame scanned the shelves. "Nothing too traditional, then. It must be subtle. The worst thing one can do is to overpower the olfactory senses. One must caress them, coddle them, seduce them. And the scent must be uniquely you. So we will persevere until we find the exact blend that will mix with your own natural essence to create a potion so enticing, so elusively sensual, that should she catch a whiff of it, Aphrodite herself would weep with envy."

The next day, armed with her new secret weapon, Mason entered the lobby of the Grand Hotel and saw Richard standing there, waiting for her. He looked particularly dashing. When he saw her, he blinked, and she caught the leap of appreciation in his eyes, registering the pains she'd taken with her appearance. He looked like a man who'd been telling himself all week that he'd overestimated her effect on him, and who, on seeing her again, had just realized how wrong he could be. She felt a trickle of anticipation flutter through her.

He surprised her by taking both her hands in his. Then he said, "I have some news. Come over here." He drew her to a cluster of chairs and sat her down. "The Exposition has embraced the idea for a Mason Caldwell Pavilion. I've hired an architect who has supplied a plan we all like. And we've raised enough funds that construction can begin tomorrow. I've also talked them into a prime location, just below the Tower by the Monaco Pavilion."

He'd done it. She thought back on that moment when she'd seen her letter of application so rudely stamped REJECTED. And now this . . . not just accepted to be placed in a room with a hundred other artists, but her own exclusive showcase!

She couldn't even imagine the argument he'd had to put up to accomplish such a miracle.

"How did you change their minds?"

"I've found that a little diplomacy goes a long way. And this didn't hurt." He reached into his jacket pocket and handed her a folded copy of the *London Times*. "Have a look."

She opened the paper and was shocked to find Cuthbert's story on the front page, positioned just below the banner as if Queen Victoria had just died.

"Go ahead, read it. We have time."

She did, and it was more than she ever could have hoped for. Despite the doubts he'd displayed during their dinner, Cuthbert had parroted most of what Richard had said to him and presented it in a way that was persuasive and heartrending. This was the legend of Mason Caldwell as Joan of Art perfectly encapsulated. A fanciful exaggeration, to be sure, but even though it bore only a peripheral relationship to her own story, she had to admit it was compelling, with all the drama and pathos of a classical Greek myth.

"I can't believe it. This is the *London Times*! They don't buy into cheap sensationalism. How did you get them to feature it so prominently? And Cuthbert—he seemed so reluctant at dinner, but he ended up saying everything you wanted him to. Word for word. How did you ever manage it?"

He grinned. "Let's just say I know where a few bodies are buried along the Thames."

This display of his prowess was unexpectedly arousing. "You make light of it; but really, this is beyond anything I could have expected. How can I ever thank you?"

"By coming up to my rooms."

"Your rooms?" Her heart leapt. This was going to be easier than she'd expected.

"Hank is there waiting for us."

"Hank?" She shook her head, trying to get her bearings.

"The man I want you to meet. He's an American, like yourself. You may have heard of him. Henry Thompson. He's a financier and entrepreneur. He's rather a legendary figure on Wall Street."

"Oh, yes. The meeting."

She didn't really want to meet this Hank Thompson, whoever he was. She wanted to be alone with Richard. But there was no way to avoid it.

"Let's go meet him, shall we?"

She reached over and put her hand on his leg. "Yes," she smiled, "let's not keep him waiting."

It was as if she'd scalded him with her hand. He jerked to his feet and she could see the hooded warning in his eyes. "Let's not," he said through clenched teeth.

She smiled at him innocently.

They strolled over to the elevator. He opened the gate for her to enter. But, glancing behind, she noticed that a family of five had just entered the lobby and were slowly heading toward them.

Stalling, she gave a faint cry of pain and pretended to stumble. "Oh dear."

"What's the matter?" he asked.

"I seem to have caught my heel on something. I hope I haven't sprained my ankle."

"Shall I have a look?"

She reached down and rubbed her ankle. As she did, she cast a quick look behind to see that the family was almost upon them. "No, thanks. I'm fine."

They stepped in and the family crowded in behind them, forcing them to the back, their bodies close, their faces almost touching.

In this position, Richard couldn't help but get a whiff of her perfume. It hit him so hard, she felt his back slam against the side of the elevator. She pressed into him further still, close enough to feel the swelling of his groin. When she looked up at him, she saw that his eyes were tightly closed as if in pain.

She'd never felt feminine power like this before. Indeed, this *was* sorcery.

Merci beaucoup, Madame Toulon!

The elevator stopped on the second floor and the family shuffled out, leaving them alone. She stepped back slightly and saw the evidence of his arousal. As the elevator began its climb again, he opened his eyes and saw her watching him with a delighted smile plastered on her face. He glared at her, and she burst out laughing.

"Are you going to be all right?" she teased.

Tersely, he ground out, "I shall manage."

The lift stopped on the fourth floor and he stood for a moment, battling down his unwanted response.

"Cold baths are wonderful for that, I'm told."

He didn't appreciate the humor.

"Well, it's hardly my fault, is it?" she asked, trying hard not to giggle.

"Not much," he grumbled.

Composed at last, he led her down the hall to his suite. She had to fight everything in her to keep from dancing down the corridor beside him.

At the door, Richard paused before turning the key. "I should warn you, Hank's a bit of a character. But he's someone I trust implicitly."

Once inside, she saw the man in question standing at the bar. He was in his late fifties, somewhat portly but distinguished in a rough-and-tumble way. He wore a grey suit with piping along the back shoulders, as one might expect on a Texas cattle baron, with a peach-colored silk bandana knotted about his throat. He'd been handsome in his day, and still bore traces of his youthful splendor with intense blue eyes in a sunburned face and attractively silvered temples. He carried about him a deceptively casual sense of authority that was in no way diminished by the vast expanse of the room.

He was drinking whiskey from a crystal tumbler when he saw them enter. He drained the glass, slammed it down on the bar, and favored her with a boisterous smile, his eyes crinkling merrily. It occurred to her that she'd never been in a room before with two more striking and charismatic, albeit completely different, men.

"You must be Amy," he boomed, charging over to grasp her hand and give it an energetic shake. "Say, they grow them pretty in Boston, don't they though? My name's Thompson. Henry Thompson on the birth records, but you can call me Hank. Everyone does. I'm not much for formalities. I've made my home in New York and Chicago these many years, but I was weaned along the Texas panhandle, and we Texicans prefer things plain. I was just fixin' myself a little hair of the dog. What can I get you, Amy girl?"

She was so astonished that she barely managed to say, "Some water will be fine, thanks."

"Water? Water's for horses, darlin'. Why don't I put some kick in it?"

She wasn't at all sure what to make of his folksy charm. "It's a little early for me to get kicked, thanks just the same."

He barked out a laugh. "Pretty and feisty to boot. Where I come from, that's a hazardous combination. But that's okay, honey, I like 'em feisty. And so does Buster as I recall, eh, boy?"

Richard scowled at the man. "They don't call me Buster here. Are you feeling up to this, Hank? Not too . . . fatigued from your trip?"

"Oh, I'm lively, son, real lively. I'm just getting started." He splashed some more whiskey into his glass and added, "Well, now, let's go sit us down, why don't we?"

Mason looked at Richard and said, "Buster?"

A muscle flexed in his jaw. "An old nickname of Hank's. Have a seat."

She did so, wondering at the man's odd familiarity with Richard. Clearly, there was more to this alliance than met the eye.

Hank sat on one of the long settees and propped the boot of one foot over the other knee. He took a gulp of whiskey, then twirled the glass as he spoke.

"Buster—all right, son—Richard here would probably like me to ease into this a tad more gracefully. But we're both Americans and I don't believe in beating around the bush."

Hypnotic blue eyes bore into her as he spoke.

"That's refreshing," Mason commented, for lack of anything better to say.

"I have a proposition for you, little lady, and I hope you'll hear me out."

Mason shifted uncomfortably in her chair, thinking this man couldn't possibly have anything to say that she'd care to hear. "I gathered that."

He watched the whiskey swirling in its glass. "I think it's safe to say all three of us here believe in the future of Impressionist pictures—Monet, Manet, Degas, and those boys. You couldn't find a sounder investment, because sooner or later every museum and millionaire worth his salt is gonna be fightin' to have one. But some folks don't have the same faith in this future that we do, because the sad truth is, with all that's been said and written about them, the Impressionists have yet to catch on with the buying public. The dealers here still have a helluva time movin' a Sisley or Pissarro off the shelf. Now, why do you think that is?"

Mason realized he was asking her. "Why don't you tell me?"

"All right, I will. Because as gifted as these painters might be, they're all still very much alive and kicking, thank you, and not one man jack of them has a life story worth telling once they *do* go. The thing is, people today need something to stir their imaginations. Something to help sell the merchandise. Something that amplifies the art and forces them to see it in a different and exciting way. A story. A face. A hero. Or in this case, a heroine."

"And that would be Mason."

He jabbed his finger at her. "Your sister. Someone whose life is so irresistibly dramatic and whose painting is so completely different—and yet so easy on the eye—that the public can't resist 'em anymore than they can resist Mark Twain or Lillie Langtry. Your sister can carry all of Impressionism on her shoulders. Now, granted, I don't know pictures the way my boy Buster does, but I know sellin', and what I sell is ideas. And what we have here, folks, is an idea whose time has come."

Mason didn't know what to make of this man. He affected the air of a bumpkin, but beneath the façade, he was undeniably shrewd and ambitious. Clearly, he held some special position in Richard's life. *Buster?* She couldn't imagine a more unlikely nickname for someone like Richard Garrett. The mystery of it intrigued her.

"You said something about a proposition?"

"That's it. I love it. Get to the point! Now I know I'm talking to an American. Okay, here's the deal: I feel so strongly about the future of Impressionism that I've decided to endow a special museum to venerate it. Mind you, this is something the French haven't come close to thinking about because the French pooh-bahs still see Impressionism as a bunch of childish scrawling. This will be the world's first museum of its kind, and we intend to stick it right dab in the middle of New England. Maybe Boston. That *is* where you're from, isn't it?"

After a brief hesitation, she said, "Yes."

"Then it'll be in your own hometown. And that's fittin' because we want Mason's paintings to be in this museum. Hell, I'll go ahead and say it. We want Mason's paintings to be the centerpiece, the top dog, of our museum. First of all, we think she'll be the biggest draw. Second, she represents a rare opportunity because all her paintings are in one place, and if we can corral them all, we can have the entire Mason Caldwell Collection under our roof, which is something no museum can say about any other great artist. Da Vinci, Caravaggio, Rembrandt, their work is spread all over the world. Third, we think her pictures belong in her own country. In the good old U.S. of A."

The centerpiece of a museum . . .

In Boston . . .

How her mother would have loved that . . .

And all those toffee-nosed Brahmins who'd scorned her . . . the crow they'd have to eat!

And her father . . . if only he were alive to see it . . .

Taking her silence for resistance, Richard interceded, "What Hank is saying is that, while Mason painted here in France and was inarguably influenced by French painters, her work shows the perspective of an American observing her adopted country as an outsider. American Impressionism, as it were. Mary Cassatt did it, and some others, but not with the riveting intensity of Mason. And as such, we feel her paintings should be given a place of their own in her own country, where they can be honored as they deserve, rather than be sold piecemeal to wealthy collectors around the world where they'll be hoarded away."

Hank slammed his drink down on the table beside him. "She don't need you to tell her that, boy. She's got sense."

Richard gave a slow nod and leaned back in his chair. It puzzled Mason that he should defer to the man so completely.

Hank turned back to her. "Now I have to tell you straight off that we don't have the resources of some of these loaded Europeans who are gonna come at you wanting to pay a truckload of cabbage for this or that painting. But, of course, we can pay you something substantial. And what we're really offering is a way for you to keep the collection in one piece in America and at the same time give it to the world."

Mason was churning inside, but she strained not to show it. After a lengthy pause, she said, "Thank you, Mr. Thompson. I'll think about it."

It wasn't the answer he was hoping for, but he said, "Good. You do that, little lady."

"What I need to do," she continued, "is to let the offer settle—maybe someplace where my mind can be diverted by something entertaining."

Hank looked at Richard. Neither man spoke.

"I know!" she added. "The opera! Do you think you could use your influence to get me a box, Mr. Thompson?"

His face brightened. "Hellfire, honey, I'll buy out tonight's performance, if you like."

"That won't be necessary. But I *will* need a handsome young man to escort me. I don't suppose you can think of someone like that?"

"Buster can take you!"

Richard's eyes narrowed suspiciously on her. "I'm not much for opera."

"Hell, you say. All those times you tried to wrangle me into going? It's not my cup of bourbon, but if it's yours, I'll get you the best seats in the house. I don't care if I have to throw out a duke and three counts to do it. Why, you young folks are gonna have the time of your lives!"

Mason grinned at Richard like the cat who'd just gulped down the canary.

Chapter 10

L'Opéra was one of the glories of Paris, often acclaimed as the foremost opera house of the world. Its architect Charles Garnier had wanted it to be "a monument to art, to luxury, to pleasure," and it had grandly fulfilled that function for the Parisian upper classes since its opening in 1875. Mason had never been there, nor had anyone she knew in Paris—it was a world apart from the milieu of struggling artists. But from what she knew about it, it would be the perfect setting for the next stage of her plan.

It was directly kitty-corner to the Grand Hotel, so Richard, looking dapper in his tuxedo and top hat, called for her at the Jockey Club and they walked the short distance. He was there under protest but was gentleman enough to disguise the fact beneath a veneer of cordial host. They went around the side to the "Millionaire's Entrance," joining the flow of fashionable guests—with their pastel silk and satin evening gowns, their jewels, their top hats and canes—through the extravagant décor, a playful mingling of Baroque and Neo-Classical. The exuberant excess, the rich paintings and statuary, the immaculately uniformed attendants, all made her feel like Cinderella at the ball. As they ascended the grand staircase to the second level, Mason spotted a crescent of open wooden doors—the private boxes that looked down on the auditorium and stage. "This is our box here," Richard said, pointing straight ahead.

They entered a vestibule with walls and a ceiling that were covered with red jacquard silk. Two padded velvet benches graced the sides, and there were curved gilt hooks to hang their coats. Crimson velvet curtains led to the box beyond. As she took her seat beside him, Mason couldn't have been more pleased. Their loge sat in the exact center of the auditorium, directly across from the stage. Unlike the others on both sides, which merely had high dividers separating them, this deluxe box was situated between two ornate columns that hid them completely from view.

As the audience found their seats and the orchestra tuned up, Richard told her about *Aida*, the opera they'd be seeing. "It's by the Italian Giuseppe Verdi, and it's my favorite of his compositions. It's set in Egypt in the time of the pharaohs. Aida is a beautiful Ethiopian slave, a conquest of war, who's loved by Radamès, a great Egyptian general. Radamès returns Aida's love, but the problem is, he's also loved by pharaoh's daughter, Amneris. So there's a great deal of conflict. It shows how complicated things can become when people give way to their passions."

She smiled inwardly at the not-so-subtle barb. Let him resist all he wanted. Tonight she intended to melt that resistance, come what may.

"I never dreamed we'd be so . . . alone in this huge box," she commented idly. "It's so private, so . . . intimate. You could do anything in here and no one would know it. No wonder the upper classes love this opera house so much. What a perfect setting for mischief."

His gaze flicked sardonically to her. He knew very well what she was trying to do, but he pointedly changed the subject. "I hope you weren't put off by Hank's manner. He hides behind a rustic exterior, but he's actually the most clever man I've ever known—also, in his own way, the most noble. I hope you'll give serious consideration to his offer. It's the best thing you could do for Mason."

"I don't know," she said with a sly smile. "I may just need some inducement."

At that moment, the conductor raised his baton, the overture began, and the lights dimmed. The sudden darkness, coupled with his nearness, was intoxicating. As the sweet, lush music filled the hall, she leaned toward him and whispered, "It's hot in here, don't you think?"

He just looked back at her guardedly, his eyes gleaming in the reflection from the stage.

She reached into her evening bag and produced the small vial of perfume, dabbing a drop or two behind each ear, on her wrists, and between her cleavage as Madame Toulon had instructed. Then she pulled out her fan, opened it, and gently began to wave it in his direction.

She watched from the corner of her eye. As the curtain rose on the Egyptian desert and Radamès stepped center stage to sing of his immense love for Aida, Richard caught a whiff of her scent and straightened rigidly in his seat. But as the tantalizing aroma enveloped him, he defensively stood up, moved his chair a few inches away from hers, and murmured, "It *is* rather sticky in here."

She let him stay there, continuing to fan the perfume his way, while Amneris came onstage, singing to Radamès, and was joined a few moments later by Aida. As the three of them sang soulfully of their respective longings, Mason scooted her chair over so she was right beside Richard once again, wedging him between her and the column, with nowhere else to escape.

She gave him time to adjust as Radamès was made leader of the Egyptian armies in a new war with Ethiopia, and Aida, torn between love of her enemy and her country, beseeched the gods, praying first for one, then the other, her anguished cry soaring through the hall. Caught up in the emotion, Mason put her hand on Richard's leg and leaned into him, whispering behind her fan, "It's magnificent. Thank you *so* much for bringing me."

She left her hand on his leg. It felt like petrified wood, braced as it was against her gentle touch. Softly, she began to massage it, moving in tandem with the music, feeling chills dash up her spine.

Angrily, he seized her hand, crushing it in his grip. She feared for an instant that he'd broken her bones. He thrust it from him, into her own lap, and she flexed her fingers, loosening the effect of his rejection. But the touch of his hand, so forceful, stirred her deeply. Her breath quickening, she felt her blood boiling in her veins.

She leaned into him again, her head on his shoulders, her far hand going to his chest. "I'm sorry," she lied softly, entreatingly. "Forgive me?"

She felt everything in him withdraw into himself, attempting to create distance without making a scene. She could sense the battle raging inside. A battle for control. Struggling valiantly to tramp down his rising rage—at her, at this enforced subjugation, at her less-than-subtle assault. But mostly, she sensed, he fought to stem the tide of his mounting lust.

"Can I help it that you make me weak with desire?" she breathed at his ear. Then she licked his inner ear with her tongue.

She felt the jolt of something raw and primal flare between them. It shocked her, as if she'd just been struck by lightning. She could feel it flow through him and into her, so intense, so nakedly carnal that her whole body coiled with longing in its wake.

He turned his head. She was so close, her face was but a fraction from his, their lips nearly touching, their eyes starkly locked. She felt suspended in the searing heat of those eyes.

"You're playing with fire," he warned.

"Am I?"

She trailed the hand that had flattened on his chest down the buttons of his shirt and felt him tense all the more. His eyes blazed, commanding her to cease. But she'd gone too far. She was simmering in her own juices, feeling reckless and daring. The danger added spice to the chase.

"Don't do it," he advised.

She met his glower defiantly and smiled. A smile as ageless as the universe itself. The smile of all the temptresses who'd known their power to rattle the most concerted obstinacy of man since the dawn of time.

She cast a glance at him to see that his eyes were tightly closed, his jaw clenched. The sweeping romance of the music, the tempting invitation of her perfume, and her nearness in the closely confined quarters were wreaking havoc with his resolve. She inched her hand downward slowly, closer, closer . . . running her fingernails along his abdomen, feeling him shudder. Ever closer, as her perfume enfolded them both in its seductive veil.

And then she touched him.

He was so hard, so stiff, that he felt like steel beneath her hand. Proof of his losing struggle. Concrete. Irrefutable.

His hand clasped hers. She thought he might snatch it away. But he held it there, pinned against his erection, his eyes closed as if in pain.

He swelled beneath her fingers, straining for release. She could feel his rough-hewn breath and realized she was breathing just as hard.

Then, all at once, his eyes flew open. He gave her a hard, impenetrable glare. His hand convulsed on hers. He lifted it, holding it between them, contracting his grip until she gave a little cry. Detaining it, imprisoned in his, he put his mouth to her ear and snarled, "All right. I've had enough."

"What?" she asked, startled.

"You win. I'm going to give you just what you want."

He stood abruptly and yanked her up out of her chair. It toppled to the floor, but the crashing of the music covered the noise. He jerked her back into the vestibule and shoved her so she went flying against the silk-lined wall. Then he gave the curtains a single yank that closed them, and they were immersed in nearly total darkness. Only a tiny crack at the edge of the drapes provided a glimmer of light with which to see.

He charged at her and took her bare shoulders in punishing fists. Jerking her up against him so she collided with his chest, he demanded, "Is this what you want?" He kissed her roughly, the force of it pushing her back into the wall, pressing into her, all but crushing her with his weight. His tongue ransacked her mouth, sending her heart leaping, making her wet between her thighs. Unleashing his pent-up fury and frustration in this blistering assault.

Then he lifted his head. She felt dizzy, clinging to the wall behind her to seek purchase. His hands moved to the low neckline of her gown and wrenched it down, baring her breasts. He lunged down, taking one of her nipples in his mouth, kneading the other in a conquering palm while he sucked on her, electrifying her. She threw her head back and moaned uncontrollably, surrendering completely to the devastating sensations. Her female triumph mingling with her rousing passion.

His hands moved up to clutch her head on either side, squeezing tight. He raised his head to hers, kissing her again so masterfully that she felt she couldn't stay on her feet.

"Is that what you want?" he insisted. "To know what you do to me? To know you drive me wild?"

"Yes," she gasped, reeling with happiness.

"It's entertaining for you, is it? Tormenting me? Watching me squirm? Taunting me with that . . . scent that scrambles my brain. Knowing that just the sight of you makes me hard? Knowing that I lie awake nights, wanting you—*not* wanting you—that you're like a fever in my blood? Until I think I'll go mad? Is *that* what you want to hear?"

"Oh, yes," she sighed.

"Then take what you asked for and the devil be damned."

He shoved her to her knees. Then he jerked his trousers

open, took himself in hand, and thrust against her lips, demanding entrance, then immersing himself inside. He was so large she choked on him. But he didn't stop. Taking her head in his hands, he fucked her mouth, standing over her like a god.

He tasted divine. Sliding in and out, moving her head where he wanted it, his authority absolute. Growing harder and larger still, bulging in her mouth, filling her throat. On her knees before him, she felt helpless and empowered all at once, a supplicant whose worship only elevates herself. She gloried in the unyielding feel of him on her tongue. The music soared, dancing at the corners of her awareness.

And then he came in her mouth. Tasting sublime. Holding himself inside, making her take all of him. She felt his energy pour into her, feeding her, nourishing her. She swallowed his manly essence greedily, feeling utterly consumed by him.

When he was done, he took her shoulders, heaving her to her feet. She swayed precariously and he had to hold her to keep her upright.

"Is that what you want?" he repeated.

She opened her eyes and saw his anguish in the dim half-light.

"I only wanted you to love me," she told him, the honesty surging from her freely, hurled from her with the force of her yearning.

He looked absolutely stricken. He stared at her for a long moment, conflicting emotions warring in his eyes. Then, unexpectedly, he pulled her to him, wrapping her in his arms. "Forgive me," he pleaded.

She eased herself back. "Oh, Richard, there's nothing to forgive."

His eyes softened. He kissed her, gently now, so sweetly that she felt her heart overflow with love. Then, as a chorus of 400 voices resounded through the hall in a rousing hymn to ancient gods, he said, "Let's see if I can't make amends."

He laid her tenderly upon the velvet bench, kissing her attentively all the while, stroking her now with the intention of pleasuring her. His kisses melting her in his arms. Moving slowly, leisurely, he called on the considerable skills at his command to carry her away in a wave of bliss. Pushing aside her skirts, he found her sticky warmth. Igniting her with practiced fingers, he knew just where to touch her to cause her body to arch into his hand. And then, only when she was ready, when she knew she couldn't wait another second, he entered her—already hard again—slowly . . . so slowly, so lovingly that she wanted to weep. The chorus flowing through her, she welcomed him into her, his mouth on hers. Moving with him to the sumptuous swell of the music, unbearably beautiful. Triumph forgotten now, games forsaken, in the majesty of his body giving everything to her.

They came together as the voices rose to a shattering crescendo. Soaring with emotion. Basking in the fulfillment of a yearning too long denied. As they lay still in each others' arms, the voices hushed, then the music ended. And on its heels, a thundering applause. It seemed in the enchantment of the moment that the audience applauded them.

Richard pushed himself up, remembering, as she was, where they were. She caught the glint of humor in his eyes and, all at once, they began to laugh.

But he sobered quickly. "Are you all right?" he asked.

"I'm so much more than all right."

"I didn't hurt you?"

"Hurt me?" She stroked his cheek. "You absolutely thrilled me."

His eyes registered something akin to gratitude before he softly kissed her lips.

They heard the audience rising for the first break. Sheepishly, they eased themselves up, righting their clothing, then noting the other's shyness, laughed again.

"I can't think why," she told him playfully, "but I seem to have developed an overpowering thirst."

He grinned and put his finger to her mouth. "I can't imagine why. Come, we'll go get something to drink."

They left the box and followed the crowd up the corridor and into the Grand Foyer. It was a spectacular rectangular chamber perhaps 200 feet long, with glass windows that looked out on Avenue de l'Opéra as it stretched all the way to the Louvre. It was modeled after the Hall of Mirrors at Versailles, but the ceiling had been painted in the style of the Sistine Chapel in Rome.

"I shall park you here for a moment while I fetch you that drink," he told her.

Suddenly alone, she felt a bit awkward. All around her, the cream of Parisian society was milling about, chatting amiably, greeting one another. Still in the afterglow of love, she smiled to herself, thinking, *If they only knew what we've just done!*

But gradually she noticed their tone change into more of a hushed buzz. Nearby she heard a woman say to her companion, "My dear, isn't that the Duchess of Wimsley?"

Before long, the name was sweeping through the crowd.

"They say she's the most beautiful woman in England."

"Her husband is as rich as Croesus."

"I hear the Prince of Wales is mad about her."

"*Mon Dieu,* that complexion!"

Curious, Mason snaked her way through the assemblage to see this fabled beauty for herself.

In the center of the hall, she spotted a small party isolated from the rest of the crowd. It took her only a moment to pick out the duchess in question. She was the most tastefully striking woman Mason had ever seen. Her features were delicate, yet sophisticated. Everything about her, from the styling of her auburn hair, to the creaminess of her complexion, to the exquisite white satin gown embroidered with real pearls, spoke of the sort of wealth and pampering most people only dreamed of. She presented a picture of effortless grace and impeccable breeding, but she smiled at her companions with a warmth that put everyone around her at their ease.

Mason watched for several minutes, then returned to her previous spot just as Richard came back with two glasses of champagne. Before long, the house lights flashed on and off to signal the end of the interval. She gave him a sly grin. "I can't wait to see what the second act has in store for us."

His eyes were warm on her face.

But just as they were exiting the foyer, fate put them in the path of the party Mason had earlier been watching. The breathtaking duchess glanced at them, then gave a small gasp. "Richard!"

Mason felt him tense beside her. When she looked up at him, she saw that his sated serenity had vanished, replaced by some flinty emotion she couldn't read. "Emma," he said matter-of-factly.

They knew each other? Richard and this paragon of regal grace? Mason was stabbed by a sudden senseless insecurity.

"How lovely to see you again, darling," the woman he'd called Emma said, recovering her composure. "What brings you to Paris?"

"I think you know," he said with concentrated effort. Mason knew this manner well. He was, once again, attempting to keep his emotions leashed. He almost looked as if he could hit the woman without a qualm.

What had happened between them to cause such a strained response?

"Don't tell me this is the sister?" Emma was saying.

They were blocking the exit, but no one was about to push their way past them.

Mason waited for Richard to make the introductions. When he didn't, the duchess did it for him. "I'm Emma. The last name is Fortescue-Wynthrop-Smythe. It's a mouthful, I know. But I should so like it if you'd call me Emma."

Mason took the hand she was offered; it was tiny and impossibly smooth. "I'm Amy Caldwell."

"You amaze me," Richard quipped to Emma. "I should think you'd want everyone to call you 'your grace.'"

Emma's smile deepened. "Not my old friends!"

"We seem to be blocking traffic. We'd best move on."

But before he could, Emma reached over and put her hand on his. "You're looking well, Richard."

The look in his eyes was hard as stone. "And you," he countered in a low tone, "look as if you have everything you deserve."

Her eyes glazed over and Mason caught a flicker of pain. She covered it with a courteous smile. "I'm staying at my dear friend the Duchess of Galliera's villa while she's away at Capri. You might stop by some time. We could . . . talk over old times."

"I think you know better than that."

She raised her chin a notch. "Well, if you change your mind, the invitation stands. Do enjoy the show. And, Amy, I'm certain we shall see each other again. Perhaps soon."

As they walked back toward their box, Mason asked, "What was *that* all about?"

"That *London Times* story must have drawn her out."

"What do you mean?"

He shot her a warning look. "She's come for Mason's paintings. And she'll do anything to get them. Do me one favor, would you? Avoid her at all costs."

"Why?"

"Because she'll just stash them away in her husband's collection and no one will ever see them again. Tomorrow or the day after, she'll come to you, oozing sweetness, and make an offer. But you can't trust anything she says. So don't see her. Don't talk to her. Just keep as wide a berth from her as you can."

He veered them toward the descending staircase.

"Where are you going?" she asked. "The box is the other way."

He looked at her apologetically, but she could see an unexpressed anger lurking at the back of his eyes. "I had an enjoyable evening, Amy, but I think we've had enough opera for one night."

Mason followed him out. She didn't understand what had happened in the foyer. But she knew two things: Richard and this Emma Fortescue-Wynthrop-Smythe had a tumultuous history, and the breathtaking duchess was still very much in love with him.

Chapter 11

The next day, Mason stood with Richard on the platform at Gare St-Lazare as her train prepared to depart. He seemed unaccountably edgy, casting glances back over his shoulder when he thought she wasn't looking. But she'd been studying him like a hawk, ever since last night, when the appearance of that extraordinary woman had served as a bucket of cold water thrown in his face.

It had, in fact, been his idea that she return to the country. He'd all but insisted on it, while taking pains to make his insistence seem casual, as if he were suggesting it for her own good. It made her wonder what he was hiding and why he didn't want her to meet with the disturbingly alluring duchess.

"I must say, you seem awfully eager to get me back to Auvers. You didn't have to bring me to the station, you know."

"Well, you did say you were enjoying your holiday, and seemed perturbed at me for dragging you back to town to meet Hank. The meeting is over, so it's just as well that you return to your rest."

"You *are* thoughtful."

"I have things to keep me occupied. Construction on the pavilion begins today, and I want to stay on top of it until I'm convinced it's moving smoothly. In a few days, I have a reporter coming in from Berlin, and hopefully I can keep the momentum going by having him do something similar to what appeared in London."

"That London piece seems to be drawing some interesting characters our way."

He arched a brow at her as if wondering if she was being sarcastic. But instead of beating the point, he said, "Another thing. The instant you get word about when and how the paintings are going to be sent from America, let me know so I can make arrangements from this end to receive them."

Was she imagining the note of challenge in his voice? She dodged him by saying, "You have enough to worry about. Getting the rest of the paintings is my problem."

"I only wanted to be of assistance."

"You seem to be full of helpful suggestions this morning."

His gaze flicked over her, but he merely shrugged. "Suit yourself. But we need them no later than mid-June. They must be cataloged, framed, and hung properly. It's quite an undertaking."

"Don't worry. They'll be there."

The conductor yelled, "*En voiture*," signaling that it was time for the train to depart.

"Well, then, off you go," he said. "Pleasant journey."

There it was again, that strange look in his eyes. He bent and gave her a quick peck on the cheek, then handed her up the step, giving the porter her valise.

The train slowly began to chug off. Satisfied, Richard turned and headed back toward the exit. Mason stuck her head out and watched him until he was completely out of sight, then snatched up her valise and, ignoring the startled porter, jumped off the moving train.

As it passed her by in a swirl of steam, she reached into her handbag and withdrew the calling card that had arrived early that morning requesting an appointment to discuss an important matter of business. She looked once again at the embossed lettering: THE DUCHESS OF WIMSLEY.

She felt a little guilty about deceiving Richard. But she was in love with him, and she had a right to know exactly what part this woman had played in his life.

She glanced at the station clock and realized she had only twenty minutes to return to her hotel. Leaving by the station's side exit, she stepped into a fiacre cab and told the driver to rush her back to Rue Scribe.

Arriving there with only minutes to spare, she hurried up to her room to find Lisette nearly ready. She wore a red wig, austere dress, and spectacles. When she saw her, Mason laughed.

"I like the wig. Where did you get it?"

"It's Mimi's, the fire-eater from the circus. It's a bit scorched here and there, but I don't think it's too noticeable."

"Have you got the story straight?"

"I think so."

"It doesn't matter too much. The story is just an excuse for you to be here. What I really want is for you to give me your expert opinion about this woman."

There was a knock on the door. Hastily, Mason smoothed her own clothing, took a breath, then went to answer it. Instead of the expected party, she found a uniformed man standing in the hall, hat in hand.

"Yes?" she asked.

"My name is Percival, Miss Caldwell. I have the honor of presenting her grace, the Duchess of Wimsley. I understand that she is expected."

"Why, yes."

He turned back toward the elevator. "Your grace is awaited," he announced.

Mason looked at Lisette, who was rolling her eyes.

From the depths of the lift stepped the duchess, a vision in feathers and fur. She walked forth with unhurried poise, so smoothly she seemed to be floating down the hall. If anything, she was even more stunning than she'd appeared the night before.

Her beauty was so majestic that it instantly changed the energy in the room. Unable to help herself, Lisette muttered, *"Mon Dieu!"*

The duchess held forth her slender gloved hand and said, "Miss Caldwell, it's terribly kind of you to allow me to impose my company upon you this way, and on such short notice. My hope is that you'll forgive my intrusion when you hear why I've come."

Mason shook her hand. The kid glove was so meltingly soft that it was an effort to keep from stroking it.

"Please come in, Mrs. . . . . duchess . . . ?"

"Now, now, you promised to call me Emma. And I shall call you Amy, if I may. I'm hoping we're going to be dear friends." She stepped inside, then spotted Lisette in her red wig and jail-matron's dress. "Oh, but have I come at an inopportune time? I seem to be interrupting something."

"This is Mademoiselle Lafarge," Mason told her. "She's the personal secretary of Monsieur Beart, who you no doubt know is the wealthiest planter in the French colony of Réunion in the Indian Ocean. It seems Monsieur Beart is determined to buy my sister's paintings to decorate his new plantation."

Emma eyed Lisette with cheerful interest. "Monsieur Beart. That wouldn't be Emile Beart, would it?"

Returning the smile easily, Lisette answered, "I have never heard of Emile Beart. My employer's name is Henri."

"Ah, *Henri* Beart. I don't believe I know the gentleman."

"He doesn't get back to Europe very often."

"And indeed, why should he? I'm told Réunion is quite lovely. But he must place a great deal of trust in you to send you on such a long journey by yourself."

"I enjoy the monsieur's full confidence."

"I'm certain you do." She walked over to Lisette, looking her over pleasantly. "And perhaps he considers you unusually appropriate for the task since, without the glasses, you would seem to bear an uncanny resemblance to the model so charmingly depicted in Mason Caldwell's paintings. Now, what was her name? Monsieur Falconier was kind enough to tell me . . . Oh, yes, I believe it was Lisette Ladoux."

The imposter couldn't think of a comeback.

Mason started to change the subject, but their visitor stepped over to Lisette and picked a long strand of blond hair from her shoulder. "But, of course, the famous trapeze artist of the Cirque Fernando is a blonde, not a redhead."

Knowing the game was up, Lisette took the wig in hand and tossed it to the vanity. "She's too sharp for me, this one."

"You mustn't distress yourself, my dear," Emma told her. "I've only just come from seeing the paintings. I would have a paltry eye should I not be able to spot a lovely face such as yours beneath the disguise."

Feeling foolish, Mason said, "I'm sorry. We were just having a little fun."

Waving a dismissive hand, Emma said, "I understand completely. You want to secure the highest possible offer for your sister's paintings, so you provided a fictitious buyer to boost the price. A clever move, but quite unnecessary, I assure you. I'm accustomed to paying handsomely for the things I want, and I've come here today with the best offer you will receive from anyone."

"Won't you sit down?" Mason offered. "We could send down for some tea or something."

Emma sat, her back ramrod straight. "Please, don't bother. I imagine you're eager to hear my proposal. As you may or may not know, my husband is the Duke of Wimsley, and one of the wealthiest collectors in England. I read about your sister's paintings in the *Times* and knew at once that I must pop across the Channel to see them for myself. I've developed quite an instinct for such things under my husband's tutelage, and I confess to being most gratified, on seeing the paintings this morning, to find that my instincts have not been unfounded. They're absolutely marvelous and we simply must have them for the Wimsley Collection."

"Must you?" Mason murmured.

Emma pretended not to hear. "I am in the position to match any offer"—she glanced at Lisette and amended— "any *legitimate* offer and raise it by a quarter."

"That's most generous of you. But as the caretaker for my sister's work, money is not the only consideration."

"Oh, but I offer so much *more* than money. I can give them the maximum exposure among the denizens of the beau monde, all of whom pass through our doors at one time or another. Our collection is the talk of Europe. You may ask anyone. All the best people come to our salon just to see it. Our influence in the art world is well-documented, I assure you. With our patronage, your late sister will become one of the most spoken-of artists of our day."

"I don't doubt it."

"But you're not going to jump at it . . . even though it's an offer no one else will be able to match?"

"I'll consider it carefully, but I'm sure you understand I have a grave responsibility."

Emma gave her a thoughtful look. "Perhaps your hesitancy has something to do with our mutual friend, Mr. Garrett."

"Richard has been quite helpful to me."

"Oh, I'm sure he has."

"I don't know what I would have done without him. He's offered sound advice and helped me navigate my way through the treacherous waters of journalists, critics, dealers, and . . . patrons of the arts," she added pointedly.

A flicker of contempt showed in the woman's eyes. "Naturally, my dear, he has an ulterior motive."

"And what would that be?"

"What has he suggested you do with the paintings?"

"He's suggested several options."

"Oh, come now, Amy. He wouldn't want them in the

hands of a speculator or collector. He detests the idea of art being cloistered away where it can't be appreciated by the masses. So he must have something else in mind."

Feeling overwhelmed by the woman, and stabbed by jealousy at her knowledge of Richard, Mason said rather irritably, "Actually, he has another buyer in mind."

"Oh? And who might that be?"

"I don't know that I'm at liberty to say. But someone he knows well and trusts implicitly."

Emma tapped the fingers of both hands together. But a moment later, they stopped and she grew still. "Not . . . Hank?" Mason's startled reaction told her she'd hit the target. "Hank Thompson?"

She threw her head back and laughed. Given her poised demeanor, it was so unexpected that Mason and Lisette exchanged a baffled glance.

"What in the world does that old bandit want with Impressionist paintings?"

Mason flushed. "If you must know, he's interested in endowing a museum devoted entirely to Impressionism."

"Hank?" She laughed again. "My dear Amy, I have no idea what they've told you, but believe me, you really must take anything those two have to say with a grain of salt. Off and on over the years, they've been partners in a number of schemes. Whatever this one is, it's not going to earn you a fraction of the money I can offer. Or do half as much for your sister's reputation."

Mason's head began to pound. "That sounds very pretty, but Richard warned me about you."

"Warned you? About *me*?" The color drained from Emma's aristocratic face. It was so satisfying that Mason took it a step further.

"In fact, he told me to avoid you at all costs. He went as far as to say you weren't to be trusted."

Emma's eyes flared like a lioness about to pounce. "He

said *that*? He said *I* was not to be trusted? When everything he says and does is a lie?"

The statement shocked Mason. "What are you talking about?"

"Lying is his profession. His whole existence is one fabrication after the other, concocted to hide the fact that he's a detective."

"Detective?"

"Of course. All of it, the flitting around the world acting like an art connoisseur . . . wealthy playboy . . . irresistible ladies' man . . . It's his cover. It gives him a certain credibility in the art world, which he uses to snare thieves, forgers, frauds—"

"Frauds?" Lisette parroted.

Mason couldn't breathe.

Emma leaned back in her chair as if realizing that, in her anger, she'd gone too far. "Oh, I know he likes to keep everything close to his vest. And I don't want to give anything away about his precious secret past. But this is different. You need to know this so you can know what—and whom— you're really dealing with."

Mason was staring at her numbly.

Speaking as if to a slow child, Emma enunciated, "Richard works for the Pinkerton Detective Agency. Hank has probably hired him to help secure the paintings. I suppose it's brilliant, if you think about it. Who better than a gorgeous man of the world to sweep the sister from America off her feet and into Hank's hands?"

She proceeded to bring the conversation back to her offer, which she outlined again in greater detail, naming a staggering financial figure, stressing that no one would be able to top it. As she spoke, Lisette crept over to Mason and silently took her hand.

But Mason didn't hear a word that was said. All she heard was that Richard Garrett was a professional detective whose specialty was tracking down art frauds.

Chapter 12

As his cab slowly proceeded down the Boulevard des Capucines, Garrett searched for her in the pedestrian traffic along the sidewalks.

Perhaps an hour earlier, the man he'd had positioned across the street from the Jockey Club had tracked him down with the news that the woman had returned to the hotel. Garrett had raced there, charged up the stairs, and banged on her door. When there was no answer, he collared a bellman and forced him to let him in. She wasn't there. He hurried back downstairs, where he learned from the doorman that she'd left the hotel just ten or fifteen minutes before. She hadn't taken a cab. The doorman had seen her march down Rue Scribe and round the corner to the boulevard.

What the hell had happened?

Obviously, she'd tricked him and returned to the hotel to meet with Emma. Whether she'd done this out of jealousy or suspicion or greed, he didn't know. He also didn't know, because his man had stupidly left his post instead of sending a message, if the meeting with Emma had actually taken place. But he had to assume it had. Why else would she go to such lengths to elude him?

Just how dangerous was this to him? Probably not catastrophic. Certainly, Emma would try to put him in a bad light and might reveal some things, but she'd never give him away.

She had too much in her own past to hide to flagrantly challenge him in the matter. There was an unspoken agreement between them: *You protect my past and I'll protect yours.*

As his gaze roamed the faces of the strollers along the boulevard, the diners in the sidewalk cafés, the figures standing before shop windows or buying crêpes from street vendors, he thought once again of the telltale clues that had been stacking up.

Her unconscious response to a waiter's question in effortless French the night of the Cuthbert dinner.

The curiously close friendship and camaraderie with Mason's model and best friend, Lisette, on such short acquaintance.

The pigment he'd spotted on her hands beneath the mud in Auvers. The elaborate effort to hide it from him.

The faint tackiness to the touch of the "recovered" catacomb painting he'd held to the light.

The lack of a birth record for an Amy Caldwell in Boston, Massachusetts—indeed, no record of the Caldwell family at all.

None of this was conclusive, of course, and might be easily explained. Still, his instincts were on fire. Amy *was* Mason Caldwell. As incredible as it might seem, the certainty of it gripped him, surged through his body, electrified his senses in a way that was almost carnal.

But how to prove it? His mind had devised and discarded a hundred maneuvers. Then, that very morning, as he'd taken the self-portrait to show the architect, it had dawned on him. The birthmark. The heart-shaped mark on her flank in the portrait. Was it an affectation of the artist? Or was it real? Surely, it *was* real. And if so, the so-called sister would also have it . . .

Suddenly, he saw her. She was sitting by herself at a sidewalk café, a glass of cognac uncharacteristically in front of her, a dazed look in her eyes. He stopped the cab, told the driver to wait, and rushed over to her.

"Amy? Am I daft, or didn't I just drop you off at Gare St-Lazare?"

She jerked at the sound of his voice. When she looked up at him, her eyes were hollow, a bit fearful, like a cornered hare. Stumblingly, she said, "I . . . felt ill."

"Ill?"

"It came upon me all at once." She was avoiding his eyes. "I left the train at the first stop and came straight back."

She actually did look sick. Her face was pale, her eyes sunken and lifeless. He sat down at the small round table. "You poor thing. You should be in bed."

She still didn't look at him. "I needed some air." Then, sharply, "What are *you* doing here?"

"It's the most remarkable coincidence. I just happened to be passing by and looked over and there you were."

Her eyes flicked to him; then she reached for the snifter and took a sip of the cognac, as if trying to steady herself. Her hand as it held the glass trembled slightly.

"I was afraid of this," he told her. "This has all been too much for you. With all you've been through, it's a wonder this hasn't happened sooner. But not to worry. I shall get you to a doctor straightaway."

"No," she answered quickly. Then in a more controlled tone, "I don't need a doctor. I just need some rest."

"Let's get you back to your rooms, then, shall we? We really must see that you take better care of yourself."

"Please don't concern yourself. I'll be fine."

He leaned toward her and put his hand to the side of her face, running his thumb along her cheek. "I know what you really need," he said softly. "But I suppose that shall have to wait until you're better. Come along, then. I'll see you safely back to your hotel."

He put a coin on the table to pay for her drink and helped her toward the waiting cab.

As he did, he watched her covertly. Her ashen pallor, the way she turned her shoulder to form a barrier between them.

There was no question about it. Something had changed. She was slipping away from him.

He had no intention of allowing that to happen.

Once again, Mason stepped over to the glass French doors that looked out over the shallow wrought-iron balcony. She couldn't spot him, but she was sure someone was out there, watching. Someone in Richard's employ. Maybe several people. For the first time, she realized she was a prisoner.

When the duchess had so casually dropped her bomb, Mason had strained not to show its devastating impact. Instead, she'd feigned interest in the woman's offer and ushered her out the door as quickly as possible. Then she'd turned to Lisette in shock.

A detective! A conniving flic!

Lisette seemed as confused as she. "*Qu'est-ce que c'est un* Pinker—"

"I can't talk now," Mason had cut her off. "I have to think."

She'd reeled out of the hotel and several blocks down the Boulevard des Capucines, until she'd finally collapsed into a chair at the sidewalk café. Then . . .

Just passing by . . .

A remarkable coincidence . . .

It was insulting. Obviously, he'd had people watching every move she made.

That's how he knew she'd gone to Auvers!

The sneaky bastard!

Ever since she'd heard those fatal words "Pinkerton Agent," she'd been running the events of the past several weeks through her mind. Those two words had cast everything he'd said and done in a poisonous new light.

Who had hired him? Duval, most likely. Who better to help the French authorities ferret out the American fraud than a helpful, handsome art expert who spoke her own language?

But to go to this length of romantic involvement . . . Why? Was it, as Emma had said, to sweep her off her feet, catch her off guard in the hopes that she'd confide in him?

If so, it had almost worked. When she thought of how close she'd come to telling him the truth that day in Montmartre, it made her shudder.

But if that was the case, why had he pulled away? Making her believe his attraction to her was so frightening that he had to protect himself?

To make her chase *him*. It was actually easier that way.

The man was diabolically clever!

But could he actually fake that passion, the obvious attraction he showed for her? Could any man do that?

Again, she heard Emma's voice: *All of it . . . wealthy playboy . . . irresistible ladies' man . . . it's his cover.*

Then she thought of the paintings, the understanding and appreciation he'd shown for them, the way they'd so powerfully moved him, his dedication to their posterity. Had he faked all that as well? He must have.

That hurt most of all.

She'd actually fallen in love with him. She'd thought he was the one man who could really glimpse her soul, could heal her wounded heart.

She'd been such an idiot. And because of it, she was in grave danger.

Good God, she could end up spending ten years in Santé Prison! Wouldn't that be bitterly ironic? She'd come to France to exonerate her family name and she would end up disgracing it even more.

She could make a run for it. Try to get out of the country. But how could she possibly accomplish that when she was, as she now knew, being watched day and night?

And if she ran and by some miracle managed to get away, would the running ever stop?

The hopelessness of it all overwhelmed her.

She turned from the window. *I can't panic. I have to think clearly.*

She fell into a nearby chair and willed her emotions to cool. There was still so much that didn't add up, that she didn't understand.

Who was this Hank and this Emma really, and how did they fit into the puzzle?

And this secret past of Garrett's to which Emma had so enigmatically alluded, wouldn't there be an advantage to her knowing what that was all about?

What she needed was information. And it suddenly occurred to her where she might find it.

Lisette.

Or more properly, Lisette's spurned but undeterred lover.

Juno Dargelos.

The gangster king of Belleville.

Chapter 13

In medieval times, the village of Belleville sat on a vine-covered slope several miles east of the city. In the eighteenth century, it became famous for its merry open-air cafés where Parisians would venture on Sundays to drink guinguet, the local specialty wine. After 1840, the village grew rapidly, becoming one of the largest towns in the Île-de-France, and in 1860, it was annexed by metropolitan Paris. But in the 1870s, it became the dumping ground for the city's poor who were displaced by the grand urban renewal of Napoléon III under Baron Haussmann. Since then, it had disintegrated into a casbah of poverty, sedition, and gangsterism—its streets ruled by competing gangs that called themselves "Apaches" after the fiercest Indians of the American West.

When Mason and Lisette crossed the invisible boundary on Rue de Ménilmontant, it was as if they'd entered a foreign country. Their cab driver automatically pulled over, fearful—like all ordinary Parisians—of entering this forbidden domain. As they stepped down, an escort of surly Apaches who'd been waiting for them came forth to offer safe conduct. They were the elite guard of Juno Dargelos, the first man to unite the perpetually warring Apache factions under a single banner.

They formed a phalanx around the two women as they walked several blocks to Rue de Belleville. By some uncanny means, word of their arrival had spread and swarms of people had come out of the shops and teeming apartment buildings to stare at them—or at least at Lisette. They'd all heard the story of Dargelos's great unrequited passion for the dazzling trapeze artist. To them, it was the greatest love story of the age, akin to Tristan and Isolde. As she passed, they cried out her name. "Lisette! Lisette!"

Acknowledging their adulation, Lisette blew a few kisses, eliciting appreciative cheers.

The warmth of the crowd bolstered Mason's spirits. Despite Belleville's fearsome reputation, she felt a huge wave of relief as they walked into its protective depths. The past week had been an ordeal as she waited for this day's meeting. She still was pretending to be sick and had endured Garrett's attentive concern and increasingly amorous overtures.

Here, she was safe. Dargelos's guards would see to it that whatever tail Garrett had put on her would stay well beyond the border of Belleville.

They came to a café where a group of a hundred or so spectators was standing respectfully at the entrance, waiting to see Lisette. Several other Apaches pushed them back to make way for the anticipated arrival. Inside, the air was thick with Gauloise smoke and several men were drinking absinthe at the bar. The sound of accordion music drifted down from an upper floor dancehall.

Dargelos was sitting at a table in the back. Unlike the last time Mason had seen him, he was very much in his own territory here, lord of the realm. Despite the shabby surroundings, he was squeaky clean, freshly shaved, dressed in his best suit, with an iris in his lapel. It was apparent that he'd dressed himself with fastidious care for this rendezvous.

When he saw them, he shot to his feet, came around the table, and approached them with both hands extended. Mason took his hand and he kissed it quickly, but Lisette ignored him completely.

He suddenly looked about him and made a sweeping gesture that instantly cleared the room except for the three of them and one other man—a massive Gascon with broad shoulders, a huge bald head, and the face of an angry cauliflower.

Ignoring Lisette's snub, Dargelos put his arm about her and led them back to the table. A small apron-clad man with a cigarette dangling from his mouth brought over a bottle of wine and three glasses. They sat at the table as the gangster's companion stood behind his chair, his gargantuan arms crossed over his chest.

Dargelos was staring at Lisette with all the love he felt for her pouring from his eyes. "*Mon Dieu!*" he exclaimed. "How is it possible? Every time I see you, you are more breathtaking."

She didn't even bother to look at him. "We came to talk business, nothing more."

Swallowing the rebuff, Dargelos said, "Very well. But before we do, I have a condition to make."

"And what is that?" Mason asked.

"Hugo." He jerked his thumb back toward the Goliath standing attendance behind him.

"What about him?"

"I have heard stories of how the fame of your sister's paintings has made my sweet Lisette the object of much attention. More than she could ever have as a performer at the circus. I laid awake nights fearing some crazed admirer might do harm to her. Hugo will prevent that from happening. Like all Gascons, he's stupid. But he's loyal to the death, fearless, and stronger than any ten men."

Lisette looked at Dargelos for the first time, her eyes blazing. "What? A bodyguard?"

"Even a goddess needs her protector."

She whirled on Hugo, then back to Dargelos. "You can't fool me, Juno. You don't want to protect me. You want to keep me under your thumb and away from other men!"

Putting his hand on his heart, Dargelos cried, "*Ma chou!*

You wound me! To think I care about anything but your safety."

Lisette made a fist at him and spat out in rapid-fire French, "I will wound you, all right! You hear me and hear me well, Juno. I don't care what you do. I don't care how many body-guards you put on me. I don't care what you say to me. I am never coming back to you. Do you hear me? *Never!*"

"All the same, that is my condition. If you want to know what I have learned about this matter, you must agree."

He looked at Mason. She turned to Lisette, took her still raised fist in her hand, and gently pushed it down onto the table. "We agree."

Contemptuously, Lisette blew a strand of hair out of her eyes, but she didn't object. Her features settled into a pretty pout.

"Excellent." Dargelos reached to the floor, picked up a folder filled with papers, and spread them out on the table. "This was not an easy task. I had to promise many favors to obtain this information."

"We deeply appreciate it," Mason assured him. "What did you learn?"

"The woman was correct. Richard Garrett is, indeed, an employee of the Pinkerton Detective Agency of Chicago, Illinois. In fact, he is one of their best agents."

"But that's an American company and he's English. Why—"

"Who can say? American, English, it's all the same to me. But here is what I *do* know. He has been in their employ these past five years. He disguises himself as a dilettante of the international art world, but it is only a ruse. He has had a remarkable string of successes in his field."

"For instance?" Mason asked.

Dargelos flipped through the papers, scanning them. "Short-ly after joining the agency, your Monsieur Garrett smashed a ring in Amsterdam that was forging Rembrandts so masterfully real-looking, they say even the artist himself would not have noticed the difference."

The word *smashed* gave her an uneasy feeling.

"Then, three years ago, he was hired by the Vatican to track down a gang of thieves who had removed a priceless Renaissance altarpiece from St. Peter's itself, posing as Dominican friars on pilgrimage to the Holy City. Each of them received an unusually stiff punishment: life in prison without possibility of parole."

Lisette gave Mason's hand a squeeze of support.

"Then, let me see—ah, yes, here it is—last year in Berlin, there was this fellow who was selling fake Egyptian antiquities to the kaiser's museum. They were the greatest copies ever to surface. So remarkable that not even the experts could tell them from the real thing. But this Garrett so ingratiated himself with the forger that the fellow confided in him what he was doing. He was so fond of this Garrett that he actually wrote him into his will!"

Dargelos chuckled appreciatively, but for Mason, this was particularly demoralizing news. Surely this was what Garrett was doing with her. But out of her depression, she had the presence of mind to ask, "You said he's worked for them for five years. What do you know about his life before that?"

"Not a thing. It is a complete blank."

"Did you try to look back that far?"

"Of course I did. But there are no records of any kind in connection with his name before he joined the agency. It is as if he came from out of nowhere. Whatever his past, he has wiped out any trace of it."

"Then you think he has something to hide?"

"Do we not all have something to hide?"

She sighed. "What about Hank Thompson? Who is he?"

"Not exactly what he appears to be. He began his career as a gambler in the Wild West of America. From this, he won a copper mine that struck a rich vein shortly after he acquired it. There were apparently rumors that he cheated in the game, but it was never proved. He used the profits from the mine to expand his fortune in railroads. There is some talk that he used less than ethical tactics to further his interests—but then, who has not? More recently, he has lost huge sums in endeavors that have not met with his earlier success. He still shows the world the face of a successful businessman, but my contacts say his back is against the wall."

Mason filed that away in her mind. "And what about the duchess?"

"She married the old duke some years ago. They divide their time between their homes in London and the family estate. His lineage is one of the oldest and most respected in England. They do all the expected things for landed gentry, attend church on Sundays, sit on the boards of charities that help the poor. Her reputation is, according to my friends in London, above reproach. She, too, comes from a wealthy, respected family, but was raised mostly in India and did not come to Europe until she was fully grown."

"How did she meet Richard?"

"That I don't know yet. Her husband is an avid art collector and they travel in the same circles as Garrett, but there is absolutely no indication that there has been any kind of relationship between her and Garrett, romantic or otherwise. As far as I can tell, their paths had not even crossed until this trip to Paris."

"But that's impossible. They both admit to knowing each other."

"That may well be, but I have no evidence of how or where that might have come about."

"So we know nothing about either one of them until he surfaced as a detective and she as a duchess."

"That's correct. Although, now that you mention it, the two things seem to have happened around the same time. I will have my people continue the search, if you wish, and see what we might come up with given more time."

"I'd appreciate that," Mason said, standing. "You've been very kind."

Dargelos rose with a shy smile. He didn't know exactly why they'd requested this information, but in his world, one didn't ask. He looked to Lisette for approval.

But she only said to him, "Leave us for a few minutes. I want to talk to Amy alone."

The two men did as they were told. Lisette took Mason's hand and sat her back down. "Listen, *chérie*. This has gone on long enough. You have to get out of the country. You heard what kind of man this Garrett is. I want you to stay here tonight. Juno will make the arrangements, and as soon as he can safely do it, he will get you to Switzerland, and then back to America."

But Mason didn't seem to hear her. "You know, there's one thing I still don't understand. He's gone to so much trouble to build my reputation as a major figure of the art world. Courting reporters, petitioning the Exposition committee, even insisting on a pavilion all my own. Why would he do that?"

"You heard his history. Rembrandt forgeries. The Vatican. The kaiser's museum. How does he possibly top those feats? Don't you see? The more famous you are, the more spectacular his success."

It was so cold-blooded, so egotistical, so cruel, she hadn't even considered that possibility. Her hatred for him hardened her heart and brought a bitter taste to her mouth.

All at once, everything seemed clear. "I'm not leaving," she declared.

"*Chérie*, you *must* leave."

"I'm not going to let him beat me like this. I'm not going to spend the rest of my life running."

"But you have no choice. There is nothing you can do."

"There *is* something I can do. This past that he guards so tightly . . . I can find it. And maybe I can find a way to use it as a weapon against him."

"That's a dangerous game."

"Maybe so, but it's the game I intend to play."

As they walked out of Belleville, Mason was feeling much better—determined, focused, and enjoying the protection of Lisette's new shadow, Hugo. But Lisette was fuming and resentful of the huge man's presence. She shook her finger up at him. "You I will put up with because I must. But let me warn you now. If you ever tell that fool Juno anything of what is said or done in your presence, I will go to him and tell him you crept into my bed and forced yourself upon me. He will believe me, because he is convinced no man can resist me. And then he will cut you up in little pieces and feed you to my dogs. Do you understand?"

Hugo's face flushed scarlet. He cast a glance back toward his employer's domain, then gave a quick, nervous nod.

"Good. Now go find us a cab."

Chapter 14

Mason and Lisette stood on the sidewalk and stared up at Garrett's fourth-story window. Beside them, holding hands with Lisette, was one of her coworkers from the circus: Bobo the Chimpanzee. It was ten o'clock. The area would be fairly deserted until the opera let out an hour or so later.

For most of this past week, Mason had been trying and failing to gain access to Richard's suite under the theory that any man who lived in hotels had to carry his important papers with him. She'd tried to bribe a maid into giving her a key, but had been rebuffed. Once, she'd allowed Richard to lure her into his lair, only to claim a recurrence of her illness and, on exiting, had slyly left the door unlatched. But when she tried to open it the next morning, when she knew he'd be gone, she discovered that it had been firmly relocked.

Nothing seemed to work.

For his part, Garrett was forging ahead with his campaign to make Mason Caldwell a household name. Besides all his other initiatives, he was now planning a gala reception next week on the site of their rising pavilion on the fairgrounds, which was occupying much of his time. Despite all this, his attentions toward Mason had increased. In fact, her backing away from him seemed to have whet his appetite. He was unfailingly solicitous. He fussed over her health, giving her brandy to kill whatever germs she might have. But the warm intoxication only weakened her defenses, so she pushed it away. He told her—in the intimate intensity of his eyes, the firm grip of his hand on her back as he helped her out of the coach, the increasing unwillingness to be put off at her door—that he was ravenous with desire for her.

Once, in her sitting room, he'd come up behind her, nuzzling the back of her neck, as his fingers had played along her spine. Without realizing just how it had happened, she discovered that the buttons along the back of her bodice had been undone. He began to slide the dress down her shoulders, kissing them in a way that made her rebellious body stir. She'd only been saved by claiming a recurrence of her convenient illness.

Another time, noticing her tension, he'd begun to rub the knotted muscles in her shoulders. "Why don't you let me give you a massage?" he'd suggested. It had felt so good that she'd had to forcibly jerk away. It was becoming increasingly difficult to be with him. Despite her secret fear and loathing, in the wake of his overwhelming charisma and charm she felt like a butterfly in the path of a hurricane.

After another week of looking into Garrett's past, Dargelos had come up with nothing new. She'd felt bitterly frustrated, at the end of her rope, when, out of nowhere, Lisette had appeared at her door in the company of her simian friend.

"He's a second-story monkey," she'd beamed. "His first owner was a burglar who trained him as an accomplice. After they put the burglar in jail, Bobo was given to the circus."

"The one I've seen standing with you on the back of a galloping horse."

"The same. It wasn't his fault that his owner got caught. Bobo is really talented. He can walk the tightrope, fly on the trapeze, all sorts of things."

At Lisette's signal, Bobo held out a hand for Mason to shake. "I'm happy to make his acquaintance, but why is he here?"

"Come on. I'll show you."

Now, on the darkened sidewalk below Garrett's suite, Lisette crouched down next to her friend and whispered some instructions in his ear. He scratched his head, showed her his teeth, and then began scampering up the side of the building. With the iron balconies on every floor, he was able to swing himself from room to room and floor to floor as if he were scaling a coconut tree. Once he reached the fourth floor, he looked down at Lisette, who raised her hand to point to the window she wanted.

As the chimp made his way toward the window, Lisette explained, "It so happens that very few hotel balconies above the second floor have a latch on their doors. So Bobo was trained to climb up and enter the rooms from the outside. There! He's done it." Mason looked up to see Bobo open the French doors, grin and salute at Lisette, then vault inside. "Let's go."

Hugo was waiting for them in the lobby. As they passed him to go upstairs, Lisette instructed him, "Garrett is at dinner with some important people. He shouldn't return before midnight. But if he does, you're not to let him step into that elevator. Whatever it takes to stop him. Understand?"

The big man nodded. Leaving him to stand guard, they took the elevator upstairs and hurried down the hallway to Garrett's suite. Its door was open and Bobo stood there grinning at them. "Good boy, Bobo," Lisette cooed. She leaned and gave him a hug. When she'd straightened, Bobo took her hand and led her inside.

The French doors were still open where Bobo had entered. A single lamp had been left on in the sitting room. As Mason followed Lisette inside, she could feel the sweat trickling down her ribs. The space was so silent that she felt her nerves prickle. Once again, as she moved through the room, she could detect the slightest trace of Richard's scent. It amplified her agitation and made her feel that he might come in at any moment.

Where to begin?

Right away she saw something interesting. A copy of *Le Figaro* lay on the coffee table, open to the society page. In ink, he'd scrawled a crude border around one of the articles. It told of how Count Dimitri Orlaf, the celebrated Russian art connoisseur, had arrived in Paris for next week's opening of the Universal Exposition. The story was accompanied by a head sketch of the debonair nobleman. But Mason couldn't make out his features because, for some reason, Garrett had scratched a violent X through the drawing.

She couldn't question it now. There was work to be done.

"These look like they could be important papers," Lisette said from the writing desk.

Bobo had helped himself to an apple from a fruit bowl on a table and was happily strutting about the suite chomping on it.

"No," Lisette amended, "these are just bills and invitations."

Mason joined her at the desk and began rifling through the drawers on the other side. Nothing significant. Finally, in the bottom drawer, she came across a leather pouch stuck in the back under some writing paper. She opened it, reached inside, and pulled out a tintype. It showed a smiling dark-haired young woman who couldn't be more than eighteen.

"She's pretty," Lisette observed over her shoulder. "Who do you think she is? A lover?"

"This is a tintype. They haven't made these in twenty years."

"His mother, then?"

Mason reached inside again and pulled out another tintype. This one showed a man in his thirties and a young boy. The man was Hank Thompson. And though she couldn't be sure, the boy looked as if he could be Richard. Though he couldn't have been more than seven or eight years old, he glared at the camera with a gaze that was so cold, so hard, that it sent a chill up her spine.

Lisette was scanning the room. "Now, where's that Bobo?"

As she wandered off looking for him, Mason reached into the file again and removed the only other thing in it: a small billfold. She flipped it open and saw his badge. It showed a huge single eye and the ominous Pinkerton slogan: WE NEVER SLEEP.

She suppressed a shudder.

Stuck into the other side of the billfold were several folded papers, his official credentials. As she read through them, the only thing of interest was the fact that he was a U.S. citizen and his place of residence at the time of joining the agency was the state of Colorado.

He was an American! From the West.

Before this had time to register, Lisette's voice called from the bedroom, "Mason, come here. You have to see this."

Quickly, she put everything back into the pouch and returned it to the bottom drawer. Then she went into the bedroom.

Standing propped on a chair next to his bed was her self-portrait. Seeing it there, so reverentially displayed, jarred her.

Lisette, holding Bobo in her arms, was staring at it as well. "Why do you think he does such a thing?"

Mason shook her head, too stunned to speak. Was it possible that, as determined as he was to trap her, he wasn't pretending his affection for the paintings?

Suddenly, Bobo patted Lisette's face and gave a tiny wail of warning. A second later, they heard the key turn in the lock. "He's back!" Lisette hissed.

Mason doused the light in the bedroom and they crouched by the door to see Richard and Hank enter. "Get out the bourbon, boy. I need me a drink. I've been to some boring shindigs in my time, but this takes the cake."

"Perhaps if you'd ever taken the trouble to learn French you'd know what was going on," Richard said mildly.

"I didn't send you to Oxford so *I* could learn French."

"In any case, it was a successful night. I was able to put a bug in President Carnot's ear about the Caldwell Collection. He's dying to see it."

"And what's been eating at you all night, Buster? You've been as prickly as a cactus. Is that filly gettin' under your skin?"

"It's Orlaf. What is that bloody bastard doing here?"

"Like everyone else in the world, he's coming to the fair."

"I don't believe that for one minute. Like Emma, the publicity we've created for the paintings has drawn him out of the woodwork."

"So what?"

"So what? As far as I'm concerned, the man is the devil incarnate. I don't want him anywhere near this operation."

"You ask me, boy, you're making a mountain out of a molehill. You been driving yourself too hard. What you need is some rest. Go to bed. Get some sleep."

"Perhaps you're right."

Go to bed?

Mason and Lisette glanced at each other from their crouched position behind the bedroom door. How were they ever going to get out of this?

As if getting an idea, Bobo began patting Lisette on the head. Lisette's eyes brightened and she whispered some instructions in his ear. Then, with absolutely no hesitation, the chimp darted into the sitting room like an arrow and threw the lamp to the floor, breaking it and casting the room into darkness.

As Mason and Lisette silently crept toward the front door, Bobo began shrieking like a banshee and leaping around the furniture. They heard Hank's voice cry out, "Good lord, boy! It's some sort of damned pygmy!"

"No, it's a bloody ape," Garrett said. "He must have come through the window."

"Careful. Don't touch it. The cursed thing might bite."

"I have no intention of touching it."

But Bobo knew when it was time to leave. Seeing that his partners had made their escape, he leapt through the still-open French doors to the balcony and was gone.

Mason and Lisette raced down the stairs, Lisette muttering, "I'm going to have that Hugo's head on a platter!"

They found their bodyguard dozing in an overstuffed chair in the lobby. Lisette hauled back and smacked the back of his bald head with all her might. "Imbecile!"

He jerked up. "I'm not asleep."

"Garrett walked right past you, you fool. He surprised us in the room."

"But I only closed my eyes for an instant," he wailed.

Mason stopped this, saying, "We'd better get out of here. They may be coming down to make a formal complaint to the manager."

Lisette began to giggle. "*'Monsieur, we have a monkey in our room . . .'*"

Mason couldn't help it; she, too, began to laugh. Soon even Hugo was joining in.

"What are you laughing at?" Lisette snapped at him, and he instantly assumed a sheepish stance.

Outside, Bobo was waiting for them. Lisette held out her arms and he climbed into them to receive her grateful kisses. "You're such a good boy, Bobo. You saved our lives."

As she continued raining kisses on his face, Bobo looked at the sulking Hugo and grinned.

Chapter 15

As April turned into May, the realization hit the city with a jolt. In a mere six days, *L'Exposition Universelle Internationale de 1889* would finally be under way. The finishing touches were being put upon the enormous glass and cast-iron exhibition halls that filled the Champ de Mars and the Esplanade des Invalides. Hotels were filling up as visitors from all over the world descended on the city like Muslims on a pilgrimage to Mecca. The restaurants and cafés, dance halls, parks, and squares—everything was crowded with tourists. The streets were alive with anticipation and a heady sense of self-importance.

Paris had reclaimed its position as center of the world.

But while the rest of the city was counting down the hours to the May 6th opening, Garrett was totally involved in his reception three days earlier on the site of the partially completed Caldwell Pavilion. Mason had no more illusions that he was doing this for her benefit, but he'd still thrown himself into the project with the zeal of a master impresario. It was important, he told her, "to steal some of the thunder" from the much larger displays of fine art that were about to open all around them, and give art patrons a taste of the excitement to come and afford them an opportunity to donate to the cause.

An outdoor event in the spring was always a risk in Paris,
but the weather cooperated. The night of the reception proved
to be a splendid May evening, warm with clear skies and no
hint of rain. Colorful Japanese lanterns had been strung all
about the area. A chamber orchestra provided a gracious atmosphere with the sweet strains of Mozart and Haydn. A
canopy sectioned off tables laden with gourmet treats and
champagne. A regiment of waiters in smart red uniforms
were poised to serve the needs of a guest list that Richard
made sure included the crème de la crème of the city's cultural, financial, and political elite, as well as the critics, dealers,
and glamorous patrons of the international art world. The
Prince of Wales and President Carnot were both expected to
make appearances. But the focal point of the evening was a
selection of Caldwell paintings displayed around the perimeter of the cordoned-off area, where the company could wan-
der about and appreciate them at their leisure.

Richard was in an especially gregarious mood. As the guests
began to appear, he turned on the full force of his charm,
amiably greeting the arrivals, making the introductions, presenting the artist's sister. As the champagne flowed freely and
the music drifted on the evening breeze, he joined the more
important guests at the paintings, discussing them so subtly
and eloquently that they never realized he was making a sales
pitch. He made certain the guests understood the paintings'
aesthetic value, their place in art history, and why he felt they
rated their own pavilion.

It was a glittering assembly. Actresses and socialites mixed
with captains of industry and Italian nobility, maharajas with
South American cattle kings and owners of African diamond
mines, critics, playwrights, and poets with Salon painters,
sculptors, explorers, army generals, and inventors whose cre-
ations would soon be featured at the fair. The conversation
was lively, intelligent, and spiked with the excitement gener-
ated by the upcoming Exposition. All in the shadow of the
Tower—this astonishing eighth wonder of the world—with a

panoply of electric lights that made it gleam like a beacon in the darkening night.

As Mason stood in the middle of this enchanted setting, watching Richard go through all these elaborate motions, his devotion to Mason Caldwell's cause seemed so touching and authentic that she had to remind herself it was all part of his carefully laid trap.

You bastard! Do you think I don't see through you? How you're doing all this for yourself? Because the more famous you make me, the more spectacular your success when you unmask me. Well, the evening isn't going to be as successful for you as you might think. With a little luck, you have a surprise in store for you!

It happened just minutes later. A tall, blond man with a formal, aristocratic bearing and sharply defined features was making his entrance.

Count Dimitri Orlaf.

As he entered the party, smiling and bowing to people he knew, Mason felt a stab of malicious anticipation. Two tigers in a cage. Now all she had to do was stand back and watch the fun—and see what kind of weapon she might gain from it.

Richard was completely unaware of the new arrival. He was at the other end of the party, talking to the author Émile Zola, pointing to a detail in one of the paintings. How long would it take him to notice the unwanted intruder in his midst?

As it turned out, it took no time at all. As if by some osmosis or sixth sense, he stopped midsentence, turned, and spotted the man at once. In a flash, his veneer of cordiality vanished, replaced by a look of raw fury.

Mason watched with a delicious smile. What was he going to do?

With an angry glare, he shot toward the man like a bullet streaking toward its target. Mason moved closer, not wanting to miss a minute.

Orlaf saw him coming. He stood where he was, amusement lifting the corners of his mustache. "Well, if it isn't my host, Richard Garrett."

"What are *you* doing here?" Richard growled.

"Why, my dear fellow, I was invited."

"I wouldn't invite you to your own funeral."

A number of the guests around them had caught the air of friction and turned to stare. Mason used them as a shield behind which to watch without being seen.

"But of course I was invited." Orlaf reached into his pocket and removed the engraved invitation Mason had sent him.

Garrett glared at it. "I don't know how you got that, and I don't much care. But if you know what's good for you, you will turn around and leave."

Garrett's raised voice aroused even more attention.

"Dear fellow, I have no intention of leaving. I'm positively itching to see these paintings I've been hearing so much about. I may even be interested in acquiring some of them."

Richard's face had turned to granite. "I'm going to give you exactly one minute to get out of my sight."

"And if I choose to ignore your little ultimatum?"

"I'll throw you out."

Orlaf chuckled. "And make a fool of yourself in front of all these salon habitués? Create a public scandal? Cause a scene at a party where you're trying to raise funds? I hardly think so."

"You think I won't create a scene?" Richard flared. The words hardly left his lips before he hauled back and slugged the Russian in the face.

The crowd gasped as Orlaf reeled into those closest to him. Mason was as shocked as everyone else. She'd never seen Richard like this. He was literally trembling with anger and hatred. The guests backed up, alarmed by the frightening intensity that radiated from him.

"I suppose you want satisfaction for that?" he snarled.

"I'll be happy to meet you any time, any place, with any weapon you might desire. Name it, Orlaf."

Shaking himself off, a taunting smile returned to the Russian's face. "Oh, I'll get satisfaction, all right, old friend. But in my own time and in my own way. And I think I will leave your little soiree right now, because I don't need to see the paintings tonight. I'll have plenty of time for that when I become their broker."

Richard charged after the man, grabbed his jacket in both hands, and gave him a single, violent shake. With his face close, he rasped out, "You listen to me, you son of a bitch. I'll see you dead before you get anywhere near these paintings."

Just then there was a commotion in the crowd and Hank Thompson came barreling through. He put his hand on Richard's shoulder. "Now, hold on, boy, that's enough. Get control of yourself. Where do you think you are?"

"If someone doesn't get him out of here, I swear to God, I'm going to kill him."

Finally losing his temper, Orlaf steamed, "You British prick. I'm going to make you pay for this. I know just how to get you."

As Hank wrestled Richard from the scene, he called out to the Russian, "You'd better get out of here, fella, while you can still walk." To the crowd, he added, "Nothing at all, folks. A couple of young bulls having a pissing match. Happens every day. Nothing at all to get excited about."

The crowd began to disperse, gossiping among themselves about the unprecedented confrontation. Mason heard a woman close to her sigh, behind her fan, "My, but wasn't that stimulating? I've never seen anything like that before. The Englishman . . . My heart is positively pounding!"

"I'm all aflutter," her female companion replied.

Mason watched as Hank spoke softly to Richard, calming him down. She waited for Hank to leave, then took him a glass of champagne. "That was quite a scene."

She could still see the anger simmering in Richard's eyes, but he reined it in, and said, "My apologies. The incident won't do much for our money-raising efforts, I'm afraid. But, as you may have noticed, the man is like a red flag in front of a bull to me. I can't imagine how he got an invitation."

"Why do you hate him so much?"

"He's a blackguard. He disguises himself as an aristocrat and a connoisseur, but he makes his money as a broker for stolen art. When a painting is lifted anywhere in the world, the thief knows he can always find a home for it in Russia through Orlaf. Even for a legitimately purchased painting, the worst thing that can happen is for it to fall into Orlaf's hands. He'll sell it to the Russian aristocracy who don't believe in museums and will just horde it away forever. Orlaf represents everything evil in the world of culture, and I detest him."

He spoke with such feeling, such passion, such wounded integrity that an unexpected guilt tugged at Mason's conscience. She'd provoked this confrontation to create a scene and see what it might tell her about Richard's past. But the genuine pain it had unleashed in him gave her no pleasure. And she'd learned nothing more than she'd known before.

The incident had only weakened her defenses against him.

She turned away. She had to fight this. If she was going to best him, she couldn't let her heart get in the way of her purpose.

She had to slam the door on the love she still felt for him.

Chapter 16

The incident with Orlaf took some of the edge off Mason's fear of Richard Garrett. She had no doubt that he was a detective on her trail in the process of patiently unmasking her. And given his idealistic love of art, it wasn't surprising that he would loathe a man like the count. But in such an eruption of raw emotion, in the midst of a scene he couldn't know was coming, could he have had the presence of mind to fake the protective passion he'd shown for her paintings? She felt confused and torn. She couldn't help thinking there was more to the enigma of Richard Garrett than she'd figured out thus far.

In the meantime, his romantic pursuit of her continued unabated. He was in no way pushy or insistent, but his campaign of seduction proceeded with charm, confidence, and good-natured persistence. Despite her guard, she felt herself weakening to him. The way he touched her at odd moments, running his finger along her palm until she felt weak with desire. The way he kissed her good night, holding her, stroking her so skillfully that it was all she could do to get away from him and lock the door behind her. Subtly, without hurrying, he was stoking the fires of her treacherous longing for him so that she paced her floor long into the night, going again and again to her window, looking out over his hotel, feeling him there, wanting the succor of his touch to ease the fever in her soul. She hated herself for wanting him, for loving him despite everything she knew about him. Each moment in his company was agony, but being without him was worse.

On May 6th, the Universal Exposition opened its gates. Along with the rest of Paris, Mason and Lisette descended upon the fairgrounds and spent the day wandering through the staggering displays of the latest advances in science and industry. Over the next three days, they ate baklava at the Greek pavilion, explored the Tonkin village, watched the Central African dancers, marveled at the Persian antiquities, browsed through displays of crystal and jewelry and photography, rode the miniature train through the grounds, and of course, took in the exhibits of art and sculpture at the Palace of Fine Arts. There was so much to see, and Mason was enjoying the respite from her ordeal.

But the air of excitement that opening week extended far beyond the Champ de Mars and seemed to transform the entire city into one mammoth celebration. One could walk from block to block for miles and never be out of earshot of people singing or bands playing or raucous toasts being offered to the glory of France. The spell even finally captured Garrett, who'd previously shown little interest in the festivities except as they related to the Caldwell Pavilion. On the third night of that golden week, he appeared at Mason's door dressed in evening attire and announced, "I'm taking you out on the town."

Mason tried to beg off. "Richard, thank you, but I'm exhausted. Lisette and I have worn our shoes out over the past few days. I don't think I have an ounce of energy left."

"Nonsense," he replied. "The world is celebrating and I feel like celebrating with it. I shall wait right here while you dress."

"I really couldn't," she protested.

He smiled at her persuasively. "Come now, of all the merriments going on in the city, there must be one you're aching to do."

"Well . . ." She reconsidered. "There *is* actually one thing I've been wanting to do, but I've tried to get tickets and it's impossible."

"Nothing is impossible. Especially in Paris. Especially not tonight." He came closer and put his hands on her shoulders. "Tell me, what is it you're dying to do?"

She moved away. The strength of his hands on her felt too welcome. "Lisette is debuting her new tightrope act all this week at the Folies-Bergères. I'd love to see it, but even she couldn't get me in. It's booked solid with a waiting list."

He gave her a cocky grin. "The Folies-Bergères it will be. You get dressed. I shall return for you in an hour."

Later that evening, the maître d' of the Folies-Bergères escorted them through the waiting crowd, across the vast floor to a ringside table. When they'd been seated, Mason said to Richard, "These are the best seats in the house. I don't suppose it would do any good to ask how you came about them?"

He shrugged. "You just have to know the right people to ask."

As he ordered a bottle of champagne, Mason penned a quick note to Lisette. Folding it and giving it to the waiter to deliver, she told Richard, "I want to let Lisette know we're here. She won't believe it."

As they sipped their champagne, the lights dimmed and the master of ceremonies stepped into the spotlight. "Ladies and gentlemen, the management of the Folies-Bergères is proud to present to you tonight the Princess of the Highwire, the tantalizing Toreadoress of the Tightrope, the Lady Godiva of the Air, the one and only Lisette Ladoux."

Dressed in a flesh-colored sequined costume that bared her legs and left little to the imagination, her blond hair flowing like sunshine, Lisette bounded onstage, then gave a curtsey to the audience and a wink to Mason. Then, with the litheness of a pixie, she mounted a white trampoline in the center of the stage, leapt up and down several times to gain height, then did a dazzling backflip onto a tightrope suspended high above.

For the next twenty minutes, she dazzled the crowd with her acrobatic feats and playful personality, purposely coming close to falling several times, eliciting gasps of apprehension from the crowd, followed by relieved laughter when they realized it was a gag. She charmed them, thrilled them, frightened them as the lights gave her costume the illusion that she was naked all the while.

When it was over, even Richard rose to his feet and applauded enthusiastically. "I had no idea she was so talented," he conceded to Mason. As they sat back down, he leaned close, and added, "Shall we go?"

"Oh, no. There's more to come."

The master of ceremonies returned to the stage, extolling Lisette's praises. Then he announced the next act. "All the way from Bucharest, Romania, the greatest mesmerist the world has ever known, Valentin the Magnificent."

Richard groaned. "Not a bloody hypnotist."

"No, no, we have to stay. Lisette says he's really amazing."

"A load of rubbish, hypnotism."

"Now, Richard, don't be a spoilsport. You wanted me to have a good time, didn't you?"

The Romanian took the stage, intrigued the audience with a few introductory remarks, then asked for volunteers. None were forthcoming. "I can see that you fear I will put you under and expose your hidden self to the world. Most wise of you. So allow me to ask this: Who among you here is the greatest doubter of my art? The one who has just said to his mate, 'The man's a fraud'?"

Mason laughed, grabbed Richard's hand, and thrust it high. He raised a brow but didn't object.

"Ah, here's a candidate. And of course, it's a man. The doubters are always men. Come on up, good sir. May we have a seat for the gentleman?"

Lisette, still in her provocative costume, came out with a

chair and received another rousing round of applause. A man in back called, "Mesmerize Lisette and have her take off her clothes!"

Valentin wagged his finger. "You would like that, would you not, my naughty friend? Alas, wouldn't we all?"

Lisette blew the man a kiss as the crowd laughed.

In the meantime, Richard had taken his seat. "Good luck, old man," he said to the hypnotist. "You'll need it."

Valentin placed a hand on Richard's pulse, asked him to look deeply into his eyes, and told him to count slowly backward from fifty.

Unable to suppress a contemptuous grin, Richard began, "Fifty . . . forty-nine . . . forty-eight . . ."

As Richard counted, the mesmerist continued to hold his gaze and murmured too softly for the audience to hear, "Relax . . . relax . . . relax . . ."

When he was finished counting, Richard asked, cheekily, "Now what?"

"Now nothing. You're in a trance."

"Am I? You could have fooled me."

The audience laughed.

"When I clap my hands, you will wake up from this state and remember absolutely nothing that has happened from the time you sat down in this chair. But for the rest of the evening, when you hear the words *World's Fair,* you will scratch your head and say, '*Viva la France.*'"

"I hardly think so."

Again, there was laughter.

Valentin nodded to Lisette and said to the audience, "I am going to have this gentleman go backstage and have a little rest. In the meantime, I'd like two more volunteers. You can see how ineffective I've been with this gentleman. Perhaps that will give you courage."

As Lisette helped Richard to his feet and led him to the wings, Mason rose and went to join them. Behind the curtain another chair had been set up. Valentin rushed back to them and said hurriedly, "Be quick about this. It makes me appear a fool." Then to Richard, he asked, "How do you feel, young man?"

"Completely in control of my senses, thanks," Richard assured him.

"He doesn't look any different," Mason said.

"Let's test it. Have you been enjoying the World's Fair?"

Instantly, Richard scratched his head and said, *"Viva la France."*

"Excellent. Now I want you to close your eyes."

He did.

The hypnotist instructed, "I want you to answer every question these women put to you with complete honesty. Do you understand?"

"I understand."

Valentin nodded to them, and said, "Go ahead."

"Are you sure?" Mason asked.

"Of course I'm sure."

He went back onstage to his two new volunteers. As his voice droned on, Mason and Lisette crouched down in front of Richard's chair.

Mason asked, "What is your occupation?"

"Lover of art," he replied.

"No. What is your employment? Your profession?"

"I work for the Pinkerton Detective Agency, Chicago, Illinois."

Mason's heart stilled. Was it possible this was going to work, after all?

"You have a tintype of a pretty dark woman that you value greatly. Who is that woman?"

A brief hesitation. Then, "My sister . . . Molly."

Mason grew excited now. This *was* going to work. It was going to give her a privileged portal to the man's soul.

Lisette asked, "How did you really like my act tonight?"

"I thought you wore a tad too much makeup."

"Stop it," Mason hissed. "Don't waste this on foolish questions."

"I could see," he added, "how someone of your aerial skills could be valuable in my profession."

"Me?" Lisette asked.

"Never mind that," Mason said. "Tell us how you really feel about the paintings of Mason Caldwell?"

"No other works of art have ever moved me so deeply. I can think of no greater privilege than to serve them and make them known to the world."

His reply warmed her, but there were tougher questions yet to come. "Have you ever suspected that Mason might not really be dead?" It frightened her just to say it out loud.

"Yes, I have suspected that."

She exchanged a glance with Lisette, who asked, "And do you still?"

"No, I gave up that notion."

"Why?"

"There's no evidence."

"None?" Mason asked.

"Nothing substantial. I realized I was only being overly suspicious. In my profession, I've learned if I can't support a thesis with concrete evidence I have to give it up."

Mason took a breath. "What are your feelings for Mason's sister Amy?"

"I've fallen in love with her. I love her sister's paintings, but I love Amy as a woman. I've never felt this way before. There's nothing I should like more than to spend the rest of my life with her. I want to hold her, protect her, cherish her until the day I die."

The words were so unmistakably from the bottom of his heart that even Lisette couldn't help but tear up. "Ooh-la-la," she sniffed.

Mason sat back on her heels. On the one hand, she was ashamed of herself for violating his privacy this way. But to hear such words coming from such a guarded man . . . She'd never loved him more.

She wanted to ask why he'd never told her, but at that moment, Valentin returned. "Your time's up," he announced. Then he grabbed Richard by the arm and took him back to the stage, where the two later volunteers were executing a humiliating duckwalk. He sat Richard back down in the chair while Mason returned to her table. Then he clapped his hands.

Momentarily, Richard asked, "Well? When do we begin?"

There was some faint snickering in the audience.

"Before we do, let me ask you a question. Have you been enjoying the World's Fair?"

Richard lightly scratched his head and said, "I've been having a jolly time. *Viva la France.*"

The audience roared.

Perplexed, Richard said, "Bloody hell . . . !"

Valentin smiled, and said, "I can see you're just too tough a subject for me. Please, take your seat."

As he did, the audience continued to laugh. "What do they find so amusing?" Richard asked Mason.

"You made a fool out of the man," she told him. "Come on, let's go."

Outside on Rue Richer, he hailed a cab. Mason turned to him with smoldering eyes. "I want to go back to your hotel room."

He looked surprised. "What brought this on?"

"Don't talk. Don't say anything. Just get me back there as fast as you can."

He handed the driver a bill and told him he would double it if he made it to the Grand Hotel in five minutes. During the ride, Mason snuggled against him, smelling his distinctive fresh scent, saying to herself, *I've been such a fool. Such a suspicious fool!*

The driver earned his bonus, and they were soon crossing the lobby of the Grand Hotel. "Just a moment," he said, then left her to have a few words with the concierge, no doubt requesting privacy. She couldn't wait to get to his room. Once he'd ushered her into the elevator, she grabbed him and kissed him on the mouth long and hard. As the grill opened, she took him by the arm and pulled him down the hall.

There was an urgency mounting in her, a need to make up for all the lost time with one grand explosive coming together. At the door, she said in a hoarse voice, "I can't tell you how much I want you."

He pulled her to him, kissing her hungrily. He quickly opened the door, then closed it behind them. Then he picked her up, carried her into the bedroom, and laid her on the bed. The room was dark, but the moonlight beaming through the window lent it a romantic enchantment.

His clothes seemed an affront to the necessity of the moment. She couldn't wait to get him out of them. She tore at his shirt, sending the buttons flying, then pushed it down his arms. She undid his trousers and helped him pull them off. The rest he did himself. Then he lay down beside her, completely naked, in a state of intense arousal.

Very slowly, he started to undress her. One by one her clothes came off and were tossed aside. She was so hungry, she couldn't wait and helped him, tugging at her corset, not caring if it ripped in the process.

And then she was as naked as he was. He came to her and she felt his body on hers, taut naked flesh on her delicate curves. He kissed her again, deeply, longingly, as if all the passion he'd pent up was suddenly unchained. His hands moved on her, stroking her, touching, cupping, gripping, as if as desperate to touch every inch of her as she was to touch him.

He rolled over, kissing her, so that she was on top of him, nuzzling her neck, her shoulders, finding the tight bud of her nipple with his mouth. She moaned, throwing back her head, relishing the moist suckling that was sending jolts of longing through her. She wanted to tell him, with her body if not her words, how sorry she was to have doubted him. To make up for all the suspicions, the avoidance, the maneuvering, the crude intrusions into his private world. To infuse him with her passion and her love for him, driving away the distance that had never had to be. Her desire was so great, so over-powering that it left her feeling stripped bare of everything save her need for him.

They'd never been completely naked together before, and she thrilled at the touch of his body against hers. The muscular sweep of his arms and shoulders. The crisp hair furring his granite chest. The junction of their hips coming together against a rigid erection. His mouth moved on her with devastating skill, kissing her everywhere, trailing his tongue down her arm, nuzzling the palm of her hand, taking her fingers, one by one, into his mouth, as if wanting to taste all the various fruits her body offered, setting her loins on fire with every masterful flick of his tongue.

Then he was rolling her onto her side, kissing the back of her shoulder, moving her onto her stomach with her face pressed into the bed as he traced the curve of her back with his mouth. Down her spine, igniting flicks of desire that seemed unbearable. Lower, lower, his hands cupping her buttocks, kneading gently, slipping underneath to find her juicy core. She gasped as he found her, already feeling ready to explode. Dear God, how she wanted him!

He moved on top of her from behind. But instead of entering her, he reached under the pillow. Suddenly, she felt something cold on her wrist, then heard a metallic click. She jerked around and realized he'd put a handcuff on her.

"What are you doing?" she gasped.

"It's over, Mason," he said in a cold voice. "You've been caught."

Chapter 17

Horrified, Mason grabbed hold of the bedspread and yanked it up to cover herself.

Richard reached over and turned on the lamp, looking down at her with cool indifference.

"You . . . miserable swine!" she spat out at him. "How could you?"

"It wasn't easy, I assure you." He clamped her handcuff to the bedpost, then began to gather up his clothes.

"You're out of your mind."

"The birthmark, Mason." He grabbed her wrist and twisted her around so he could see her flank. "You forgot the birthmark. The damning proof."

Jesus! She *had* forgotten it. It was in a place she never saw in the course of her day. But she'd put it in her own portrait because she'd been using mirrors to see herself from behind. She'd never thought of it again.

What a simpleton!

She thought quickly. "You fool. All the Caldwells have this birthmark."

He was systematically dressing himself, making her feel more vulnerable in her nakedness. "Come now, Mason. The chance of two siblings having the exact same birthmark in the exact same spot is perhaps many billions to one."

Again, she scrambled for an explanation. "Who said it

was a self-portrait? Falconier gave it that title. It's actually Mason's painting of me. I just didn't tell you that because you seemed so attached to the idea of it being her that I didn't want to disillusion you. It's me."

He couldn't help but smile. "My, but you *are* a worthy opponent. A marvelous defense tactic, I admit. But that's not the only way you slipped up. There were other little things. And one big one: your eyelashes. Everyone who knew Mason remembers her unusually long lashes. Which, I hasten to remind you, are prominent in the self-portrait. Amy's lashes, on the other hand, are quite short. But the oddest thing happened. During the time I've known you, they seemed to be growing. I thought it was my imagination at first. But then, quite suddenly, they were short again. Which had to mean only one thing. You were cutting them. Now, why would a woman go out of her way to sabotage something that adds to her allure?"

The man had the eyes of a microscope. But she wasn't about to give in. "Eyelashes are also a family trait. I just don't happen to like them. Have you ever thought of that, you smug bastard?"

Unfazed, Richard continued, "But it became even more apparent when you began to fight back. I realized you were on to me. Somehow you found out I was a Pinkerton man. Emma, no doubt. So you went looking for information to use against me. That felonious ape. Who else would have access to such a creature but someone whose best friend was a circus performer?"

"Why shouldn't I fight back and try to find the truth when I learn that everything you told me about yourself is a lie?"

"The monkey was clever, even imaginative," he went on. "But the mesmerist—now, that was pathetic. Do you honestly think my mind is so undisciplined that I'd allow myself to fall under your power? It was all I could do to keep from laughing aloud. *Viva la France*, indeed. Did you take me for a complete amateur?"

She felt her heart sink even further. "Those things you said. They were just to trick me, to get me into your bed so you could see my birthmark."

Fully dressed now, he pulled his pocket watch from his vest, glanced at it, and said, "Time to go."

He stepped to the bed, unlocked the handcuff, and watched her get dressed. She was so hurt—so furious—she was cursing him as she did. "I'm going to sue you for this. You and the Pinkertons of Chicago, and anyone else who helped you. You're going to be so sorry."

As they got to the door, he snapped the handcuffs on both her wrists and quipped, "Sorry about the restraints, but worthy opponents are not to be underestimated."

"I'd gladly strangle you with them if I could."

"Ah," he smiled coldly, "hell hath no fury like a crook who's been caught."

She reached around to kick him, but he sidestepped it and said, "I think we'll avoid the lobby tonight and take the back way out."

They walked down the four flights of stairs and left by the back entrance. As they did, they ran into one of the bellboys, who jerked in surprise at the sight of the handcuffs. Mason had never felt more humiliated in all her life.

"Lovers' spat," Garrett explained, nodding to him pleasantly, as if it were the most natural thing in the world.

She was surprised to find the coach waiting as they left the back entrance. "You were pretty sure of yourself," she grumbled.

"I had the concierge make a few arrangements. You see, I've had this evening planned for some time."

The coach headed down Avenue de l'Opéra in the direction of the Prefecture of Police. Mason sat as far away from him as she could, but she couldn't keep the fear from gripping her.

"Let's just say, for a moment, that you're able to convince

the authorities that I'm masquerading as my sister. What do you think they'll do to me?"

"Hard to say. For the crime of fraud, I should estimate perhaps eight to ten years in the women's wing of Santé Prison. But the French, as you know, can be rather harsh in the meting out of their justice, and might be vengeful toward someone who'd made fools of so many important people. They might decide to make an example out of such a person, in which case the term could be . . . far greater."

The reality of her predicament paralyzed her. She spent the rest of the journey down the avenue staring morosely out the window.

Soon they came to the Palais Royal. But instead of turning left on Rue de Rivoli toward the Prefecture, the carriage pulled up and stopped.

"We're here," Richard said.

Mason looked around. "The Louvre?"

"Very perceptive. Get out."

She did, feeling confused and slightly absurd being in shackles at the north entrance of the world's supreme sanctuary of art.

"Up the stairs, please."

He gave her a nudge to get her started. It must have been midnight by now, but a guard was standing at the door. As they approached, he bowed slightly at Richard and opened it for him.

"What's going on?" she asked.

"Just keep walking."

They started down a long corridor lined with paintings by Poussin, Boucher, and Fragonard that they could barely see in the moonlight shining through the curved glass ceiling. As they rounded the corner, another guard was standing sentry. Displaying no surprise at their presence, he handed Richard a key.

"Keep going, please," Richard said to her.

They proceeded down another corridor, their footsteps

echoing in the vast, empty temple of art. It was eerie being there at night. The hush seemed almost ghostly. The huge paintings, now by Renaissance artists, hung in the gloom like darkened windows to other impenetrable worlds.

"This is vicious," she told him. "I demand that you tell me where we're going and why."

"Oh, I'll do the demanding here."

They took a left and started down a smaller corridor where a night maid curtsied to Richard and said, "Everything has been prepared, Monsieur."

He tipped her and they kept walking.

Where could they be going? Mason couldn't think of anything that made any sense. Except, perhaps, that he'd arranged for Duval to meet them here, so she could be turned over to the police in a setting that would emphasize the particularly heinous nature of her crime to a nation that treasured art above all else. A perfect coda for a sanctimonious detective who prided himself in nailing defrauders of his sacred religion.

The darkness of the halls, the unearthly silence, the echo of their footsteps all served to increase Mason's trepidation.

They came to a closed door. Using the key the guard had provided, Richard opened it and then stepped back.

Inside, she saw an incredible sight. The large rococo chamber was lighted by dozens of white candles. To one side, two paintings were positioned on stands, facing a chaise lounge. An end table beside it was laid with a bottle of champagne and a couple of glasses.

As he locked the door behind them, she noticed that the smaller of the two paintings was Leonardo da Vinci's *Mona Lisa*. The other was her own self-portrait.

Mason was flabbergasted. She couldn't speak. She turned and looked at Richard numbly for some explanation. But he said nothing. Instead, he unlocked her handcuffs and let them fall to the carpeted floor.

"What is all this?" she managed.

He dropped his cold indifference and his eyes softened on her. "A celebration."

"A celebration? Of what?"

"Of our coming together at last."

Coming together? What was he saying? "You're not arresting me?"

"I'm arresting you, but not in the way you think."

"But . . . I don't understand."

"Don't you see? This is my way of showing you how much I love you. How much I admire you."

Her legs buckled. He caught her and guided her to the lounge where he gently sat her down.

"I must be dreaming."

He took a seat beside her. "I *wanted* it to be like a dream. I wanted to create a moment that was not of this world. You see, I've never told a woman I loved her before, and I wanted it to be . . . magical."

"This has to be a trick."

"We're through with tricks. This is real."

She looked up at him. "You *love* me?"

"I think I've loved you since the moment I first saw your painting."

"You love a woman you think is a fraud?"

"You're no fraud. You're everything I thought you were, and more."

"More?"

He took her hand in his. "You're a woman after my own heart. A woman who's not afraid to spit in the face of fate and create her own destiny."

"But all your talk about purity and honesty . . ."

"The purity I admire is the purity of your painting. The honesty I admire is your devotion to do whatever it takes to give that purity to the world. *Whatever* it takes."

"You admire what I've done?"

"More than you'll ever know. The world couldn't see the brilliance of what you were doing. So when chance placed a unique opportunity in your path, you took it, fearlessly, risking everything. I did what I did tonight to show you what could have happened, to show you how courageous your sacrifice really was. As a way of honoring the risk you took."

She was beginning to believe it. "You honored me by scaring me to death?"

He dropped her hand. "I'm doing this badly. I told you how I figured out you were Mason from the standpoint of a detective. But it wasn't the truth. Not the real truth."

He rose and went to stand before her portrait. "That first day in Falconier's," he said softly, "I stood before this very painting and fell in love. I saw in your work something that touched me on such a deep level it rocked the very foundations of my soul. It utterly seduced me. It was as if I hadn't lived until that moment. But on the heels of this revelation came sadness. All I could think was, if only I'd known her. If only I'd been here to help her, love her, while she was still alive. Maybe I could have saved her."

He turned to her. "And then I looked at you, the sister. And I wanted you. I wasn't even sure why. And when we made love in the coach . . . It was so much more fulfilling than anything I'd ever experienced. It shook me as deeply and almost in the same way as when I saw your portrait. I couldn't understand it. I thought perhaps I wanted you as a way of being close to Mason, so I tried to stay away. But I couldn't. It was driving me out of my mind. Then I saw the paint on your hands in Auvers. And I thought, could it be? I didn't even dare to hope. But I set out to discover the truth— not to bring you to some false justice, but because I wanted, *needed* it to be true."

He came back and sat down beside her once again. "I think I knew it in my heart all along. But I couldn't be sure. And I couldn't confront you, couldn't risk scaring you away. So it became a game between us. I actually enjoyed the game. In a way, it was a form of making love with you. Back and forth, give and take. It was exciting to watch you try and best me. Truly you *were* a worthy opponent. And so imaginative!" He laughed. "Who but you could come up with such entertaining maneuvers?" He took her hand, growing serious once more. "I knew tonight was the night. I planned everything carefully in advance. But there was still an unanswered question in my mind. Something I needed to know before confessing everything to you."

"What was that?"

"I didn't know how you felt about me. I didn't know if the discoveries you'd made about me had spoiled any hope that you might love me. So I told you the truth when you thought I was hypnotized. I told you I loved you. To see your reaction. To see if, underneath your sense of betrayal, your anger, there might be some spark of feeling for me. Some reason to hope that this wasn't all for nothing."

"You wanted to know if I love you?"

Mason could see a flicker of doubt, of vulnerability in the dark recesses of Richard's eyes. "Yes."

She just stared at him for a moment. There was no doubt in her mind that the hope she read in his eyes was real. She turned to him fully and put both hands on his face. "With all my heart and soul, Richard. With everything I have."

In a savage move, he yanked her to him, holding her close. She could feel the thundering of his heart. "Thank God," he whispered.

Feeling his love pouring into her, she clutched him to her, tears of gratitude welling in her eyes.

"Now we can start over," he murmured. "All barriers down between us."

She eased away. She didn't want to spoil the moment, but she had the presence of mind to say, "My barriers are down. But what about yours? There's so much about you I don't know."

"You know I love you."

"That's all I know. What about your past?"

He blinked. "My . . . past?"

"Before you became the pride of the Pinkerton Detective Agency."

"Oh. You mean, what did I do?"

"For starters, yes."

"You really want to know?"

"Of course I do."

"I warn you, it's something rather shocking."

"More shocking than finding myself in a candlelit room with the *Mona Lisa*?"

Richard chuckled, then stood up. Looking down on her, he gave a mischievous smile. "I was a thief."

"You were not!"

"I was. An art thief. Actually, one of the world's foremost art thieves. I could try to impress you with tales of my exploits, but as accomplished as I was, in the end I was caught. I was given the choice of a long jail sentence or joining the agency and using my skill and experience to serve the other side of the law. It wasn't a difficult choice."

Mason sat there somberly for a moment, taking it all in. Then, suddenly, she threw her head back and laughed. She laughed so hard her sides began to ache.

"And to think," she finally gasped, "I was terrified you'd find out *I'd* done something dishonest!"

He saw the humor and laughed with her. It was so funny, so wonderful, the two of them, outlaws, masters of deception. She jumped up and threw her arms around him, hugging him joyously. "I adore you!"

She'd never seen him look so happy. He hugged her again, lifting her off her feet.

But when he put her down, she looked around her at the room, the candles, the paintings. "You must have had to grease a few palms in the Ministry of Culture to pull *this* off."

"Let's just say it helps to know where a few bodies are buried along the Seine."

"But . . . the *Mona Lisa* . . . What does *that* mean?"

"It means I think your self-portrait is the equal of Leonardo's masterpiece. And I believe, Mason or Amy, it's your destiny to be one of the most important painters in the history of Western art."

Mason had to catch her breath. "You mean . . . You want everything to go on as before? Our mission to make Mason—me—famous?"

"That's exactly what I'm saying."

"But . . . Mason can't very well just suddenly come to life, can she?"

"I'm afraid not. Her legend demands a martyr. Nobody planned that, it just happened. But the myth that's coming out of it has a power and a will of its own and we can't stand in its way."

"Then I have to stay dead. I have to be Amy."

"But when you paint, you'll be Mason."

She paused a moment to let that sink in.

"If you feel you can't do it, I shall understand. But if you choose to rejoin me in this quest, I promise I shall give everything I have to it . . . to you."

He said this with a sincerity that made her dizzy. In one evening, this man was telling her he loved her, he forgave—no, celebrated—her fraud, and he wanted to dedicate his life to her. What woman could resist that?

She had no intention of resisting.

She reached up, took his face in her hands, and gave him the deepest, most heartfelt, most surrendering kiss she'd ever bestowed in her life.

"Are you sure the door's locked?" she asked.

He smiled and held up the key. "We're shut off from the world. The three of us here. You, me, and *La Gioconda*."

"Good."

Mason reached behind her and unbuttoned the back of her gown, then let it drop to the floor. Her petticoats followed, then her shoes, her stockings, her corset. Until she was standing before him, completely nude. "I've never been so exposed before. I never dreamed it could be so liberating."

Richard came to her and slowly turned her so her back was to him. He kissed her shoulders. Then he left a trail of stirring kisses along her back, moving lower, dropping to his knees. He glanced over at her self-portrait, looked at the heart-shaped birthmark, then at its inspiration on her flank. He kissed it, tenderly, reverently, worshipfully.

The intimacy of this devotion sent a jolt of excitement through Mason. She turned around and said, "Take off your clothes. I want to see you as naked as I am. I want us to be like Adam and Eve, here in our own Garden of Eden."

He stood again and began to undress. She'd only caught a brief glimpse of his naked body for the first time earlier that night. But at the time, she'd been so angry she hadn't been able to appreciate its exhilarating contours. Now she sat back on the softly padded lounge and watched as, bit by bit, it was revealed to her gaze. A strong body, powerful and wholly masculine, a chest of iron, massive, sumptuously sculpted, with dark hair that made her want to run her fingers through it. Lean waist, trim but muscled thighs. Every inch of him ruggedly beautiful, like a stallion in the wild. And his cock— bold, tumescent, but quickly rising to the occasion. So perfectly formed that Apollo himself would be envious.

He joined her on the chaise. "Take a moment and feel the spirit of this place," he murmured. "All the history these walls have seen. The energy possessed in all these glorious works of art concentrated in one contained space. Energy we love, energy that has always called out to us, that speaks to us so clearly and powerfully. Let it come into us, let it possess us, let it give us strength for what's to come. Let it merge us into one."

She felt his words seep into her soul. She felt that energy, the essence of all these great masters, all their pain and suffering and genius, permeating the spirit of this grand palace of beauty, pouring into her, giving her a confidence, a certainty, a mandate the gods were telling her she could, and should, merge with him.

She took him into her mouth and felt him swell and fill the vacant hollow. Filling, too, the hollow she'd carried in her heart for too many years to count. The feeling that took hold of her was beyond bliss. It was as if she were being carried off to some higher plane of existence. As he slid in and out of her mouth, she lost all track of time, of who she was, of what tomorrow or next week or next month might bring. She felt a satisfaction and gratification and exquisite oneness that was beyond anything she might have imagined, and that she never wanted to end.

Finally, however, he withdrew from her, leaned her back, and knelt before her. "I'm going to devour you," he said. Then he buried his face between her legs.

His tongue was like a hot flame. As it found her tender clit and skillfully set to work, she was transported to that place where she'd been moments before, where time was meaningless, where there was only pleasure. Pleasure that built . . . and built . . . and built . . . until all of her—body, mind, and soul—opened to him, rejoicing in the spirals of ecstasy, erupting on his tongue, spilling her juices into his mouth.

He was on her even before the delicious spasms ended, plunging into her, carrying her again to a world of sheer delight. As he pounded into her, she rising up to meet him, they held each other so close it was hard to tell where one began and the other left off.

"Go deeper," he commanded, his mouth at her ear. "Deeper . . . deeper . . . deeper than you've ever been before . . . don't hold back . . . leave the earth behind . . . deeper . . . *deeper* . . ."

He gasped and his head jerked back. As he poured into her, she felt herself transported, transformed, merging with him . . . merging . . . merging . . . She couldn't contain herself. She screamed, her cry echoing through the vast citadel. *Oh God . . . oh God . . . ohhhhh God . . .*

And when it was over, she lay clutched in his arms in an afterglow of divine rapture. Dreamily, she looked over at Leonardo's masterpiece.

The mystery of the ages was solved.

She knew why *La Gioconda* was smiling.

Chapter 18

It was a miracle! In the wake of all the worry, suspicion, and fear that had consumed her since Emma had revealed Richard's true identity, everything had fallen into place for Mason as if some fairy godmother had waved her wand and made all her dreams come true. Everything. The work, the recognition, the support and love of a man who truly knew and appreciated her. The caveat of having to continue her masquerade to the outside world seemed a small price to pay for such total fulfillment. And now she no longer had the burden of having to lie to the man she loved so dearly. She didn't care who the rest of the world thought she was, as long as she could be herself with him.

The two days since the Louvre had been a time of increasing intimacy. They'd returned to Richard's suite and made love again and again, taking their meals in bed, not bothering to get dressed. Richard seemed a different man, completely relaxed, witty and amusing, boyishly playful one minute, insatiably amorous the next. By an unspoken agreement, they didn't talk of anything that had gone on before or was going on outside their walls, intent on sustaining the magic of their experience at the Louvre as long as possible. It was as if they were the only two people in the world. Even the appearance of a bellboy delivering their meals or a maid coming in to tidy the room seemed an intrusion on their sanctuary.

But on the third night, she was startled out of sleep by Richard's voice crying out. He shot up in bed, breathing erratically, bathed in sweat. Alarmed, Mason rolled over, and asked, "What is it?"

"Nothing." His voice sounded strained. "Just a bad dream."

She put her arms around him. "You're trembling."

"I'll be all right in a minute. Just hold me."

He held on to her so tightly she could barely breathe. "What did you dream?"

He was still shuddering in her arms. "Nothing specific," he whispered. "Just a nightmare. I have them from time to time. Probably, it's just my body's way of telling me it's time for us to get back to work." He turned on the lamp, flooding the room with light. "Let me just hold you a minute and I'll be fine."

She cradled him in her arms, feeling his heart hammering in his chest. Gradually, it returned to a normal rhythm and he drifted off to sleep. She left the light on, not wanting to disturb his peace by stretching over him and extinguishing it.

The next morning when Mason woke up, Richard was already awake. He greeted her with a smile and said, "I have to go to Rome."

"Rome? What's in Rome?"

"Signore Alberto Lugini."

"Lugini? The critic?"

"Not just a critic, the most esteemed art scholar and historian in Europe."

It gave Mason a wistful stab to see him focused on something besides her. She'd been spoiled these last few days, when the world had seemed so far away. "Surely you don't have to go now. We're having such fun. Stay here with me."

She leaned over and kissed him enticingly.

"Unfortunately, I must. The twenty-first of June is coming quickly and we don't have anywhere near the critical support I'd hoped to have by now. Morrel, Wolfe, and the other important French critics have been resistant to us, no matter what I've tried. We need to outflank them, and fast."

"Outflank? What do you mean?"

"If a man with Lugini's prestige were to see your paintings and lose his head over them, the rest of the critics would have to fall in line. He carries that much weight."

"But he's even more of a traditionalist than Morrel and the others."

"True. But I'm hoping to make him see the light."

"And how are you going to do that?"

He grinned. "Let's just say I know where some bodies are buried along the Tiber as well."

"Are there *any* rivers in Europe whose secrets are safe from you?"

He kissed her on the nose. "Damn few." He smiled.

"I don't know what I'm going to do without you," she grumbled.

"You can get some painting done. That should occupy you nicely."

"A pale substitute for being here with you."

"One more thing. Who else knows you're really Mason?"

"Only Lisette."

"Is she trustworthy?"

"She's the most trustworthy person I've ever known in my life."

He still seemed uneasy but said, "Very well. But let's make certain the secret stays between the three of us. The fewer people that know, the better."

As he rose and slipped a robe over his magnificent naked body, Mason slumped down in the bed and gave him a mock pout.

That afternoon, at Gare de Lyon, they stood on the platform drawing out their good-byes as the train was about to depart. Mason did her best to present a good face, but all she really wanted to do was beg him not to leave.

The train whistle blew. "I have to go," he said.

"How long will you be gone?"

"About a week, or as long as it takes to make our case to the man." In a rush of sudden passion, as if realizing how much he'd miss her, he hooked his arm about her waist and yanked her to him, giving her a blinding kiss.

"Oh, dear," she murmured against his lips. "If you kiss me like that, I won't let you go."

"Don't forget, your job while I'm gone is to get some painting done. Close yourself off and get some focus and concentration. Try to return to the frame of mind you had when you did the self-portrait. Don't think about anything else."

"I'll try."

He kissed her again and headed for the train. But suddenly, he stopped, turned to look at her, then hurried back for one last kiss. "Remember. We're in this together." Then he was gone.

Mason watched the train until it disappeared, then started back to her hotel, already feeling lonely. A whole week without Richard. How could she stand it? But she remembered what he'd said. Close yourself off . . . paint . . . she'd do it for him. She could already see the reunion in her mind. Showing him the new paintings. The pleasure on his face when he saw them. Taking her into his arms and rewarding her for her toil. The image heartened her.

It had been days since she'd been back to her own rooms. When she entered the lobby and approached the reception desk, the clerk gave her an alarmed look. "Mademoiselle Caldwell, we were growing concerned."

"I should have told you. I was staying with friends."

"The police were here yesterday looking for you."

"Police?" The word brought her crashing back to reality.

"They left a message." The clerk looked under the counter. "Now, where *is* it?" Finally, he pulled out an envelope with the name Amy Caldwell on it.

She tore it open and unfolded the single page, a request for her to appear at the office of Inspector Duval at her earliest possible convenience.

The prospect frightened her. But if she put it off, it would only grow in her mind. Without going to her room, she went out and hailed a cab, willing herself to remain calm and find out what was going on.

Duval's office, on the second floor of the massive Prefecture of Police building on Ile de la Cité, looked across a square at the Cathedral of Notre Dame. Duval came out to the waiting room to greet her, walked her inside, sat her down, then stood over her, watching her closely. He said nothing for several moments. It seemed so hot in the office that she had to resist the urge to wipe her brow.

Finally, he spoke. "As you may recall, Mademoiselle, certain aspects of your sister's suicide have troubled me." He paused.

"Yes, I recall."

"Since our last meeting, I have continued to look into the matter. And my inquiry has turned up several other irregularities." Again, he paused.

"Irregularities?" She pressed her palms together.

"I must now inform you that I believe it is more than possible that a crime has been committed in connection with this incident."

A crime. *Dear God, what does he know?*

"What kind of crime?"

"At this point, I prefer not to say."

"What evidence do you have to support this conclusion?"

"Again, I am not prepared to divulge that information."

His gaze never once left her face. *Don't let him see your fear.*

Carefully, she asked, "Then why did you summon me here, Inspector?"

"To officially inform you that the Sûreté is launching a full investigation of the matter. And to request that you not leave

THE ART OF SEDUCTION   183

the country until the investigation is concluded. May I assure myself of your cooperation?"

"Of course. If there are any doubts about my sister's death, I want them to be satisfied before I go home."

She stood to leave.

"One thing more, Mademoiselle."

Mason froze. "Yes, Inspector?"

"You have been seen frequently in the company of a British gentleman, Richard Garrett. May I ask the nature of your relationship?"

She forced herself to look innocent and surprised. "Why, we're friends. He's a great admirer of my sister's work and has been helping me settle her affairs."

"Was he a friend of your sister?"

"No, they never met. It was only in the wake of her death that he learned of her work."

"What do you know about this man? His background?"

"I know that he's a well-connected and well-respected figure in the art world."

"I see. Very well, you may go."

Dully, she walked out of the office and down the stairs. As she left the building, two policemen were carrying a woman kicking and screaming through the entrance. Mason had no idea what her crime was, but the woman was respectably dressed and her terror was palpable. Was that Mason's future? She choked on her own panic as she left the Prefecture and started back across the Pont au Change toward the Right Bank.

Irregularities in the death of Mason Caldwell.

A crime has been committed.

A full-scale investigation by the Sûreté.

What do you know about the background of this man Richard Garrett?

But what exactly did Duval know? If he knew everything, surely he would have arrested her on the spot. So he was fishing, trying to rattle her and see what she might give away. She thought back on their conversation. Had she let anything slip? She didn't think so, but who knew what an expert like Duval would pick up from her responses?

Her first impulse was to send a wire to Rome and tell Richard, warn him what was happening. But what if Duval was having her watched? He could intercept the telegram. And if he *was* watching, how could she possibly do the new paintings? She couldn't very well work in her hotel room, or even rent a studio here in Paris. He'd know in an instant what she was doing.

She felt physically ill.

Just that morning she'd been so happy. Now this. The truth was, she didn't feel like doing any painting, she didn't want Richard to go to Rome, and this quest to make her into an artistic immortal suddenly just didn't seem worth the risk.

Stop it! I can't let this get to me.

She looked down into the Seine to try and calm herself.

This was exactly what Duval wanted, for her to go to pieces and give herself away. She had to think. What was it Richard had said? Focus. Concentration. Forget about everything else.

But how could she do that now?

Auvers.

She would go back to Auvers.

Go to Lisette and ask her to come along.

Get away from all of this in the serenity of the country.

The canvases and paints were still there. She'd lose herself in the work, as she always had. Away from Duval's prying eyes.

Don't think. Don't lose your nerve.

When Richard returned, he'd know what to do.

Just keep calm.

And don't do anything stupid.

Chapter 19

Summer had come early to Auvers. The wildflowers, in full bloom, filled the air with their sweet perfume. The days were warm and lazy, the nights cool and refreshing. Villas were filling up with summer renters, and the Oise River was alive with pleasure boats and swimmers. As Mason and Lisette moved back into their country retreat, with the dogs and Hugo in tow, Mason settled in to paint, determined to do good work and blot out the clouds that threatened her new existence.

Lisette, for her part, was enjoying the vacation immensely. When not posing, she took the dogs for long walks along the riverbank and through the wheat fields on the plateau, with Hugo trailing behind. Away from the pressure of the city, Lisette found she actually had a kind of rapport with her clumsy bodyguard and was even beginning to like him. She discovered he'd once been a strong man for a circus in Lille, and he was able to help her with the new acrobatic routine she was developing for the upcoming summer session of the Cirque Fernando. Hugo even bought the materials and built her a trampoline in the field outside the house so she could practice. He had a real fondness for animals, and there was nothing he enjoyed more than lavishing her dogs with attention—the one sure way to Lisette's heart. "You know," she told Mason in her off-handed way, "this Hugo, he's not so bad."

But Mason had no time to join in their frivolity. She'd thrown herself into an idea derived from the Folies-Bergères. She would paint Lisette on the tightrope, as seen from the midst of a ghoulishly impersonal audience. It was very much in the vein of the pictures she'd painted that Richard had loved so much, and she wanted it to be the best thing she'd ever done. For three straight days and most of the nights, she toiled away until it was completed. But when she stood back to look at it with some perspective, she wasn't at all sure of its quality. Unlike her other paintings in this vein, it left her with no swell of satisfaction.

Was it because of all the turmoil surrounding her? Or was it possible that, with all her recent happiness, she simply no longer had such a grim vision of the world to convey? She honestly didn't know.

But the dissatisfaction of it made her feel restless and empty inside. She tried to catch up on her sleep, but she couldn't find a comfortable position. She tossed and turned, feeling as if she wanted to crawl out of her skin. She recognized it as the feeling she had when she needed to paint. But she'd just spent three days working and it had done nothing to alleviate the craving.

Finally, Mason threw back the covers, went to the small room she'd set up as a studio, put a new canvas on the easel, and in a sudden flash of inspiration, began to paint a portrait of Richard. Her hand flew across the canvas, her strokes bold and sure, the glorious image she held in her mind unfolding with an ease and swiftness and burst of skill that was nothing like the agony of the last three days. She was done within an hour. The result was far from a photographic likeness, but it captured his cleverness, his sexual confidence, his physical beauty, his streak of larceny. It captured, not so much the way he looked to the world, but how he looked to her and how he made her feel—wanted, understood, appreciated, cherished, complete as a human being.

It was the best thing she'd ever done, and it filled her with satisfaction and joy. She took it with her to her bedroom and slept in its shadow, the soundest, most peaceful sleep she could remember in years. She felt as if she were wrapped in the glow of Richard's love.

She awoke before daybreak, completely revitalized. Lying in bed, looking at the fruit of her late-night inspiration, she was suddenly seized by an impulse to paint the rising sun. Without even bothering to dress, she snatched up her supplies and went, in nightgown and bare feet, out into the dewy freshness of the encroaching dawn. She found a spot down on the lawn where she'd have an unobstructed view of the rising sun. As the sky began to brighten with pink and orange hues, she set to work, feverishly trying to capture the fleeting moment—the early light on the river, the shadows of the willows, the bloodred of the sun just beginning to peek its head over the horizon in the distance.

Mason had just placed a few dabs of citron yellow on the canvas to indicate a patch of waking wildflowers when she looked up to see a man staring at her. He was down by the river, just outside the property line. He was dressed in a business suit, so he was obviously not a vacationer or one of the local workers. When he saw that she'd noticed him, he quickly stepped back behind a tree.

Duval's man!

Had he followed her? Had he been watching the house all this time? *Oh, God, I'm painting! Amy doesn't paint!* A dead giveaway. What would he do? Close in and make an arrest?

Slowly, she began replacing the tubes of paint into her box and snapped it shut. Then she took the canvas off the easel, picked up the palette and paint box, and started back for the house. Glancing nervously over her shoulder, she saw that the man wasn't following her.

Back at the house, she bolted the door behind her and rushed up to her room. The first thing she saw was the portrait of Richard—the most damning evidence imaginable. The trapeze picture could be explained as Mason's earlier work, and the sunrise just an amateurish attempt by her sister. But this . . . There was nothing amateurish about it. And as far as the world was concerned, Mason Caldwell had never even met Richard Garrett.

She sat back in a chair and looked at it. She knew what she had to do. But could she? To destroy it was like destroying a part of herself.

But there was no choice.

With a heavy heart, she stood, loaded a large brush with liquid white, and before she could think better of it, covered the entire surface with rapid strokes, until all that was left was a blank canvas.

Then she locked her door, lay down on her bed, and wept.

When the others were up, she told Hugo what had happened. He went out to investigate, but the man was nowhere to be found. Mason was so jangled by the intrusion that she didn't leave the house for the rest of the day. She just stayed in her room, feeling trapped. She went to bed early that night but had a difficult time falling asleep, imagining the forces of Inspector Duval surrounding the grounds. It was long after midnight when she finally drifted off.

Sometime in the night, she awoke with a start. What was it? A noise outside. Was she imagining it? No, there it was again. Footsteps in the gravel. Noises that sounded like the rustling of leaves in the trellis outside her window. The faint squeal of an unoiled hinge. She sat up in bed, terrified, clutching the covers to her. The window was opening! As it did, she could make out the form of a man's arm pushing it inward.

Her heart was pounding like a sledgehammer. A shadowy figure mounted the ledge and swiveled his legs around to the floor.

"I have a gun," she lied, her voice trembling.

The intruder froze. The silence was dense.

Then a low voice said, "Not exactly the welcome I'd expected."

She recognized the fluid, faintly Scots-accented voice and the humor lurking beneath the words. In an instant, she was out of bed and throwing herself into Richard's arms in a rush of relief.

He held her so tightly her feet left the floor as he kissed her. He seemed so strong and solid, and she instantly felt safe in his arms.

"I didn't mean to frighten you," he said between kisses. "I got word Duval is on your tail. He even had the Italian police question me in Rome. In case you're being watched, I decided the less he knows about us, the better."

"They *are* watching the house. I've been so frightened."

"I'm here. Everything's fine now."

She was still shaking. "Make love to me, Richard. Please."

He kissed her, holding her close, as if sensing that she needed his strength. "God, I've missed you." He picked her up and held her in his arms, and she felt some of his vitality ease away the fear.

And then he was laying her softly on the bed. Shedding his clothes swiftly, he tossed them aside as she tugged the night-gown over her head. He covered her with his warmth, with the granite power of his body. He kissed her, touched her, made her feel wanted and cherished. Taking both her hands, he entwined his fingers with hers and held them up above her head on either side as he entered her. "I'm here," he kept whispering in her ear. "There's nothing to fear."

Mason had never felt so exquisitely reassured. Richard used his body, his long, slow thrusts, to soothe and uplift her. And when the fright had at last seeped away, replaced by the pleasure and sustenance of his love, she left it all behind and rejoiced in their tender union. She lost herself in him, in the heat of his tongue, the vibrancy of his gentle might, the potency of his devotion.

They laid in each other's arms for a long time afterward in the dark, saying nothing, listening to the rhythms of one another's breath. Mason sensed that he was giving her time, not pushing, allowing her to tell him what had happened when she was ready.

She didn't want to talk about it. She wanted it to all go away. To stay here, lying in the warmth and safety of his arms, suspended in time. But she knew she'd have to tell him sooner or later.

"Duval called me in to the Sûreté."

He kissed her temple. "Take your time and tell me everything he said."

She did.

"He's suspicious, that's certain," he mused when she was done. "But he doesn't have anything. He's just trying to scare you into doing something foolish."

"That's what I thought. But with all his resources, surely he'll check in Boston and find out there's no record of Amy there."

"There is now. I had an associate insert some documentation there. Birth record, baptism, graduation from Miss Hanover's College for Women. It's all on file in various Boston institutions. There's also a notation in the books of the Cunard Line proving Amy bought a ticket to France."

Mason was astounded that he'd had the foresight to do such a thing. It was almost eerie. But it was ingenious. It brightened her spirits considerably. She snuggled closer to him, tangling her fingers in the thick hair of his chest, feeling his strong pulse.

"You've taken care of everything, haven't you?"

"I've tried."

"And Lugini? How did it go with him?"

"He was a bit resistant at first, but I was persuasive."

"Is he going to give us the endorsement we need?"

"We'll soon see . . . Which reminds me, did you manage to get any work done through this ordeal?"

"I finished one painting."

"Let's have a look."

She slipped on her nightgown and went to the studio to fetch it. He'd already turned on the bedside lamp. She propped it up against the iron footboard.

He stared at it for a long time, giving no indication of his feelings.

Finally, she said, "I don't think it's that good. Something seems to be missing."

He cocked his head. "I like the concept. The tightrope at the Folies-Bergères. But the contrast between the radiance of the tightrope-walker and the venality of the crowd isn't quite sharp enough to give it the impact it needs."

"Maybe the problem is I just don't feel that way anymore."

"No, the problem is you've been under a great deal of strain and pressure, and you've momentarily lost your muse." He kept staring at it.

Mason felt awful, as if she'd failed him. The other three paintings and now this one. They clearly did nothing for him.

"I'll knuckle under and do better," she promised.

For a long time, he continued to look at the canvas without speaking. Finally, he said, "No, I think we'd better give up this part of the scheme. For one thing, it's too dangerous. With Duval watching as closely as he is, there's no way we shall be able to fake a shipment from the States. So we'll just go with the eighteen masterpieces we have. They'll be enough."

Still, he seemed preoccupied with the disappointing painting. It was as if he was searching it for something and was troubled that he couldn't find it. She saw in his eyes a kind of veiled disbelief that was so upsetting to her she walked over and snatched the painting away.

"Let me get rid of this thing."

When she came back into the room, Richard seemed himself again. She turned off the light and slipped into bed beside him. He kissed her forehead tenderly. But as she settled in against his body, she couldn't help but feel that his disappointment over the painting had jarred something elemental between them.

She tried to fall asleep, to recapture the feeling of being protected in his arms. But she was very much aware that he wasn't relaxed. He was still propped against the pillows, one arm behind his head. She could feel his distance.

That night, Richard had another nightmare. He awoke as he had before, crying out in terror. Mason turned on the light and held him close, but it took much longer this time for him to escape the clutches of the dream.

"Won't you tell me about it?" she pleaded. "I want to help you. I can't stand to see you in such pain."

He shook his head. "It's impossible to describe. Just a jumble. Nothing that makes any sense. I suppose it's just something I have to live with."

"But if you try to talk about it, it might help—"

"What might help," he said, laying his head back in exhaustion, "is a successful conclusion to this thing we're trying to do. I can't explain it, but I have a feeling that my entire life has been pushing me toward this single mission. And I can't help but feel that once we've completed it, and Mason has become to the world what she *must* become, the nightmares will simply go away."

He finally went back to sleep, but Mason didn't. Something about the way he'd referred to her in the third person . . . on the heels of his obvious letdown over the painting . . .

It was unsettling.

Chapter 20

The following week, the celebrated art collector Edouard André and his society-portraitist wife, Nélie Jacquemart, hosted a Sunday afternoon gathering at their townhouse on the Boulevard Haussmann. The occasion was a rare Parisian lecture by the art world's most respected figure, Alberto Lugini of Rome's Academy of Fine Arts. Though the topic of Signore Lugini's talk was undisclosed, it was suspected that he was about to take a position on the subject that had so vehemently divided the Parisian critical establishment over the past few months—the rising posthumous fame of the American Impressionist Mason Caldwell. It was expected that, like his colleagues, Lugini would denounce the phenomenon, but no one could be sure, and the uncertainty created an air of titillating speculation.

The days since returning from Auvers had been lonely and depressing for Mason. With no painting to be done and Lisette occupied with the new season at the circus, she had little to do but dwell on the investigation to which Duval was no doubt assiduously devoting himself. At the same time, Richard had been absorbed by the financial difficulties of the pavilion, which was now entering its final stages of construction. They'd made love once since returning to Paris, but the spark and magic of the Louvre was missing. And while polite and attentive, his overall manner had changed toward her in a way she couldn't quite put her finger on. It seemed to her that her inability to do the kind of painting he wanted her to do had affected his feelings for her. But since he was adamant that she not continue, there was no way of exonerating herself in his eyes. He insisted it was too dangerous for her to paint, but she knew it was more than that. She sensed that he no longer *wanted* her to paint.

But on that fateful Sunday afternoon, he was in a buoyant mood as he chatted amiably on the short drive from the Opéra district to the Jacquemart-André mansion. Their carriage entered a driveway that took them out of the hustle of the city and curved around the unimpressive façade that faced Boulevard Haussmann to pull up in front of a pair of stone lions flanking a colonnaded entrance. High, curved walls on either side cut it off from the other row mansions so effectively that Mason had the feeling she was at a country estate.

A majordomo met their coach and ushered them into a vestibule that led into a grand reception hall crowded with the cultural elite of the Belle Époque. Mason's eyes picked out the art dealers Flaconier, Durand-Ruel, Georges Petite, and Theo van Gogh. Emma, Duchess of Wimsley, was there, and so were the painters Renoir, Fantin-Latour, and Caillebotte. As Richard began handshaking his way into the crowd, Mason caught a glimpse of Hank Thompson on the far side of the room speaking to Dimitri Orlaf, perhaps warning the Russian to keep his distance. But when he saw that Richard had arrived, he abruptly left the man and headed his way.

Mason felt awkward and conspicuous in the crowd and she had to be careful, since everyone here was speaking French and it would be easy for her to slip. Gradually, she made her way to an area of the room where she heard English being spoken. Here, Mary Cassatt, the painter from Pennsylvania, introduced her to Mrs. Potter Palmer—"Call me Bertha, dear"—the wife of a Chicago millionaire and an avid art collector who'd goaded her husband into making some of the first significant purchases of Impressionist paintings for their family collection. "We're sticking around straight through July fourteenth," she told Mason as she fanned herself. "They tell us they're convoying in boatloads of fireworks from as far away as Russia and Hong Kong for the biggest bang-up Bastille Day ever seen by man. That's a show we want to see."

Momentarily, there was a rustle in the rear of the crowd and word spread that it was time for the lecture to begin. Richard found Mason and led her to the music room, where rows of straight-backed chairs had been set up for the hundred or so guests. They sat down and waited until the rest of the assembly had found seats. Finally, heads turned and a round of applause greeted an authoritative white-haired man with a Van Dyck beard who walked to the front of the room and stepped to the podium.

"Ladies and gentlemen," he began in Italian-accented French, "my name is Alberto Lugini and I have come here today to talk to you about Mason Caldwell, who represents the most significant artistic event in our lifetimes."

There was a gasp in the audience. No one, even those foolish enough to believe the Italian might endorse the controversial American, had expected anything so unequivocal and definitive. Except maybe one person.

Richard reached over and took Mason's hand, giving it a squeeze.

For the next forty minutes, Professor Lugini spoke of how the eighteen Caldwell masterpieces amalgamated, fused, and underscored everything that was important in Impressionism and Neo-Impressionism, and at the same time, carried painting into an entirely new realm. "This new realm is not what the artist sees with his eyes, but what he—or she—feels in his heart. This is something startlingly new, something revolutionary. It is the art of the coming twentieth century and the millennium that will follow it."

He poured himself a glass of water and took a sip. The room was so quiet the guests could hear him swallow.

"But the career of this remarkable young woman is even more important than this. She embodies a radical new idea of the very nature and identity of the artist in human society. She is not a sycophant who serves the aristocracy, the church, or the court. She is not a craftsman who cares about selling her work or pleasing her critics. She is a purist, outsider, rebel, true to her inner self and sacred calling at the expense of everything else, even her life."

He continued along this line with great power and conviction, spellbinding his audience. As he spoke, Mason glanced at Richard and noticed that he was mouthing the words even before Lugini voiced them. Richard had written the script and Lugini was merely an actor giving a performance.

"And perhaps most important of all," the professor continued, "Mason Caldwell is a new kind of cultural figure who is more alive in death than she was in life. She is a true Joan of Art, an inspiration for the downtrodden, a martyr whose suffering is frozen in time. She is a painter whose saga grips us so emotionally and whose vision stirs us so profoundly that we cannot see her paintings except through our own tears . . ."

Hearing these words, Mason felt as if she were at her own funeral. Except that it wasn't *her* funeral. This apparition he was talking about bore no relation to her whatsoever. She was a figment of the imagination of the man mouthing the words next to her.

The next thing she knew, everyone was giving the speaker a standing ovation.

As the applause died down, Mason and Richard joined the crowd as it moved out into the reception hall. When they passed the critic Morrel, he was speaking with two of the reporters who'd also been at the Falconier Gallery that first afternoon. "Yes, it is true that I had some initial misgivings regarding the Caldwell métier," he was explaining. "But when I went back and studied the paintings more carefully, I immediately recognized their merit. I was her earliest critical supporter."

Mason stared after him in disbelief.

Lugini was now making his way toward them through the crowd as people kept trying to stop him and shake his hand. But he ignored them all and headed directly for Richard. His face, which had looked so benign and sincere during his lecture, was now red with suppressed rage. "Our business is completed," he said to Richard in a low, tight voice. "From this day forward I want nothing to do with you, or this monstrosity you've shoved down my throat. I hope you rot in hell for what you've made me do."

Then he turned and stormed from the chamber. As more well-wishers attempted to stop him for a word or slap him on the back, he angrily sloughed them off.

Watching the humiliated man leaving the scene of his crime, Mason said, "He didn't mean a word he said."

"Maybe not, but what's important is that he said it."

She turned to Richard. "What did you do to get him to compromise himself so completely? And please don't tell me you know where some bodies are buried."

"But it's true. The man has some terrible things to hide. I wouldn't waste my time feeling sorry for a man like that."

"You blackmailed him?"

"I wouldn't use that word. I merely offered an exchange. My silence about his adventures with *les jeune filles,* and I do mean *jeune,* for his speech here today."

Mason's stomach was in knots. "Richard, this is *wrong.*"

"Wrong? Putting some pressure on a dirty old man is wrong? Look what we've done here today for the legacy of Mason Caldwell."

"*I'm* Mason Caldwell."

"Of course you are." He bent to kiss her cheek. While his

lips were close to her ear, he added, "But please don't say that so loudly. You're going to have to get used to not saying that anymore. Even in private."

He said this in a kindly way, but she felt as if he'd just slapped her in the face.

He was distracted by something across the room. "Hank is waving at me. I'd better go see what he wants. Will you be all right here for a moment?"

She watched him leave. She felt so dejected that she didn't know what to do with herself. She just stood there on the fringes of the excitedly chatting crowd, feeling wobbly on her feet.

Just then she heard a voice behind her.

"Amy, how lovely to see you again."

She turned to find Emma standing beside her. "Oh, hello."

Emma's face was glowing. "Isn't he something?"

"Lugini?"

"Good heavens no, my dear. Our Richard. We two are the only ones in this room who know who *really* wrote that historic little speech."

Mason felt the heat in her face. She didn't relish having this reminder of what had just happened. She wished the woman would go away.

But Emma didn't seem to notice. "I have to hand it to him. He really pulled it off. Every time I underestimate him, he proves me wrong. But Lugini of all people! What a coup!"

Tartly, Mason said, "I don't know what you mean."

Emma laughed delightedly. "My darling girl, you needn't pretend with me. I know Richard pulled the strings on that old man as if he were a marionette." She paused, peering at Mason, for the first time noting her discomfiture. "But perhaps it's just a bit much for a sheltered Boston girl?"

It was a deliberate barb and Mason knew it. To get back at her, she said, "I think I should tell you, your grace, that I've definitely decided *not* to sell you my sister's paintings."

Emma only smiled. "Oh, don't concern yourself. I gave up

on that idea some weeks ago. I know Richard well enough to know he'll move heaven and earth to make certain they go to Hank. In any case, as luck would have it, I've just found my own Caldwell painting."

This stopped Mason cold. "What are you talking about?"

"I've found an independent dealer who is going to sell me the most marvelous Caldwell you've ever seen."

"That's impossible!"

"Why is it impossible? Your sister lived and worked here for five years. Surely she must have turned out more than eighteen paintings."

"It's a forgery."

"I assure you, it's not. Wait until you see it. You'll have no doubts."

Mason didn't know what to say. She'd never considered the possibility that she might become so famous that she would be the target of forgers.

Piece by piece, she was being robbed of her self. She couldn't paint. Critics who'd never met her were giving her a personality she'd never had. Crooks were counterfeiting her pictures and signing her name.

At the end of this process, Mason would be gone. And she would *be* Amy.

Chapter 21

Eager to be away from all this, Mason waded into the crowd and looked for Richard. It took her some time to find him in the winter garden in conversation with Hank, Mary Cassatt, and Mrs. Potter Palmer. She watched him for a moment. He was the center of attention, lionized by the others and very much enjoying his triumph.

As she waited for a lull in the conversation that would allow her to approach, she glanced about the room and her gaze once again came to rest on Count Orlaf. He was standing by himself in an unguarded moment, glaring at Richard with naked hatred in his eyes. It was quickly masked as he was joined by several other guests. But that momentary glimpse of his hatred added to the sense of menace that seemed to be closing in on all sides.

Mason had to get out of there. She went to Richard and stood beside him, waiting to be noticed. When he did, she told him, "I'd like to leave."

He stepped away from the conversation and said in a lowered tone, "Hank has arranged for us to go to dinner with Mrs. Palmer. He thinks she may write a bank draft to cover all the rest of the expenses for the pavilion."

"I have a headache. I really want to go back to the hotel."

"This could be really important."

"You go ahead with them. It's a pretty day and we're not far away. I'll just walk back."

"Are you certain you don't mind?"

"It's fine."

"I'll drop in after dinner and see how you're feeling."

"No, don't bother. I think I'll just go to bed early."

She walked down Boulevard Haussmann, past the long, geometrical rows of Second Empire façades, only vaguely aware of the afternoon sun dancing in the leaves of the almond trees like an effect in a Monet landscape. The Sunday strollers passed by in a blur. By the time she reached her hotel, her head was splitting. She couldn't eat, so she went to bed early, but she couldn't sleeep.

What was happening to her? She wasn't sure. Much of it was the terrifying sense of self-loss that had come upon her at the lecture. But it was more than that. For the first time, she was seized by doubt about what they were doing and how they were doing it.

For her part, Mason was finding that this fame she'd once thought would be the solution to all her problems was not just cheap and unsatisfying, but a kind of ludicrous joke. Witness the scene today. Moreover, she no longer wanted to—or had the ability to, apparently—paint the kind of pictures the world wanted to see from her. Her love for Richard had filled that hole and healed her need to express that particular vision. She'd be happy to just walk away from all this and spend the rest of her life with him, painting whatever struck her fancy.

But Richard needed this. His nightmares told her that he was being driven by dark forces he didn't even understand to create, celebrate, and immortalize a false Mason. A Mason he now seemed to be distancing from her—the real Mason— in his mind. And in this quest, he was willing to go to any lengths, no matter how immoral.

She finally drifted off around three in the morning, feeling exhausted and emotionally spent.

She awoke late and ordered breakfast in her room. When it came with the usual morning edition of *Le Figaro*, she noticed the front-page story detailing Signore Lugini's crowning of Mason Caldwell as the "martyred messiah of art." The lead had picked up on his poignant assertion that "we cannot see her paintings except through our own tears." Beside the main article was a secondary story about an incident yesterday afternoon on the fairgrounds when a display of three Caldwell paintings had elicited an unusually emotional response from the crowd. A succession of viewers had broken down in front of them, sobbing uncontrollably. It was an outpouring of grief, the paper noted, the likes of which had not been seen in the city since the death of Victor Hugo.

There was a knock on the door, Richard's distinctive double rap. She went downstairs and let him in. He took in her nightgown and said, "You're not up?"

"No, I didn't sleep well last night."

"I hope you're not still feeling sorry for Lugini."

"I don't feel good about it. But I'm actually more upset about something else. Your old friend Emma told me yesterday that she's just acquired a Mason Caldwell painting on her own."

Something flicked in Richard's eyes that looked more like annoyance than surprise. "A forgery, naturally."

"*Of course* it's a forgery!"

He shrugged. "Well, you have to expect that. When an artist becomes famous, forgers will follow. Anyway, she may just have been trying to get your goat. That's her style."

"And what's this about displaying paintings on the fairgrounds? You didn't tell me you were going to do that."

"I thought it best to keep them in the public eye."

"I find it rather strange that on the same day Lugini coins that poignant phrase about seeing the paintings through tears, people start breaking into sobs in front of them and there just happen to be reporters there to witness the spectacle."

He gave her a mysterious smile.

"You paid them to break into tears, didn't you?"

"Only the first few. After that, they started doing it on their own. It was contagious. They're still doing it. I was just there. It's something to behold, to see how deeply the paintings touch people."

"They only did that because you manipulated them into it!"

"I may have started the ball rolling, but go see for yourself. Hundreds of people have filed through already this morning, and their tears couldn't be more genuine. They're moved to tears, and the process is cleansing for them."

"But it's false."

"It's not false. It's real. Mason's paintings are—"

"Dammit! Will you stop talking about me as if I'm dead?"

He chuckled. "Believe me, I know you're very much alive."

She sighed her exasperation. "Richard, may I ask you a question?"

"Of course."

"The other night in Auvers, after you had the nightmare, you said that something was pushing you to do all this. What exactly did you mean?"

"Did I say that? I don't recall. I often talk a lot of rot after one of my screaming terrors."

"Why is this so important to you?"

He gave her a blank look. "This?"

"What we're doing. Why do you need to do it so much that it's become your calling in life?"

He still looked puzzled. "You know why. Because I love art. I love these paintings and the story behind them. I want to share that love with the world."

"But why *these* paintings? What is it in them that speaks to you, that made you bond with them so instantly?"

He was peering at her as if he'd never thought about it,

didn't even want to think about it. "Why don't you tell me what's really bothering you?"

"Richard, I'm losing myself! Everything that makes me who I am is slipping away. Now you've even planted records that say I'm Amy. I couldn't even prove in a court of law that I'm *not* Amy Caldwell."

He came to her and took her shoulders in his hands. "Look, you've been through a lot, and you're tired. Duval's bluff has you spooked. The trouble you've had painting probably rests uneasily on your mind. No doubt, you saw that bastard Orlaf at the reception, lurking in the wings. And granted, it's a sobering experience to see your sister canonized in the pantheon of art."

"My sister?"

He smiled. "You know what I mean. But what we're creating here for posterity is important. It's the most important thing we will ever do in our lives. We're like the people who saved the scrolls containing the Greek myths from the Turks. It doesn't matter whether Zeus and Hera really lived. What matters is what their stories give to the world. Hope. Succor. Wisdom. Inspiration."

He kissed her then. It took a while for her to soften in his arms. But when she finally did, he picked her up and carried her to the bedroom and made love to her. It was wonderful, and she desperately needed it. But when he dressed and returned to his hotel room, she was left with a curious uncertainty about who he loved the most: the flesh and blood woman, or the legend he'd just so passionately defended.

The next morning brought another blow.

The front page of *Le Figaro* had yet another story about Mason Caldwell. This one gleefully reported that England's illustrious Duchess of Wimsley had acquired not one but *three* previously unknown paintings by the tragic young artist. They'd been authenticated by several experts, were declared to be of the highest quality, and through the generosity of the new owner, were being displayed today in the window of the Durand-Ruel Gallery on Rue Peletier.

In a fury, Mason dressed and stormed the five blocks to the gallery. Already, there was a considerable crowd in front of the window. Several young women were sobbing. Mason pushed her way to the front. What she saw nearly knocked her to the ground.

Positioned in the window were three size-thirty canvases, each depicting a scene very much in her style. Each contained an exquisitely beautiful model who might have been Lisette, surrounded by a foreboding, hostile universe. Each study was imaginatively conceived and stylishly rendered. They were so much like what she'd done in the past that she had to search her memory to make certain she hadn't painted them and merely forgotten.

But no, they were masterful counterfeits.

She felt utterly violated, as if she'd just been raped.

She remembered the morning when this unique vision had hit her. How satisfying it was. How it seemed to encompass everything she'd experienced and everything she'd felt up to that moment. Of the weeks and months and years she'd worked to reach that point.

And though she'd now outgrown this vision, the pain she felt on seeing it usurped by some faceless criminal who'd signed her name in the corner was excruciating.

Only another artist could know what she now felt, standing in that spot, looking in that window.

She slowly trudged away, through the sobbing crowd of shopgirls and back to her hotel. The sensation she'd had before of losing herself, of being swept away by malevolent forces, engulfed her completely.

But this wasn't to be the end of her bad day. For when Mason retrieved her key at the desk, the clerk said, "There's a gentleman waiting for you over there."

She turned to see Inspector Duval sitting in a chair by the fireplace at the far end of the lobby.

Oh, God, not now.

But what could she do?

She tried to assume a pleasant look and walked over to him. As she approached, he stood and eyed her shrewdly.

"I have some news for you," he said, "regarding the death of your sister. Join me, please." He indicated the chair beside him and they sat down. "We have finally had a breakthrough."

"Breakthrough?"

He seemed to be examining her, judging her reaction to this. "Yes," he said, with agonizing deliberation, "a witness has finally turned up."

"What kind of witness?"

"One who was passing the bridge shortly before the alleged suicide."

"I don't understand. Who would be—?"

"A *latier*. What you call a milkman. And what he had to say was most interesting."

She braced herself. "What did he say?"

"That there were two women on the bridge that night. Two women conversing."

"How could he possibly remember such a thing?"

"It was the foulest night in our city that he'd ever seen. His wife hadn't wanted him to go out, but he insisted because his customers would expect their milk in the morning."

"But that was four months ago!"

"Even so, they were the only people he saw during his entire route. He remembers thinking they were crazy, standing in the wind and rain at the edge of the Pont de l'Alma."

"And what does the milkman's testimony lead you to conclude, Inspector?" she had to ask.

"I am not prepared to say at this juncture. But I *will* say that it confirms all of my worst suspicions about this case and gives me the confidence to assure you, Mademoiselle, that an arrest will soon be forthcoming."

Chapter 22

Mason rushed across the street to the Grand Hotel, but Richard wasn't there; he wasn't at the adjoining Café de la Paix, where he often took his meals, or at the pavilion on the fairgrounds. It wasn't until hours later that, on a hunch, she found him at her old apartment near Place du Tertre on the top of the Montmartre butte, which he'd been converting into a sort of shrine.

It was the first time she'd been there since the night of her plunge into the Seine. The garden was the same, as was the sloping vineyard out back. But the building itself had been sandblasted to sparkling cleanliness. The floors and stairwell had been freshly varnished and the walls painted a warm terra cotta hue. As she stepped into her old living space on the upper floor, she found that it had been stripped of the charming French country accoutrements with which she'd decorated it. In their place were the spartan furnishings more befitting Richard's concept of a noble, starving artist: a ragged, narrow cot, a single commode, a broken mirror, all worn with age.

And in the midst of this museum-like memorial, Richard sat at a shabby table with pen in hand, surrounded by stacks of stationery. On the floor below were several pieces of wadded-up pages that he'd discarded. His sleeves were rolled up and he was deep in concentration.

"Duval is on to us," she told him.

He looked up at her as if still in the grip of his other thought. "I beg your pardon?"

She told him about her meeting with the inspector, her voice seething with agitation. "He knows there was another woman on the bridge. He's figured out that the other woman jumped and it was her body that was found and mistaken for me."

"We have nothing to worry about," he assured her calmly.

"How can you say that?" she cried. "He says an arrest is imminent."

"He can't arrest you for something he can never prove."

"What if he finds out who the other woman was?"

"He can't."

"And why the hell not?"

"Because I've taken care of that. I've erased every record of her existence."

"But . . . We don't even know who she is."

He put the pen in the inkwell. "I'm a detective. It just took a little digging. Her name was Blanche Cauvereaux. Born in Bordeaux, 1860. A widow, no children, no living family. Her birth record and baptismal certificate are back at the hotel, if you'd care to see them."

Mason remembered the brief glimpse she'd had of the woman's face. Saw her being carried to her death by the current. Now she had a name. Blanche. "My God," she breathed. "That woman was a human being. And now you've made her disappear as if she'd never existed. Is there no end to what you'll do to get what you want?"

"What I want is to protect you. Is that so wrong? Had I left that to chance, Duval wouldn't be making idle threats. He'd have you in irons."

The truth of what he said took the wind out of her. She sat down on the cot she'd never slept in. Even so, what an unconscionable thing to do. Kill the woman a second time. And

for what? To protect a fraudulent fame that was bringing her
nothing but misery.

Be careful what you wish for. . . .

"I assume you read about the forgeries," he was saying.

Vacantly, she told him, "I went to see them."

"I still wouldn't worry about them either. They can't be
much."

"They're so good they almost knocked me off my feet."

"There are a number of excellent Rembrandt fakes floating about. Hasn't hurt his reputation one bit. You aren't
upset, are you?"

"When I first saw them, I thought it was the end of the
world. But after Duval's threat . . . after discovering we've
erased a woman's life . . . it seems a small matter."

"You've had a bad day. You'll feel better tomorrow." He
turned back to whatever he'd been writing. "Let me just finish this and we'll talk some more."

Lost in her own thoughts, Mason just sat there, feeling
battered and lifeless. But eventually, the scratching sound of
Richard's pen began to grate on her nerves. She rose from the
bed and picked up one of the wadded pieces of paper on the
floor. When she uncrumpled it, she saw some bold lines of
handwriting that had been crossed out. It was the start of a
letter dated March 6, 1885, and the greeting read, "Dear
Amy."

"What is *this*?"

He glanced up at her. "I was just going to tell you. I've had
a marvelous idea. Just a minute." He finished a line, then put
the pen down and turned to her. "It struck me when I saw
how emotional people were becoming in front of the paintings that there was another way we could make the story
come alive. It occurred to me that we could communicate her
character and give substance to her voice in a series of intimate letters to her sister. I've made arrangements with a pub-
lisher. If we can dash off a few dozen or so in the next week,

he'll have a deluxe volume printed and in the bookshops in time for the pavilion opening. A rush job to be sure, but it can be done. I only wish I'd thought of it sooner."

Mason couldn't quite believe what she was hearing. "And you're going to be the *author* of these letters?"

"There's no time to procrastinate over this, so I just jumped right in."

She stepped to the desk and picked up one of the finished letters. Her eyes scanned the page. In bravely poetic language, this fictional Mason was describing to her confidant sister how she'd starved herself to buy paints to finish her self-portrait, only to have it ridiculed by every dealer. She spoke of how she would struggle on despite this, how she would do whatever it took to stay alive, keep painting, fulfill the vision that burned in her consciousness like a fever. Even if she had to sell herself on the streets to do it.

Slowly, she looked up at him. "So now you've turned me into a whore."

The word made him flinch. More firmly, he said, "The fact that Mason was willing to sell herself for what she believed in hardly makes her a whore. It ennobles her spirit. Shows that she was capable of such devotion, she would pay any price to protect what she loved most."

She shook her head. "You just can't stop yourself, can you?"

"Don't you understand the beauty of this? With these letters, we can make Mason really come alive to people—even people who might never see her paintings."

The page dropped from Mason's fingers. "This is too much. I can't take any more."

"I think these letters could be vital to what we're trying to do."

"It has to stop. All of it."

"It can't stop. It's too important."

She rubbed her face with her hands. "Richard, I'm not

blaming you. I'm as responsible for all this as you are. More so. I wanted the fame, the immortality."

"And you can have it."

"But I don't want it. I thought I did. But I hate it. I hate everything about it! The whole process has stripped me of my identity. For days I've been terrified of this, fighting to hang on to what was left of me. But what I didn't realize until this very moment is that I no longer care. About any of it. I don't want to hang on to that Mason, the Mason who needed to paint those pictures, who had that vision. Because of what you gave me, I've grown beyond that, and I don't want to go back. What I want is you. I want to stop this sick charade before it destroys us both. I don't care what happens to the paintings or how many people forge them. I don't care if I have to go to jail. I just want it to end."

He stood up. "It can't."

"Why can't it? Let's just get out of here. Leave the country and never come back. We could have so much together, if you'd just give us a chance."

"I told you, I can't."

"Don't you love me, just a little?"

"You know I love you."

"No, Richard. You don't love me. You love . . . this." She motioned around the room.

"That's ridiculous."

"Is it? Then why have you never once asked me anything about myself? You don't give a damn about the real me, or why I painted those paintings. All you care about is the vision of Mason Caldwell that *you* created and *you* control. It has nothing to do with me."

Richard's face tightened. He started to speak but couldn't find the words. Balling his hand into a fist, he ground out, "I've told you. I think this is a crucial story that must be—"

"But why, Richard? Why is it so important to you? What is it in your past that's driving you to such extremes? What is the thing you won't tell me that's haunting your sleep? What was it that turned you into an art thief?"

"My past has nothing to do with this."

"It has *everything* to do with it. Don't you see that this whole campaign of yours is just one more theft?"

"Who am I stealing from?"

"From me, Richard. From *me*. But I don't even care about *that* anymore. I care about you. You're scaring me. You've let this consume your life—*become* your life—to the point that there's nothing else left. You've created this monster who doesn't even bear the slightest resemblance to me. And your devotion to it is destroying you. Richard, I love you. I want to help you. You can trust me. Won't you please tell me what it is that's making you do this?"

He was looking at her with tortured eyes. His fist was clenched so tightly, it was turning white. "I never wanted to take anything from you. I only wanted to give to you. I wanted to give Mason to the world."

"Are you going to tell me or not?"

"There's nothing to tell."

"All right, then, I'm going to find out on my own." She turned to leave.

"Where are you going?" He sounded angry now.

She swung on him. "Richard, you're in the grip of something you don't understand, won't face, and can't control. I'm going to find *some* way to set you free from it."

As she moved to leave, he grabbed her. "I said *where* do you think you're going?"

"Wherever I have to."

Mason pulled herself free.

"You're not going anywhere." He blocked the path to the door.

Determined, she sidestepped him and made a lunge for the table. She grabbed a stack of letters and flung them out the open window. When he charged after them, she seized the opportunity to flee from the room and down the stairs to make her escape into the streets of Montmartre.

Mason stepped off the omnibus in the fashionable Chaillot district. Up ahead, she could see the grandiose Renaissance mansion of the Duchess of Galliera, which took up the entire block. This was normally one of the most sedate corners of upper-crust Paris, but as Mason approached the entrance of the stately building, she was met by incongruous sounds of raucous laughter and bawdy-house singing coming from every open window.

Percival, the same uniformed attendant who'd heralded Emma's arrival at Mason's door, answered her knock. "Miss Caldwell," he greeted over the noise, "how lovely to see you once again. We weren't expecting you."

"I'm sorry to have come at a bad time, but I really have to see the duchess."

"Not in the least. You're always welcome here. Her grace is just hosting a little reception."

She looked past him into the connecting rooms, which were filled with the customary crowd of society swells intermingled with rough men wearing western frontier garb and Colt Peacemakers strapped to their hips. Some drank Dom Perignon from the bottle, passing it around like a canteen at the campfire. A sudden gunshot rang out, followed by a crescendo of laughter.

"Oh dear," Percival clicked. "They *are* an energetic bunch. I do hope no one has been injured."

"Reception for what?" she asked.

"Why, Colonel Cody, naturally. If you'd care to wait a moment, I shall find her grace and inform her that you're here."

As he left her, a group of men standing at a side bar began to sing at the top of their lungs:

Buffalo Bill, Buffalo Bill
Never missed and never will;

Always aims and shoots to kill,
And the comp'ny pays his
Buffalo Bill."

They dissolved into guffaws, slapping each other on the back in drunken appreciation.

Just then, Emma entered the foyer with a flourish and a smile. "Why, Amy, what a pleasant surprise." She looked lovelier than ever, positively glowing in her apricot-colored day gown, perfectly relaxed in the tumult of the bacchanal. "We're entertaining some of your countrymen here today. The guest of honor is yet to arrive, but I can introduce you to some of his saddle-mates."

"I need to talk to you," Mason said urgently.

"My dear, you look positively white. Come, let's find a quiet spot, if that's possible, and you may tell me what I can do for you."

Emma led her through the crowded front salon. Some of the ambassadors from the Wild West ogled Mason as she passed, and one of them let out a low whistle. Emma laughed. "Aren't they colorful?"

As they bypassed an even more crowded room, more sounds of gunshots erupted from it. Some rowdy was using the crystal ornaments of the chandelier for target practice.

"What is the Duchess of Galliera going to think when she gets back and sees the damage?" Mason asked.

Emma waved a dismissive hand. "She won't mind the damage. She'll be ecstatic to discover that I scored this social coup for her. All the crowned heads of Europe are competing for the honor of hosting Buffalo Bill and his troupe on their tour of the Continent. She'll only be livid that she missed all the excitement."

They found a settee in a relatively tranquil corner of a cavernous room. "This is about as quiet as it's going to get today, I'm afraid. Now, you wanted to speak with me."

Stiffly, Mason said, "I want you to tell me everything you know about Richard's past."

"My goodness! That's rather an odd thing to come here and ask."

"I need to know. And I need to know now."

"I'm afraid you've braved this rambunctious spectacle for nothing. You see . . . Richard and I have an understanding. We don't talk about one another's past."

The sound of breaking glass reached them from the room beyond. Then cries of "Fight! Fight!"

Mason tried to ignore it. "He's in deep trouble. I need you to tell me what you know so I can help him get out of it."

"Trouble? I find that difficult to believe. He was positively ebullient the other day over his triumph with Signore Lugini."

"He's drowning in a delusion. I've got to find out why."

"A delusion?"

"Emma, before he was a Pinkerton man, he was a thief. . . ."

Emma's polite façade cracked a little. "He told you about that?"

"Then you knew."

"Yes," Emma confirmed cautiously, "I knew."

"What can you tell me about those days?"

Somewhat testily, Emma responded, "If you're on such close terms with him, why don't you simply ask him yourself?"

"I've tried, but he won't say anything. It's as if there's something there he can't look at, yet which still has a power over him. I was hoping you could tell me what that might be."

"I'm afraid you're wasting your time. With him *and* with me."

Some of the more boisterous of the cowboys began to flood into the room, laughing and shouting, waving their pistols in the air.

Raising her voice to be heard, Mason said, "If you tell me, there's something I can give you in return."

"Oh? And what might that be?"

"Information that can save you a great deal of embarrassment."

More people stumbled in the room. One of the frontiersmen was about to give his society companions a demonstration of the western fast draw.

But Emma was now completely focused on Mason. "And what sort of information would do that?"

"I've seen the paintings you bought and I can tell you with absolute certainty that they're forgeries."

Emma's violet eyes narrowed. "How can you possibly say such a thing with absolute certainty?"

Mason hesitated a moment. She hadn't come for this purpose. But forced to the precipice, she decided to take the leap. There was no other way.

"I can say with absolute certainty that those pictures were not painted by Mason Caldwell because I *am* Mason Caldwell."

The blood drained from Emma's face. "That's . . . ridiculous. You're her sister."

"I have no sister."

The woman's shock was palpable. For a moment, Mason feared she might faint. "You can't be!"

"I assure you, I am."

Emma's eyes were flitting in her sockets. "Mason Caldwell committed suicide. Why would you say such a thing?"

"There was no suicide. It was another woman's body they found. It was all a big mistake, which, I'm sorry to say, I compounded."

Emma closed her eyes. A shudder passed through her. Then, without warning, she shot to her feet, wrenched the Colt .45 from the holster of the nearest cowboy, pointed it at Mason, and pulled the trigger.

Chapter 23

Mason dove for the floor as the bullet whizzed over her head and shattered the vase of flowers behind her. In a daze of disbelief, she looked up and saw Emma cock the hammer and pull the trigger again. Mason vaulted aside as the bullet splintered the parquet floor behind her.

Taking the attack as a cue for more fun, several of the other showmen drew their pistols and fired them at the ceiling, whooping and hollering like drovers hurrahing Dodge City. Mason bounded to her feet and hurtled past Emma in a race for the door. Charging after her, Emma fired a third time. The bullet nicked the doorway as Mason flew through it.

Mason ran across the courtyard. At the front gate, she paused and looked back. Emma was standing at the front portico holding the gun outstretched. She fired three more times in rapid succession. But Mason was well out of range.

She whirled and ran down the street in no particular direction. She just had to get as far away as possible. There was no time to think, no time to reason out what had just happened.

She was running so furiously that she collided with a group of men coming out of a restaurant. They called after her as she barreled past, but she ignored them, pushing on. She was vaguely aware that she was presenting a spectacle of herself and that people were staring at her. But she couldn't stop.

Finally, after a mile or more of zigzagging through the streets to lose anyone who might be in pursuit, she darted down a side street and fell back against the stone wall. She was gasping for air, her lungs on fire, exhausted and terrified.

The woman was trying to kill her!

For God's sake, why?

It made no sense. For some reason, finding out that Mason Caldwell was alive threatened her to the point that she'd become unhinged. The scene was so unexpected and bizarre that Mason still couldn't believe it had actually transpired. The only thing she was sure of was that it was the act of a pathologically jealous woman.

A terrible thought seized her. If Emma was jealous and unbalanced enough to try and kill her in front of a hundred witnesses, might she not also be crazed enough to try and kill the real object of her rage: Richard? And if, after their fight earlier that day, he was shrewd enough to figure out where Mason had gone, wouldn't he also likely try to intercept her?

He could have been right behind me!

In her mind's eye, she saw him walking into the Galliera estate, saw Emma aiming the gun at him, and saw her pull the trigger.

She couldn't very well go back. Emma would shoot her on sight. She could try to cut Richard off, but she had no way of knowing if he was coming at all, or from which direction. And what if Emma, having gone this far, decided to go after him? She could go to the Grand Hotel and be waiting for him there. She felt the threat to him on all sides. She was utterly powerless to negate it.

Unless . . .

By telling Emma who she really was, Mason had crossed a bridge from which there was no turning back.

Suddenly, she knew what she had to do.

The situation had spiraled lethally out of control. She had to put a stop to it. All of it.

She went out onto the boulevard and hailed a passing fiacre. The driver gave her a peculiar look, making her aware of her harried state. She told him, "Take me to the Prefecture of Police as fast as you can. It's a matter of life and death."

He cracked his whip and they were off. Racing through the streets, Mason could only think that Richard, mindless of the peril, was in mortal danger. "Faster, please," she urged the driver.

After what seemed hours, the cab pulled up to the gate of the Prefecture of Police. "Wait here. I'll pay you when I come out," she called as she jumped down and made for the courtyard. The driver yelled after her, but she ignored him, rushing past two guards to enter the building. They stepped forward to stop her, but she said, "I have an appointment with Inspector Duval. Don't you dare get in my way!"

The authority in her voice caused them to step back to let her pass. She charged up the two flights of stairs, her heart in her throat. But as she entered the antechamber of his office and approached his secretary, she discovered that he wasn't in.

"Where is he?" she demanded.

"He's upstairs in a meeting in the Salle Voltaire," the man told her.

"I must see him. It's urgent."

"That's impossible. He's meeting with the Minister of Justice. There is no way you could interrupt such a conference."

Mason turned on her heels, ran up to the third floor, and entered a wide hallway. Down at the end of the corridor, she saw a set of double doors below an ornate fleur-de-lis. Two guards stood sentry. She headed straight for them. Without slowing down or offering explanation, she barged through the doors before the guards knew what was happening.

She entered a large, high-ceilinged chamber so grandiose that it seemed to reflect all the power and glory of France itself. Duval was sitting at a Louis XIV table opposite a bureaucrat with thinning red hair. As they looked at her in surprise, she heard a voice behind her scream, "*Arrêt!*"

She rushed toward Duval, and the voice cried, "Stop or I'll shoot!"

But Duval was on his feet with his hand raised. "No, wait."

Mason half fell into his arms. "Inspector, you've got to help me! I'm here to confess everything."

Duval glanced at the minister and said, "Monsieur, I am afraid I must deal with this. It could be vital to the case we were just discussing."

He told the two guards to escort her to his interrogation room. "I'll join you there presently," he promised.

"You must come at once," she insisted. "Please. There's no time to waste. A life is at stake."

The guards took her to a small room that was just off the antechamber of Duval's office. Its single window stared across the courtyard at Notre Dame. When he didn't come at once, she stood up to pace. Where was he? What was he doing? Didn't she say it was urgent?

At last the door opened and the inspector entered. He sat down at the sparse table and said, "Very well, Mademoiselle, I am ready for you."

"I want to confess everything. I'm sick of the lies."

His eyes widened. "Very well, Mademoiselle."

"I'm not going to do anything until you send some men to find Richard Garrett. His life is in danger." In a jumble, Mason told him what had just happened, adding, "If he's not already at the Galliera, he might be at the Montmartre apartment or his suite at the Grand Hotel. Wherever he is, you have to find him and protect him from that crazy woman."

After a brief hesitation, Duval rose, stepped to the door, opened it, and gave the order to the guard outside. When she heard the words, she finally felt her body relax. Thank God.

Now at least Richard would be safe. The relief was so great that she collapsed into the other chair beside the table.

Duval returned and sat across from her. "Now, start from the beginning."

There was no stopping now. "Mason Caldwell did not commit suicide."

"I am most aware of that. But tell me, how do you know it?"

"Because I *am* Mason Caldwell."

He jerked back as if he'd just accidentally put his hand on a hot stove. He was clearly surprised. But how could he be? He'd been hinting that he knew the truth. He had proof that there'd been another woman on the bridge.

In an icy voice, he ordered, "Tell me everything you know."

She did. Standing and pacing before him, she related the entire story from the beginning. Every detail, no matter how bad it made her look.

He listened, sitting ramrod straight in his seat, never once taking his eyes from her as she paced. When she was finally finished, she dropped into the chair, feeling drained but relieved.

He remained seated for what seemed an interminable time, deep in thought. Then he stood and slowly crossed the room to stand before the window, looking down onto the courtyard below.

After another eternity of silence, he finally spoke, "I am going to have to take you into custody."

"I assumed that. I'm ready to face the consequences for what I've done."

"I am afraid," he said, still staring out the window, "that the consequences you are going to face are not at all what you expect."

"I don't care what you do to me. Just so it's over and Richard's safe."

"Unfortunately, I cannot accept your story, as detailed as it is and as persuasively as you have presented it."

She looked up at him in alarm. "But it's true. Every word."

"It can't be true, Mademoiselle. You cannot possibly be Mason Caldwell, because Mason Caldwell's body was found washed up on the bank of the Seine."

"I told you. That was Blanche Cauvereaux."

"And yet you say there are no records of such a woman."

"No, I told you. Richard had them removed."

"How very convenient."

"Stop playing games with me, Inspector. I told you. I didn't kill myself."

"That much is true. Mason Caldwell did not kill herself."

"Finally!"

"She was murdered."

The word seemed to reverberate in the hushed aftermath. "Murdered!"

"Foully murdered by the woman she was seen with earlier that evening. The woman who hurled her from the bridge."

Mason shot to her feet. "No, no. You have it all wrong. I told you—"

"The murderess whose identity I have painstakingly deduced over these past few weeks. Whose name will be released to the press this very day."

"This is insane! What murderess?"

"Come here. I will show you." He gestured her toward the window. "Look. She is arriving now."

Through the window, she could see that a police wagon had pulled into the courtyard. Two officers were hauling a handcuffed prisoner from its interior.

A woman.

Fighting them heatedly.

Sunlight glinting off her golden hair.

Lisette.

Chapter 24

Mason paced the confined width of her cell, back and forth in a continuous path that led nowhere. Frantic with worry for Richard and Lisette. Confused by the barrage of impossible developments. Terrified of where this monster of her own making might be carrying them all.

After her catastrophic meeting with Duval, he'd summoned a jailer who'd handcuffed her, gagged her, and placed a black hood over her head before forcing her down four flights of stairs to an empty basement dungeon. There she'd been freed of her restraints and prodded into a cell with padded walls. As he supervised her incarceration, Duval told her, "This is a holding pen for criminally insane patients on their way to the Charenton asylum. You are the only detainee we have down here at the moment. You might as well save your breath, because the guards will assume everything you say is the babbling of a lunatic."

As he left, she begged him, "You can't do this, Duval. Even if you have to do it to me, please don't do it to Lisette. It's unspeakable. She never harmed a creature in her life."

The door clanged shut behind him.

A day and a night had passed since then. She'd worn herself out banging on the door, trying to get the guards to listen to her. She tried to assuage her anxiety by telling herself Duval couldn't possibly keep this up. What did he intend to do, anyway? Throw her in Charenton for the rest of her life? Try Lisette for her murder? It was beyond belief! He would have to come to his senses and see the absurdity of his scenario. Once he talked to Lisette and she corroborated the story, he would realize his mistake and set them both free.

But in her bleaker moments, she thought of the injustice that was so prevalent in the French legal system. It was a major theme in their literature. Half the novels of Balzac, Jean Valjean in *Les Miserables*, Edmond Dantes in *The Count of Monte Cristo*. Hadn't they'd put Dantes in prison and thrown away the key?

Another day and night passed. A jailer sat on a stool outside her cell for much of the day. She demanded to see the inspector, begged to be taken to Lisette, asked the whereabouts of Richard. But all of it fell on deaf ears. He sat reading his newspaper, as oblivious to her as if she were a raving madwoman.

If only she knew what was going on. She'd asked for news and he'd ignored her. He'd always snuck in a bottle of wine and nipped at it during the day. By late afternoon, he was usually asleep. She heard him snoring and got an idea. Looking through the slot in the bottom of the door through which a plate of food was shoved twice a day, she could see that he'd put the newspaper he was reading on the floor beside him. Her hand was slender, and if she could just reach it a little farther . . . just a little more . . . It was really tight now, but pushing just a tiny bit harder, she was able to get the end of it between her two extended fingers and pull it through the slot and into the cell.

Its front page headlines screamed the scandalous story. The American painter Mason Caldwell had not committed suicide: She'd been murdered . . . her best friend, the popular circus performer Lisette Ladoux, had been arrested and refused to comment on her guilt or innocence . . . a speedy trial date had been set . . . Inspector Honoré Duval, who had miraculously solved the crime, was the hero of the hour . . .

the scandal had explosively boosted the interest in the artist's paintings and in her upcoming retrospective on the Champ de Mars . . . the victim's sister, broken by the revelation of the murder, had gone into strict seclusion . . .

The paper dropped from her hands and she curled up in a ball on the floor, feeling queasy. It was even worse than she'd imagined. Lisette awaiting trial for murder, too loyal to Mason to defend herself. Strict seclusion . . . Did that mean they intended to keep Mason locked up forever? And Richard . . . Where was he? What was happening to him? Had they reached him in time? It was all such a mess.

What she would give to go back to the Pont de l'Alma and start all over.

Finally, Mason had worn herself out and fell into a deep sleep. But she was awakened by the sound of a metallic clang, then voices, one of them Duval's. She had no idea what time it was, but it had to be some early hour of the morning.

Momentarily, she heard the key turn in her lock. The door squealed open. The light hit her eyes, briefly blinding her. "What's happening?" she asked groggily.

"We are going for a ride," the inspector answered calmly.

A ride? "Charenton?" Mason asked.

"It is best if you not ask questions, Mademoiselle."

"Inspector, you're an intelligent man. You must know the sequence of events you've outlined can't possibly be true. You must know I'm telling the truth."

"I *do* know you're telling the truth," he said gently.

Her heart lifted. "Then . . . you're here to set me free?"

"Sadly, no."

No?

He gestured to the two men accompanying him and they lifted her to her feet. All three men wore rain slickers. One of the guards asked, "Should we use the hood, sir?"

"Never mind. There will be no one about at this hour."

They took her upstairs and out into the courtyard where a

tempest was raging. The wind was howling and the rain pouring in a way it hadn't since the night this had all started for her. A coach and three mounted men were waiting. She had no coat and was soaked to the skin before Duval could hustle her into the coach.

It pulled out of the courtyard, crossed the Pont Notre Dame to the Right Bank, and headed off into the night, the mounted escort leading the way. As they rumbled along, the inspector seemed to have lapsed into deep contemplation. After a moment, she said to him, bitterly, "You're a policeman. Your business is uncovering the truth. How can you turn your back on it now?"

Mason detected an air of melancholy. "It brings me no pleasure."

"Then, why?"

"Because I have no choice."

She stared at him. "No choice?"

"They are going to make me a member of the Legion of Honor."

Mason didn't understand. "For what?"

"For solving the murder of the decade."

"But you know now there *was* no murder."

"Yes, but by the time you told me who you really were, it was too late. I had already convinced the Minister of Justice, the Minister of Culture, and President Carnot himself that a dastardly murder had been committed. Your friend Mademoiselle Ladoux had already been arrested. The press conference announcing my 'spectacular detective work' had already been scheduled. I was the man of the hour. So you see, I could hardly step forward at that point and admit that I had been a complete fool. It would ruin my career, my reputation . . . my very life."

"You'd let an innocent woman die for a crime she didn't commit to save your *career?*"

He shifted uncomfortably. "I do not expect you to understand. But a man's reputation is everything. Without it, he is nothing—a pariah. Even if I could weather the storm, my wife could not. She comes from an old and proud family, and she married a mere policeman. The promise of the Legion of Honor will exonerate her—and me—in her family's eyes. Besides, her health is poor, and the scandal would kill her. So you see, my course is clear."

"So it came down to a choice between your wife or Lisette."

He averted his eyes. The silence was deafening.

Suddenly she *did* understand. "It's not just Lisette, is it? You won't be able to get a night's sleep as long as anyone who knows the truth is still around. It's not enough for Mason's 'sister' to be in seclusion or off in a mental institution. After all, she might escape. She might convince someone of the truth. No, that's much too risky."

"Regrettably, true."

At that moment the coach pulled up at its destination and Duval opened the door. "I am afraid the only logical end for Amy is that she join her sister in Mother Seine."

As they helped her out into the wind and rain, Mason realized they were at the Pont de l'Alma. It was only then that Mason came face-to-face with the full, impossible dimensions of her dilemma, of what was about to happen to her.

And the unavoidable truth was that she'd done it all to herself. Her desire for success, and her willingness to take shortcuts to achieve it, had been the cause of a mountain of misery.

She turned to Duval with tears in her eyes. "What about Richard?"

"It is too late to worry about him, child."

Of course. They couldn't very well have let him live either.

"It's time to make your peace with God. I promise you won't suffer. One quick blow and it will be over. You will simply go to sleep in the Seine's embrace."

A poetic ending. Distraught over her sister's murder, Amy goes to the scene of the crime and hurls herself into the river.

Kindly, he added, "You can go to your rest knowing you will not be forgotten. Your paintings will be confiscated and become part of the national heritage of France. The campaign you started to make yourself immortal will go on as before. The retrospective at the Exposition will open on schedule under my personal charge with all the amenities you would have wanted. You see, my child, the greater the name of Mason Caldwell, the better it is for France, and the better it is for the reputation of the man who solved her murder."

She looked down at the raging water below, barely discernable in the storm. It had been her fate all along to die in its depths. If only it had happened that first time, months ago. If she'd known what would come of it, she'd never have fought to stay alive.

She stepped to the rail, no longer minding her fate. She deserved it.

But before she closed her eyes, she looked about her and thought of the symmetry of the situation. This bridge. This night. A night so eerily like that other. And even . . . another pedestrian suddenly appearing from the darkness behind the coach, coming her way.

But this time, it wasn't a suicidal woman. It was just some man crossing the bridge. He was slumped over, weaving from side to side. A drunk on his way home from some late night revel. As he came closer, she could hear him slurring the words of a popular cabaret song.

They would have to wait until he passed. The policemen raised their collars so he wouldn't see their faces.

"*Bonsoir, messieurs,*" he greeted them.

"*Bonsoir,*" they called back curtly.

But he didn't continue on. He stopped before them and gave them a drunken smile.

For a moment, she thought she was seeing a ghost.

Richard!

Chapter 25

Richard staggered toward the nearest of Duval's men. "Such a miserable night. Might you spare a few sous for a poor unfortunate with no dry spot to lay his head?"

"Be gone, impudent lout," the man retorted.

He reeled closer to the man, taking his arm beseechingly. "Have pity, kind sir."

The man shook him off. "If you're not out of my sight at once, I will give you my boot."

"Your boot? Ah . . . You mean like this?" Richard leapt into the air and kicked the man squarely in the face, sending him tumbling against the rail with such force that he fell careening backward over the edge and into the water below.

This had happened in less than half a minute, which was all the time the second man needed to unholster and aim his revolver. But in a lightning draw, Richard had produced his own pistol from his belt and, without aiming, fired a shot that hit his opponent's hand, sending his gun clattering along the bridge.

With that, the inspector reached for his own weapon, but Richard was on him like a panther. In one swift movement, he grabbed him by the arm and leg, raised him above his head, and flung him into the Seine, kicking and screaming and flailing his arms as he dropped.

Mason rushed to him. "I thought you were dead."

"Far from it. Are you all right?"

She went into his arms. "I am now."

He held her for a moment, then said, "We have to go."

As he turned, he spotted the three men on horses in the distance: Duval's escort, which had stopped and was standing vigil several leagues from the bridge. One of them had a rifle. In the pouring rain, they couldn't see exactly what had happened; for all they knew, it had been Inspector Duval who'd fired the shot at his intended victim. But their rapt attention indicated a suspicion that something might be going wrong.

Richard quickly unfastened the horse from the coach, leapt onto its back, grabbed Mason by the arm, and hoisted her up behind him. The escort, seeing this, moved into position to block the fugitives' easy escape. They could cross the bridge to the Left Bank, but that would make them an easy target for the marksman with the rifle. Instead, Richard kicked his heels and charged the three men head-on. They hadn't expected this, nor had their horses. Two of them reared, unbalancing their riders. The third Richard kicked off his mount as he barreled past.

They galloped down the cobblestone street. As Mason tightened her arms around his waist, the sound of gunfire echoed behind them. She felt a sting in her upper back, as if she'd been hit by a flying stone chipped off a building. It hurt, but only for a moment, and then the pain went away. She clutched Richard with all her might as the rain beat against them.

"They came and arrested me," he called back to her. "But I managed to get away from them in the crowded lobby."

"It's my fault. I went to Duval. I had no idea he would do anything like this. I was so confused. I just wanted to make it go away and start over."

"It's not your fault. Nothing is your fault."

She felt so strange. Her head was spinning. She wasn't even cold anymore. "I told Emma who I really am and she tried to kill me. So I went to Duval and told him, and *he* tried to kill me. Can this really be happening?" Her voice sounded to her as if it were coming from a tunnel far away.

"Don't think about it now. Just hold on."

Her body felt numb and weak. It was all she could do to force out the words. "We have to help Lisette."

"They have her locked up in Santé Prison. We'll have to figure out some way to get her out."

"How did you . . . find me?" Again, it was an effort to wring out the words. Every ounce of energy had drained from her body. It was taking everything she had just to hang on.

"I had a feeling they were going to try something like this. I've been keeping watch outside the Prefecture, waiting. As your coach left the Cité, I jumped onto the back of it. Luckily, the escort went ahead, so they didn't see me."

Mason felt herself losing her grip on him. She began to slip to the side.

"What's the matter?" he called back.

She couldn't answer. He reached around to keep her steady and slowed the animal. When he withdrew his hand, it was covered in blood. "Christ, you've been hit!"

Abruptly, he reined in the horse beneath a gaslight, slid down, and pulled her off into his arms. As he held her, he tore the back of her dress and examined the wound. Propping her against him, he yanked his shirt from out of his trousers and ripped it to make a bandage, which he pressed to her back with great pressure to stop the bleeding.

"I've got to get you to a doctor, but I have to keep the pressure on this wound with my hand or it will start bleeding again. So we're going to have to do this on foot. I'm going to carry you. All you have to do is just try to stay awake. Can you do that?"

Mason tried to speak, to reassure him, but she was so lightheaded she couldn't tell if she'd spoken aloud.

As he trotted through the empty streets, holding her as gently as he could, the deluge continuing to pelt against them, she could hear his words coming to her as if from a dream. "What have I done to you? This is all my fault. How can I ever make it up to you? You've got to hang on so I can find a way. Do you understand, Mason?"

The tenderness with which he said her name buoyed her. She rested her cheek on his chest, feeling his strength pour into her. It wasn't long before they stopped. She heard his fist pounding on a wooden door. It was met by silence. He pounded harder, not stopping. Finally, she heard the door crack open and Richard's voice, demanding, "I need the doctor at once."

"The doctor is asleep," a female voice complained. "Do you have any idea what time it is?"

Still holding her as gently as possible, he pushed his way through the door and past the startled maid. "Wake him up."

After that, there was a series of sensations. Arguing voices. A bright light shining in her eyes. The feel of a hard wood table against her stomach and face. Richard's tormented voice saying, "She has to pull through, doctor. Do you understand? She's—got—to—pull—through!"

Then the smell of alcohol, a burning pain in her back, the sound of a metallic object hitting a tin pan. The pain dissolved into darkness.

That darkness was broken by Richard's voice. "I've got to get you to a place of safety. Duval's had time to be fished out of the river by now and to have wired every precinct in the city regarding our escape. They'll be paying visits on everyone we ever knew and watching all the roads. The doctor says it's dangerous for you to be moved, but I have to get you out of here. Can you hang on, just a little while longer?"

It took all her strength to nod her head.

She felt him pick her up again, and soon after that he laid her onto an upholstered surface, wrapping several blankets around her. "I'm commandeering the doctor's carriage," he told her. "I'll take it as gently as I can."

The concern in his voice was cradling, giving her a sense of safety and well-being. It was warm inside the blankets, cozy and dry. But where was he taking her? He was going relatively slowly for her sake, and the pleasant sensation continued. In the distance she could hear the hum of his deep voice, talking to her, gentling her. She couldn't hear what he was saying, but it didn't matter.

Time passed. She had no idea how much. Then the carriage pulled to a tentative halt.

"Good evening, *messieurs*," Richard's voice said.

"Get down," a male voice responded. "We have to search your vehicle."

"Working on a night like this?" Richard commented dryly. "How barbaric."

"Stand aside and hold your tongue."

A moment passed before she heard a thud, then sounds of scuffling and cries of alarm. Then gunshots. *Dear God, please keep him safe!*

Someone jumped back into the driver's seat, a whip cracked, and the horse raced off, this time at a full gallop. Now she was bouncing up and down in the carriage and the pain shot through her. Before long, she felt the damp stickiness and realized she was bleeding once again.

After several minutes of racing through the night at breakneck speed, the carriage pulled to a sudden halt. She felt herself being lifted in powerful arms, smelled Richard's sweet breath against her cheek as he said, "You're bleeding again. I've got to keep the pressure on the wound, so I'll carry you the rest of the way. It shouldn't be that far now. Just stay with me."

He held her to him, keeping pressure on the wound as he ran. Soon his breath became labored. She felt herself slipping away again.

As if sensing this, his voice sought to steady her.

"I don't know why I've treated you the way I have. I've never understood myself, or why I do the things I do. But I do know this. I love you, Mason. I've never loved anyone else. I can't lose you. I can't. I won't! Hold on, my love. Hold on . . . hold on . . . hold on . . ."

Finally, he stopped, dropping to his knees as he held her, breathing so heavily she feared his heart might burst. "We made it," he panted.

"Where . . . ?"

"Belleville."

He waited for his breathing to slow, then stood again, taking her with him. Another banging on the door. More voices. Being laid on a soft bed. Her bandage being changed. Someone putting cognac to her lips. Her clothes being removed with infinite care. A warm cloth sponging her.

Then it was dark again. She felt someone sit beside her on the bed, felt his warm lips on her cheek. Then he shifted, lying down beside her, to tenderly pull her into his arms.

Blackness claimed her again. But every time she awoke in the night she was aware of him beside her, holding her close.

Chapter 26

Darkness.
A comfortable, sheltered void.

Then, somewhere in the distance, a flickering light.

Voices.

"I can't stand to see her in such agony," Richard's voice said.

And another older, more grave, French voice replied, "She has a very high fever. Infection, I'm afraid. I will leave a tincture. Be sure she swallows a spoonful every few hours."

Her mouth was being opened . . . The bitter liquid slid down her throat. "It will help her sleep more peacefully."

She sank into darkness once again. And then she was looking down on herself, as if watching a play. The blue sky of a summer day in Massachusetts. A carefree young girl running barefoot through the woods. Coming home across a covered bridge to the gabled white house with green shutters. Padding upstairs, going into her mother's studio. Her mother painting by the window. Curling up at her feet, feeling loved and secure, happily watching as she squeezed the pigment from the tube onto the palette, mixing it with the other colors to find just the right shade. Applying it to the canvas with loving strokes. Her soft voice explaining to the child what she was doing.

"Why do you paint all the time, Mama?"

"To try and add a little beauty to this cruel world."

Suddenly, she was pulled out of her contented viewpoint, and she felt her body convulse in pain. The light came from above again, and the voices. But this time another male voice, vaguely familiar. The gangster Dargelos?

"I must get you both out of here. The flics are making a search of every building in Belleville. I need to move you to a better hiding place."

Richard's voice again, "I'm not sure she can take it. I'm afraid we're losing her."

"I can't protect you here. There is another place, just two blocks away, that has a sealed-off room in the attic. They'll never find you there."

Silence. Then Richard's voice again, closer to her ear, "We're going to have to pick you up and move you somewhere. It may hurt, but it won't be for long, I promise you. And then I'll see to it that nothing hurts you ever again. Hold on for me, love, just a little longer."

She felt her body being lifted, and then a sudden sharp pain. She heard her own cry. But the pain quickly disappeared and she felt herself slip back into that netherworld where nothing hurt.

She saw herself again, as if looking at someone else, but she was different now—older, grown. Stepping off the ship in Le Havre. Hungry for success and fame. Determined to do whatever it took, to prevail at any cost. Grabbing the opportunity—the temptation—that was laid before her and . . . bringing herself and those she loved most in the world to a desperate situation. Lisette facing the guillotine, Richard a hunted criminal, herself slowly dying in a Belleville attic from a policeman's bullet.

How did it happen? What was the demon in her that had brought them to this point? Where had it all begun?

Once again, she felt herself being pulled away from this vantage point. The light pierced her eyes, and she heard Richard's voice, "I think she's coming around."

She opened her eyes and saw a haggard face with a week's growth of beard and bleary eyes.

The other voice, the doctor's, said, "Her fever is broken. I think she might make it, after all. See if you can get some soup down her."

She tried to speak but couldn't. She felt the cold spoon against her dry, cracked lips, and then the warm liquid, salty, like chicken broth. She swallowed and it filled her with a delicious sense of nourishment. But she instantly sank back again into the blackness.

She saw herself standing with her mother before the rolling Pennsylvania countryside. The peaceful green pasture broken, scarred by rows upon rows of white headstones that seemed to stretch to infinity. Hearing, as her mother described it, the shriek of horses, the thunder of cannons, the cries of the wounded and dying. The tears in her mother's eyes as she sank to her knees, grabbed two handfuls of dirt, and rubbed them on her face, sobbing now. "This is what we've done. This is the stain on our family name. This is the legacy you must overcome."

Mason jerked awake.

It took her a moment to realize where she was. A low, sloped ceiling. An iron bed. No windows. A single kerosene lamp. She had no idea whether it was day or night.

Then she felt something wet and warm. Richard, looking much as he had before, was bathing her legs with a sponge. Slowly, weakly, she reached for him, murmuring his name. He turned to look at her. When he saw that she was conscious, tears welled in his eyes.

He dropped the sponge and came to her, holding her head in his hands, kissing her face with deep emotion, like a condemned man saved from execution.

"Richard," she repeated. It was barely a whisper.

"Don't try to talk, love. You've been through hell. You'll have to take things slowly."

"Something . . . something's happened. I need . . . to tell you . . ."

"It'll have to wait. There'll be plenty of time later. I was so afraid I was going to lose you."

He was clutching her tightly, as if afraid to let her go.

She stroked his head. "Everything's going to be all right now," she told him. "Just hold me."

He eased down beside her and held her, careful not to hurt her. His lips in her hair, he spoke softly, wretchedly, "When I thought I was going to lose you, I didn't want to go on. I never thought anyone could be as important to me as you've become. I find that I love you so much, it actually scares me. And when I think that it was because of me that you've had to suffer so—" His voice broke.

"No," she told him haltingly, "it was me . . . I did it . . . That's what's happened. I see that now. That's what I want . . . need . . . to tell you."

He held her tighter, stroking her hair. "It doesn't matter now. Nothing matters except that you're going to be all right. We won't talk of anything yet. We're just going to make you well. That's the only thing that means anything to me now."

He continued to gently kiss her face, holding her, whispering to her, until his voice became a pleasant hum and she slept.

But she was soon awakened by a sense of intense agitation. "I'm so sorry," he said in the dark. "It's just another of these damned nightmares. I probably shouldn't be sleeping here."

She reached for him. "No, I want you here."

"It usually only happens once a week or so. I don't think I'll have it again for a while."

"I wish I could fix it so you'd never have to have them again," she murmured.

Several days passed. As Mason was able to take more nourishment, her strength began to return. She was still sore and stiff, but her head had never seemed so clear. Richard continued to spoon feed her even after she was able to do so herself. It seemed to give him pleasure to care for her. He'd found a volume of Balzac, and at night he read to her, lying beside her, his voice soothing. Those were the times she loved most. No one read to her since her mother had, so long ago.

Several times, Dargelos came to the door in a distraught manner, but Richard always took him downstairs to talk. He didn't want any outside news to intrude on her progress. Every time she tried to ask about Lisette, he assured her, "There will be plenty of time for that later."

Finally, she was able to get up and tentatively walk around the room. When she'd passed this threshold, she decided it was finally time to tell Richard everything the perspective of her near-death had taught her about herself.

"I have to talk to you," she said.

He looked at her, gauging her progress. "Are you quite certain you feel strong enough?"

"It will make me feel better."

"Very well."

"You see, you're not the only one haunted by a nightmare. I have one of my own. I think I'm finally ready to tell you about it. It's something I buried when I came to France and thought I'd never look at again. No one knows about it, not even Lisette. But I've found you can't really bury these things. You think you can. You try to. But in the end, it comes back to haunt you. And it keeps haunting you until you face it. In a way, it's the story of what made me an artist."

He grabbed hold of a chair and brought it over with its back facing the bed, then straddled it, crossing his arms over the seat back. "I'd like to hear it."

She swallowed nervously. "They say there's a moment in every artist's life—usually when they're young—that twists them and gives them a terrible need—a void, if you will— that only the act of creation can fill. Most artists can't even identify what that moment is. It can be something monumental or something so incidental they barely remember it. I didn't want to look at it before, because it was too painful. But while I've been lying here, slipping in and out of consciousness, I couldn't help but see that it's the seed from which my whole life has grown."

She looked up at him to find him listening with rapt attention. "Your mother?"

"It happened when I was about thirteen. My father was away on business. I'd come home from school and as I entered the house, I saw that a bag had been packed. Mother was in a somber mood, the way she often was after my father had been harping on her about spending all her time painting. She told me we were going on a trip. When I asked where, she said she wanted to show me something important, something my father would never show me, but something I had to see with my own eyes. So we boarded the train and took the journey to Pennsylvania. To the site of what had been, the year before I was born, the Battle of Gettysburg. Do you know what that is?"

"The Civil War battle. The turning point of the war."

"It was so strange. As far as I knew, she'd never been there before, but she'd studied and memorized every aspect of the campaign and knew every inch of the battlefield. She took me on a tour of the place, describing the slaughter so vividly that I could see the minié balls in the air, smell the burning flesh, hear the agonized cries of men falling in the wake of Pickett's charge."

A light came to his eyes. "Your self-portrait. That's Gettysburg in the background."

"Yes. I didn't understand why she was showing me all this. Until, standing on the crest of Seminary Ridge, she suddenly fell to her knees, rubbed its hallowed soil on her face, and told me that everything we were, every piece of bread we ate, every article of clothing on our backs was the fruit of this holocaust. It was *our* doing. We had profited from its blood. And there wasn't enough water in all the world to wash its stain from our souls."

Chapter 27

Mason paused, wincing at the pain in her voice. Richard reached over and took her hand. "That's a terrible thing to say to a child."

"What she said was true."

"How can it be true?"

"First, I have to tell you I'm not from Boston. I made that up. My family is from a town called Greenfield, on the other side of the state."

"That's why there were no records in Boston."

"I wanted to leave my past behind when I came here, so I invented a new history for myself. Greenfield is my home. When my parents married in 1860, my father owned a small foundry there. He'd been trained as a gunsmith, and he had a knack for anything mechanical. He was also, as it turned out, a natural businessman. Anyway, when the war broke out the next year, like all the other small manufacturers in New England, he retooled his shop to serve the war effort. But he did it with much more imagination and skill than his competitors, and by 1862, the Amos Caldwell Foundry was the largest arms manufacturer in the state of Massachusetts. By the next year, it was the largest in all of New England. Almost all the munitions used at Gettysburg, Chickamauga, and The Wilderness by the Union side were made by us."

"Someone had to do it."

"Don't get me wrong. At first, we were proud of it, even bragged about it. They gave my father testimonial dinners. President Lincoln presented him with a medal and letter of commendation. Our neighbors wanted him to run for congress. And this good will continued for years after the war. But then, gradually, things began to change. Jealous of my father's fortune, some of the good people of Greenfield began to whisper that it had been made off the blood of a generation of young Americans. When I was ten, a Boston newspaper published a long article detailing the genesis of the Caldwell family fortune, listing battles we'd supplied and the number of men who'd died in them. Shortly after that, a crazed woman who'd lost all three of her sons at Shiloh stopped my father on the street and publicly accused him of being a murderer."

His hand tightened on hers. "That's hardly fair."

"Fair or not, incidents like that started happening with terrifying regularity. Both my parents took it hard. My father outwardly steeled himself and tried to appear unconcerned, but inwardly, it ate him up. He grew bitter and took to drinking. My mother, who'd always been sensitive and artistic by nature, was nearly destroyed by it. She was dropped by all her so-called friends. She became ashamed of all the advantages we had and began to hide away from the world behind the gates of our estate. She became fatalistic. Over and over again, as I was growing up, she cautioned to me, 'Your father wanted to be the most important manufacturer in New England, and he succeeded. Be careful what you wish for, Mason.'

"The next ten years of our lives were especially difficult. My mother finally made me fully aware of our family stain when I was thirteen and she took me to Gettysburg. She wanted me to understand the cloud I'd been born under and to realize that, in some way, my life had to make amends for it. Over the next seven years, there were more articles, the whispering campaign grew louder, and the guilt continued to grow in our eyes. My mother withdrew even deeper into her painting, and my father grew even more angry about what had happened to him. He began to resent her withdrawal from him. They had horrible fights. He kept insisting her painting was making her unhappy, but he didn't realize it was a gift, the only thing keeping her sane."

"She passed on that gift to you."

"Yes, she taught me how to draw and work in oils, and I loved it from the beginning. I loved the peace, the two of us painting quietly together. The escape from a world that now seemed ugly and threatening to me. She took me to art shows in Boston and New York, to show me what others were doing. It was wonderful. But every time we returned, there was a price to be paid. My father accused her of trying to make me just like her. He told me painting would only make me miserable, the way it had my mother. Meanwhile, he was drinking more and more, trying to escape in *his* way. I had no friends at all. The family had become pariahs in the community. Our house was falling apart from lack of care—not because we didn't have the money, but because we didn't notice. We were like something out of a Hawthorne novel. When I look back on it, it doesn't even seem real."

"What happened to your parents?" he asked.

"My mother died when I was eighteen. I blamed my father for it. I said the most awful things imaginable. I told him he'd murdered her, just as he'd murdered all those boys in Gettysburg. I actually said that. It crushed him, because I think he loved me in his own way. But all I could see was that he was the cause of all our misery. I just lashed out at him. After that, I left. My mother had a small family inheritance, which she willed me. I took it and went to Boston, then to Paris. When I left the country, my father tried to give me money, but I spit on it. I told him I wouldn't touch his blood money. That was the last time I ever spoke to him. Several years ago, I received a letter from his attorney notifying me that he'd gone down in a shipwreck off the coast of Brazil."

"The *Simon Bolivar*?"

"How did you know?"

"It was a major disaster. The agency was hired by a consortium of insurance companies to investigate it. A great many people lost their lives."

"My father was one of them."

"So you never resolved your differences."

"No. I can see now how unfair it was to blame him for the brutality of war. After all, he was only serving his country, trying to end slavery. It was an injustice to make him a scapegoat because he was so successful at doing what had to be done. I wish I'd told him so. But at the time, I didn't even want to. The only thing I wanted was to vindicate my mother, erase the family stain, and clear the Caldwell name. I thought if I could find a way to take all the horror of my past and transform it into something beautiful, the world would love me for it. In time, I found that vision. But it wasn't enough. Because, as satisfying as it was to me personally, the rest of the world didn't give a damn about it."

He smiled gently. "They do now."

"Yes, they do. Because I lied and cheated and took a shortcut to immortality. That's what I'm trying to tell you with my story. My upbringing left me with a gaping hole in my soul. The need to fill that hole brought me to Paris, drove me to create, and made me grab for fame when the chance was presented. But the truth I've come to realize is that, even though I'm now more famous than I ever dreamed of being, it hasn't filled the hole. It's only made me feel more empty and lost, and driven us to where we are now. What I now know is, the things I always thought would fill the hole only made it larger. The only thing that will fill it is my love for you. The rest is meaningless. That's what I've learned. That's what all this has taught me."

"You might feel that way now, but—"

"No, I got that dark need out of my system by doing those paintings, and now they mean nothing to me. They're just something I passed through. I'm on the other side of them. You, Richard, have healed me of the need to express that vision, and of the need for the world's approval. Loving you has taught me that it's not the receiving of love that fills the hole inside us, it's the *giving* of love."

As she spoke, his eyes grew misty. He rose, then stretched out on the bed beside her, cradling her in his arms. "Thank you," he said hoarsely. "For trusting me, for sharing all this with me, for loving me. It makes me feel so close to you I can't express it."

She nestled into his warmth, feeling her heart swell with love for him as he gently stroked her hair. "I've told you my nightmare. Won't you tell me about yours?"

His hand stopped momentarily. Then he pulled her closer and kissed the top of her head. "You're tired," he told her. "You need sleep. I don't want you to think about anything else. Just let me take care of you for now."

By the end of the week, Mason was feeling almost fully recovered and even a bit restless at being cooped up in their hiding place. One morning, the door suddenly swung open and a pack of dogs flooded the room, leaping on the bed, licking her face, competing for her attention. Lisette's dogs! She'd asked about them earlier and learned that Dargelos had rescued them after Lisette's arrest and had put them up in a Belleville apartment where Hugo had been taking care of them.

Richard was right behind them. "The sun is shining and you need some air. I thought it might do us both some good to give these fellows a walk."

The sight of them was a painful reminder of Lisette's dilemma, for which she was responsible. She took them in her arms, one at a time, and tenderly hugged them to her, thinking how Lisette must be worrying about them.

They strolled down Rue de Belleville and took a side street to a park that held a sweeping view of Paris from the east. As the dogs romped around the green space, Mason and Richard looked out at the Pantheon, the gleaming gold dome of Les Invalides, and far in the distance, the peak of the Eiffel Tower, below which preparations for the opening of the Mason Caldwell retrospective were proceeding under the personal scrutiny of Inspector Honoré Duval.

Holding Richard's hand, Mason asked, "What are we going to do about Lisette?"

"I'm not sure what we *can* do."

"I can't live with myself if something happens to her."

"I don't know her very well, but she strikes me as a clever girl. She'll figure out some way to protect herself. She knows the truth and she'll tell it before going to the guillotine."

"You don't know her at all. Lisette is like all the frustrating, surprising, and magnificent things about France all rolled up into one person. She'll keep you at arm's length for an agonizingly long time, but once she accepts you, it's with a loyalty and fierce devotion that we're not capable of. I'm telling you she *will* go to the guillotine without saying a word in her defense if she thinks that word will betray me in any way."

"Sadly, I fear you may be right in that assessment."

"There must be someone *we* can go to with the truth. The press. The American ambassador. Someone who will listen and help us."

"Duval will figure that out right away. If we try, he'll cut us off. We'll be shot on sight. Getting us has to be his chief imperative right now."

"What about Juno? Can he do anything?"

"God knows he's going to try. The man is half out of his mind with grief. It's all I can do to talk him out of doing something foolish."

"Does he know who I really am?"

"No, I thought it best not to complicate the situation. He thinks you're Amy and you're being hunted because you know Lisette's innocent and could ruin their case against her."

She shook her head in despair. "There must be something. I won't accept the fact that there's nothing we can do."

"As dire as her situation is, she still has a trial to go through, so she's not in any immediate danger of the guillotine. In the meantime, we have something else we have to do."

She couldn't think what he meant. "What's that?"

"The French government has confiscated the paintings."

"I know that."

"We have to get them back."

"The paintings?"

"They stole them from us, we'll steal them back."

She couldn't believe what she was hearing. "You still want those paintings?"

"Of course I do."

She dropped his hand. "Did you hear nothing I said? I don't care about the paintings anymore. They can do whatever they want with them as far as I'm concerned."

"I heard you and I understand. But you must understand that, no matter how you might feel about them at this moment, those eighteen paintings constitute a masterpiece of art. They're a part of you, they're important to the world, and they're a responsibility we can't walk away from."

"Even if that were true, how do you think you're going to accomplish such a feat?"

"We have Dargelos and the Parisian underworld as our allies. We can find a way."

"All right, say we pull off the impossible and steal the paintings back. Then what?"

"We get them to Hank, who'll arrange to take them secretly back to America."

She stared at him in disbelief. After all that had happened to them, the one thing dominating his thoughts was *still* the paintings.

A wave of frustration swept through her. For a long time,

she didn't speak. Then she took a breath and said, "Richard, I've told you the secret of my past. Won't you tell me yours?"

She saw the flash of something unreadable in his eyes, but all he said was, "There's really nothing to tell."

"You can tell me about the nightmares. I know they're eating you up. You're having them more often. You try to hide them from me, but I know they're getting worse. Can't you try and confide in me?"

She saw the reflexive hardening of his features. Then he took both her hands in his. "I know you're trying to help. But you have to understand, I really don't want to talk about them. It's not that I want to hide things from you. It's just that it's bad enough to have to live through them at night without having to rehash them during the day. They go away. I turn on the light, I give you a hug, and I'm fine. So please, Mason, don't make it hard for me. *Please.* If you want to help me, let's mobilize ourselves toward getting your paintings where they belong."

He was shutting the door in her face again. But this time, it didn't anger her. She felt, instead, a rush of sympathy and love for him. It only made it more apparent that he was a prisoner of this thing in his past, and it was up to her to set him free.

Chapter 28

Lisette's trial began in the first week of June. The bravely silent defendant, dressed in somber convict grey, was led out of the prison wagon surrounded by a phalanx of police guards and marched into the Palais de Justice, past a swarm of reporters and a jeering multitude of spectators.

In an unprecedented move, the courtroom had been sealed off from all but court officials, and its proceedings were to take place in strict secrecy. This extreme measure was necessary, the Sûreté had argued, because of the intense passion the case had engendered in the mob, and because the defendant's links to organized crime made some sort of rescue attempt a strong possibility.

Despite the blackout, the press unanimously speculated that the trial would not be lengthy. As the editorial writer of *Le Figaro* saw it, there were three significant elements to the prosecution's case.

First, the testimony of some twelve witnesses who'd seen the defendant with the victim at the Café Tambourine on the night of her death, plying her with drink and even, according to the waiter who served them, insisting that she consume the highly debilitating liqueur absinthe.

Second, and most damning, the testimony of a milkman who'd seen the defendant standing with the deceased on the

Pont de l'Alma just moments before she was swept away in the Seine.

Third, the fact that, in the notoriety following her friend's death, the defendant had immediately sought to profit by her demise, illegally seizing several of her paintings and selling them to the public.

Also working against the defendant was her strangely steadfast refusal to speak out or cooperate with the trial in any way. Rumor had it that she didn't intend to put up a defense at all, so when the time came to present her side of the case, the attorney appointed her by the court would have to stand and merely shrug his shoulders.

Reading the papers, looking at the sketches of her lonely, defiant friend entering the building, Mason was beside herself. But she wasn't alone. Lisette's bodyguard, Hugo, frequently came by to check on her progress and express his anguish. It had taken ten policemen to beat him down the day they'd come to arrest Lisette. He still bore the lumps and lacerations of their clubs. But he held himself responsible. He was tortured by guilt and begged Dargelos to put a bullet in his brain.

Dargelos, however, didn't blame him and had no time for disciplining underlings. He was out of his mind with his own grief, desperate to take action—any action that might save Lisette. He tried to send his own attorney, but Duval made sure he was unacceptable to the court. After that, he began to recruit a small gangster army with the intention of storming the courthouse and rescuing her, come what may.

For his part, Richard was mindful of Lisette's plight and feeling his own anxiety about it. But while he was willing to follow Dargelos into such a fray, if no other solution presented itself, he strained to be the voice of reason in a highly charged situation, pointing out that such a reckless action would more likely cause everyone's death, including Lisette's.

Through the long, frustrating nights, Richard, Dargelos, and Mason sequestered themselves, coming up with plan after plan, and in the end, rejecting each as impractical. As Dargelos went without sleep and food, driving himself to the breaking point, Mason began to realize the depth of his feeling for Lisette, and her heart went out to him. "You have to eat something," she told him one night. "You're going to collapse if you don't."

Dargelos put his head in his hands. "I can't. I can't eat. I can't sleep. I can't think of anything else. When I think of what she's going through, how she's suffering . . ." He couldn't continue.

Mason put her arm about his shoulders. She felt his body relax somewhat, as if he needed her empathy. He reached back and patted her arm. "You're the only one who really understands," he told her in a muffled tone. "Because you love your Richard in the same way I love Lisette. It doesn't matter if they love us back as much, does it?"

He saw more of what was going on in her life than she'd realized. There was a compassion underneath his rough exterior that was genuinely touching and a quiet strength that gave her courage. She was beginning to feel both respect and a special kinship with the gangster king of Belleville.

After the trial had been in session for a week, another adjacent story joined the massive newspaper coverage given the Lisette Ladoux murder trial. Several more of the victim's earlier paintings had come to light, all purchased by the Duchess of Wimsley.

Mason was beyond caring about this development, but Richard was unaccountably furious. When he read about it, he slammed the paper down on the table and said, "The market's being flooded by these damn things. You were right. I should have put a stop to it at once."

"I don't understand. Why does anyone want to keep forging them, and why does Emma keep buying them? Hasn't the French government made it clear they plan to confiscate anything with my name on it?"

"I know why," he said.

She waited for him to elaborate, but he didn't. He just sat there fuming. She had a sense that he was formulating a plan to do something about it. But what could he do?

It struck her as odd that he should care so much about this now, in the midst of all that was going on, when he hadn't before. But she knew him well enough to recognize the stone-wall face that told her any questions she might ask would go unanswered.

Instead, she decided to wait and see what he did. She didn't have to wait for long.

That night, about an hour after going to bed, when he thought she was asleep, she felt him slip from out of the covers and quietly sneak from the room with his clothes in hand. As the door closed behind him, she rose and quickly dressed. Then she tiptoed down the three flights of stairs just in time to hear him leave from the front door.

She scrambled after him. He disappeared around the corner onto Rue de Belleville. It wasn't so late that the streets were completely deserted, and she had no trouble following him down the hill at a respectful distance without being noticed. He found a cab just beyond the borders of Belleville and headed west. She hailed her own cab and told the driver to follow.

After they passed through central Paris and entered the 16th arrondissement, it became obvious to her that he was going to see Emma. When his cab pulled into the courtyard of the Galliera mansion, she left her cab and followed him into the courtyard on foot, keeping in the shadows. The area wasn't well lit, and when he paid off his driver and stepped to the door, she was able to creep to a hiding place behind one of the tress only a few yards away.

Emma opened the door herself. "Richard. You came!" Her voice sounded breathy, full of emotion.

"Isn't that what you intended?"

"It's what I'd hoped. But I was beginning to think you weren't getting my messages."

"I thought I'd better stop by and see what you were up to." His voice sounded casual, but Mason detected a hint of something underneath that told her he was anything but.

Emma opened the door wider so the light from inside spilled out. As Richard stepped in, Mason reached into her bag and extracted a calling card; then as Emma closed the door behind him, she raced from her hiding place to stand at the side of the door, slipping the card in between the doorjamb and the lock to keep it from latching.

She waited a few moments, then eased the door open and peered in. By now they'd moved into the main salon, leaving the foyer empty. She entered quietly, making sure the door made no noise as she closed it, then crept to the doorway of the salon to peek inside.

"I understand you were using this place for a little un-scheduled target practice," Richard commented in the same neutral tone.

"Oh, that. Let's forget that for now. You know I don't take surprises well. Would you like to see the paintings? They're over here. I've arranged them in the order I want you to see them. No, no, start over here with this one."

As Mason watched from the shadows, they moved across the room to where the six forged canvases were lined up on display stands. For what seemed an eternity, no one spoke. Richard shifted his weight several times as he stood, but he seemed to be transfixed.

Finally, with vulnerability underscoring her confidence, Emma said, "Nothing I've ever done has come as easily or felt as satisfying as these works. For the first time, I wasn't just copying a style, I was creating within it. I just hope you feel the same way."

What was she saying? *Emma* was the forger?

In a rather professional manner, Richard said, "Your use

of complementary colors really is quite striking in this one. You've turned into quite the colorist."

"Really? You think so?" The vulnerability had been replaced with undisguised joy.

Was Mason losing her mind? Was he actually discussing these fakes with the woman who'd forged them as casually as if he was strolling through the Louvre?

Emma gazed up at Richard, her eyes shining. "Come and take a look at this. I really love this one." They moved down the line to another canvas. "What do you think of the light on the parasol?"

"Oh, yes. Big improvement. I remember how the texture of light was always the thing that gave you the most trouble."

They sounded like two longtime conspirators, partners in crime discussing her handiwork with the chatty courtesy of two doctors over a patient.

Richard had known all along that it was Emma who was forging the paintings! Why hadn't he just said so? Why was he protecting her?

Emma was speaking in a soft, intimate tone. "This style of painting doesn't just suit me, it's liberated me. It's made me an artist in my own right for the first time. And though I went crazy when I found out she was still alive, I see now that it doesn't make one bit of difference. Because the inescapable truth, Richard, is that I'm a better Mason Caldwell than she is. Step over here and look at these."

Richard stared at the next painting. "The off-center composition of this one is interesting. Rather like a Japanese woodcut. Hiroshige in particular."

She beamed at him like a child who'd just been given a gold star. "Morrel was here yesterday," she went on excitedly. "He couldn't say enough nice things about this one. He called it the summit of the art of Mason Caldwell. He thinks it should go at the very front of the Caldwell retrospective at the fair." She glanced up at him, her heart in her eyes.

Mason watched Richard move from canvas to canvas, taking the time to study each one carefully. At last, he turned to Emma. "All right, Emma. I've seen them. Now, tell me: What are you trying to do here?"

"Can't you guess? I'm trying to make it right between us again."

He frowned slightly, not quite comprehending. "Make it right?"

"I know how much you love art. More than you love people, really. I know how much you hate me—blame me for what happened to the Poussins. I've always known the only person you could ever love would have to be someone who could create art on that level. I've seen how you were devoting yourself completely to a woman artist everyone believed was dead. Suddenly, it seemed so clear. A way to wipe the slate clean, to make up for everything that happened between us. A way to make you forgive me. Make you love me. I could *become* Mason Caldwell! I could show you that I'm more than a copyist, that I'm a true artist. I could assume her style and paint better than she ever did. And when you saw the paintings, and fell in love with them, I'd tell you I'd done them. And you'd be so proud. That's why I lost my head when I found out the woman was alive. Because I thought it would ruin everything. But now . . . now that you've seen the paintings . . . I'm hoping . . . I'm praying, Richard, that it won't matter. That you'll see that, whether the real Mason Caldwell is dead or alive, *I* am the woman for you."

She was watching him pleadingly, adoringly, as tears ran down her cheeks.

"You did all this—"

"For you, Richard. For love of *you*."

For a while, he just stared at her. Mason clenched her fists so hard the nails bit into her palm. Her whole future stood suspended waiting for his response.

Finally, he said, "Emma . . . *Emma*." He shook his head. "There's just one thing wrong."

She blinked. "Wrong?"

His voice lowered a notch as he said, "They're . . . simply . . . not . . . very . . . good."

Emma's face became a porcelain mask.

He went on, "They have line, color, composition. Technically, they're fine. But underneath the technique, there's nothing there. The backgrounds merely look repulsive. The passion of the artist and the purity of the female figures don't have the power to transform them into something beautiful. There's nothing transcendent in the paintings—any of them. Mason's unmistakable spark of originality and genius—her soul—isn't there."

A dense silence. Then Emma's seething voice, "You son of a bitch!"

"You know I know what I'm talking about, Emma. I'm never fooled when it comes to art."

She slapped his face. The smack resounded through the chamber.

Enraged, she flew into him, beat him with her fists, used her nails as claws to scratch at him. His face bleeding, he grabbed her wrists and twisted them to make her submit. Then, as she lost her strength, he let her drop to the floor.

"You wasted your time, Emma. You can't take Mason's place. Not in the art world. And not in my heart."

With that, he turned on his heels. As Mason jumped back to hide behind a column, he stormed past her and out of the house.

Chapter 29

Emma lay crumpled in a heap on the floor, sobbing as if her world had just come to an end—the kind of wrenching sobs a woman succumbed to only when she thought herself alone. Even a few short weeks ago, Mason would have left without a word, satisfied that justice had been done. But she'd changed; her heart had opened, softened. As the wracking cries filled the empty hall, she felt neither anger nor reproach. And strangely, given the fact that weeks before this same woman had tried to kill her on this very spot, no fear.

Quietly, Mason went into the room and stood looking down at the duchess. Her shoulders were shaking with the force of her outpouring of grief and despair. Crouching, Mason touched her gently.

Emma shot up, startled. Her eyes were red and her face was streaked with tears. "What are *you* doing here?" she hissed.

"I'm sorry, I—"

"You heard all that?" Emma looked about wildly. "Well, I hope you're happy." She shrugged Mason's hand off and pushed herself to her feet. "I've lost everything. Everything I ever wanted or hoped for. And you . . . You've won."

Mason stood. "I don't feel like such a winner."

"You've won the only thing that matters to me."

Mason just looked at her and said, "We're so much alike, you and I."

"I'm nothing like you," Emma shrieked. "Nothing! Haven't I just admitted it? I'm not an artist. I'm nothing but a cheap copier of artists."

Mason said, "When I first saw you, I thought you were the luckiest woman in the world. I wanted everything you had. Money. Position. Respect. Confidence. And to get it, I pretended to be something I'm not. My impersonation is really no different from yours. We're both imposters. So you see, we're not so different after all."

"Don't talk like this. I want to despise you. I *need* to despise you."

"You're right to despise me. What I did was despicable. I wanted something I wasn't supposed to have, and I didn't care how I got it. And I've hurt so many people in the process. But I, too, want to make things right. And the first thing I can do is forgive you."

"*You* forgive *me*? Why, you arrogant little doxy! I don't want your pity!"

"I don't pity you, Emma. I understand you. I know why you did what you did. After all," she added softly, "I love Richard, too."

Suddenly, Emma crumbled. She burst into tears, hiding her face in her hands. Her heart aching, Mason went to her. But when Emma tried to fight her off, she ignored her, pulling the sobbing woman into her arms and holding her until she went limp, crying on Mason's shoulder. Mason gave her the time she needed, stroking her back, murmuring soothing words, feeling herself close to tears.

When Emma had finally quieted, she straightened up and fished a handkerchief from her sleeve, wiping her eyes. "Why are you doing this? After all I did to you . . . I wanted to kill you!"

Mason reached forth and straightened a lock of hair that had fallen onto Emma's brow. "Because I think Richard is a deeply scarred and trapped man who doesn't know how to free himself. I feel his pain, but he won't talk about it. He won't let me help him. Whatever it is, it's twisting his mind. If it goes on, I'm afraid it will destroy him. I have to save him. And I need you to help me."

"Me?" Emma sniffed. "Even if I wanted to, how can I possibly help you?"

"By telling me what you wouldn't before. What you know about his past."

"He'll hate me if I do. That doesn't matter now. But he'll hate you just as much for going behind his back."

"That's a chance I'll have to take. Whatever happens, whatever the consequences to me, I have to help him. While you and I are here talking, the only thing he's thinking about is how to steal my paintings back from the French government. Something he doesn't understand and can't control is driving him to do this, and it's going to end up killing him. Don't you see, Emma? We have to help him. I believe we can. Who better than the two women who love him? Don't you want to save him from himself? Isn't that more important than anything?"

Emma was staring at her as if she'd never seen her before. Finally, she said, wondrously, "You really *do* love Richard, don't you?"

"Of course I do."

"In all the years that I've loved him, I always thought of myself, of what I wanted. I never once stopped to think of what I could do for him."

"You can do something now."

Emma turned and took a few thoughtful steps. "I always thought I loved Richard more than any other woman ever could. I thought he was mine by right. But the truth is, I *wanted* him. I wanted him back. But you *really* love him."

Mason followed, taking the woman by the arm and turning her to face her. "Emma, please, for God's sake, help me to help him!"

Emma studied her for what seemed like ages. Finally, she sighed. "What do you want me to do?"

Mason stepped over to the side bar filled with crystal decanters and poured a brandy, then took it and handed it to Emma. "Just tell me your story. Tell me everything you know about him."

Emma took a sip and gave a small self-deprecating laugh. "I'm not accustomed to telling the truth."

"Neither am I. We're sisters under the skin."

"More so than you know. Very well." Emma sat down and Mason sat beside her. Emma's eyes glazed over as she thought back for a moment, then took a breath and said, "I may be as rich as Croesus now, but for most of my life I've been poor. Poor the way someone like you can't even imagine. The kind of poverty that sinks into your bones and wipes out your spirit. I left the East End of London when I was seventeen and went to St. Louis, hoping to move in with my father's sister. But when I arrived, she wasn't one bit interested in taking me in. So I pushed west to seek my fortune."

"That must have been hard, a woman alone."

"No, actually, it wasn't so bad. It was rather a lark, if you want to know the truth. I had what westerners call grit, and I also had a talent. I could draw. Sometimes I sketched local news events that were made into woodcuts for the newspapers. But mostly I did caricatures of patrons in saloons. They got a good laugh out of those and paid pretty well, too."

"How did you meet Richard?"

"One day I was working in a saloon in Crede, Colorado, and I noticed this handsome young cowboy staring at me. Now, this happened all the time when I was working in mining towns, but what was different this time was the fact that my admirer was looking at my drawing and not at my body. He was absolutely fascinated with what I was doing."

"Richard? A cowboy?"

Emma smiled, her face glowing in remembrance. "He rode shotgun for Wells Fargo. And did he cut a dashing figure. I'm talking tall in the saddle! A fast draw and a straight shooter who stepped out of the way for no man. He was all rough edges in those days, but I fell in love with him on the spot. How could I not? Besides everything else, he had this incredible respect for my work. It was so flattering."

Mason shifted in her chair. This was hard to hear, but she had to hear it. Everything.

"The other thing we had in common," Emma continued, "was that we were both from England. He came west as a child with an older sister, who I think died along the way. He never talked about that part of his past with me. But soon after being on his own, he was adopted by a man who became a kind of substitute father for him. That man," she said, turning to give Mason a steady look, "was Hank Thompson."

Mason remembered the picture she'd seen of Hank with a small boy.

"Hank's a respected businessman now, but he wasn't then. He was a swindler, a con man, a gambler, and everything else bad you can think of. He trained Richard, taught him to gamble, even sent him back to England to school to put some polish on him. Richard thinks he did it with his best interest at heart, but I think it's because Hank wanted to use Richard, and he realized a sophisticated man of the world would be more valuable to him."

"But how did he become an art thief?"

"I can tell you exactly because I was there when it happened. It was eighty-three—no, eighty-two. The spring. There was this Denver silver king who'd just built the town's showiest mansion. To top it off, he'd bought himself a Delacroix painting, which he'd hung with great fanfare over his mantle for all of Denver society to marvel at. Hank got the idea that he would steal that painting. So he had Richard and me invited to the party he was giving to show it off. I can still see the moment Richard laid eyes on the painting for the first time. He'd never seen anything so beautiful before. It was as if he'd just touched the hand of God. He didn't move for I don't know how long, just stood there, staring at it. Finally, I pulled him away. Someone might remember how much time he'd spent looking at it later, after it was stolen."

"So you stole it?"

"Well, yes and no. The problem was not stealing it, it was getting away with it, because it was large, and there were only so many ways of getting out of a town like Denver. Richard said, 'If only there was some way of copying it.' I looked at the painting and, I'm not sure why, but I just had the sense that if I memorized it, every detail, I could paint one just like it. I told him I wanted to try. The next day, he bought a canvas and paint kit, and I set to work. I closed my eyes and concentrated; then I opened them and started to paint. Within a fortnight, I had made a copy that not even Delacroix's wife could tell from the real thing. Because you see, I do have this gift for mimicry. Anyway, a few nights after it was finished, we sneaked it into the mansion and replaced it for the genuine article. As far as I know, that silver king never did find out he had a fake on his wall. He's probably still showing it to people to this day. Hank sold the real one to some South American cattle king."

"So it was Hank's doing."

"Hank may have got him started, but Richard carried on. He loved it. Everything about it. The research, the excitement, the intrigue. Steeping himself in the history of art. He had no qualms about the robberies because he always felt that he was liberating the paintings from people who wanted to horde them for themselves, that he was doing the world a service by keeping the paintings in circulation. Also, it just gave him an excuse to be around the art he loved so much. After the first job, Hank wanted him to quit."

"Why, when it had been his idea in the first place?"

"Because that wasn't the direction he had in mind for his protégé. Hank always had this dream of becoming a Wall Street tycoon. He used the money he got from selling the painting to buy himself into a high-stakes poker game. In the

THE ART OF SEDUCTION   263

course of it, he won himself a copper mine in Montana that, shortly after, struck a mother lode. After that, he went legitimate and started grooming Richard to be his right-hand man. Every so often, he'd send him away to school, and this is when he decided he needed a year at Oxford. But it didn't work. Richard stayed there just long enough to learn how to pass himself off as a cultured gentleman, which he could use in his career as an art thief."

"And you were part of that career."

"I was an *integral* part of it. Even while he was going to school, we'd spend his holidays bouncing around Europe pulling heists. We used the same method that had worked in Denver. Conned our way inside, chose the target; then I copied it, and we substituted the copy for the real one. Oh, what times we had! I loved it almost as much as Richard did. We were a team, we were doing something delicious. In those days, Richard loved the fact that I was such a proficient forger. He respected me for it. I really believed he loved me. Hank hated the fact that we were doing this, and hated me in particular for 'leading him astray.' But even though Richard bowed to Hank in just about every other way, he stood his ground on this one issue. He liked being an art thief. And I think he'd still be doing it if it hadn't been for a couple of things that happened at the same time."

"What things?"

"The first had to do with a trio of stolen Poussins. Our broker in that deal was Dimitri Orlaf."

"The count?"

"Count!" Emma gave a brittle laugh. "No account is more like it. He was born even poorer than I was. He had his coat of arms made up by the same counterfeiter who supplied my phony family tree. The world of high society is filled with frauds, deary. Anyway, Orlaf took possession of the goods and stored them in a dock warehouse the night before they were bound for shipment to a buyer in Stockholm. Somehow, the police got wind of the transaction. To protect the operation, Orlaf destroyed the evidence. He set fire to the warehouse, and those Poussins went up in flames."

"So that's why he hates Orlaf so much."

"Yes, and it's also why he hates *me* so much. I was at the warehouse that night, and I threw the match on the paintings after Dimitri soaked them with kerosene. By the code of our profession, we did what we had to do. I didn't even know who Poussin was and, frankly, couldn't care less. But Richard was crushed. To him, destroying those 'irreplaceable masterpieces' was a crime against humanity. He never forgave himself, and he certainly never forgave me."

Mason thought back to the day they'd walked the dogs to the Belleville park. The things he'd said about her paintings . . . *important to the world . . . a responsibility we can't walk away from . . .*

"It also shook his nerve a bit, I think. Because when he pulled himself together and tried another job, he got caught. Whether it was fate or sloppiness, I can't say. I think he suspects me of turning him in because our parting was bitter, to say the least. But though I can't prove it, I've always strongly suspected that Hank turned him in."

"Why would Hank do that?"

"He didn't want Richard to be a thief. He had bigger plans for his boy than that. And though Richard hasn't followed him into the world of robber barons, he's been extremely valuable to Hank over the years in his capacity as a Pinkerton Agent. I wouldn't be a bit surprised if Hank had gone to the Pinkertons and *suggested* they offer him the deal they did."

"And Richard never suspected that Hank might have done such a thing?"

"I wanted to tell him, but he'd have knocked me down if I even hinted at it. He has a blind spot about that man. For some reason, he sees everything Hank does, no matter how crooked, as being not just justified, but *noble*."

"Did Richard ever forgive you for destroying the Poussins?"

"He wouldn't even speak to me. But that wasn't enough for Hank. You see, Hank always hated me. Before and after the Poussins, he saw me as a threat to Richard's future. So he got rid of me by putting a temptation in my path that he knew I couldn't resist. He moved mountains to match me up with one of the wealthiest men in England. A *duke,* for Christ's sake! Knowing full well that a girl like me, who'd grown up as poor as I did, couldn't possibly refuse the attentions of a man like that."

"You married him."

"I jumped at the chance. If there had been the slightest glimmer of hope that Richard would take me back, I would have turned down even the duke. But there wasn't and I didn't. After the glow of that golden life began to dim, I hated myself for it. I began to think if only I'd stayed and fought for Richard, in time he would have softened to me again and found some place for me in his life. It haunted me, made every day of my life an ordeal. I would have given it all back— the respectability, the position, even the wealth—for one more glorious caper with Richard."

Emma stopped and closed her eyes. Tears were once again rolling down her cheeks.

Mason didn't want to prod her too much, but she couldn't stop now. "What I'm still trying to figure out is . . . this thing that drives Richard . . . his fanatical devotion to art . . . Where does it come from? What is its *source?* Do you have any clue?"

Emma straightened, sniffing. "I never thought about it."

"He has a picture of his sister that he keeps hidden. Besides a picture of Hank, it's the only thing he's kept from his past. I wonder if it could have anything to do with her?"

"It might, because I never could get him to talk about her. He became distant when I asked, so I didn't."

"Do you know about the nightmares?"

"His screaming terrors? Do I!"

"Did he ever tell you what they were about?"

"Not a word. I asked once and he bit my head off."

"They're getting worse. He has one almost every night now. It kills me to see him in such pain and not be able to help him. He's being devoured by some demon, and it's driving him to do something really crazy now. I'd hoped you could tell me what the genesis of his pain is, but obviously he's kept it from you, too. Emma, I'm at my wit's end. What can I do to learn this secret so I can keep it from pushing him over the edge?"

Emma considered this carefully. "What you're trying to do is extremely difficult. Because if there is a secret that 'explains' Richard, we can be sure there's one person who *does* know it. Hank. Hank was there from the beginning. He was his father, his confessor, his mentor, his everything. Hank has been the one constant in his life and the source of most of the security and love he's known. As long as he has that stable base that shares, protects, and understands his little secret, he doesn't need to share it with anyone else. So if you're ever to reach that private place deep in his heart, you're going to have to break that security and make Richard see Hank as what I know him to be: a totally corrupt and evil man."

Chapter 30

When Mason returned to Belleville later that night, Richard met her at the door with concerned relief. "It's three A.M. Where the hell have you been?"

"I woke up and you were gone," she responded innocently. "I was terrified something had happened. I've been out looking for you."

He pulled her to him, hugging her close. "You scared the life out of me. Please don't do that again."

"I won't," she assured him. Then added, wondering if he'd tell her the truth, "Where were you?"

He stilled, then said, "I couldn't sleep so I went for a walk."

"You scratched your face."

"It's nothing. Come on, let's go back to bed."

She went with him upstairs, accepting his reticence as a part of the challenge she was determined to overcome.

Richard and Juno spent most of the next day holed up in their usual brainstorming session, with their usual lack of results. But that night, what might be the long-awaited break in their dilemma came in the form of a gaunt man with a black beard who appeared at Dargelos's headquarters claiming to be a messenger from Hank Thompson.

Hank, he told them, had assembled a band of mercenaries: some fifty cutthroats, brigands, and street criminals he'd recruited mostly in London and brought over as "employees of the Thompson Holding Company." If Dargelos could assemble fifty more men and reconnoiter with him on the Champ de Mars on the day before the retrospective opened, they could storm the pavilion and abscond with the paintings. Then it was a matter of taking a chartered train to Calais where he would have a fast ship waiting.

Dargelos demanded, "What about Lisette?"

"Mr. Thompson said nothing about that," the messenger replied.

"The way she's being guarded, even a hundred men wouldn't be able to rescue her from Duval's clutches," Dargelos grumbled.

"We'll figure out how to get Lisette later," Richard promised him. "We have plenty of time. Even when the trial is over, it will be months before the sentence is carried out. In the meantime, can you help us out with the fifty men?"

Dargelos nodded. "I can do it."

Richard turned to the messenger. "Tell Hank we're with him. Just let us know when and where to meet."

Mason saw her opportunity. "Wait a minute," she said, stopping the man as he was about to leave. To Richard, she added, "Don't you think we should meet Hank in person? I mean no offense, but all we have is this man's word that he's from Hank. Shouldn't we see him in person before jumping into something like this?"

"She's right, you know," Dargelos agreed.

After a moment of deliberation, Richard said to the messenger, "It's no good having him come here. He could be followed. Better we meet somewhere else."

Dargelos cautioned, "It is dangerous for you to go into central Paris. Your description will be in the mind of every flic on every street corner."

"I know just the spot," Mason said. "The Observatoire. Louis XIV's observatory. It's in its own little park in an obscure corner of Montparnasse. No one ever goes there at night."

"Perfect. Relay that message to Hank. We'll meet him at the Observatoire at ten o'clock tomorrow night."

A ghostly twilight was descending upon them as their carriage pulled up. The outline of the seventeenth century observatory was only faintly visible in the distance as Richard and Mason left the coach and walked across the surrounding park toward it. It was the oldest functioning observatory in the world, where the dimensions of the solar system had been first calculated and the planet Neptune had been discovered. A single light was on in an upper story window where some scientist was, no doubt, hard at work pondering the mysteries of the universe.

Soon, they could make out the dim forms of a group of men standing off to the side. Richard paused to observe them carefully. Then the men started toward them. "Well, it's not a trap," Richard said happily. "I'd know that bowlegged walk anywhere."

A voice boomed out, "That you, Buster?"

"It's me."

They moved closer.

Hank said, "It's a fine thing when two upright citizens like ourselves have to meet like criminals in the dark."

"I do find myself in a bit of a fix," Richard acknowledged.

"Well, your old partner is here to get you out."

The two men embraced. The relief and joy in Richard's manner was unmistakable. Hank kept his arm about Richard's shoulders in a paternal manner as they turned and walked a little, talking softly. Mason followed a few steps behind but didn't bother to try and enter into their conversation.

The four men who'd accompanied Hank stayed several steps behind her. They chatted among themselves in Cockney accents.

Finally, Richard and Hank seemed to be in agreement on all points. Hank stopped and turned slightly so that Mason was included. "It's gonna be tricky, there's no doubt about that. But we can do it. The most important thing we've got going for us is the element of surprise. They might be expecting something, but they sure as hell aren't goin' to expect a full frontal attack. And once we get to Calais, we'll be home clear, 'cause I'm gonna have the fastest damn ship money can buy waiting for us there."

Mason, who'd been silent through their conversation, spoke up now. "May I ask a question?"

"Sure can, little lady."

"Why Calais? The French Navy is in Le Havre, and you'll have to go all the way through the Channel to get past them to make your way to the Atlantic. Wouldn't it make more sense to leave from Cherbourg or even Brest?"

"That's a fair question, and I'll tell you the answer. Because the fastest damn ship money can buy is right now on its way to Calais."

"Would that ship be the *Princess Alexandra*?" she asked.

He jerked a bit in surprise. "It is. Have you heard of it?"

"That's a Russian ship, isn't it?"

"That's right. It's bringing in a load of Russian fireworks for the Bastille Day Centennial. They're ordering all they can get from the four corners of the world, you know. Now, are there any other questions, sweet pea?"

"No, no other questions, but I do have something to say."

In the encroaching darkness, she couldn't gauge Richard's expression, but she could feel his uneasiness with her statement.

"Oh?" said Hank in a patronizing tone. "And what is that, Amy girl?"

"There's something that other people know about this matter that you don't. I think it's time you learned it."

She felt Richard tense beside her. "Amy," he said pointedly. "Perhaps we shouldn't—"

"Well, don't just leave me hanging, gal. Fire away."

She shook off Richard's cautioning hand and told Hank, "I'm not Mason Caldwell's sister Amy. I'm Mason Caldwell."

Hank turned to Richard. "Has this filly gone loco on us, son?"

"She's telling the truth," Richard confirmed evenly. "I didn't know it when we started."

Before Hank could react, Mason went on, "There's something else you *both* should know. I'll be leaving your company tomorrow and leaving France. I don't care what you do with my paintings, but you can't have my identity. I'm taking that back. I'm going to Rome, where I intend to paint a picture for Signore Lugini, the world's greatest art authority, and he's going to take one look at it and know I'm the real Mason Caldwell. And not you or Inspector Duval or anyone else is going to be able to dispute him. So I'm just going to wish you luck and be on my way. Or . . . How do you say it in the Wild West? Happy trails?"

She turned to head back toward the waiting coach.

"Hold on there, little sister," Hank's voice pierced the night.

She stopped and turned back to him. "Oh? You have something else to say?" There was a taunting edge to her tone.

"You're not going anywhere," Hank told her.

"Why is that?" she asked. "Could it be that a live Mason Caldwell torpedoes your plans?"

When this was met with silence from Hank, Richard stepped between them and said, "Now, wait a minute, both of you. Let's just cool down."

But Mason gently pushed him aside. "You stay out of this. This is between Hank and me."

Turning to Richard, Hank ground out through his teeth, "You shoulda told me this, boy. This complicates matters in a most unfortunate way."

"And why is that, Hank?" Mason resumed her attack. "If what you really want is to donate my paintings to a museum, what difference does it make if I'm alive or dead? Or could it be that's not your plan at all?"

"What are you talkin' about?" Hank snarled.

"I happen to know that you're in deep financial difficulty. Much more than you've let on to Richard or anyone else. In fact, your back is against the wall."

"Is that true, Hank?" Richard asked.

Hank demanded of her, "How would you know anything about my personal business?"

"Juno told me months ago. I started thinking about that recently and, after your courageous proposal yesterday, asked him to wire an associate of his in Calais to do some checking. And guess what, Hank? It turns out the bill of charter you signed for the fastest damn ship money can buy distinctly states 'Destination: St. Petersburg.'"

Mason could feel the shock jolt through Richard's body.

Hank, trying to repair the damage, spoke in a conciliatory tone. "Now, hang on everybody. Let's don't go off half-cocked here. Now, I don't care what it said, it isn't—"

Mason cut him off. "On a hunch, I also had him send a wire to St. Petersburg, asking who had recently rented some warehouse space anywhere near the home berth of the *Princess Alexandra*. And guess whose distinguished name popped up? Count Dimitri Orlaf."

In the deepening darkness, Richard's voice was pure ice. "Is this true?"

Actually, as Hank stood there thinking how to respond, Mason had no idea if it was true. It was a bluff she'd deduced from seeing Hank and Orlaf with their heads together at the Jacquemart mansion. She held her breath. Was the bluff about to blow up in her face?

Hank stepped to Richard, took the gun from his belt, and said, "I'm afraid it's true, boy."

"How *could* you?" Richard cried, his voice an agony.

"Like she said, my back's to the wall. One catastrophe after another, and the bill collector beating at the door. Doesn't take much. I bet high and didn't get the cards I needed. It happens. But this little deal will put me right back in the swing again. You wouldn't believe what those Russians are willing to pay for those paintings. They have more faith in the future of Impressionism than the French ever had! And you've done such a bang-up job of promoting the Caldwell brand that Russian collectors are clamoring for them. Orlaf has the connections I need to the czar and his inner circle. I have to deal with him."

Richard could barely speak. "Hank! This can't be true!"

"It's just one of those things. Business is business, son. I've tried to teach you that."

"And business," Mason cut in, "won't be very good when Orlaf and company find out I'm not dead, will it?"

"Sad to say, little sister, you're right on the money."

Richard couldn't quite comprehend what was happening. "Then . . . What? You're going to kill her?"

"It's not that I want to, son. It's the last thing I want to do. But what choice do I have?"

At that, Mason reached into her handbag and removed the pistol Dargelos had provided her. She thrust it into Richard's hand. He raised it to Hank's face and the four thugs suddenly drew their weapons in response.

"Hold on," Hank bellowed, holding his hands in the air. "Let's don't any of us do anything stupid here."

Richard's arm was shaking, but he kept the pistol aimed at Hank's head. "You're not going to do this, Hank."

"Then you better go ahead and pull that trigger. Because if this deal falls through, I'm as good as dead anyway. But you know, I don't think you want to kill your old partner after all we've been through together. After all I've done for you. Hell, boy, I'm the closest thing you got to family."

Richard kept the gun leveled at him, but his hand was trembling badly now. His thumb pulled back on the hammer. It was so quiet they heard it click.

But suddenly, he lowered the gun and shoved Hank into

the four men who were still bunched behind him with their weapons drawn; then he grabbed Mason and pulled her in the direction of their coach. They ran. A shot rang out over their heads. Hank's voice roared, "Don't hit *him*. Aim for the girl."

Two more shots followed. As they approached the coach, Mason stopped short. "No," she cried, "they'll shoot the horses. Follow me. I know a place where they'll never find us."

As they heard the running footsteps behind them, they darted into the empty square, then around a building where Mason led him down an alley to a manhole cover. She pried it open and said, "We can hide down here."

"What is this place?" he asked skeptically.

"The catacombs."

Chapter 31

"Wait." Richard pulled back on Mason's hand. "It's too dark." After closing the cover behind them and descending a metal ladder, they'd run fifty feet down a long, black passageway. It was cool and dank, and the air was stale. "We're going to get lost."

"I have a light." She reached into her handbag, withdrew a match and handkerchief, struck the match against the wall, and lit the bottom of the cloth. The yellow light flared and illuminated the narrow tunnel leading into the distance.

"Let's wait here. I don't think they're following us."

"I hear footsteps," she insisted. "We've got to go farther." Holding the handkerchief before her like a torch, she led the way. "There's an exit we can take up ahead about half a mile."

He saw a line of human skulls up ahead. "Is this where you painted Lisette?"

"Yes, right up here."

Medieval Paris had been built from the limestone that was quarried from these shafts. They weaved their way through almost every quarter of the city, a vast network of underground tunnels. This particular section had become the depository of hundreds of thousands of bones transferred here from the cemeteries of Central Paris in the eighteenth century. The bones and skulls were stacked against the walls, giving the place a particularly ghoulish aspect that Mason had used in a trio of paintings. She held up the lighted handkerchief before a lintel in which an inscription had been carved: STOP, FOR THIS IS THE KINGDOM OF DEATH.

"Let's wait a minute and see if we hear any more footsteps."

"No, we've got to keep going."

The path before them suddenly forked in four different directions. Without allowing him time to think about it, she pulled on his hand. "This way." She gripped his palm tightly, guiding him into one of the shafts.

Soon, they came upon another fork and she took its left branch. Then another three-way division. Then another. And another. At that point, she dropped the burning handkerchief to the ground and stepped on it, stamping it out.

The darkness was intense, smothering.

"What are you *doing*?" he demanded. His voice was shrill.

"We're here."

"Where?"

"Where we're going to have our talk."

"Would you please strike another match?"

"Sorry, I don't have another one."

"Then we've got to get out of here."

"We're not going anywhere until you tell me what I want to know."

"This isn't funny, Mason."

"I don't intend it to be funny. I know the way out, but you don't. If you try to leave, you're sure to get lost. These passages go on forever without end. People become disoriented down here and never find their way out. Someone stumbles on their skeletons fifty years later. So you have two choices: You can either talk to me honestly and I'll lead you out, or we can stay here in this darkness forever. Take your pick."

"You don't know what you're doing."

"I know exactly what I'm doing. I've tried everything else,

and you've stonewalled me. This is the only course left to me."

"You don't understand. You know about my nightmares."

"That's why we're here, so you can tell me about them."

"What you don't know is they're about darkness. I don't *like* darkness. And I have a fear of falling asleep, having a nightmare, and not having a light to bring me out of it. Just this kind of situation. So please . . . For Christ's sake, Mason, get me out of here. Now."

"Do you think this is easy for me? Do you think I wouldn't do anything else if I thought it would make you talk to me? But I've tried, Richard, again and *again*. I'm not doing this for me. I'm doing it for you. So we're not going to take one step out of here until you tell me what I need to hear."

She felt him fall back against the wall and slide to a sitting position on the floor. She sat beside him. His breath was coming deep and hard. "This was quite an evening you planned. You really wanted to strip me bare, didn't you?"

"I'm sorry I had to do that back there with Hank. But I had to force the issue because I didn't think you'd believe me if I just told you."

He didn't respond.

She tried again. "Did you have any idea that he might betray you?"

After a moment, he said acridly, "None. Hank was the one person I thought I could count on."

"You have someone else you can count on now. Me."

"You. Who dragged me into the darkness."

"Yes, me. The only person who cares enough about you to fight for you. Hank wanted to mold you into a copy of himself. I don't think he *ever* loved you. He used you. But I love you, Richard. I love you so much that I don't care what happens to me or what you think of me. I only care about you. But unless you tell me everything, this has all been for nothing. You've got to trust me, Richard, please."

"I can't," he groaned.

She could feel his torment. "If you don't tell me, Hank has won. I know it's hard. I know it hurts. But I know you can do it. Just think back and tell me what happened. Try, Richard, please. For me. For us."

He still didn't answer. It was as if the barriers to his heart were so strongly fortified that it was impossible for him to let her in.

She prompted him. "Go back. To the beginning. What is the first thing you see?"

For a long time, he didn't respond and her heart began to sink. Then, just as she'd given up hope, she felt his head drop back against the wall behind him. "I see a little boy . . ."

The words shook her. Was he actually going to do it? "Tell me about him. What is he like?"

"He's a scruffy, rebellious little smart aleck . . . His father had died in England and his mother, a Scot, succumbed to pneumonia on the ship to America, leaving him an orphan."

"But he's not alone, is he?"

"No. He has something wonderful in his life that he's not smart enough to appreciate."

"What?"

A brief hesitation. "An older sister."

"Molly?"

"Molly. She's eight years older. And she's lovely, with clear skin and bright eyes and a smile that lights up the world. She's a saint. And more protective of me than my parents ever were. We landed in America with nothing. And we survived thanks to her determination and ingenuity and faith in the future. God"—his voice cracked—"Molly was something!"

Mason put her hand on his leg, offering support. "Tell me about her."

"She was the strongest and most loving person I ever knew. She had a magic about her that charmed people, and a basic goodness that tended to restore people's faith in humanity. And she was fearless. When we landed in New York harbor, she grabbed me by the hand and didn't look back. We pushed west from one town to another. Mostly, she worked in dance halls. And she could sing a little. We always got by. We eventually landed in Virginia City just before the Comstock Lode came through . . ." His voice trailed off.

Afraid he wouldn't go on, Mason asked, "What did the two of you do there?"

"She worked in a saloon, and she put me in school for the first time. I hated it. I went because Molly wanted me to, but I just couldn't stand sitting in that classroom day after day. 'Education is the most important thing in life,' she kept telling me. 'You're going to school, and you're going to be there every day, and you're going to excel.' But I just wanted my freedom. So one morning, instead of going to the schoolhouse, I just lit out for the mountains."

Once again, he stopped. Mason squeezed his leg. "What happened?"

"She came after me, of course." Suddenly, there was an agony in his voice that she'd never heard before. "Even though she could barely ride, she got herself a horse from the livery and set out to track me down. But she didn't find me." His voice choked. "Something got in her way. Something unforeseen. Something . . . unimaginable."

He couldn't go on. He was breathing rapidly now. He reached for her hand, gripping it so tightly that she thought he'd crush it. She pulled his hand to her lips and kissed it tenderly. That simple motion seemed to open the floodgates.

"Molly got to within half a mile of where I was hiding out," he rasped, "when she ran into a group of men who'd spent the day there on the creekbed drinking whiskey. The Murphy brothers—Clint, Chad, and Rufus—and their toady Harp Childers. The worst batch of no-accounts God ever created. They pulled her down from her horse . . ." Richard couldn't keep from sobbing. "They tore off her clothes . . . and they raped her one by one . . . and then again . . . I heard her screams, Mason. They drew me there. And I saw it from high up on that hill. I couldn't understand what was happening. I didn't know what to do."

She felt his tears on her hand. Awash with pain, she turned and pulled him to her, and he cried on her shoulder, pouring out his grief.

"When they were done," he sobbed, "she was dazed. She tried to stand, and she stumbled toward Harp as if she might be reaching for his gun. Clint Murphy shot her down as casually as he'd shoot a rattlesnake. And the other two Murphys laughed at it. They laughed!"

She stroked his hair, giving him time, saying nothing.

"I was only seven, and it was beyond my comprehension. I ran down to them. I cried to Clint Murphy, 'Why did you do that? Why did you hurt her?' I couldn't even conceive that she could be dead. 'Why did you hurt her?' And Clint Murphy said to me, with a smile I'll never forget, 'I wouldn't waste any tears on a saloon whore, boy.' Then he spurred his horse and they all rode away. I went to her and put my hand on the bullet wound and tried to coax her back to life. But of course I couldn't. So I just lay there with her, holding her . . . crying . . . praying . . . not knowing what to do . . . out of my mind, really. Hours passed before a horseman happened by. A passing gambler who took pity on me. He tied Molly to her horse and took us both back to town. The funeral was two days later, and the gambler paid for it. But before that, I went to the mortuary to see her. She was laid out in her coffin in her best blue dress. The undertaker had done his job well. She'd never looked more radiant. Everyone who came to see her said she looked like an angel. And she did. For hours, I just stood there at Stampler's Mortuary and stared at her. The coal-black hair. The white skin. The blue, blue dress. The bluest blue I'd ever seen. It gave me a kind of strength, that beauty. Otherwise, I don't know what I would have done. A world that had that kind of beauty in it couldn't be all bad."

He sat up and took a breath. "I stayed there all night, looking at her by candlelight, finding a kind of peace. But the next morning, they came and nailed the coffin shut and carried it up to Boot Hill. I tried to stop them. When they put her in that hole and shoveled the dirt on her, it took five men to hold me back. You see, I wanted to keep that image. Because without it, I had nothing. I was so crazy that they were in the process of tying me up when the kindly gambler came and calmed me down. He looked me in the eye, and said, 'You don't have time for this, son. We've got some important business to take care of.'"

"The gambler was Hank."

"Hank." Again, Richard's voice choked. "You should have seen him in those days, before the good life turned him soft. He was lean and cagey, and a dead-eye shot. The kind of man they wrote dime novels about. He got me a horse, and the two of us went after those animals who'd done that to Molly. They heard we were on their trail and split up. But one by one, we tracked them down. Hank gunned down Harp in Carson City and got the drop on the two lesser Murphy brothers in Laramie. He made them get on their knees and apologize to me before he shot each one in the head. It took us another two months before we could corner Clint Murphy himself in some little rat-hole town in New Mexico Territory. Hank pistol-whipped him for a good five minutes. Then he handed me the gun. He told me, 'Take it, son. It's time for you to become a man . . .'" His voice trailed off.

"What did you do?" she croaked.

"I stuck the barrel in Clint Murphy's ugly face and pulled the trigger. And I enjoyed every minute of it."

The tears that had been welling up in Mason's eyes spilled over now. "What an awful thing to do to a little boy."

"I suppose it was. But it didn't seem like it at the time. It felt like sweet justice to me. And I worshiped Hank for giving me the opportunity. After that, he more or less adopted me. He put me with a foster family now and again. He came in and out of my life. He saw to my education. After I'd grown a bit, he kept me with him permanently. He was good to me,

Mason. I can't deny that. But I never really could become the kind of man he wanted me to be. Because I never really did get over Molly. The strongest thing in my life wasn't Hank. It was the image of my sister in her coffin in that blue dress. That indelible, transcendent image. That indescribable beauty. Whenever things got really rough for me, I'd close my eyes and bring back that image, and it pulled me through. In a way, that's what my dream is about."

"What do you mean?"

"In the dream, I'm always surrounded by nameless horror, things reaching out of the dark and trying to pull me into the pit. But up ahead is a blue light that I know can save me. So I'm trying to get to it. But I can't. Never. When I wake up, I don't want to think about it anymore. But I'd be pretty stupid if I didn't realize that blue light is Molly's blue dress, and it's disappearing the same way Molly disappeared into the earth. What I never realized until this moment, though, is that my entire life has been a search for that blue dress."

"You mean your love of art?"

"Yes. The first great painting I ever saw was a Delacroix in Denver. It shook me to the core. When I saw that painting— that magnificent work of art with its rich colors and the cobalt blue dress of the woman—it was as if Molly had suddenly come back to life for me. It was just like her in the coffin, this vision of beauty. I can't tell you what a revelation it was to see that painting. It changed me in an instant. Changed everything in my life. From that moment, the only thing I cared about was art."

"And when you saw my paintings?"

"When I saw your paintings, it was an even greater revelation. Not only were they innovative and masterfully done and seemed to point art in a whole new direction, they reflected *my* own vision of the world. The contrast of unspeakable terror and angelic purity. It was as if you'd looked into my mind and painted what was there. All of them, but especially the self-portrait with that enigmatic figure of transcendent grace and sexual confidence in a Prussian blue dress."

Mason could see that now. "But once you found them, and after you discovered I was alive, why did you want to turn me into a lie?"

He thought for a moment. "You know when Clint Murphy said to me, 'Don't waste your tears on a saloon whore?' Well, as I grew older and learned what that meant, I blocked it out. I couldn't accept the fact that Molly probably had to sell herself to keep us alive. So I substituted the real Molly with that image of her, the image of purity. In a way, that wasn't fair to her. Or to the noble sacrifice she was willing to make for me. I don't think I've ever understood that until just now. I made her into a paper saint."

"And that's what you were trying to do with me?"

"I suppose I was. I didn't realize it, of course. The way I twisted your story, the letters I wrote for her . . . It seems crazy when I think about it now. But at the time it seemed necessary, vital to the mission we'd started. But the woman in the legend I was trying to create wasn't really you, was it? It never was. It was Molly . . . the whole time. I can see that now. I suppose some part of me was just trying to bring her back to life. Because deep down . . . I *knew* . . . not only was I responsible for her death . . . but I watched it happen . . . and I didn't do anything to stop it."

"But you were just a little boy!" Mason clutched him to her. "You *weren't* responsible. And there was *nothing* you could have done to stop it."

In the long silence that followed, Mason felt an overwhelming tenderness for this man who'd shared the deepest secret of his soul. There was no doubt in her mind that he'd told her everything, had held nothing back. "I'm so proud of you," she told him.

He returned the embrace, holding her, allowing the healing energy of her love to seep into him. She could feel his gratitude, feel his body release its tension in her arms, as if a terrible weight had been lifted.

"How do you feel?" she asked after a while.

He pondered the question, then said, sounding faintly surprised, "Relieved."

"Are you ready to get out of here?"

"I'm ready."

She took a small candle from her bag and lit it. The light seemed almost intrusive after the intimacy of their cocoon. When her eyes had adjusted to it, she saw that he was looking at her wondrously. "You must love me a great deal to go to such pains."

She touched his face. "Oh, Richard. I love you more than I ever thought it was possible to love anything or anyone. You gave me a great gift. Your love has healed me. I wanted to return the favor, if I could."

He kissed her sweetly, gratefully. She felt so happy, so relieved. Everything would be all right, after all.

They retraced their steps through the labyrinth and climbed the ladder. Richard tipped the manhole cover and saw that the alley was deserted. They climbed out into the fresh night air. But as he was replacing the lid behind them, he suddenly stopped short. "I just thought of something. These catacombs honeycomb all of Paris, don't they?"

"That's what they say."

"Then there must be some under the Champ de Mars, wouldn't you think?"

"I suppose so. Why?" She didn't like where this was going.

"That's it. That's how we'll get the paintings. We shall tunnel under them!"

She could feel his excitement, but her own spirits plummeted. He *still* wanted the paintings.

"But we don't need them anymore," she protested.

"We can't just forget about them."

"Why not? Let the French have them."

"Just walk away from them?"

"That's right. Just walk away."

He raked a hand through his hair. "I don't think I can do that."

"If you had them, what would you do with them?"

"I'm not sure. Take them to some safe place. Care for them. After all the work you put into them, I'm hardly going to let them fall into the hands of people who want to kill you."

She could taste her frustration. "Can't we just let them go?"

"Absolutely not. Mason, those paintings are a part of you. Turning my back on them would be like turning my back on you."

He still wasn't free. Even though he understood the forces that drove him, understanding wasn't enough. There was nothing she could say to change his mind. He would find a hundred different ways to rationalize his need. He was like a drunkard who knew now why he drank but still couldn't give up the crutch around which his whole life had revolved.

Chapter 32

Inspector Honoré Duval spent the morning pacing a worried path in front of the cordoned-off pavilion where the Caldwell Collection would be opened to an eager public the following morning. Art critics, dealers, brokers, and connoisseurs from all over the globe had made the journey to Paris for the event, which had been heightened by the sensational news of the artist's murder and the ongoing trial of her murderess.

Two steps behind him, Duval's assistant Daniel followed closely—a cocky young man who smugly prided himself on being on top of everything. Duval couldn't stand him, but the boy was a nephew of the Minister of Justice and had been thrust upon him. He strained not to let his annoyance show but secretly delighted in catching the pup with any detail left undone.

Without stopping, he turned toward the young man. "What's the latest on Thompson?"

Duval well knew that the American tycoon was a bosom friend of Garrett and had gathered a force of lowlife thugs, no doubt with hopes of helping him recapture the paintings and smuggle them out of the country.

"He's in Calais with his men," Daniel said, just barely stopping before plowing into the inspector. "He still has his ship in readiness, but he has made no move to bring his people to Paris. Cold feet, no doubt."

Duval assumed the American would try to join forces with the fugitives' Belleville allies, but so far, he'd made no moves in that direction. If he had such a strategy, surely he'd act before tomorrow, when the opening would firmly establish the collection as a French possession.

If he did try something before then, it would be futile, because Duval had convinced the Minister of Defense to bring in an entire regiment of crack troops that was positioned in platoons all over this end of the Champ de Mars and was more than capable of squelching any uprising of petty criminals.

As he resumed walking, his eyes watched the curious faces staring at the pavilion from the other side of the cordon. Just behind them, a crew was doing some kind of construction work. The hammering had been going on all morning, resounding in his head. He stopped again and peered at Daniel. "And how are things progressing at the prison?"

"Everything is set. The execution of the young murderess will take place tomorrow morning at ten sharp. As you requested, there will be no prior announcement and the press will not be told about her conviction until after the execution has been carried out."

"Good."

Duval had convinced the Minister of Justice and the President of the Republic to extend the secrecy under which they'd cloaked the trial by not announcing her conviction last week. He'd prevailed upon them to carry out her sentence in privacy and at once, to avoid a bloody and potentially embarrassing rescue attempt by elements of the Belleville underworld. He also reasoned that once the young woman was dead, her gang chieftain admirer would be so crushed that he would have no stomach to aid the fugitives in any foolhardy attempt to rescue the paintings.

Duval turned to walk another lap that would take him away from the irksome hammering of the workmen. He strode another twenty feet in deep thought, then stopped and shot a glance at his companion. "And what about the artist's sister? Has there been any breakthrough in the search?"

"None, sir. We have had information that they may have left their Belleville hideout, and we are intensifying our efforts in the city's center. Every policeman has their description and knows that capturing or killing them constitutes the highest priority."

Duval wasn't enjoying this. He felt no animosity toward the young American woman and even less toward the beautiful trapeze artist who was about to lose her head. They were all victims—he included—of a situation that seemed to have been ordained by fate and now had a will of its own. The ironic truth was these people had to die so he could save his reputation.

And yet, with the fugitives still running around loose, determined to foul up his plans, and allied with two criminal armies, the potential for a career embarrassment—no, disaster—hadn't vanished. So he had to be diligent.

Well, if they were stupid enough to make a move on the paintings, he'd be ready for them.

He turned again and headed back the way he'd come. As he walked, the hammering of the road crew, the repetitious rat-tat-tat, over and over again, suddenly made him flare with anger. "What are those people doing?" he snapped out.

His assistant reddened. "Apparently, sir, they are doing some work on the waterline to the Tower."

"When will they be done? We cannot have the dignitaries tomorrow subjected to that racket. Tell them they're to finish up and be out of here by eight A.M. I don't care if they have to work all night to do it!"

Richard pushed his shovel into the loose pile of dirt and limestone and deposited the rubble into a wicker basket.

Behind him, another man picked up the basket and passed it to another behind him, sending it down a long bucket brigade that led to the wider shaft of the catacombs. Richard was grimy, sweaty, tired, and hot from the kerosene lamp he had to keep perpetually by the side of his face. Without the lamps, it was pitch-black and painfully claustrophobic. It was miserable work, but he couldn't afford to let up, and he preferred doing the digging himself.

They'd entered the catacombs through an opening in an old building that faced the south end of the Champ de Mars. The tunnel had stretched almost three quarters of the way down the long fairgrounds before it took a sharp diversion toward the Seine. By his calculation, that put them within a hundred feet of the pavilion. They'd been digging their way through that hundred feet and it was tough going. The procedure was to use a sledgehammer to break up the hard rock, then shovel it into containers to be removed. A slow procedure, but they were making progress. Soon, he estimated, they would hit surface clay and it would become much easier.

As he toiled, Richard thought again about Mason. She'd been surprisingly reticent the past few days, even a bit withdrawn. They'd seemed so close after his confession. In fact, he'd never felt more connected with anyone in his life. It had tortured him to strip away the layers of his past, but when he'd finished, some of its treacherous hold had drained out of him. He'd ended up feeling grateful for her patience, her understanding, and yes, even for having forced him to see the real Hank.

But then he'd told her his idea about the tunnels and her face had fallen. Since then, she'd been distracted, remote. He was determined to finish this job on time, and had thrown himself into the task with ferocious vigor. And yet . . . that look on her face. He couldn't get it out of his mind.

Another man crawled to his side. It was Pierre, a good-natured Corsican and Dargelos's chief lieutenant; he knew the catacombs and had led them to this branch of them. "Time for me to relieve you," he said.

"Just a minute. I want to get this one big rock that's loose."

"Have you hit any clay yet?"

"No, but I expect to soon."

"We must be close," Pierre said.

"I just hope we've calculated correctly. It's so easy to get disoriented down here. It wouldn't do to tunnel into the river."

Pierre crossed himself.

"I'm concerned about the time," Richard continued. "We only have until eight tomorrow morning, because they've ordered the work crew to stop by then. After that, if we keep tunneling, they're likely to hear us."

"Then I think you had better let me take my turn. You must be tired. I will dig as quickly as I can."

The sumptuous carriage pulled off the Boulevard des Capucines and into the driveway of the Grand Hotel. As it drew to a halt, the driver announced to the smartly uniformed valet, "The Count of Deauville."

The attendant quickly opened the door and the count stepped out. He was a short, slight figure with a sneer on his full lips that twisted the close-clipped mustache. He looked about haughtily, then walked up the steps, entered the hotel, and crossed the lobby, stopping short when he spotted her grace, the Duchess of Wimsley, sitting with an older gentleman in a corner area. Pausing a moment to run his fingers along his mustache, the count approached the aristocratic couple. When he reached them, he made a curt bow, and when the lady extended her hand, he brought it to his lips, just barely grazing it.

"Please join us," the lady offered graciously.

When the count took the offered chair, the lady leaned forward and said in a low, conspiratorial whisper, "The disguise is marvelous. You fooled me right up to the moment you bowed."

It was Emma's idea for them to hide in plain sight for this meeting, just in case the Galliera was being watched. She'd sent the carriage and the necessary accoutrements. Percival, with his customary unflappability, had picked Mason up just outside of Belleville, and she'd donned her disguise on the drive into the city.

"This is my husband, Smedley," Emma told her. "And this, darling, is the"—she hesitated—"*person* I spoke of."

Smedley Fortescue-Wynthrop-Smythe, Duke of Wimsley, leaned forward to shake hands with Mason. "I'm delighted to know you, although discretion dictates that I not address you by name."

Mason grinned. "You may call me 'count' for the time being. Did you have any luck?"

"We managed to procure exactly what Richard wanted. Actually, Smedley arranged it. Tell the count about the plans, Smedley dear."

"I've arranged through a personal acquaintance, the Earl of Hambersham—charming fellow, by the way, with an excellent wine cellar, although he tends to be a bit of a snob when it comes to his preferred vintages—to have the fastest cutter in the British Isles at your disposal. It's currently docked at Cherbourg, which offers the safest escape route from the country."

Emma patted his arm proudly. "Smed's being much too modest. He had to pay a bloody fortune to the earl to convince him to go along."

Smedley blushed. "What's the use of having a fortune if one can't use it to help one's friends?"

Mason leaned closer to him. "What you're doing is enormously risky. I want you to know how much we all appreciate your efforts."

"Not at all, my good young—fellow. It's nothing compared to the kind of capers—Is that what you called them, dear?—my Emma used to perpetrate. Why, did you know she was a daring counterfeiter living by her wits in the Wild West? All these years I hadn't the foggiest. She finally told me. I knew she was a glamorous figure, but I had no idea how truly glamorous she really is. I must say, it's rather a delicious development, being married to an adventuress. I feel enormously privileged that she finally cares enough about me to bring me into her full confidence."

"Just so you know," Emma said, taking her husband's hand, "we destroyed my forgeries of your paintings. We did it together."

"And a jolly good bonfire they made, too."

Emma smiled at him and said, "Smed, do be a dear and go get us something cool. We ladies need to have a little chat."

When he left, Mason observed, "So you threw caution to the wind and told him."

"Thanks to you I did. Ever since I've been married, I was afraid my secret would come out. I lived in constant fear of that. But when I told him, I think he fell in love with me all over again. Perhaps for the first time. With the real me. Oh, Mason, I've been such a fool! This man is the best thing that ever happened in my life and I didn't know it."

"Are you over Richard now?" Mason asked.

"Completely. I've never been as happy as in the last two days. I've been released from a passion that really had no meaning anymore. By forcing me to face the truth, you've given me a second chance at happiness—perhaps the first I've ever had. I intend to seize that chance. Mason, dear, I don't know how I can ever thank you."

"You already have. Your help is going to prove invaluable to us. Richard appreciates it as much as I do."

Emma laughed. "I rather doubt that."

"It's true. I told him I followed him the night he went to see you. He knows about our conversation. He was a little reluctant to trust you, I admit. But, Emma, he's really trying to change. He wants to change. He knows he *needs* to change. What you thought was impossible has happened. He's broken with Hank. I took your advice and forced the issue."

Emma's eyes widened. "Darling, do tell!"

She related the scene at the observatory.

"That snake Hank! I knew he had to be up to no good. But a complete betrayal? Dimitri Orlaf of all people! Heavens! How did Richard take it?"

"Just as you said he would. It turned out to be the key to unlocking his past. He shared it all with me, Emma. Everything."

Emma's eyes sparkled. "A few short days ago, I would have died to know what that 'everything' is. But that's for the two of you alone. I'm so happy for you. Now we both have what we want."

"Not completely. Richard has opened himself up to the thing that haunts him, but that hasn't freed him from its power. He's still having the nightmares. And as you can see, his obsession with the paintings—and the legend they represent—is still the thing that drives him. I don't care a thing about those paintings, and I'll never be happy until they're out of our lives."

Emma nodded sympathetically. She was the one person capable of fully understanding Mason's dilemma. After all, hadn't Richard found a trio of Poussins more important than her? "What are you going to do?"

For a moment, Mason didn't answer. Then she looked at Emma, and said, "I'm going to force him to make a choice between me and my paintings."

After digging all night, Richard pushed his shovel into the hole and, finally, mercifully, felt its resistance give way. As he pulled it back, a beam of light hit his face. They'd made it, and with no time to spare. He yelled back, "We've broken through. Get ready to move."

He plunged the tool into the opening and moved it around

until he heard it clang against a metallic object. Then he pulled the shovel back and jabbed it against the object with all his might, piercing it and unleashing an ominous hissing sound.

He yelled back, "The gas main is broken. Get the hell out of here!"

Grabbing his kerosene lamp, he crawled back down the cramped tunnel to the larger catacomb shaft. But as he stepped through, he dropped the lamp. It shattered and a rivulet of lighted kerosene streamed onto the stone floor.

Swiftly, he turned and raced down the larger tunnel. But he couldn't quite escape the exploding gas behind him. A wave of hot air picked him off the floor and hurtled him down the corridor.

Chapter 33

Father Gaston arrived at Santé Prison in southern Paris promptly at eight A.M., two hours before the execution was secretly scheduled to take place. As he was escorted through the prison gate, he noted that the institution was an armed camp. The encircling streets of Montparnasse were lined with soldiers and the inner courtyard, where the guillotine was already in place, was filled with another platoon standing in tight formation with bayonets affixed to their rifles.

"See that white grandstand by the guillotine, Father?" his accompanying turnkey pointed out. "That's for the President of France. The warden received word late last night that his excellency may be gracing the execution with his presence."

Father Gaston took the large wooden crucifix dangling from his neck and kissed it. "God's will be done," he muttered.

When they reached the second-floor cell block where the condemned woman was living out her final hours, the guard said, "I'm sorry, Father, but I must search you."

"Search me? I'm here to receive the woman's final confession."

"Everyone must be searched. The orders are most explicit. The pope himself, if he happens to show up."

The priest sighed. "Very well."

Embarrassed, the guard patted him down. "That's fine, Father. Again, I'm very sorry."

"You are forgiven, my son."

"I'm afraid I will have to be with you when you hear the confession."

"But I cannot allow that!" the priest protested.

"Again, apologies, Father, but these are my orders."

"Very well. It goes against tradition, but I suppose we all must live with our orders."

As their footsteps echoed down the cold, bleak walkway, the priest inquired, "The condemned. How is she?"

"Defiant to the end, Father. She may spit in your face."

"The poor misguided child."

"She's so beautiful, Father. It seems tragic that she must lose her head."

"The devil seems to have a penchant for the beautiful, my son."

"True, Father. So true."

The guard put the key in the lock, gave it a turn, and pulled the heavy door open. Lisette sat on the bare cot, her legs folded beneath her, staring at the wall. Her blond hair was hanging loose and was slightly disheveled. She was barefoot, her shoes lying discarded beneath the cot.

"I am here to grant you final absolution," the priest announced.

Without looking up at him, Lisette said, "Save your breath. I have nothing to confess."

"Look at me, child. Look into my eyes."

She did. Amusement flickered in her eyes. "So you think you can save me, do you, Father?"

"That is God's promise to the world."

After a moment, she gave a surly shrug. "*Et bien.* Why not?" Then she stood and dropped down on her knees. "Forgive me, Father, for I have sinned."

* * *

When the explosion rocked the earth beneath him, Duval was standing twenty feet in front of the Caldwell Pavilion, up early and issuing more last-minute instructions to his eager assistant. Both men were thrown to the ground by the impact. As Duval rose to his feet, jarred, he struggled to figure out what had happened. Then it occurred to him. The one thing he'd never considered. They were tunneling *underneath* the pavilion! Using the catacombs to get as close as possible, then digging the rest of the way. Brilliant! Why hadn't he thought of it? But what had happened? Obviously, they'd struck a gas main. Bad luck for them . . .

But before his thoughts could go any further, he heard the scream: "Fire!" Smoke was funneling out from under the pavilion door. His two men who were stationed inside came running out, coughing.

Behind them, he could see the flames themselves.

Mon Dieu! The paintings!

He shouted at the sergeant who led the nearest platoon of soldiers, "Get in there! Save the paintings before it's too late!"

Reluctantly, the men trooped inside and began to pull the paintings from the walls and carry them from the burning edifice. As they did, Duval's assistant rushed up to him. "What do we do with them? We can't just leave them sitting out here exposed and vulnerable."

Duval saw that he was right. The fairground was already crowded with workers setting up for the day ahead. They'd all gravitated toward the explosion and were now watching the burning building. Some had run for buckets and were gathering water from nearby fountains. Who knew what criminal elements might be hiding among the gathering crowd?

What to do?

Improvise.

He looked around and saw the line of wagons from Buffalo

Bill Cody's Wild West Show. To Daniel, he barked, "Commandeer those wagons. We'll load them up with paintings and take them to the Prefecture."

Duval could hear the bells of the fire department rushing to the scene. He watched anxiously as the pictures were hauled out. "Careful with that one, you idiot!" he yelled at one of the men dragging a large canvas on the ground behind him as he tried to balance another.

When they were securely loaded in the three wagons, the inspector ordered, "Get these to my office as fast as you can."

"Like hell you will!" A man and woman were rushing through the crowd toward him. The man had long grey hair and beard and wore buckskins with two pistols strapped to his waist. The woman with him was dressed as a cowgirl and carried a Winchester rifle. "Where do you think you're going with my wagons?" he demanded.

Daniel, standing beside Duval, half whispered in his ear, "That's Buffalo Bill, sir, the famous American cowboy. That must be Annie Oakley with him."

"In the name of France, I am seizing your wagons."

"In the name of America, I say the hell you are!"

Reddening, Duval retorted, "I must get these priceless paintings to safety at once."

"I don't care what you must do, you're not going to rustle my wagons."

"Don't be a fool. Your wagons will be returned. I am just borrowing them for a few hours."

"And I say you are not. I have a performance to give this morning and most of the equipment I need is still in those wagons."

The vein in Duval's temple was bulging. "Please get out of the way. I do not have time for this. If I have to arrest you, I will."

"And who's going to be doing the arresting? You?"

"Yes. And if you're so foolish to resist, all I have to do is give the word and those soldiers over there will shoot you down."

"That might be so, but before they can get a shot off, I guarantee that you two varmints will have breathed your last breath. You take the little fellow, Annie. I'll get the boss man."

"Sure thing, Bill." The woman raised her rifle.

"Sir!" Daniel pulled on Duval's sleeve. "They can do it! I read in Ned Buntline's 'Scouts of the Plains' "—

"Shut up, you idiot!" Duval flared. Then, trying a different approach, he moderated his tone. "I implore you, Monsieur Cody, France needs your help in this moment of crisis."

The buckskinned man shrugged, and said, "Well, if you put it that way, of course we'll be neighborly. But I want my own teamsters on those wagons. These here are the best mustangs in the West, and I don't want any of your fancy city boys treating them like pack mules. You gotta know just how to handle them." To his own men, a group dressed as cowboys and Indians who'd been gathering around him, he said, "Hop on board, boys, and take these pictures wherever the man wants them to go."

"I need to put one of my men with each of the drivers," Duval said.

"You do that. Come on, Annie, we're going, too." To Duval, he offered, "Want to tag along?"

"Unfortunately, I cannot," Duval said. "I have a disaster on my hands here. I will have dignitaries from all over the world showing up to find a smoldering ruin."

Duval and Daniel watched the convoy move out. As it rumbled from the fairgrounds, one of his detectives stepped forward with a quizzical look on his face. "The Indians, sir. One of my men said he recognized one of them. He said he's an Apache."

"But of course, imbecile," Daniel scoffed. "Buffalo Bill uses real Indians in his show."

"No, sir. Not Apache Indians. *Un Apache de Belleville*. An Apache of Juno Dargelos."

Duval wheeled to his assistant and his face fell as the realization sank in. He turned toward the disappearing convoy. "Go after them," he screamed. "Stop them. Shoot to kill!"

"But, sir, we have nothing to chase them with. And if we shoot, we might hit our own men."

Duval realized he'd been completely outmaneuvered. For now.

But he wasn't out of this race. Not by a long shot.

To Daniel, he ordered, "Get my coach."

Lisette, Father Gaston, and the captain of the guard walked across the courtyard to the cadence of a military drummer. Lisette's hair had been tied back at the base of her neck, and her hands were bound in front of her. As they walked, the priest read from the Bible he carried. The executioner—a huge, burly man with a black hood over his head—stood beside his horrific instrument, the guillotine. To one side of the raised platform on which he stood was the white dais on which the President of France was supposed to witness the swift retribution. But it was empty. Apparently, he'd changed his mind.

The trio marched up to the executioner. Ceremoniously, the captain of the guard said to him, "I hereby turn over custody of this prisoner to you. Let justice be done."

The huge man nodded to him, then turned around, reached into his satchel, and removed a round black object with a fuse in it. From his pocket, he withdrew a match, which he struck against the heel of his boot, then lit the fuse. As the others watched in amazement, he hauled back and, with all his might, flung the burning object several hundred feet over the far wall toward the front entrance of the prison. It landed with a tremendous explosion.

That done, he removed his hood.

Hugo.

Before the platoon of dazed soldiers below him could recover their wits, he dived into them, knocking them over like so many tenpins. As the huge man proceeded to further immobilize the guards by picking them up and knocking their heads together, the priest—who was no priest at all, but Juno Dargelos—reached over, unsheathed the saber of the captain of the guard, and ran him through. Then, in a quick movement, he sliced the ropes that bound Lisette's hands.

"That white dais is a trampoline," he told her. "If you can use it to jump to the top of the wall behind us, your friends will be along at any moment with some wagons. All you have to do is jump down to them. But you must hurry. Hugo's bomb has diverted the guards from the street along this side of the prison, but they'll soon return to their post."

"What fun!" Lisette cried with a giggle. She descended the platform of the guillotine and ran over to climb the steps of the dais. Leaping onto the trampoline, she jumped twice to gain height, then executed a backward somersault into a standing position on the high prison wall. She glanced down to see the wagons of Buffalo Bill Cody's Wild West Show pulling up below her. She looked back at Dargelos. "They're here!"

Some of the soldiers who'd been neutralized by Hugo were regaining their senses and reaching for their weapons. Juno had grabbed the captain's pistol and was firing at them. "Go!" he screamed at her.

"What about you?"

"Never mind us. We'll hold them off here while you get away. Now go!"

But Lisette put her hands on her hips and gave him a pouty glare. "I'm not going anywhere without you."

He fired again, dropping a man who was about to shoot at her. "Don't be stubborn. Go!"

"If you think I intend to have Hugo's death on my conscience, you're even more of a fool than I thought!"

Dargelos shot a steely glance at Hugo, who had his hands full with a couple of guards. "Hugo, join her."

"But, *Patron*—"

"I said move!"

Hugo knocked the heads together, then, as ordered, rushed up the steps, jumped onto the trampoline, and made the wall in one bound.

"Now you," Lisette yelled down.

"I'm not coming. I'm going to stay here and hold them off." He raised his pistol and shot down another charging soldier. "They'll be coming back around from the front at any minute. Now get out of here."

"So you can die like a hero for me? Oh, you'd love that, wouldn't you? For me to spend the rest of my life being the woman you sacrificed yourself for. Well, it's not going to happen, Juno. You get up here right this minute."

"I told you, I'm not coming."

"But why?"

He didn't respond.

Suddenly, it dawned on her. "You're afraid . . . You're afraid of heights, aren't you?"

He shot her a furious glare. "Will you shut up and get out of here?"

"That's it! Juno Dargelos, the man in whose wake all Paris trembles, the scourge of decent citizens everywhere, is afraid of heights! No wonder he's so attracted to the Flying Princess of the Air!" She laughed uncontrollably. She laughed so hard that Hugo grabbed hold of her, afraid she might topple. "It's the funniest thing I've ever heard."

"That does it," Juno snapped out. "I'll show you who's afraid."

Two soldiers charged toward him, intending to impale him with their out-thrust bayonets. Like a matador, he nimbly stepped aside and let them tumble into the wall behind him.

"Afraid, am I?"

He quickly ran up the steps and, without allowing himself

to think about it, leapt onto the trampoline. But as he rose high into the air, he lost his balance and approached the wall heels over head. Hugo reached out and grabbed him. With Lisette's help, the flailing Dargelos was pulled onto the parapet.

At that moment, a volley of fire came from the courtyard. Bullets whizzed by them. Dargelos jerked back so sharply that they nearly lost their hold on him. As they straightened him, Lisette saw the blood seeping from the sleeve of his clerical robe.

In an instant, the dam broke and her heart gave way. She threw her arms around him. "Juno, my love! My poor, sweet, brave turtledove!"

Chapter 34

In the port of Calais, Hank Thompson was enjoying a cigar as he lay stretched out in a deck chair on the fantail of the SS *Princess Alexandra*. Sitting nearby, Dimitri Orlaf looked at his pocket watch and shook his head. It had been a frustrating week for both men since the observatory fiasco, but Hank was displaying none of the emotional Russian's agitation. He drew on the cigar, rolled it in his fingers, and blew the smoke leisurely into the air. On the dock below them, the mercenaries they'd hired were sitting around playing cards, throwing dice, telling lewd stories, waiting to be called to action.

"How much longer are we going to sit here and do nothing?" Orlaf whined.

"What do you suggest we do?"

"How can you be so calm about it? If we don't get those paintings, we will both be ruined. I have already made arrangements for their disposal in Moscow and spent most of the original deposits. These are not people I can toy with. If I turn up empty-handed after all the promises I have made, my life won't be worth a single kopeck."

"There's really nothing we can do, is there? The French have regular army troops on the Champ de Mars. Even if we had Dargelos's people, we wouldn't stand a chance against them."

"So you are just going to give up?"

"No, I'm not giving up. The way I figure it, we still have a good shot at those pictures."

"Bah! You make no sense."

"There's nothing you and I can do because we don't have the necessary genius to surmount this situation. But Richard Garrett does. He wants those pictures bad, so somehow he's gonna get 'em. I'll stake everything I own on that fact."

"*How* will he get them?"

"I don't know how. If I knew how, I'd get them myself. But young Garrett is the most gifted man in a pinch like this I've ever known. I can't even imagine how he'll do it. But he'll do it. I know my man. He'll get those pictures, and then we'll get 'em from him."

"This is insanity!" Orlaf exploded. "How did I ever get involved with something like this?"

Hank just looked at him and smiled. "Relax. I told you, I know my man."

He saw someone coming their way, a telegram delivery boy. "Monsieur Thompson?"

Hank took the telegram and said to Orlaf, "Give the boy a coin, Dimitri." As the disgruntled Russian did so, Hank tore open the envelope. As he read it, he broke into a broad smile. "What did I tell you? Do I know my boy or what?"

"He stole the paintings?"

"Every single damn one of 'em. And he's got 'em on a train already."

"Going where?"

"Cherbourg."

"That's a hundred miles away!"

"It don't matter. We can intercept him."

"You planned for this?"

"I didn't know which port they'd leave from, but I figured once he'd got those pictures, he'd have to vamoose from one of the northern ports. Hand me that map on the table there."

As Hank unfolded the map of France, Orlaf asked him, "How do you know all this? Who sent you the telegram?"

"Now, Dimitri, you don't think I'd venture into an operation like this without having a scout in the enemy camp, do you?"

Orlaf brightened. "A spy?"

"And a damn good one. One of Dargelos's inner circle. A fellow with some mighty inventive ideas, as you'll see."

"What are we going to do, then?"

Hank squinted at the map showing the rail lines crisscrossing the country and found the route from Paris to Cherbourg. "What we're gonna do, my friend, is use our own train to cut him off right here—where the line south from Calais intersects the Paris-to-Cherbourg track. In this big valley here, just before the town of Bernay." He stabbed the butt of his cigar at a spot on the map.

"Cut him off? What do you mean? Block the tracks?"

"Damn right."

"What good will that do? If he has enough speed, he can plow right through you. Railroad box cars are just made of wood and only loosely attached to one another."

"Maybe, partner, but the box cars on the train we're gonna take will be different."

"Different? How?"

"These boxcars are gonna be packed tight, floor to ceiling, with the fireworks that have just been taken off the ship. They were due to head out for Paris this afternoon, but we're gonna borrow them for a while. The cars will be clearly marked as dangerous explosives. And he sure as shootin' ain't gonna pile into that."

Orlaf could see the beauty of it, but he still didn't like the idea. "What if you guess wrong about him? We will be sitting on top of a mountain of explosives!"

"I haven't guessed wrong. I told you, I know my man. When the chips are down, he's not gonna do anything to hurt ole Hank. And he sure ain't gonna do anything to hurt those paintings."

From the locomotive of the Paris-to-Cherbourg Express, Richard, no longer dressed as Buffalo Bill, leaned his head as far out as he could and looked behind them. Another train was definitely in pursuit—he could see the telltale plume of smoke in the distance—but it was at least a mile behind them. If he kept at full steam, the pursuers would never be able to catch them. "Keep shoveling that coal, lads," he called to two of Dargelos's Apaches, still dressed as Apache Indians.

When word of Lisette's early execution had reached them via Dargelos's network inside Santé Prison, they'd only had hours to put together their daring plan. The easiest part had been using that inside resource to place the trampoline in the courtyard of the prison and substitute Dargelos and Hugo for the priest and executioner. It also hadn't been difficult to use Emma's friendship with Buffalo Bill—forged in her saloon days—to arrange to borrow the wagons and costumes needed for the snatching of the paintings. But the rest of it . . . deliberately starting the fire under the pavilion . . . getting out of the tunnel and into costume and face-to-face with Duval within minutes . . . dislodging the inspector's men from the wagons and racing across Paris in time to catch the high-flying Lisette and her rescuers . . . and getting to Gare Montparnasse in time to commandeer the Cherbourg Express . . . *that* had been no easy task.

Richard went back to the first passenger car. It was crammed with paintings. Lisette was binding Dargelos's arm with a bandage she'd torn from the dress Mason had brought along for her to change into. "How is the patient?" Richard asked.

"The bullet just grazed him," Mason said. "He'll be fine."

"Fine?" scoffed Lisette. "Look how he suffers. My poor Juno, who wanted to give his life for me."

Basking in her attention, the gangster said to Richard, "Did you see me up there? I flew through the air."

Richard smiled. "You looked like a bird. Make that a hawk."

Dargelos thought a moment, then suggested, "How about an eagle?"

"Just so. An eagle."

Dargelos beamed.

"Juno and I need to have a conversation about what we're going to do once we get to Cherbourg," Richard said.

Lisette smoothed Dargelos's brow with a tender hand. "I'll go. But I won't be far away. If you need me, *mon chou,* you just call me and I will fly to your side, my brave eagle." She bent and kissed him soundly before standing. As Mason moved with her to the back of the car, she saw the delighted smile on Dargelos's face.

"She loves me," he told Richard.

The two women sat down on one of the plush first-class seats. It was the first time they'd been alone for ages. So much had happened. Mason turned to Lisette and put her hands on her shoulders. "You are the best friend anyone has ever had."

Lisette seemed genuinely surprised. "But you rescued *me.*"

Tears welled in Mason's eyes. "Lisette, you were willing to go to the guillotine for me. You didn't even consider telling them the truth to save yourself. You were willing to die before you'd say a word, for fear it might harm me. They could have tortured you for weeks, and you still wouldn't have given in. You're the most loyal, noble person I've ever known. No one has ever had a truer friend."

Lisette shrugged, disguising her emotion as was her way. "It was nothing."

"No," Mason insisted, "it was very much something." Overcome, she pulled her friend into her arms and held her. By the time she let her go, there were tears in Lisette's eyes as well.

She swiped them away, sniffing. "Don't make me cry. I still have an image to uphold. I can't let these men think I'm made of mush."

Mason laughed and wiped her own tears away. "Speaking of which, I see you've made your peace with Juno."

"I've decided to forgive him." She tried to sound nonchalant, but Mason could see through it. "If he can risk so much for me, then I can be merciful."

Lisette cast a loving glance at Dargelos. Mason watched her a moment, realizing she'd never seen her friend look so happy. "Now that you've decided to put it behind you, I'm dying to know. What did he do that was so unforgivable?"

"Not did. *Does.*"

Mason leaned closer. "What is it?"

Lisette cast a sly glance at Dargelos, as if trying to decide whether to divulge the awful truth.

"Come on, Lisette. You know I won't tell a soul."

Another brief hesitation. Then Lisette put her finger to her lips, leaned close to Mason's ear, and whispered, "He slurps his soup!" She straightened in her seat, put her hands in her lap, and added, "There. I've said it."

Mason's jaw dropped. "He—slurps—his—soup?"

Lisette shuddered. "It's so disgusting, I can't even think about it."

"*That's* why you've rejected him all this time? Not because he's the most notorious gangster in Paris? But because he slurps his soup?"

Lisette peered at her as if she were daft. "Well, how would you like to sit across from a man for the rest of your life and listen to that horrible sound? Slurp, slurp, slurp. I'm going to have to buy cotton by the bale to stuff in my ears!"

Mason glared at her for a moment, then threw her head back and laughed. She laughed so hard her sides began to ache and tears streamed down her face. Finally, when she could catch her breath enough to speak, she said, "Just tell him not to do it!"

Lisette looked puzzled for a moment. "But men don't like bossy women." She glanced over at him. Richard had finished his conversation and was returning to the locomotive. She turned back to Mason and winked. Then she squeezed Mason's hand, rose, and went to kneel by Dargelos's side.

Mason watched as the two of them put their heads together. She felt suddenly envious of the love that filled the room. As Richard left, her own situation came rushing back at her. Could he ever feel the totality of affection that Juno so obviously carried in his heart?

She would soon find out.

All at once, the enormity of what was about to happen hit her.

I hope I'm doing the right thing!

A half hour later, Mason looked out and saw from a passing sign that the town of Bernay was five kilometers away. The time had come.

She went to join Richard in the locomotive. The train was chugging its way up a steep hillside now, and he was helping the men shovel coal into the blazing furnace. As they came to the crest of the hill, she stepped to his side.

"It won't be long now," he told her, laying down his shovel.

"No, it won't be long."

As the train cleared the crest and started its downhill descent, Richard looked out and saw an unexpected sight. Below them, across a sweeping valley, on the track that crisscrossed their own, a locomotive with five cars was stopped, blocking their path.

Richard swore beneath his breath. "Duval must have telegraphed ahead."

"What are we going to do?" Mason asked.

"The only thing we can. Build up as much speed as possible and go right through them. If we have enough momentum, we'll be able to stay on the tracks."

Mason reached over and unhooked a pair of binoculars hanging from a peg. "Maybe you'd better take a closer look."

He took the binoculars and put them to his eyes. Standing in the other locomotive, staring at him through another pair of binoculars, was Hank. And beside him, his partner Orlaf.

"Look at all of it," she said.

He scanned the line of cars. Each of them was marked with a scull and crossbones and big red letters warning, DANGER! HIGH EXPLOSIVES!

"You're really in a spot, aren't you?" she asked.

He swiveled, his eyes narrowing on her face.

"You've got Duval behind you and Hank and all his men in front of you. So what are your options? We could jump off and let the train keep going, but that would kill Hank and destroy the paintings. You could stop and Hank would kill me, but at least he and the paintings would be safe. He'd have them, but they'd survive. So what's it going to be, Richard? You don't have much time."

His jaw clenched, he glanced in the direction of Hank and the stationary train, which they were rapidly approaching, then back at her again.

"*You* did this."

"Yes, I wired Hank and gave him the idea."

"So I would . . . have to make a choice between you . . . and the paintings."

She nodded, her lip trembling.

For an instant, she feared he might hit her. She couldn't help remembering that he'd never forgiven Emma for destroying the Poussins. But these—her own paintings—meant so much more to him. Could he do it? Finally let them go?

He was glowering at her, his hands clenched into fists. The seconds ticked by . . . the trains were getting closer . . .

Then, very slowly, his dazed, angry face relaxed into a smile of admiration.

He turned to the two Apaches, and said, "Everyone off.

Go back and tell the others to jump. Now. There's no time to think about it."

"Jump?" they cried in unison.

Returning his gaze to Mason, he widened his grin. "That's right, lads. We're going to abandon ship."

They scrambled back to the compartment, frantically calling out the orders. The passengers, seeing the obstacle ahead, instantly obeyed.

For a moment, Richard just stood there, smiling at Mason. Then he shoved the accelerator all the way forward, gave her a kiss, grabbed her hand, and together they leapt from the speeding train.

A few hundred feet away, Hank, still gazing through the binoculars, couldn't believe what he was seeing. The train was speeding up and its occupants were jumping from it like grasshoppers from a hot grill.

Orlaf sneered contemptuously, "*I know my man!*"

It was the last thing he ever said. An instant later, the trains collided with a massive impact, followed by a ripple of explosions as each of the boxcars ignited in a chain reaction.

Rising stiffly to their feet, Mason and Richard stood hand in hand, watching the fireworks color the midday sky like a Monet poppy field.

Epilogue

14 July, 1889
Bastille Day

"Oh, isn't that one spectacular?" Mason marveled. She and Richard were standing on the Pont de l'Alma, gazing up at the Eiffel Tower and the fireworks that illuminated the night sky. In the distance, in every direction, the bells of the churches of Paris were pealing nonstop. This was the climactic moment of the grandest celebration in the history of France. A commemoration of its glorious past—its commitment to liberty, equality, fraternity—and an affirmation of its rebirth and determination to be a beacon of the future.

For Richard and Mason, it was a celebration of their own union and freedom from the trials and dangers that had begun six months earlier on this very bridge. But as the crowd around them spontaneously began to sing "La Marseillaise," they, too, were caught up in the irresistible patriotic sentiment. The song was picked up by those in the fairgrounds, echoing through the night, a chorus of hope and pride. Mason, in particular, felt moved and appreciative. She'd come to this nation as a refugee and exile, and it had made good on its promise, giving her, ultimately, everything that was missing in her life.

With tears in her eyes, she said to Richard, "I love this country."

It had now been more than three weeks since the two trains had collided in a Normandy field, and they'd stood watching the explosions as Duval's train had arrived and he'd taken them into custody.

But Richard, unfazed, had said to him, "In a bit of a pickle, aren't you, old chap?"

"You are going to wish you had never been born," Duval had threatened.

"I suppose it does look rather grim for us," Richard had conceded. "But it looks even worse for you, doesn't it?"

Duval had glared at him suspiciously. "What do you mean?"

"Think about it. You've allowed a notorious murderess to escape. You've let an irreplaceable collection of paintings be stolen. And now, through your negligence, they've been destroyed. Not exactly the accolades one cares to read about one's self in the press."

"Or much of a recommendation for the Legion of Honor," Mason chimed in.

Duval flinched. But he rallied, saying, "My consolation is that the two of you will spend the rest of your lives in prison."

"And how will *you* spend the rest of your life?" Richard persisted.

Mason, seeing the color drain from Duval's face, answered for him. "Disgraced. Dismissed. Reviled forever. A humiliation to the Sûreté and an embarrassment to France. Not to mention what it will do to poor Madame Duval and her delicate health."

"Wouldn't you prefer being the conquering hero instead?" Richard offered.

"Hero?" Duval blinked.

"I think *this* might sound better. The American swindler Hank Thompson and his fiendish Russian accomplice stole the paintings and were racing to smuggle them out of France. Both the artist's sister and myself were trying to stop them. We managed to do that and justice was done; but, unfortunately, in the process, we crashed our train into theirs and the paintings were destroyed."

Duval's eyes remained steady. "Where was I during all this?"

"You weren't here because, in the meantime, through your clever detective work, you discovered that Mason Caldwell's death was, indeed, a suicide, and the conspirators Thompson and Orlaf were attempting to frame the brave and innocent Lisette Ladoux. You couldn't get here in time to save the paintings because you had to go out of your way to rescue the poor wronged victim—such a favorite with the crowds of Paris—from losing her head. When the chips were down, you chose the life of a beautiful young woman over a batch of lifeless oil paintings. A difficult choice, but the only one for a man of character. What Parisian would not applaud you for that decision? Why, my eyes water at the thought of it. Let me shake your hand."

Duval's eyes had grown vacant as if he might be reading the news story in his mind. Finally, he said, "Yes . . . That was a heroic choice, was it not?"

"When we return to Paris, we will no doubt be met with legions of reporters. The late artist's sister and I intend to sing your praises to them as if you were Charlemagne, St. Louis, and Sherlock Holmes all rolled into one."

Just then, Duval's assistant Daniel came rushing up with handcuffs and said, "I think you will be needing these, Inspector."

"Handcuffs?" Duval cried. "Imbecile! Get my two compatriots something to drink. They will be meeting the press soon and will need their strength."

"But, Inspector—"

Duval cut him off. "Your incompetence never ceases to amaze me. Did you never even suspect that these two innocents were, in reality, my allies, working undercover to foil the scheme of the American villain and his Russian cohort? Really, Daniel, if you are ever to make detective, you are going to have to show more perspicacity than you have thus far demonstrated."

Back in Paris, after praising Duval to the heavens for more than an hour at a Gare Montparnasse press conference, they'd finally arrived back at Richard's suite in the Grand Hotel. As the door closed them off from the world, Mason was feeling relieved and excited, yet strangely apprehensive. Richard had made the ultimate commitment to her, but once the dust settled, would he come to regret it? Had the slate really been wiped clean, or would there always be a slight doubt, a nagging holding back?

The moment of truth was upon them.

They stood looking at one another. Their eyes locked, her heart beating fast, Mason asked, "Are we all right?"

He didn't answer. He just crossed the distance between them with two determined strides and pulled her to him. He held her for a moment, his arms strong and warm about her. She could feel the beating of his own heart thundering in his chest. He held her as if holding on for dear life, and she felt tears of relief and joy well in her eyes.

But there was no time for tears. He moved away slightly, just enough to dip his head and kiss her. Kissing her as he never had before—deeply, wondrously, cherishingly. His mouth still moving on hers, their tongues entwined, he lifted her up into his arms and carried her through the sitting room to the bedroom beyond. He laid her gently on the bed, then kissed her again and began to undress her, slowly, taking his time, relishing every moment.

"I have this extraordinary feeling that I'm doing this for the first time," he told her, smiling down into her eyes.

He removed his own clothes and joined her on the bed. He kissed her again, long and hard, holding her head in possessive hands. Then he began to move, trailing her with passionate kisses, her chin, her neck, the back of her ear, moving ever downward to her collarbone, her breasts. He feasted on her as his skillful hands ignited her with a passion that felt new and fresh and deeply moving.

"You're trembling," he noted.

"I'm a little frightened."

"I am, too, a bit."

He put his hand on her breast and kneaded the nipple between this thumb and finger. Then he reached down and licked it with his tongue. A thrill shot through her. She realized that all the other times they'd made love, there'd been some barrier between them, some secret, some doubt, some unanswered question. But those barriers had blown up on a field in Normandy. She could feel his energy flowing into her in a way it never had before. So powerful, so unrestrained, so utterly committed. It ennobled her, buoyed her, filled her completely.

When he entered her, he'd never seemed harder, more forceful, more confident. He held her in his arms, thrusting into her deeper and harder, merging himself with her, giving the totality of himself with reverence and devotion, like an offering to a goddess. She felt reborn in his arms, newly risen from her self-made ashes, clean and gloriously whole. Truly alive for the first time.

The next two weeks were like a honeymoon. They made love for hours at a time. Richard always coming back for more. Asking her to put on that divine scent she'd worn the night of the opera, which, he admitted, "Seems to have a remarkable effect on my prowess."

During the days they walked hand in hand along the Seine. Picnicked by the columned pond in the jewel-like Parc Monceau. Rode horses in the Bois de Bologne, where Richard showed her some of the roughriding tricks he'd learned back in his days in the frontier West, accompanied by Mason's appreciative laughter.

They went to the Exposition with Juno and Lisette, wandering through the exhibits, climbing the Tower and paying the two-franc fee to drop balloons to the delighted children below. Later, sitting crosslegged at dinner in the Moroccan café, Richard made an unlikely proposition.

"Juno, you're the best colleague I've ever had the honor to work with. So here's a thought. Pinkerton is planning to open a Paris bureau next year. How would you like to head it up?"

Dargelos chuckled. "Me?"

"You won't make as much money as you would in your current position. But you'll have just as much adventure, and you're likely to live longer."

"And think of the respectability," Mason seconded.

Dargelos angled a look at Lisette as she clapped her hands together like a little girl in excited encouragement.

"Hmmm," he murmured. "Juno Dargelos, Pinkerton Agent. Wouldn't that make a distinguished calling card? And think of the look on Duval's face when I hand it to him! There we'll be, two men of the law, working side by side, selflessly serving the cause of justice."

In gratitude for all they'd risked to help them, they invited Emma and her husband Smedley for an afternoon of racing at Longchamps. But instead, Emma insisted on taking them all to a performance of Buffalo Bill Cody's Wild West Show. They were given Bill's personal seats, and later, backstage, reduced him to hysterics with their tale of how they'd impersonated him and his supporting players. To their surprise, the two couples got along famously, bonded by the duke's boundless enjoyment. Richard and Emma had actually embraced at the end, two old friends, their former grievances forgotten.

Best of all, during these weeks of bliss, Richard's nightmares had vanished completely. He slept with Mason enfolded in his arms, and if he woke in the night, it was only to make love to her again.

Mason had never been happier.

But gradually, she began to notice a subtle change in Richard's behavior. Sometimes, he would make some excuse and go out without her. When she asked where he'd been, he'd pointedly changed the subject. Once, she'd spotted him in the hotel telegraph office sending a wire. Another time, she'd caught him hastily shoving a reply into his pocket. This time, when she'd questioned him, he'd mumbled something about an "old bit of Pinkerton business" and left the room. Then someone had knocked on the door. He'd gone out into the hall, and she'd heard whispering. After all they'd been through, his desire to keep whatever it was from her troubled her and made her fear that their hard-won state of grace had been only temporary.

Then one morning, he'd told her, "I have to go somewhere for about an hour, and then I'll be back. I'd really like you to be here, if you could." He'd seemed slightly edgy, almost nervous.

"All right," she'd assured him. "I'll be here." But inside, she was dying.

An hour later, he'd returned as promised. Somewhat more relaxed, he'd said, "I have a surprise for you downstairs. I hope it's a good one, but good or bad, I think it's a necessary one for you. Will you come down with me?"

His earnestness reassured her, but she was filled with trepidation. What kind of surprise might prove bad but necessary?

Apprehensive, she followed him to the elevator. They rode the four flights down, saying nothing. When it stopped, she started to step out, but he halted her with a hand on her arm. "I have to tell you now so you can turn around if you want to."

"What is it? You're scaring me."

"Your father."

The earth moved beneath her feet. "My father's dead."

"He's not. He survived the wreck of the *Simon Bolivar*. I was hoping he might have because I knew a number of the passengers originally reported dead actually made it to shore. It took some doing, but I tracked him down through the agency. He's been living in Brazil ever since he washed up there, mostly in the deep recesses of the Amazon. Do you want to talk to him?"

Her father? Alive? "Yes, I want to see him . . . of course . . . but . . . oh, God, Richard! I'm not ready . . ."

"You can't prepare yourself for something like this. That's why I didn't warn you. You just have to do it."

"But . . . How do I look? . . . No, I can't . . . it's just too . . ." Her head was spinning around in circles. She took a breath and tried to think. Then, in a rush, she said, "Yes, I can. I want to talk to him. Where is he?"

"He's not the same man you remember. He's been working for a missionary society all this time. He's given away all his money and has spent the last several years helping people. It's a life that's given him peace, and he intends to go back to it."

"Why didn't he let me know he was alive?"

"He thought you never wanted to see him again."

"Of course. After all those mean things I said to him. I have so much to make up for."

Richard smiled. "That's funny. He said almost the same thing to me. That he had so much to make up for. Shall we go see him?"

"Richard . . . I'm stunned. This was . . . an *amazing* thing for you to do."

He put his hand on her face. "Mason, I love you. I'd do anything for you. You told me I'd healed you, but I knew it would never be complete as long as the guilt you felt about your father was unresolved."

She turned her cheek and kissed his hand, then looked across the lobby. Her father was standing there, hat in hand, looking smaller and more stooped than she remembered, but radiating a tranquility she'd never seen before.

She headed toward him, at first slowly, hesitantly. Then, seeing the welcome in his eyes as he recognized her, she ran to him.

* * *

Now, a week after her miraculous reunion with her father, Mason still couldn't get over what an extraordinary act of love it had been on Richard's part. As she tucked her arm through his, watching the sky erupt in a kaleidoscopic blaze of color, the voices raised in song all around them, she felt so close and grateful that her heart seemed to be overflowing.

As the voices died down, the bells finally ceased their jubilation, and everyone around them wiped their teary eyes, Richard asked, "So what do you think is next?"

"Next?" She wasn't quite sure what he meant.

"For us. Have you thought about it? As much as I should like to, we can't very well lounge about the hotel forever."

"Why not?"

"Eventually, I have to get back to work."

"You *do* enjoy your work, don't you?"

"I do. But I've learned something on this particular case. I enjoy it even more with a gifted and oh-so-alluring ally." He gave the tip of her nose a playful kiss. "But you haven't answered my question."

"Oh, sooner or later I want to start painting again. I have a few new ideas. But this time, I want to paint only to please myself . . . and you. I'm all out of torment to express. I just want to paint because I love to, because the doing of it makes me feel connected to something greater than myself."

"Did you see the Morrel piece this morning?"

"No. Was it about me?"

"Not specifically. It was a general piece about the art on display at the Exposition. But he did mention you."

"What did he say?"

He struck a pose and quoted, "'As the tragic loss of the Caldwell oeuvre recedes into history, her name, if remembered at all, will likely be only a footnote to the story of Impressionism. But those of us privileged enough to have seen her works will never forget them . . . their genius, their virtuosity, their sweeping vision, their bold grasp of the medium . . .' Are you quite certain you're not going to miss that kind of adulation? The power to seduce the world with your brush?"

Mason laughed. "As long as I can seduce you, that's all that matters to me."

He gave her a wicked grin. "That's a given. But what about your name? Won't you miss that?"

"No, I'm tired of it. Come to think of it, I'm tired of Amy, too. A fresh start needs a new name, don't you think?"

"Hmmm, I suppose you're right."

"Good, we're agreed. Now we only have to come up with something. How about . . . Louisa May Caldwell?"

He shook his head. "Don't like it."

"All right. How about . . . Lillie Langtry Caldwell?"

"You can't be serious."

"My, you're picky. Then what do you think of . . . Elizabeth Barrett Caldwell."

He considered it. "I rather like the Elizabeth. Without the Caldwell, though. If you're going for a new name, you might as well go full measure."

"Then Elizabeth Barrett it is."

He was still running it through his mind. "That's better, but it needs a little work. There's something about the 'B' that's not quite right."

Slowly, her gaze rose to his face. There was a decided twinkle in the depths of his dark eyes.

"Perhaps," he suggested, "if you were to substitute a 'G' for the 'B.'"

Her heart began to flit erratically in her chest. She forced herself to assume an insouciant air. "Elizabeth Garrett," she mused. "Artist . . . garret . . . they do go together, don't they?"

He gave her a seductive smile. "Only this will be one instance in which the Garrett spends more time in the artist than the artist does in the garret."

Overjoyed by the proposal and the delicious image he'd just tacked on to it, Mason jumped to embrace him just as he heard another skyrocket burst and stepped away to look.

She missed him completely and her impact carried her careening over the rail.

As she felt herself helplessly falling, she could see the dark rushing waters of the Seine below her. In that terrifying instant, her life seemed to be coming full circle.

But this time, Richard's strong hands grabbed her around the waist just as she cleared the railing and pulled her into his sheltering arms.

Here's a peek at MaryJanice Davidson's
sexy and hilarious new novel,
DOING IT RIGHT
available now from Brava!

*T*ap-tap-tap.

"What the hell *is* that?" Jared muttered, getting up and crossing the room. He had a flashback to one of his literature classes. "Who is that tapping, tapping at my chamber door?" he boomed, pulling back the curtain and expecting to see . . . he wasn't sure. A branch, rasping across the glass? A pigeon? Instead, he found himself gazing into a face ten inches from his own. "Aaiiggh!"

It was her. Crouched on the ledge, perfectly balanced on the balls of her feet, she had one small fist raised, doubtless ready to knock again. When she saw him, she gestured patiently to the lock. He dimly noticed she was dressed like a normal person instead of a burglar—navy leggings and a matching turtleneck—and wondered why she wasn't shivering with cold.

He groped for the latch, dry-mouthed with fear for her. They were three stories up! If she should lose her balance . . . if a gust of wind should come up . . . the latch finally yielded to his fumbling fingers and he wrenched the window open, grabbing for her. She leaned back, out of the reach of his arms, and his heart stopped—actually stopped, ka-THUD!—in his chest. He backpedaled away from the window. "Okay, okay, sorry, didn't mean to startle you. Now would you please get your ass in here?"

She raised her eyebrows at him and complied, swinging one leg over the ledge and stepping down into the room as lightly as a ballerina. He collapsed on the cot, clutching his chest. "Could you please not ever, *ever* do that again?" he gasped. "Christ! My heart! What's going on? How'd you get up there?"

"Quoth the raven, nevermore," she said and helped herself to a cup of coffee from the pot set up next to the window. At his surprised gape, she smiled a little and tapped her ear. "Thin glass. I heard you through the window. 'While I pondered, nearly napping, suddenly there came a rapping, rapping at my chamber door.' I think that's how it goes. Poe was high most of the time, so it's hard to tell. Also, the man you saw me bludgeon into unconsciousness dropped a dime on you today."

"He what?"

"Dropped a dime. Rolled you over. Put you out. Phoned you in. Wants to clock you. Wants to drop you. Made arrangements to have you killed, pronto. Sugar?"

"No thanks," he said numbly.

"I mean," she said patiently, "is there sugar?"

He pointed to the last locker on the left and thought to warn her too late. When she opened it (first wrapping her sleeve around her hand, he noticed, as she had with the coffee pot handle), several hundred tea bags, salt packets and sugar cubes tumbled out, free of their overstuffed, poorly stacked boxes. She quickly stepped back, avoiding the rain of sweetener, then bent, picked a cube off the floor, blew on it, and dropped it into her cup. She shoved the locker door with her knee until it grudgingly shut, trapping a dozen or so tea bags and sugar packets in the bottom with a grinding sound that set his teeth on edge.

She went to the door, thumbed the lock with her sleeve, then came back and sat down at the rickety table opposite the cot. She took a tentative sip of her coffee and then another, not so tentative. He was impressed—the hospital coffee tasted like primeval mud, as it boiled and reboiled all day and night. "So that's the scoop," she said casually.

"You're here to kill me?" he asked, trying to keep up with the twists and turns of the last forty seconds. "You're the hitman? Hitperson?" *Who knocked for entry?* he added silently.

"Me? Do wet work?" She threw her head back and pealed laughter at the ceiling. She had, he noticed admiringly, a great laugh. Her hair was plaited in a long blond braid, halfway down her back. He wondered what it would look like unbound and spread across his pillow. "Oh, that's very funny, Dr. Dean."

"Thanks, I've got a million of 'em." Pause. "How did you know my name?"

She smiled. It was a nice smile, warm, with no condescension. "It wasn't hard to find out."

"What's *your* name?" he asked boldly. He should have been nervous about the locked door, about the threat to his life. He wasn't. Instead, he was delighted at the chance to talk to her, after a day of thinking about her and wondering how she was . . . who she was.

"Kara."

"That's gorgeous," he informed her, "and I, of course, am not surprised. You're so pretty! And so deadly," he added with relish. "You're like one of those flowers that people can't resist picking and then—bam! Big-time rash."

"Thanks," she said, "I think." She blushed, which gave her high color and made her eyes bluer. He stared, besotted. He didn't think women blushed anymore. He didn't think women who beat up thugs blushed at all. He was very much afraid. His mouth was hanging open and he was unable to do a thing about it. "Dr. Dean—"

"Umm?"

"—I'm not sure you understand the seriousness of the situation—"

"Long, tall, and ugly is out to get me," he said, sitting down opposite her. He shoved a pile of charts aside; several clattered to the floor and she watched them fall, bemused. "But since you're not the hitman, I'm not too worried."

"Actually, I'm your self-appointed bodyguard."

"Oh, well, then I'm not worried at all," he said with feigned carelessness, while his brain chewed that one . . . *bodyguard?* . . . over.

We're sure you don't want to miss
Robin Schone's eagerly awaited return with
SCANDALOUS LOVERS
available now from Brava!

*With a seductive style all her own, Robin Schone captures
the erotic imagination as she explores the deepest hungers of
a woman's soul in a story that breaks all the rules . . .*

DESIRE AWAKENED

Married at fifteen and widowed at forty-nine, country-bred
Frances Hart has known only the duties of a wife and
mother, and never the joys of a woman. Determined to
broaden her horizon on every level, she daringly dyes her
hair and sets out alone to explore London in all its
sensual glory.

A successful London barrister and now a widower, James
Whitecox knows duty but has never known passion. He
joins an exclusive society founded to discuss sexual
relations—but talking of the pleasures of the flesh is a far
cry from actually experiencing them. Then Frances Hart accidentally barges into a meeting, enlightening the Men and
Women's Club about a woman's needs—and tempting James
to put his theories into practice . . .

Surrendering to the pleasures of the flesh, Frances finds
herself in the arms of a younger man whose ideas shock her,
whose gaze rivets her, and whose touch will change her
forever . . .

**"Combining the erotic with the romantic, Robin Schone
tests the boundaries of romance fiction."**
–*The Literary Times*

Take a look at E.C. Sheedy's
scintillating new romance
WITHOUT A WORD
coming next month from Brava!

"I want to talk about tonight," she said. "What happened here."

"I don't." He picked up a sandwich, bit into it.

"What *do* you want to do?"

"Eat this sandwich." He took another man-sized bite and another drink of wine, then added, "And go to bed."

"Here?"

"Here."

"And you want to stay here because . . ."

"My daughter asked me to. I promised her I'd be here when she woke up."

"You can do that by going to your motel and coming back early in the morning," she said, trying on some logic that something in her hoped he'd ignore.

"True. But that would mean leaving you." His gaze drifted over her face. A face she knew was drawn and tired. A face that warmed under his scrutiny. "I don't intend to leave, Camryn." His eyes dropped to her mouth. Stayed there. "And I don't think you want me to." He lowered his head, looked at her across his wineglass. "Do you?"

With that two word question, Camryn's kitchen shrank in size; its oxygen depleted by half, and its perimeter blurred. All that remained was a man, a woman, and a razor sharp awareness. A high-voltage sensual jolt that caught Camryn wildly off guard. She hadn't planned on this, hadn't seen it coming—hadn't seen Dan Lambert coming; over six feet of man and muscle, who turned into mush when he looked at the little girl who called him Daddy, and somehow turned into a potent, seductive male when he looked at her. A male who left *everything* to the imagination.

"I repeat, do you want me to go, Camryn?"

Her breathing, uncertain under his steady gaze, leveled off. She told herself not to forget he had an agenda, like Paul Grantman . . . like Adam. She told herself she was a fool for feeling anything, sensual or otherwise, for a man who'd come here solely to take his "daughter" from her. All these rattling emotions were aftershocks from the evening's events, nothing more. Perhaps he was as opportunistic as Adam and saw her weariness as weakness, a chance to shorten that straight line he was so keen on. She told herself all of that, looked into his quietly waiting eyes, and said, "No. I think you should stay." She swallowed, rose from the table, and picked up her plate and glass. She gave him another glance when she added, "After tonight, Kylie needs all the reassurance we can give her."

"Is that a *but*, I don't hear at the end of that sentence?" He stayed seated, following her with his eyes as she walked to the dishwasher.

When she'd put her dishes away, she rested her hip against the counter. Her gaze, when it again met his, was level. "Yes, and what follows that 'but' is this—your staying here, doesn't mean I want you messing with my head—or my hormones."

He stood, and wineglass in hand, walked toward her. When he was solidly in front of her, he reached around her and set his glass on the counter. He was so close the scent of his clean skin, the lingering hint of his aftershave, musk and cedar, drifted up her nose. All of it man scent, strong and primal. Even though hemmed in by his size and strength, she had no desire to cut and run.

He trailed the back of his hand along her cheek and followed its path with a reflective, focused gaze, finally smoothing her hair gently behind her ear. "You were right, you know, about my ulterior motives." His eyes met hers, dark and intense, faintly sorrowful. "I'd do anything to keep my daughter. And I did consider the idea that seducing you might be the way to do that." His lips curved briefly into a smile, but it left his face as quickly as it had come. "I thought it would be less time-consuming, a way to avoid a messy and complicated legal battle, that Paul Grantman wouldn't stand a chance against the two of us." He rested his hand on her shoulder, caressed her throat with his thumb. The gesture both heated and idle. "But now . . ."

When he didn't go on, Camryn waited, then raised a brow. "Now?"

"Now all I want to do is mess with those hormones you mentioned—without a base motive in sight." He leaned toward her and kissed her, a lingering kiss that touched her lips like a shadow, an inquisitive kiss that slammed those hormones she was so worried about into overdrive. "Well, maybe a little base," he whispered over her lips.

And finally here's a taste of Amy J. Fetzer's
searing new romance,
INTIMATE DANGER.
Coming next month from Brava!

When the woman came flying over the gate, Mike couldn't have been more surprised—and disappointed. He'd expected to find his men. One, at least. She dropped to the ground, and he thought, that's gonna leave a mark. Then he heard the troops, the gunshots, and didn't think about his decision to help. But she fought him, landing a kick to his shin, and all he could do was drag her.

Out of sight, he gritted, "Stop fighting me, dammit."

Clancy turned wide eyes toward the voice. An American. Where did he come from?

He didn't give her the chance to ask, moving on long legs, pulling her with him, then paused long enough to toss her unceremoniously over his shoulder and grab something off the ground. Then he was off again, running hard, each jolt punching the air out of her lungs and making her want to puke down the back of his trousers.

"Stop," she choked. "Stop!"

He didn't.

So she cupped his rear and squeezed. He nearly stumbled. "Stop dammit, please!" she hissed. "I can run."

Mike set her on her feet.

Clancy pushed hair from her eyes, then reached out when the world tilted. Her hand landed on his hard shoulder. "That was unnecessary. Nice butt, by the way."

"We have to move."

She met his gaze and thought *he's huge*. "Who are you?"

"Help?"

"Yeah well, I was doing okay, sorta."

"If you wanted a bullet in your head, sure. Get moving."

Clancy was about to bitch when she glanced back and, through the trees, saw troops. She looked at him. All he did was arch a dark brow.

Big, handsome, *and* arrogant? "Lead the way."

He didn't wait for her, and Clancy struggled to keep up. For a big thing, he was agile, leaping chunks of ground while she raced over it.

"They took my jeep," she said into the silence.

He glared at her and thumped a finger to his lips. He waded into the water, his machete in his hand as he turned back for her. She held out her hand. He stared at it for a second and she wiggled her fingers, her expression pleading for help. He grabbed her hand, pulled her the last couple feet to the shore. She smacked into him, her nose to his chest.

She met his gaze. *Thank you*, she mouthed exaggeratedly and his lips curved. She had a feeling he didn't do that often. He turned away, kept the steady pace, and she thought, somewhere at the end of this better be a bed and a hot bath, and lots of room service.

No such luck. Just more jungle.

Mike listened for her footsteps instead of looking behind himself. She barely made a sound. What the heck she was doing in jail was something he'd learn later. Right now, getting out of here was essential. He didn't want to be noticed, and pissing off the *Federales* wasn't good any way you looked at it.

When he felt they'd lost the troops, he stopped. She slammed into his back. He twisted, grabbing her before she fell. She was winded, sweating, not unusual in this country, but she looked like a drowned cat. Wisely, he didn't say so.

"Okay, chief, you're gonna have to cut the pace a little." She bent over, her hands on her knees as she dragged in air.

"It was only a mile."

"At top speed when it's a hundred ten out here?" She tried to put some force in her words, but it just sounded like whining to Clancy. She hated whiners. "I run five miles, three times a week for years. But you . . . you'd clean up in the Olympics."

"Keep up or I leave you behind," he said coldly, then frowned at the GPS.

Cute and crabby, who knew? "Well, that would just ruin my day," she bit back.

His gaze flashed to hers. "You want to be a fugitive?"

"No, but I'm still wondering why they wouldn't let me contact the consulate."

"Maybe because the nearest one is in the capital."

"You're kidding."

His frown deepened. "Who arrested you?"

"Some *jefe* . . . Richora?" His features smoothed and Clancy said, "What?"

"You pissed off the wrong guy, lady. He's corrupt as hell."

She figured that out easy enough. "Abusive, too."

Mike just noticed her swollen lip. "Richora won't let this go. This is his jungle."

Clancy didn't need an explanation. He owned the people, not the land. Richora ruled and she didn't doubt that the smugglers who took her jeep handed it right over to him.

Mike's gaze moved over her slowly and she felt, well . . . so thoroughly undressed she looked down to see if her clothes had suddenly melted off.

"If they search you, what will they find?"

She cocked her hip. "Tits, ass and a gun."

Both brows shot up this time.

"What could I be hiding? They killed Fuad, took my jeep and have my good panties and makeup." She wanted to shout, to really let it loose, but that was just plain stupid. But whispering at him like a mad woman wasn't helping her case either.

Mike grabbed her bag, and since it was still looped around her, the motion pulled her close. He dug in it.

"All you had to do was ask," she said, yet understood this man didn't ask for anything.

Mike fished and found what he was looking for. He opened her passport. "Grace Murray?"

"Here, teacher." She grabbed for it.

He held it away, then found her wallet. It was empty except for some cash and a credit card. "No other I.D.? Who are you?"

Clancy just tipped her chin up, refusing to answer, and for a moment, she thought he'd give up till he pulled her close and ran his hands firmly over her body. A little gasp escaped when his hand smoothed between her legs, then up the back of her thighs.

"Shouldn't we date before you get this familiar?"

Mike ignored the sound of her voice, but this close, her words skipped down his spine. His hand slid over her tight little rear and his look went dark as the ocean floor.

"Interesting hiding place."

His big hand dove down the back of her slacks and pulled out the passport. Inside it was her Virginia driver's license. He took a step back, examining it, then only his gaze shifted. "So Clancy Moira McRae, why two passports? CIA?"

"You know, that's the second time someone's asked me that. What is this area, spy central?"

"Other than intel operatives, people who are dealing in illegal contraband need more than one passport."

"I'm neither."

He studied both, then waved one. "This is the fake."

She grabbed them back. "How did you know?" And did Phil screw it up on purpose?

"I just do." He inspected her gun, checking the ammo. "Can you even fire this?"

She took it back. "Yes I can, and lay the hell off." She cocked the slide and pushed it down behind her back. "I'm not your problem."

"You are right now."